MOLLY CL
SUSAN SETTL

Mary 'Molly' Clavering was born in Glasgow in 1900. Her father was a Glasgow businessman, and her mother's grandfather had been a doctor in Moffat, where the author would live for nearly 50 years after World War Two.

She had little interest in conventional schooling as a child, but enjoyed studying nature, and read and wrote compulsively, considering herself a 'poetess' by the age of seven.

She returned to Scotland after her school days, and published three novels in the late 1920s, as well as being active in her local girl guides and writing two scenarios for ambitious historical pageants.

In 1936, the first of four novels under the pseudonym 'B. Mollett' appeared. Molly Clavering's war service in the WRNS interrupted her writing career, and in 1947 she moved to Moffat, in the Scottish border country, where she lived alone, but was active in local community activities. She resumed writing fiction, producing seven post-war novels and numerous serialized novels and novellas in the *People's Friend* magazine.

Molly Clavering died in Moffat on February 12, 1995.

TITLES BY MOLLY CLAVERING

Fiction

Georgina and the Stairs (1927)
The Leech of Life (1928)
Wantonwalls (1929)
Susan Settles Down (1936, as 'B. Mollett')
Love Comes Home (1938, as 'B. Mollett')
Yoked with a Lamb (1938, as 'B. Mollett')
Touch Not the Nettle (1939, as 'B. Mollett')
Mrs. Lorimer's Quiet Summer (1953)
Because of Sam (1954)
Dear Hugo (1955)
Near Neighbours (1956)
Result of the Finals (1957)
Dr. Glasgow's Family (1960)
Spring Adventure (1962)

Non-Fiction

From the Border Hills (1953)

Between 1952 and 1976, Molly Clavering also serialized at least two dozen novels or novellas in the *People's Friend* under the names Marion Moffatt and Emma Munro. Some of these were reprinted as 'pocket novels' as late as 1994.

MOLLY CLAVERING

SUSAN SETTLES DOWN

With an introduction by
Elizabeth Crawford

DEAN STREET PRESS

A Furrowed Middlebrow Book
FM65

Published by Dean Street Press 2021

Copyright © 1936 Molly Clavering

Introduction © 2021 Elizabeth Crawford

All Rights Reserved

First published in 1936 by Stanley Paul & Co

Cover by DSP

ISBN 978 1 914150 43 2

www.deanstreetpress.co.uk

INTRODUCTION

'A JOLLY Lowland fling', was the verdict of the *Birmingham Gazette* (1 April 1936) on *Susan Settles Down*, neatly placing the novel in southern Scotland, while indicating that it was one to lighten the spirits. Molly Clavering had already published three novels under her own name but, after a gap of six years, was now re-launched as 'B. Mollett'. The change of name was most likely a whim of her new publisher, indicating neither, it would seem, any desire for privacy or change of style or genre. Whether writing as 'B. Mollett' or as herself, Molly Clavering centres her fiction on life in the Scottish countryside, with occasional forays into Edinburgh, the novels reflecting the society of the day, with characters drawn from all strata, their gradations finely delineated, the plots fuelled by sherry parties and small-town gossip, rendered on occasion very effectively in demotic Scots. She is peculiarly adept at describing, in all seasons, the scenery and atmosphere of the Borders, the area in which she eventually chose to settle.

For Molly Clavering had been born, on 23 October 1900, in Glasgow, the eldest child of John Mollett Clavering (1858-1936) and his wife, Esther (1874-1943). Named 'Mary' for her paternal grandmother, she was always known by the diminutive, 'Molly'. Her brother, Alan, was born in 1903 and her sister, Esther, in 1907. Although John Clavering, as his father before him, worked from an office in central Glasgow, brokering both iron and grain, by 1911 the family had moved to the Stirlingshire countryside eleven miles north of the city, to Alreoch House outside the village of Blanefield. In an autobiographical article Molly Clavering later commented, 'I was brought up in the country, and until I went to school ran wild more or less'. She was taught by her father to be a close observer of nature and 'to know the birds and flowers, the weather and the hills round our house'. From this knowledge, learned so early, were to spring the descriptions of the countryside that give readers of her novels such pleasure.

By the age of seven Molly was sufficiently confident in her literary attainment to consider herself a 'poetess', a view with which her father enthusiastically concurred. Happily, her mother, while also entirely supportive, balanced paternal adulation with a perhaps necessary element of gentle criticism. In these early years Molly was probably educated at home, remembering that she read 'everything I could lay hands on (we were never restricted in our reading)' and having little 'time for orthodox lessons, though I liked history and Latin'. She was later sent away to boarding school, to Mortimer House in Clifton, Bristol, the choice perhaps dictated by the reputation of its founder and principal, Mrs Meyrick Heath, whom Molly later described as 'a woman of wide culture and great character [who] influenced all the girls who went there'. However, despite a congenial environment, life at Mortimer House was so different from the freedom she enjoyed at home that Molly 'found the society of girls and the regular hours very difficult at first'. Although she later admitted that she preferred devoting time and effort to her own writing rather than school-work, she did sufficiently well academically to be offered a place at Oxford. Her parents, however, ruled against this, perhaps for reasons of finance. It is noticeable that in her novels Molly makes little mention of the education of her heroines, although they do demonstrate a close and loving knowledge of Shakespeare, Dickens, Thackeray, and Trollope.

After leaving school Molly returned home to Arleoch House and, with no need to take paid employment, was able to concentrate on her writing, publishing her first novel in 1927. Always sociable, she took an active interest in local activities, particularly in the Girl Guides, with which her sister Esther, until her tragically early death in 1926, was also involved. Although friends from later life never remember Molly speaking of Esther, she did use her name (which was also that of her mother and grandmother) in several novels. For instance, in Susan Settles Down 'Esther' is the name Molly gives to Peggy Cunningham's dead sister.

During these years at home Molly not only acted as an officer for the Girl Guides Association but was able to put her literary talents to fund-raising effect for them by writing scenarios for two ambitious Scottish history pageants. The first, in which she took the pivotal part of 'Fate', was staged in Stirlingshire in 1929, with a cast of 500. However, for the second in 1930 she moved south and wrote the 'Border Historical Pageant' in aid of the Roxburgh Girl Guides. Performed at Minto House, Roxburghshire, in the presence of royalty, this pageant featured a large choir and a cast of 700, with Molly in the leading part as 'The Spirit of Borderland Legend'. For Molly was already devoted to the Border country, often visiting the area to stay with relations and, on occasion, attending a hunt ball. Novels such as *Susan Settles Down* drew on her knowledge of Border society, high and low, the introduction of a novelist, 'Susan Parsons', into the life of a Border village perhaps reflecting an element of personal desire. Like the author, 'Susan' is in her mid-thirties and apparently destined for spinsterhood before moving to 'Muirsfoot' and embarking on a new way of life.

During the remainder of the 1930s Molly Clavering published three further novels as 'B. Mollett' before, on the outbreak of the Second World War, joining the Women's Royal Naval Service, based for the duration at Greenock, then an important and frenetic naval station. Serving in the Signals Cypher Branch, she eventually achieved the rank of second officer. Although there was no obvious family connection to the Navy it is noticeable that even in her pre-war novels, such as *Susan Settles Down*, many of the most attractive male characters are associated with the Senior Service.

After she was demobbed Molly did follow in the footsteps of the heroine of *Susan Settles Down* and moved to the Borders, setting up home in Moffat, the Dumfriesshire town in which her great-grandfather had been a doctor. She shared 'Clover Cottage', a more modest establishment than Susan's 'Easter Hartrigg', with a series of black standard poodles, one of them a present from D.E. Stevenson, another of the town's novelists, whom she had known since the 1930s. The latter's granddaughter, Penny Kent, remembers how 'Molly used to breeze and bluster into North Park (my Grandmother's house) a rush of fresh air, gaberdine flapping, grey hair flying with her large, bouncy black poodles, Ham and Pam (and later Bramble), shaking, dripping and muddy from some wild walk through Tank Wood or over Gallow Hill'. Molly's love of the area was made evident in her only non-fiction book, *From the Border Hills* (1953).

During these post-war years Molly Clavering continued her work with the Girl Guides, serving for nine years as County Commissioner, was president of the local Scottish Country Dance Association, and active in the Women's Rural Institute (meetings of which feature in many of her novels). She was a member of Moffat town council,

1951-60, and for three years from 1957 was the town's first and only woman magistrate. She continued writing, publishing seven more novels, as well as a steady stream of the stories she referred to as her 'bread and butter', issued, under a variety of pseudonyms, by that very popular women's magazine, the *People's Friend*.

When Molly Clavering's long and fruitful life finally ended on 12 February 1995 her obituary was written by Wendy Simpson, another of D.E. Stevenson's granddaughters. Citing exactly the attributes that characterise Molly Clavering's novels, she remembered her as 'A convivial and warm human being who enjoyed the company of friends, especially young people, with her entertaining wit and a sense of fun allied to a robustness to stand up for what she believed in.'.

Elizabeth Crawford

CHAPTER ONE

1

SUNDAY was the busiest day of the seven at the Manse of Muirfoot. In her rare moments of rebellion Peggy Cunningham, the minister's daughter, sometimes thought it was the longest and dreariest. Waking early one dark Monday morning in January, her first feeling of thankfulness that the so-called day of rest was behind her for another week was tempered by the remembrance that this particular Sunday had been drearier than usual. Bun and Colin had gone south to their other grandparents by the night express, and would not be back at the Manse for six months.

Peggy's heart sank. Six months . . . ! Tiresome though her nephew and niece, children of her elder sister who had married and since died in India, could be on occasion, they certainly added interest and variety to life, especially to Peggy. She played with them, bathed and dressed them, taught them elementary lessons in an unconventional but effective manner of her own, and grudged every minute that they spent with their father's parents, the Richardsons, in Hampshire. Of course it was fair enough; they were Christopher's children as well as Elspeth's; but somehow Peggy was illogically but firmly convinced that "the Infantry" really belonged to the Manse, and were only on loan during their six months in England. They had no young aunt to play with there, and a girl of six, a little boy of not quite four, must surely be happier running wild in a place like Muirfoot, than carefully watched over by an expensive nurse on the crowded sands of a south-coast seaside resort, or going for guarded walks along prim English roads. Be that as it may, the Infantry were shared with scrupulous fairness between the two sets of grandparents, and until July, Peggy would have to resign herself to their absence, softened by an occasional letter in staggering script to "Deer pegy" from Bun, adorned with Colin's row of enormous crosses. . . . She sighed and wriggled farther down under her sheets and blankets until only the tip of her nose could be nipped by the chill air stealing in at the faint grey oblong which was her open window. At least it was Monday.

Breakfast brought a little compensation in the shape of a piece of news.

"I hear," said Mr. Cunningham, as he finished his porridge and cream, "that the new owner of Easter Hartrigg has arrived."

He was not disappointed of the mild sensation he had hoped to cause. With one accord his wife and daughter stopped eating and gave him their undivided attention.

"Who is he, James?" asked Mrs. Cunningham.

And: "Tell us, father, quickly!" begged his daughter, her blue eyes alight with interest.

"Well . . ." began Mr. Cunningham deliberately, and with what seemed to Peggy infuriating slowness, "He's a godson of old Sir Hugh Blackburn, and used to be a sailor, or so I heard."

"A sailor!" from Peggy, charming memories of the "Flag Lieutenant," "The Middle Watch," and stories by Bartimeus thronging her romantic mind.

Mrs. Cunningham said: "He'll not be coming to live at Easter Hartrigg, though, James? Won't he just let the house again?"

"Not at all. Not at all. He means to live there. He told Jed Armstrong so."

"That house will require a lot done to it before anyone else lives there," Mrs. Cunningham said. "The Morgans really neglected it shamefully. And as for the garden, it doesn't bear thinking about."

"He told Jed Armstrong he hadn't a penny," said the minister doubtfully. "But maybe that would only be his way of talking. I'm sure I hope so, for his own sake, poor fellow, as well as for the place."

"Oh, well, some people's idea of not having a penny is riches to others," answered Mrs. Cunningham. "And if he is really meaning to settle down at Easter Hartrigg he must have *something*."

"Time will tell." Mr. Cunningham's conversation frequently consisted of platitudes, which the good man uttered as if for the first time. "Now, Peggy, is that my tea beside you? Pass it up, my dear, before it gets stone cold."

Peggy, with an obedient start, passed the large cup of strong milky tea, generously sweetened, to her father. But though she did so, though she mechanically ate and drank, her thoughts were far away from the breakfast-table, picturing a figure, blend of Prosper le Gai and all the sailor heroes of fiction about whom she had read. Life, even without the Infantry, began to assume a faintly roseate hue.

While she was supposed to be making the beds, she spent some minutes in surveying herself earnestly in her mother's wardrobe mirror, since she had only a small round one, dim with age, in her own room. The sight of her ingenuous healthily pink face, framed in hair of dull gold, failed to please her. It was far too round, far too childish. "Babyish" was the term she herself applied to it. In fact, with her slender unformed figure and lack of height, she looked even younger than her nineteen years.

"No one could possibly realize how grown-up I feel inside," she thought ruefully, and wished she could look like the heroine of a novel. As it was, the only heroine she resembled at all, and that in nothing but appearance, was Amelia Sedley, a young woman for whom she had felt the utmost contempt since she had first read "Vanity Fair" at the ripe age of twelve.

The sound of a voice floated up to her from the hall below, "Peggy! Are you not nearly done yet?" With guilty haste she turned from the mirror and started to make the wide old-fashioned bed in which her parents spent their placid nights. Still the glimpses of herself which she caught from time to time offended her, and with sudden irritation she picked up her mother's crimson ripple-cloth dressing-gown and threw it so that it hung right over the wardrobe, completely hiding the looking-glass.

She had smoothed down the white counterpane and was laying the quilt over it when Mrs. Cunningham came in.

"Oh, you *are* finished," she said. "I began to think you were never coming. Your father wants you to go a message for him, and—Mercy me! What's my dressing-gown doing up there?"

Peggy, her cheeks as red as the garment in question, mumbled something incoherently, and tugged vainly at the dressing-gown.

"It won't come down," she said at last.

"So I see," said her mother drily. "I'd like to know how it got up! No, don't drag at it, you'll only tear it. Stand on a chair—not that one, Peggy! The cover's clean. . . ."

By the time the dressing-gown had been freed and hung on its rightful hook behind the door, Peggy was too breathless to bother about her own appearance or that of the unknown who had come to Easter Hartrigg. Meekly she listened to her father's message, and sticking a navy-blue beret on her head without troubling to see what it looked like, she shrugged herself into her old school overcoat and went out.

2

The Manse of Muirfoot was set, as a good shepherd's dwelling should be, where it overlooked the houses of his flock without seeming to interfere with that flock on its lawful occasions. Half-way along the village, which consisted only of a straggling double row of cottages, facing each other across the road, a high wall, pierced by a gateway, marked the ministerial out-buildings. These were substantial, and included a barn, lofts, and stable, used to house the minister's cow and horse in the more pastoral days of other centuries, now occupied only by sacks of hens' food, lawn-mowers of advanced age, and during the vacations, when he was home from Cambridge, the somewhat noisome motor-bicycle of Peggy's only brother, Jim. The Manse itself was further separated from the road by a pleasant expanse of green lawn, and the rose-garden which was Mr. Cunningham's pride and delight. Directly opposite the gate was the post office, a small cottage with an old thatched roof, and by craning his neck a little from a window in the upper passage of his house, the minister could see, had he wanted to, whoever entered or left the solitary public-house.

But Muirfoot was a well-behaved, douce place, and the post office rather than the Kirkhouse Inn was the real centre of its social and commercial activities. By watching that doorway it was possible to know exactly what was going on in the village, and Mrs. Davidson, the indefatigable post-mistress, occupied a strategic position of whose importance she was perfectly aware.

There was no telephone installed in the Manse, but the Cunninghams had never regarded this as a drawback. They found it quite as easy and very much more interesting to dart across the road and use that instrument in the cosy gloom of the post office. The arrangement also suited Mrs. Davidson admirably, for it enabled her to remain up to date with all that happened at the Manse, a privilege which she would have sadly missed had the minister possessed what was locally known as a "foam" of his own.

Indeed, intending callers on Mr. Cunningham were in the habit of first inquiring at the post office if the meenister was ben the hoose;

and more than once, on seeing a chance visitor about to open the Manse gate without observing this ceremony, Mrs. Davidson, leaving her post, had sprung from behind her well-polished counter to shrill across the road: "Ye needna gang up till the hoose. They're a' awa' oot tae their tea!"

On a Monday morning the village emporium was usually deserted, and Peggy, well aware of this, was abashed by her reception when she came running in with a gay "Good morning, Mrs. Davidson!"

There was a loud and sibilant "Wheesht!" and the postmistress, a horny forefinger pressed to her lip, nodded vigorously towards the stuffy glass cage which shrined the telephone. It was occupied, as Peggy, her eyes by this time accustomed to the dark interior of the shop, could see, and by a stranger.

"The new gentleman at Easter Hartrigg!" mouthed Mrs. Davidson, and Peggy, who had politely averted her eyes, looked again. Acute disappointment was her first sensation, for this was by no means what her imagination had led her to hope for. Farewell to the compound of Prosper le Gai and Mr. Henry Edwards which she had pictured to herself. The man who was speaking into the mouthpiece in clear, indignant, and "dreadfully English" tones was only of medium height. His hair was black, his face pale, and well-marked eyebrows were drawn by a scowl into a single black bar above the bridge of a shapely but distinctly large nose.

"I'll come back. It doesn't matter," she whispered hastily to Mrs. Davidson, knowing that nothing short of an earthquake would drag that lady from her absorbing occupation of listening to the one-sided conversation being carried on in the telephone booth.

"Juist a meenit. He's near feenished," said the postmistress, and as if in answer, the new owner of Easter Hartrigg put down the receiver and came out into the shop, still scowling. He passed Peggy over with one entirely uninterested glance, and addressed himself to the presiding authority.

"Thanks very much. What do I owe you for that?" he said. His hand was in the trousers-pocket of his brown tweeds, rattling coppers as if in impatience to pay and be gone.

But that was not Mrs. Davidson's way, and Peggy found herself pitying his innocence. Did the poor man really suppose he could escape so easily?

Leaning her arms, bare to the elbows, and above them hidden by the rolled-up sleeves of the grey-and-black overall which covered her capacious person, comfortably on the counter, the most important woman in Muirfoot now proceeded to make amiable talk, chiefly in the form of adroit questions.

"I doot ye'll no' be finding things juist as ye might hae liked up at Easter Hartrigg, Mr. Parsons?" she began.

"No. I am not," said Mr. Parsons, some long-smouldering irritation struggling to the surface and making itself heard. "The house was supposed to be ready for me to go into it to-day, and now I find it won't be fit for habitation for at least a week. And as there's no telephone, I have to send messages over from the nearest house that possesses one, which doesn't save time."

"Eh, dear me! That's bad," replied Mrs. Davidson, uttering a clucking sound indicative of sympathy. "Have ye no' had a wumman in tae redd up the place?"

"There have been two able-bodied women there since the last tenants left," he said grimly.

"Eh, my, my! They're surely no' stirrin' themsel's," said Mrs. Davidson.

"Quite evidently not." Thus Mr. Parsons, even more grimly, and with such a scowl that Peggy once more began to edge her way out of the post office. Her departure was stopped.

"Dinna gang, Miss Peggy! I've a message aboot the Women's Guild for Mistress Cunningham!" cried the postmistress urgently. Peggy halted uncertainly in the doorway, and now Oliver Parsons looked at her with more attention.

"Mrs. Cunningham? Are you by any chance a daughter of Mr. Cunningham? The vicar—I mean, the minister?" he asked. "I wonder if I might come and see your father sometime? Armstrong said he could advise me about the garden better than anyone."

"'Deed, an' Mr. Armstrang was richt," said Mrs. Davidson decidedly. "Awa' you up tae the Manse the noo. Monday's the meenister's easy day, an' ye'll get him in. Here, Miss Peggy, here's the message, a' written doon, an' say that I've ordered the paraffeen frae the man, an' it'll be here come Thursday. That wad be what ye cam' aboot. An' a dizzen o' stamps. The meenister aye gets them on a Monday."

In a minute Peggy and Oliver Parsons, the latter slightly dazed, were outside on the road in the pale January sunlight, staring at each other.

"Lord, what a masterful female!" said the man, smiling for the first time, and showing a glimpse of white teeth, a sparkle in dark eyes. "I thought we'd never get away from her, didn't you?"

Peggy dimpled in reply, but said sedately: "I'm used to her. You see, I've lived here all my life."

"Have you, though?" Oliver said, thinking with faint amusement, "I suppose that means about fourteen or fifteen years at the outside! She seems a nice child, but painfully shy."

As they crossed to the Manse gate, Peggy noticed that he limped slightly and that above his ears the dark hair was beginning to go grey. When he was not talking, his brows drew together in a frown, his expression was bitter, his eyes gloomy. "I wonder why?" she thought, filled with half-pitying curiosity.

"Are there many of you?" asked Oliver Parsons, more to make conversation than from any interest in the subject.

Peggy's ingenuous face clouded. "The Infantry went away yesterday and won't be back for six months," she said dolefully. "It's horrid without them, so dull and quiet."

"The Infantry?"

"Yes. My niece and nephew," said Peggy.

"Good Lord! Are you an aunt already?"

"Of course I'm an aunt. Why shouldn't I be?" she asked indignantly, forgetting her shyness of this strange gloomy Englishman.

"Well, you haven't left the schoolroom yourself yet—"

Peggy drew herself up. "I left *school*," she said with immense dignity, "very nearly two years ago. I am nineteen."

"I say, I'm frightfully sorry, but you do look rather young for your age, you know."

"I know I do," said Peggy mournfully, her dignity fled. "It's a great trouble to me in the parish. Everyone treats me as if I were a child."

They were almost at the Manse door by this time, and Oliver Parsons stopped for a moment in his halting walk to say seriously, "I wouldn't let it trouble you, Miss Cunningham. Believe me, you'll grow old quite quickly enough, as you will find."

Peggy could find nothing to say in answer. Something about the effect of sudden intimacy produced by his earnestness frightened her. She wished desperately to make a laughing reply, to restore the conversation to its former lightness, but she lacked the necessary *savoir-faire*. She could only stand tongue-tied, her blue eyes staring at him in resentful perplexity, while he, on his side, was conscious of acute embarrassment and annoyance at having allowed a momentary impulse to get the better of his reserve.

He spoke first, though it was only to say "Well?" with an interrogative glance at the hall-door.

"I'm so sorry," said Peggy, blushing from chin to broad white forehead. "Do come in."

She led him into a long, rather dark hall, and opening a door to the left, showed him into a small room where a fire burned cheerfully. "I'll go and tell father," she said, and was gone.

Oliver was relieved. This was not the kind of girl to whom he was accustomed, and though at first, supposing her to be the schoolgirl she looked, he had been willing to be amused by her unsophisticated chatter, this passing interest had vanished. With a far greater liveliness he looked about him, glad to be alone.

The room in which he stood waiting was evidently the minister's study. A high book-case, crammed with theological works, filled one wall entirely, and on a large business-like desk opposite the window was a pile of church magazines in paper covers of an unprepossessing pink. There were photographs on the walls and mantelpiece: photographs of men in clerical collars, photographs of what he took to be former Manses, groups of grim-looking parishioners, stiff in their Sunday blacks. Not an aesthetically pleasing room, yet it had an atmosphere which soothed and attracted Oliver. The hall, and this cool, prim, high-ceiled study, were plain enough, and spoke of genteel poverty, yet everything was kept with a scrupulous spotlessness which gave the house a curious modest charm. "Susan would like this," he thought, and decided to spend the evening which passed drearily for him at the Kirkhouse Inn, in writing to her. She would be worrying about him, wondering when she could come and keep house for him at Easter Hartrigg.... Well, at the present rate of progress there, it would be a deuce of a long time, he thought ruefully.

The door opened with a brisk rattle of the handle, and Mr. Cunningham strode in, his ruddy face, so like that of a prosperous farmer that his dark-grey clerical suit and dog-collar seemed a little incongruous on him, beaming a welcome. Below a thatch of silver hair his shrewd but kindly blue eyes darted keen appraising glances at the young man who moved to meet him.

"Ah, poor fellow! He's seen trouble and disappointment," was the minister's immediate summing-up, made even while he shook hands. Aloud he said with a genuine cordiality which was one of his most endearing characteristics, "Mr. Parsons, I'm delighted to meet you—or should I be calling you 'Commander?'"

"Thank you, sir. The 'Commander' isn't really necessary. It's just a sort of courtesy title. I am—I was—a Lieutenant-Commander," said Oliver. "And by the way, I must apologize for troubling you already, but Armstrong told me you could help me—"

"No trouble, no trouble at all, my dear sir!" cried Mr. Cunningham. "You'll just tell me anything I can do and I'll be only too pleased. Jed Armstrong is your nearest neighbour, of course, at Easter Hartrigg, and a very fine fellow, none finer in the parish, or indeed the county. A sterling character, Commander Parsons. A bit of a rough diamond, perhaps, but a sterling character. Ay, yes, indeed. 'The man's the gowd, for a' that!' Now draw in your chair to the fire, and light a cigarette, and let me know how I can help you."

When Oliver Parsons left the Manse about an hour later, he took with him the pleasant conviction that he had found some new friends. If the daughter was gauche, country-bred, supremely uninteresting, both her parents were well worth knowing, and he sincerely hoped to know them better when he had settled in at Easter Hartrigg.

3

"My dear," wrote Susan Parsons to Charles Crawley, "we are embarked on the maddest venture you can imagine. You have heard us speak of Oliver's godfather, Sir Hugh Blackburn? The dear old man is dead, but he has left Oliver a small farm on the borders of Scotland, which was not entailed, a place called Easter Hartrigg. Up to date it has always been let furnished, but the tenants' lease expired last November, and Oliver's insane scheme is to *live* there. With me, of course, to keep house for him. I hope I'm a sensible woman, and I think the whole arrangement sheer folly, but Oliver was so set on it that I simply hadn't the heart to make even a feeble objection.

"You know—no one better, Charles dear—how miserably depressed he has been for months, ever since that dreadful accident that broke his leg so badly, and how he 'retired at his own request,' having had a strong hint that he'd be axed if he didn't. The poor dear has been like a fish out of water, and this is the first gleam of interest he has shown in anything. How could I damp his enthusiasm with wet blankets of common sense? If he weren't so pleased with his unexpected legacy I should set it down as the most snowy of white elephants. As it is, he is already in the wilds of Scotland, where I am pledged to follow him as soon as the house is fit to be lived in.

"Don't, please, write and tell me that we're mad. I know it already; and even if I didn't, every friend we possess has pointed it out. My spirit is quailing at the prospect of life at Easter Hartrigg, because I know what pitiful figures we shall cut as landowners in a country quite strange to us. Oliver talks blithely of shooting and fishing, and has told me to buy a smelly Harris-tweed suit and clumping brogues and a walking-stick, but these outward semblances won't make country-dwellers out of us. I feel just as the children of Israel must have felt when Moses dragged them into the uncharted perils of the wilderness out of the land of Egypt—a place in which, however unpleasant their lot, they were at least at home!

"Fortunately I haven't much time for dismal speculation, as I have all the packing-up to do at this end. Would you were here to help, instead of floating about the Mediterranean on the spring cruise! What fun we had buying the furniture for our little flat, and now I've got to try to sell it again—a much less easy task. Isn't it queer how expensive things are to buy, and how terribly cheap to sell? There is a faint hope that some service people who have looked at the flat may take over our gear when I leave. I devoutly hope so, for Easter

Hartrigg is probably so full of stuff that there won't be a corner left for any of our own surplus.

"Oliver sent me a telegram to announce his safe arrival at Muirfoot, the nearest village, where he spent two miserable weeks, in the Kirkhouse Inn (local pub). After a fortnight I had a picture-postcard from him. It showed a long uneven row of singularly depressing cottages and a small grim church. More local colour was supplied by a shoulder of hill in the distant background, and nearest the camera, a group of inhabitants dressed in the style predominant during the early days of Edward VII. Below was the legend: 'A Greeting Frae Muirfoot'; and on the back Oliver had scrawled, 'Not a bad place, and the village much less awful than it looks from this. Have met one or two decentish blokes.'

"It isn't very helpful, is it? I can't get a word out of him about lighting arrangements, or what is needed in the house, or whether the drains are all right. However, it is quite useless to moan. Oliver is my only brother—in fact, my only relative nearer than a few fourth or fifth cousins in Australia, and we must stick together. I loved living with him while he was still in the Service, and having tremendous fun at Pompey and Weymouth and on the China station. Now I shall have to share this entirely unknown life, even if it's only to see that he doesn't do something incredibly foolish. You know he is still very far from fit.

"If we survive, you must come and stay with us, and I will pour all my woes into your sympathetic ears. In the meantime, Charles darling, *don't* scold us, but write a nice kind letter to cheer us up, for I go to Easter Hartrigg in four days, and if my things weren't all packed and ready, and most of them gone in advance, I really think I'd back out of it. Oliver writes in his last letter, just arrived: 'By the way, I'm afraid the first thing you'll have to do will be to sack the cook, Mrs. Bald, for various reasons, one of them being that she drinks like a fish. With whisky at twelve-and-six a bottle I can't afford it, but I haven't the necessary guts to tell her so.'

"What a prospect! After a long, tiresome journey, I'm to be embroiled with a whisky-drinking cook as soon as my foot is over the threshold. Wish me good luck. . . .

"P.S. I've just read a line of verse written by a peevish Englishman which seems to describe Oliver exactly: 'A laird and twenty pence, pronounc'd with noise . . . !'"

CHAPTER TWO

1

A SLOW train from Berwick brought Susan Parsons, after an hour of cross-country meandering, to the little country town of Abbeyshiels, where she was met by her brother, with a hired car which had obviously begun life as a private landaulette of the early days of motoring, for among its fittings were a handless clock and an imposing array of scent and smelling-salt bottles with tarnished gilt tops. The driver, a rather toothless but cheerful and talkative young man, told her at once how lucky she was to secure it, and she gathered that another unsuccessful client had wanted it in order to attend a funeral in suitable state.

"Tell me one thing," she said nervously as they lulled out of the station yard, "is the cook likely to be drunk when we arrive?"

"If she is," said Oliver, "it won't be on my whisky, because I took jolly good care to lock it up before I left!"

After this somewhat dubious reassurance they gradually sank into silence, while the driver, nursed his ancient car over villainous roads in the half-dark, at a stately pace singularly reminiscent of the funeral which had been his alternative hire. The lights flashed wanly on hawthorn hedges, leafless as yet, on an occasional wayside cottage, on passing carts. In the west a pale afterglow coloured the sky, and the evening star began to wink, doubtfully at first, but with ever-rising confidence. The air was cold, but wonderfully fresh and fragrant. Above the wheezing of the asthmatic engine came drifting the sound of birds—restless, fretful, complaining of invisible plover; thrilling, eerie cry of curlews; bleating and drumming of snipe, which had already begun their courting in the low-lying marshy ground; and, dominating all the rest, the bold halloo of an owl from some wood close to the road. Susan, though chilled, was excited by the strangeness of that drive in the dark, by the sounds which she could not name, by the thought of her unknown destination. She sat very still, her face turned to the half-open window, wondering what life was going to be like in this place which she could not even see yet.

"Not much farther now," said Oliver as they went round a corner so sharply that Susan was flung into his lap. And as she recovered her balance the car came to a standstill before a gaunt house which rose blackly in front of them, darker than the night's darkness, and without a single gleam of lighted window to relieve the general gloom.

"I doot," said the driver cheerily as he groped his way into an ice-cold, pitch-black hall with an assortment of luggage, "Mrs. Bald's forgot ye."

A vengeful voice made answer with terrifying suddenness in that Stygian interior. "I'll ha'e the law on ye, Gibbie Johnston, for misca'in' an honest wumman that's auld enough tae be yer mither—ay, an' wad ha'e been if ye hadna cast oot wi' ma puir wee lass!"

The words were quite incomprehensible to Susan, but the tone in which they were uttered boded ill for any who came in contact with the speaker. She withdrew hastily to the gravel outside, where Oliver was grappling with hat-box and dressing-case.

"Wrong?" he echoed in reply to his sister's quavering question. "Oh, no, nothing's wrong. It's only Mrs. Bald and Gibbie. He used to walk out with her daughter before he married someone else, and she bears him a grudge. It will be all right, Susan. Don't worry."

A flickering light in the hall, and a cry from the faithless Gibbie of: "Come awa' in, Miss Parsons. The lamp's lighted!" seemed to bear witness to the truth of his words, and not without some inward trepidation, Susan entered the house of Easter Hartrigg.

The evil-smelling oil-lamp which burned sulkily on a table showed a vista of dark hall, and a forlorn heap of rugs and suit-cases planted in the centre of the floor, where no one coming in could avoid falling over them. Oliver promptly did so, and cursed heartily, to the evident amusement of Gibbie, who uttered a hoarse chuckle from the darkness outside. Susan was more than thankful to find that of the voice, or its owner, there was no trace, except a distant booming and a clattering of pots behind some closed door in the rear. She had no desire to cope with a possibly drunk and certainly angry cook in her present state of weariness.

"There's one thing certain," she said about an hour later, sniffing. "We are going to dine off fried fish, Oliver."

"Well—perhaps—" he answered doubtfully. "And perhaps not. It's Friday, you see—"

Before Susan had time to ask the meaning of this cryptic remark, the door of the dingy room in which they were sitting beside a smouldering fire, was thrown open, and a tousle-headed young woman in a dirty apron bounced in.

"Yer supper's waitin' on ye!" she announced and, bursting into wild giggles, instantly fled.

Meeting Oliver's glance of apologetic pride as he said, "I told her that when you came she was to announce dinner properly," Susan suppressed a wish to giggle wildly herself.

"Is that Mrs. Bald's daughter?" she asked instead.

"Yes; that's Bernice."

"Bernice! How—how overpowering." Susan was awed by this grandeur. "Bernice Bald. And is she the girl the taxi-driver didn't marry?"

"Yes, the same," said Oliver. "I think myself she's a bit weak in the top story, but she's quite well-meaning."

As they proceeded down an uncarpeted stair, Susan could not help thinking that Gibbie Johnston had shown remarkably good sense in not marrying Miss Bald, who added to her lack of intelligence a face like that of an elderly rabbit, with a rabbit's bulging eyes and prominent teeth.

The dining-room was enveloped in an atmosphere of thick blue smoke strongly redolent of fried fish, through which the beams of an unshaded lamp on the table struggled fitfully, like a lighthouse in a fog.

"Do you still tell me that we aren't going to have fish?" asked Susan, coughing, as they seated themselves at a table which looked as though an earthquake had disarranged it after it had been laid.

"I'm absolutely certain we're not," Oliver asserted, peering through the haze at the mutton-bone with a few unappetizing scraps of dry meat clinging to it, which lay in a plate before him. Susan was confronted by a lordly dish of waxen boiled potatoes. Their numerous black eyes seemed to return her stare malevolently. An enamelled kitchen pie-dish beside them held tinned peaches floating wanly in pale syrup. While she gazed in stupefied silence at this astonishing repast, he went on desperately: "Mrs. Bald and Bernice are Catholics, you see, and it's Friday. They always have fried fish on Fridays."

"But don't they let you have it too?"

"No," he admitted, "they don't. And after once eating fish fried by Mrs. Bald I decided that there are worse meals than cold mutton and bread and cheese. But I told her she'd have to manage to produce some sort of a sweet when you came."

"She—she has," said Susan shakily, and pointed to the peaches.

For a second brother and sister sat staring at each other, then with one accord they burst into helpless laughter—and ate bread and cheese.

Susan, tired with her journey, went early to bed, but sleep refused to visit her, for a variety of reasons, one of which undoubtedly was Bernice's, or Mrs. Bald's, inability to make a bed. The intense stillness of the night, after the continuous hum of town which usually lulled her, helped to keep her wakeful. She found a place between two of the mattress's many humps, and kicked a stone hot-water bottle, which had given her unwary feet a frigid welcome, out of the bed. It promptly revenged itself by breaking on the floor.

"Damn!" murmured Susan wearily. "Let it lie there till morning!"

Resigned to wakefulness, she began to make plans for the reorganization of the whole establishment. The chairs and sofas would have to be shrouded in fresh loose covers, the heavy old curtains which hung dismally at every window must be torn down; the chimneys, which apparently had not been swept for a quarter of a century at least, should receive the attentions of the nearest sweep at once. Above all, Mrs. Bald and her daughter would be gently but firmly told that their services were no longer required at Easter Hartrigg. And on this last comforting thought Susan finally drifted off into uneasy slumber.

2

Heavy and prolonged thumping on the door woke her after an interval of what seemed like five minutes of blessed oblivion.

Sleepily she called: "Come in!" and there entered to her Bernice, who by the cold light of day presented an appearance even less pleasing than when seen in the oil-lamp's sultry gleam. Susan mastered the impulse to shut her eyes tightly, and asked if the bath water was hot.

"There's nae watter," announced the handmaiden in tones of gloomy pride. "The tank's dry."

This was a complication which Susan had never foreseen, and it left her dumb.

"Ma mither says," Bernice pursued, "are ye for an egg tae yer breakfast?"

"Certainly," said Susan, rallying. "In fact, I could eat two eggs, Bernice, lightly boiled. Three-and-a-half minutes will do."

"There's juist the ae egg in the hoose," Bernice made answer stolidly. "But it's a fine big one—ay, a juck's egg we got frae m'auntie that wis keepin' them for settin' in ablow the clockin' hen. But the hen got rin ower by a cawr—"

Susan hastily countermanded the egg and asked for tea and toast. As Bernice left the room, she sank back against her nobbly pillow with a feeling of complete disillusionment. Somehow—it must have been the result of reading H.V. Morton, she supposed—she had expected to find reasonable food at least in these wilds, good cooks, charming shy country housemaids, a welcoming manner. . . . Evidently they existed only in the hotels patronized by happy Mr. Morton. . . .

A deep voice rose from downstairs. "Bairniss! Bairniss! A meenit!"

"I'm comin'!" answered Bernice in tones of peahen stridency.

"Whit wis she wantin'?" demanded the voice.

"She wis wantin' a bath, an' two eggs biled for three-an'-a-hauf meenits!" shrilled Bernice, descending.

"Three-an'-a-hauf meenits! I wonder whit next she'll be seekin'? I'll ha'e naethin' to dae wi' her an' her hauf meenits." Mrs. Bald's voice rose passionately to a magnificent fortissimo. "As for meenits, hoo am I tae ken them, wi' yon 'larmin' clock that disna' gang the ae time-piece in the hoose?"

It seemed to Susan that the time had come for her to take a hand. She rose, flung on a dressing-gown and, emerging from her room, said clearly and firmly over the banisters:

"Thank yon, Mrs. Bald, but I do not wish an egg for breakfast. Tea and toast in half an hour, please."

A silence as of death fell over the lower regions, broken at last by a gusty whisper. "Presairve us! She's heard a' we said!"

Susan retreated, feeling that victory had attended her so far, and thoroughly pleased with her own astonishing courage. The travesty of a meal which Mrs. Bald dignified by the name of breakfast left her, if anything, hungrier after than before it, and she tugged at the antiquated bell-cord in the sitting-room with no uncertain hand. Bernice appeared with a sulky air, after an interval long enough to assert her own independence and to fan Susan's smouldering anger to white heat.

"I wish to see Mrs. Bald here at once, please, Bernice."

Mrs. Bald, however, was engaged on an operation darkly alluded to as "warkin' wi' the range" and was not able to attend anyone's pleasure.

"Very well," said Susan with an iciness that masked intense wrath. "Then I shall go to her in the kitchen myself. In the meantime, Bernice, you can dust this room."

"It was dustit afore ye got yer breakfast," she replied.

"Then," said Susan, "you can dust it again, and this time please remember that I like the dust removed."

Feeling like a dragon breathing fire and smoke, she made her way through a baize-covered door to the kitchen premises along a passage highly scented with mouse and damp; but her spirit quailed when she reached Mrs. Bald's domain and confronted her. With a dust-cap askew on her grizzled locks, with the natural purple of her complexion striving to make itself seen through a coating of soot and coal-dust, with her massive form enveloped in a man's old waterproof, she made a sufficiently intimidating spectacle, and only extreme anger kept Susan from trembling visibly.

"Good morning, Mrs. Bald," she began at once, before the cook could launch into the recital of complaints that obviously hovered on the tip of her tongue. "I hope you are going to give us a better dinner this evening than the one we had last night."

"Is it a better denner?" cried Mrs. Bald, brandishing a dirty flue-brush so close to Susan's nose that she thought it prudent to retreat a step in self-defence. "Whit mair could ye ask than a nice wee bit cauld mutton wi' pitawties, an' thae peaches? I'm sure puir Bairniss had the feet fair walked aff her, traichlin' awa' tae Muirfoot for them in a' the mud, an' her buits lettin' in, puir lassie!"

"I'm sorry, Mrs. Bald," said Susan bravely. "Would you mind putting down that brush while I am talking to you? . . . I'm sorry, but I do expect a dinner that is a good deal better, and if you can't give us one—"

She was cut short by a torrent of explanation, excuse and abuse which she found very difficult to follow. She did gather, however, among other items, that Mrs. Bald wasna used wi' these late denners, and that the range was a burnin' and a cryin' shame. There were obscure references to her sister in Oriorio—a place-name unrecognizable to the half-deafened Susan—who would be glad to gi'e her a hame; and to other prospective employers, all imploring her services, whom she had had to disappoint for the sake of the Parsons family. Indeed, if it hadna' been for leavin' the Commander, puir fallow, she and Bairniss wad ha'e packit up an' been awa' three weeks syne, so worn out were they with warstlin' wi' the establishment at Easter Hartrigg.

One salient point impressed itself on Susan's mind, and as soon as Mrs. Bald paused for breath, she pounced on it. "I take it, then, Mrs. Bald," she said with deceptive sweetness, "that you are not pleased with the place?"

Darkly Mrs. Bald muttered that the place was well enough, but some fowk were never satisfied, though you worked your fingers to the bare bane for them. . . . "Ay, an' there's an awfu' nice family in Edinburgh wantin' me an' Bairniss. A fine wee hoose wi' gas-stoves an' 'lectrick licht. I wis wae tae disappint them, so I wis."

"Then *don't* disappoint them," said Susan cordially. "Go to them at once, you and Bernice. Don't wait until your week is up. I'm sure you will be very much happier in Edinburgh, Mrs. Bald."

For a moment it seemed to Susan that she would be attacked with the flue-brush, and she laid her hand, as if casually, on the only likely weapon she could find, which happened to be an exceedingly dirty dishcloth lying on the table in unpleasant proximity to a plate of butter. But while cook and mistress faced one another, Bernice burst upon them in her usual manner of one pursued by a mad bull, and proclaimed breathlessly: "There a man in the droyn-room seekin' the Commander, an' a gentleman at the back-door sellin' combs!"

By mutual though tacit consent Susan and Mrs. Bald postponed the remainder of their interview. Leaving her domestic staff to deal with the "gentleman at the back-door," Susan made her way to the drawing-room to explain to this early caller that Oliver was out looking at some fence which was in urgent need of repair.

An enormous man turned from a window, the light of which, it seemed to Susan's prejudiced eye, he almost blocked out, and in a deep rumbling voice told her that it was a fine morning.

"Is it?" said Susan bleakly, shivering in the vault-like atmosphere of the unused room, which smelt of mould. "I haven't been out yet—"

She was disturbed by her crossing of swords with Mrs. Bald, appalled at the prospect of the work that must be done before the house would be comfortable, and in no mood to be sociable, particularly as she knew she must be looking anything but her best.

Anyhow, it was a most uncivilized hour for a call, and this person in his riding-breeches and muddy boots and leggings ought to have known it.

"You wanted to see my brother, I think?" she said distantly. "I'm afraid he's out looking at a fence or something—"

"He's taken very kindly to this country," said the stranger in his deep voice. "Will he be farming the place himself, do you know?"

"Farming the place?" Susan almost laughed at the absurdity of this question. Oliver farming! Perhaps only those who knew him could appreciate how entirely ridiculous such a suggestion was. "No, I think not."

"Well, I'll go and look him up. He'll be at the fence I came to see him about, likely," said he, and made for the door. Reaching it, he turned and said gruffly: "My name's Armstrong. I march with you."

"Oh ... why?" was all that Susan could find to say in reply. Was this some Scottish form of leave-taking? Apparently not.

"Why?" he stared at her; then a slow smile began to spread over his wind- and weather-beaten countenance. Looking down at Susan who, a tall young woman, was accustomed to meet the eyes of most men on a level, he explained with an indulgent grin: "I have the place next to Easter Hartrigg."

To be caught out in such an idiotic townswoman's mistake so soon after her arrival, to be laughed at kindly by this gigantic clod-hopping Scotsman, was almost more than Susan could bear. "Indeed?" she said, still more distantly. "Don't let me keep you from going to find my brother."

But he seemed to have abandoned the idea of going. He leaned comfortably against the door, looking at her.

"And how d'you think you're going to like living at Easter Hartrigg, Miss Parsons?"

Thinking of the Herculean tasks that lay in wait, not least among them the summary dismissal of Mrs. Bald and daughter, Susan answered promptly, "Not at all."

He nodded. "You don't look as if it would suit you. Too die-away. But it's a pity, for your brother's settling in well—and it was time there was somebody here to take an interest in the place. Tenants aren't the same, and the last lot here were a poor crowd. You'll need to remember that your brother is laird of Easter Hartrigg now, you know."

"'A laird and twenty pence, pronounc'd with noise,'" Susan quoted with a rueful smile, forgetting that she was speaking to this extraordinarily rude man, and thinking only of the tiny income, so inadequate for a landowner, who needed capital in these hard times, no matter how small his property.

He looked puzzled. Evidently the words had no meaning for him, and he turned once more to the door. "I'll go down to the march fence, then," he said abruptly. "I can find my own way out. Good morning."

Susan said "Good morning," and parted from him without regret. She did not doubt that, as he went with a quick, short stride down the sloping grass field towards a hollow screened by bushes, followed from the window by her resentful stare, he was thinking her an epitome of all that the country-dweller scorns.

"I daresay he's laughing at me over that imbecile mistake about the march," she thought angrily. "And he called me 'die-away!' Odious man! And, *what* an oaf."

3

The remainder of the morning was spent in a dreary pilgrimage from room to room of the neglected house, finding here a large rat-hole in the skirting-boards, there a loose piece of wallpaper flapping, or a badly cracked window-pane, and cobwebs, and the reek of damp everywhere. The repairs spoken of so grandly by Oliver seemed, to his sister's disgusted amusement, to have consisted solely in putting a few new slates on the roof, though he had nailed unsightly pieces of tin over one or two of the largest rat-holes. Mrs. Bald and Bernice appeared to have done nothing whatsoever.

"What passes my comprehension," murmured Susan aloud, leaving the last room to find herself in the upper hall, "is *how*, in a house where every mirror and picture-glass is clouded as if with steam, and where the walls are discoloured by moist patches, the tank can come to be empty! I must ask Mrs. Bald."

Mrs. Bald, being questioned, expressed the pious but singularly unhelpful opinion that it was "the hand o' Goad." Bernice, as usual, merely giggled.

After a deplorable luncheon, eaten alone, as Oliver had sent a message to say that he was too busy to come back, Susan sat down in the drawing-room to make out a list of the most urgently necessary improvements. The sun had retreated with an air of finality behind a bank of heavy doud, and a sharp shower of rain, beating smartly on the windows, added to her depression.

"I shall cry in a minute," she thought desperately, looking about the dismal room and remembering the pleasant little flat which she had left for it. "Perhaps a fire would help things a little. It's bitterly cold in here."

The grate was furnished only with a small piece of newspaper, yellowed by age. Susan rang the bell. The summons remained unanswered for so long that at last she went out into the hall and called loudly. Still there was no reply, except for the defiant strains of a mouth-organ, played discordantly but with considerable verve, in the back premises. Advancing to the baize-covered door and throwing it open, Susan once again called for Bernice.

The mouth-organ ceased abruptly, and Bernice, her face flushed with musical effort, came scuttling along the passage.

"Didn't you hear the bell?" asked Susan.

She giggled. "Och, I thocht it wad juist be the baker, an' I wisna heedin' *him!*" she responded with a coquettish toss of her untidy head.

"I shall be obliged if you will answer any bell that is rung at once," Susan said; but the dignity of this reproof was spoiled by her wonder that the baker, or, indeed, any male, should have fallen a victim to Bernice's rabbit-like charms, as her pleased simper seemed to declare. "Please bring sticks and paper and coals, and light the drawing-room fire," said Susan, and retired to wait for her longed-for blaze.

It was not to be. Bernice, wearing a somewhat chastened look, entered in a few minutes with the announcement: "Ma mither says the coals is near done, and onywey there canna be a fire lichtit ben in the droyn-room, for the chimley's chockit wi' sterlings' nests."

("I've sometimes wondered," Susan wrote later to Charles Crawley, "how the principals in a Greek tragedy felt towards the messenger who is always popping in with tidings of fresh woe. Now I think I know. If the messenger wore the look of half-terrified delight in bad news which is plainly to be seen in Bernice's protruding eyes, death, instant and painful, would have been his portion. In fact, I really believe that only the lack of a handy weapon prevented me from killing her on the drawing-room hearthrug!")

Controlling herself, she dismissed Bernice from the room in such a peremptory manner that the girl ran all the way to the kitchen, where her shrill tones could be heard proclaiming: "Eh, she's awfu' vexed. She's lookin' like murrder!"

As she relieved her feelings by slamming the drawing-room door, Susan tried to find some comfort in the thought that the day had become so awful as to leave no further depths to be plumbed before nightfall. She brewed herself tea over her picnic spirit lamp, and, refreshed and a little heartened, shrouded herself in a rug and opened a book. Minutes passed, and drowsiness began to overtake her. The book had fallen from her hand, and she was in that pleasant borderland which immediately precedes sleep, when a succession of thrilling screams, increasing in volume as their utterer approached the door of her haven, roused her with horrid suddenness. She was springing from the sofa when the door burst open and the Messenger of Fate, capless, draggled apron-strings streaming like a comet's tail, rushed in. Her mouth was opening to give vent to one final yell when Susan stopped her by demanding what was wrong.

"Is it whit's wrang?" screamed Bernice, her voice, hitherto muted to an indistinct pipe in her mistress's presence, now given full freedom with ear-shattering results. "There's ma mither in the kitchen, fechting drunk, an' seekin' ma bluid!"

Susan knew a second's fleeting sympathy with Mrs. Bald, and then the horror of the situation began to come home to her, sharpened by the ominous sounds of crashing crockery and hoarse bellowing from the kitchen.

Bernice broke into loud hysterical sobbing. "The Commander'll fin' us baith deid when he wins hame!" she cried, weeping.

"The Commander will do no such thing," Susan retorted angrily. "Stop behaving like a fool, Bernice, and tell me, if you can, where your mother got anything to drink."

Hiccupping sobs made Bernice almost entirely incoherent, but Susan was at last able to elicit that Mrs. Bald, her appetite whetted by a bottle of cooking sherry, had drunk some methylated spirits, and had then demanded whisky. Bernice, who had seen where Oliver had put the key of the cupboard containing the whisky-bottle, had been forced to disclose its whereabouts at the point of the poker, Mrs. Bald's favourite weapon.

"Well," said Susan, "you must go to—Reiverslaw, is it?—and tell Commander Parsons to come back here at once, and bring a policeman with him."

"Is it the polis?" echoed Bernice with a look half of pity, half of misplaced pride in her parent's reputation. "Guid save us, the polis is as feared for ma mither as ony o' them!"

A ring at the bell caused an interruption, and Bernice, darting to the window, said, "It's Wullie Blair wi' the breid."

"Is he afraid of Mrs. Bald too?" asked Susan, her hopes rising at the thought of possible succour.

"Ay, is he!" quoth Bernice.

Susan's heart sank, and certainly the appearance of the weedy shambling youth on the gravel outside, who held two loaves, innocent of wrapping, in his grimy hands, was not inspiring. Obviously he was no match for Mrs. Bald.

"But he'll gi'e me a lift tae Reiverslaw!" said Bernice with the first glimmering of intelligence her mistress had yet perceived in her. "I'll awa' oot an' speir him!"

She sped to the door, and Susan heard their conversation, punctuated by loud exclamations from the youth and neighing laughter from Bernice. The request evidently met with a favourable reply, for presently both darted round the side of the house and disappeared from view. In a few seconds from the back window, to which she had hurried, Susan saw the baker's van, with Bernice seated on the box, her arm lovingly round her swain's neck, lurch perilously off along the road, the horse between the shafts breaking into a stumbling gallop as roars from the kitchen told that their flight had not passed unnoticed by Mrs. Bald.

They were scarcely out of sight before Susan began to regret most bitterly that she had not thrown pride to the winds and accompanied them. The prospect of bearding the cook in her den was far from alluring, and she had serious thoughts of locking herself into the drawing-room to await Oliver's return in safety.

There was a sudden lull in the noises from the kitchen, and an ominous silence began to settle down and brood over the whole house. Susan, who had plenty of courage, decided that Mrs. Bald was by this time reduced to a state of stupor; so, leaving the drawing-room, she went towards the kitchen passage to see for herself. It was getting dark in the house, though outside a queer grey half-light still prevailed. As Susan stood uncertainly in the passage with the swinging baize door between her and safety, she hesitated again. Perhaps, after all, discretion was really the better part, and it would only be foolish to interfere? It was the striking of a match in the kitchen that turned the scales. She could not leave a drunken old woman to set the house on fire without making some effort to prevent it.

Mrs. Bald was trying with a palsied hand to light a lamp on the table. Several matches lay on the floor; one, still alight, was burning a hole in a rug. Susan stamped out its smouldering end, and striving to hide her disgust at the old woman's appearance and the fumes of alcohol which filled the kitchen, said in a voice which succeeded in being both firm and conciliatory, "Let me do that for you, Mrs. Bald."

Rather to her surprise, for she had expected a violent refusal, Mrs. Bald gave up the matches and sank into a chair. By the time the lamp had yielded to Susan's inexperienced fumbling and was properly lighted, stertorous breathing, broken from time to time by a pig-like snore, led her to hope that the cook had fallen asleep. She tiptoed from the kitchen thankfully, but had not reached the door when Mrs. Bald roused herself to demand querulously:

"Whaur's Bairniss? Whaur's ma wee lassie?"

Susan found herself quite unequal to the task of telling Mrs. Bald that her daughter had gone to summon those who would remove her from Easter Hartrigg without delay; and while she hesitated there was a lamentable howl from the figure slumped in the chair.

"Ye needna tell me. I ken whaur she is! She's aff wi' yon guid-for-naethin' Wullie Blair! Ma bonnie wee Bairniss that micht ha'e mairret on the sanitary inspector frae Kaleford if he hadna' catched the 'fluenzy an' dee'd on her! Eh, ma wee lassie!" Then, with a sudden appalling change from maternal sorrow to ferocity: "Eh, wait you till I get ma haunds on her! I'll sort her, so I wull!"

Susan trembled for Bernice, but thought it probable that by the time she returned Mrs. Bald would be completely comatose.

"Eh, dearie, dearie me!" moaned the stricken parent. "I'm feelin' that badly. I doot whit I need's a wee drap whusky!"

"A cup of tea will do you all the good in the world," Susan said firmly, and turned to move the kettle farther on to the fire. When she looked round, it was to see Mrs. Bald withdrawing a bottle, with stealthy cunning, from a little cupboard below the sink.

"Mrs. Bald," she cried, "you must give me that—that bottle at once! If you drink any more out of it you'll be ill." Without allowing herself time to hesitate, she advanced and, before Mrs. Bald's bemused brain could gather her intention, snatched the bottle, now only one-third full, and poured the remaining contents down the sink. Then, indeed, Susan shrank back, appalled at the consequences of her action, for the gibbering creature mouthing incoherent curses and threats who came wavering towards her seemed barely human.

"Mrs. Bald—" she began bravely, to be cut short by a tea-cup which, fortunately wide of the mark, flew past her and was shattered against the wall at her back. Several plates followed, and Susan wished with all her heart that Mrs. Bald were not between her and the door. It was when the cook seized the lamp that her nerve gave way, and she uttered a cry of horror.

Then a good many things seemed to happen at once. There were screams easily recognizable as Bernice's in the hall, quick, heavy footsteps along the passage, and a man burst into the kitchen. Without an instant's pause he tore the smoking lamp from Mrs. Bald and, holding it out of her reach, pushed her down into a chair.

"Take the lamp, can't you?" he roared.

Susan threw down the whisky-bottle to which, as a drowning man to his straw, she had been clinging convulsively, and did as she was told with a shaking hand. Still holding the overflowing bulk of Mrs. Bald down easily, the rescuer, whom Susan now realized was her unwanted caller of the morning, said: "It's all right. Your brother will be here in a minute, and we'll put her inside the baker's van and send her home to Kaleford."

The white, scared faces of Bernice and the baker's boy were now to be seen peering round the door, and shortly afterwards Oliver limped in. Within a few minutes the shelves, empty of loaves now, had been taken from the van by Bernice and her young man in loving co-operation, and the portly figure of Mrs. Bald was inserted in their place as a tigress in its cage, by Oliver and the gigantic Mr. Armstrong. The door was slammed on her bellowing, the baker's boy and the housemaid mounted the box once more, and the weary horse with its roaring freight plunged off into the darkness.

Oliver mopped his brow. "What a day!" he said. He put an arm about his sister's still trembling form. "Sure you're all right, old lady? *What* a day!"

Susan, with a shaky laugh, confessed to feeling rather the worse for wear; but her recovery was speeded by her sudden spurt of anger, for Mr. Armstrong, with a reproachful glance at her, merely remarked: "It's a pity you were so hasty with that good whisky. We could have done with some of it ourselves."

4

As though the mere presence of Mrs. Bald and her daughter had cast a blight over the place which vanished with their departure, the major discomforts of Easter Hartrigg seemed to have melted away on the following morning. If Susan still felt indignant with Mr. Armstrong for his callousness, she had to admit that he had been as good as his word, for he had promised help and duly sent it in the form of the grieve's wife from Reiverslaw.

This gaunt, grim but capable woman had served Oliver and his sister with an excellent breakfast, and Susan, going to thank her, found her giving the kitchen what she called a "redd up." The tank, so far from being empty, was overflowing, the coal-cellar in like case, and the grieve's wife darkly uttered her opinion of Mrs. Bald as she scrubbed the table.

"Bane-idle, baith the twa o' them, like a' the Irish," she said, her words keeping time to violent movements of her bony arms. "They're no' Kaleford fowk, ye ken. It wad be tae spare hersel' the trouble, mem, o' heatin' watter or cairryin' coal that she tellt ye a pack o' lees. This kitchen's no' fit for pigs' meat tae be mixed in, let alane cookin' for gentry! But I'll sort it. Awa' you ootbye an' tak' a bit daunder tae yersel', it'll dae ye guid, and ye'll no' ken the place or ye come back."

Cheered by this promise, Susan gladly took herself out of doors to look for the first time since her arrival at her brother's inheritance. Shafts of March sunshine, slanting between the leafless branches of the trees which pressed too closely about the sides and back of the house, lighted the first daffodils to pale-yellow fire. A mating blackbird somewhere aloft had opened his orange bill and was pouring out a love-song more exquisite than any by which mortal maid was ever wooed. Susan walked slowly across the sweep of nobbly gravel to the verge of a sloping unkempt lawn and stood there, staring about her.

The house, two-storied, square, stolid, its rough-cast walls stained by damp, was a little too low-lying, but a great improvement could be made by cutting down some of the trees, and she ruthlessly marked several future victims with a calculating eye. Once these were out of the way, a view of the rolling wooded country beyond would be cleared; and if Oliver demurred on the grounds that trees should not be felled for a view alone, she could point out more prosaic advantages.

"It would be so much less damp without the trees," she murmured aloud, "and think what splendid logs they'll make for all sorts of things—"

"What are you muttering about?" suddenly demanded Oliver, coming up behind her on the grass. "I see destruction in your eye, a sort of horrible spring-cleaning look. But if it's anything that will cost a lot, you can think again."

Susan repeated her words. "We can use the logs on the sitting-room fire," she urged. "And the house is dreadfully damp, Oliver."

"So we can. So it is."

"And we'd have such a lovely view—"

"So we should."

"And I hope you are going to have them cut down," she went on, a little daunted by this hearty agreement where she had expected to be overwhelmed by a flood of objections.

"So I am," he said. "Armstrong told me we ought to have 'em all down, and down they shall come."

"What? Not *all*?" cried Susan perversely, annoyed by this intrusion of what she was beginning to call to herself "the inevitable Armstrong."

"Every blessed one of them."

"Oh, no! Leave a few—for shade, you know—" she began weakly, and he broke into loud and derisive laughter.

"Oliver," said his sister, "you are a brute, and so is your great galumphing Mr. Armstrong."

He took her by the arm. "Never mind, old lady. Come and look at what used to be the garden. Lord knows what the last tenants did to pass the time, but I'll take my oath it wasn't gardening."

A garden run to waste, the hardier plants struggling valiantly but unavailingly against the encroaching weeds, is a melancholy sight, and as brother and sister went down the sloping pathless lawn towards the half-broken rustic trellis of spruce branches which marked its upper boundary, they both fell silent.

"Mercifully it's not very large," said Susan at last, when her eyes had taken in the desolation of overgrown paths, borders now rampant with nettles, beds where young weeds were springing up in gay green confidence.

"It lies beautifully—southern exposure, sheltered on the east by that brick wall," said Oliver more hopefully. "I believe it used to be a sight to see. It's good soil, too, so Armstrong says—"

"*Blow* Armstrong! And it's a sight now. Do you suppose anything will ever make it look like a garden again?"

"We'll get it dug, anyhow. I don't know the first thing about gardening, but the minister is an expert, and he's offered to help."

"Very kind of him," said Susan absently, for she was thinking of something else, and presently she voiced her thought. "How much of what we see belongs to you, Oliver?"

On this, the only side of the house that was not shut in by trees, the ground fell away gently. Following the slope of the lawn came the garden, and below it again fields descended to a long, green hollow fringed with thorn bushes. Oliver nodded towards these and said: "There's our march. Beyond the hawthorns is Armstrong's place, Reiverslaw, and we have a couple of fields across the road behind the house."

"All that?" Susan was horrified.

"All that? It's a small property—"

"Yes, but—my dear! It will have to be looked after. Ploughed or—or something," said Susan helplessly. "And you know nothing about farming, any more than I do."

"I don't have to," he said. "Luckily, the land always seems to have been let separately from the house, and we get quite a decent rent for it, as land goes nowadays."

"Thank goodness!" sighed Susan.

Relieved of her chief anxiety, she felt as she turned back to the house quite an affection for Easter Hartrigg. True, it was a house which, if not definitely ugly, was extremely plain; but it suited the surroundings in its simplicity, and there was not a hint of pretentious villadom about it. When she walked into the hall, reduced to cleanliness and order by the grieve's wife, she was conscious of a pleasant sense of homecoming.

"After all," she said to Oliver that evening, "I believe I was really intended for a rural life. There's something about this, with all its drawbacks, that town entirely lacked."

His face, which had grown browner and slightly less haggard in the two months since he had left London, brightened.

"I'm glad you feel like that, Susan. I hoped you would," he said. "It's—I can't explain it, exactly, but this is my own place. *Our* place. . . ."

CHAPTER THREE

1

THE "long-lie-in" which his parishioners enjoyed on the Sabbath morning was denied to Mr. Cunningham and his family. After breakfast there were dishes to wash, beds to make, the hens to feed, and preparations for the midday dinner to be started, all before eleven o'clock, when the Sunday School was timed to begin.

Peggy went through the usual routine in a frame of mind far from exemplary. The lovely clearness of the March morning had made her restless. For just one Sunday, she thought, she would like to stay away from church if she wished, as other girls of her acquaintance were free to do. She paused in her task of arranging a bowl of evergreens to be placed on the Communion table in the little chancel, to plan what she would do with this morning if it were her very own. A book beside the fire in the study, perhaps; or, far better on such a day, a tramp along the high ridge past Reiverslaw, wearing comfortable old clothes instead of her Sunday dress of deep-blue with its white collar. There would be yellowhammers flitting about the hedges, and pussy-willows, powdered with gold, in the sheltered hollows. . . . She shook herself free of useless wishes with a sigh, and carried the big jar of glossy rhododendron leaves and a few of the earlier daffodils into the church.

But while she told her class of small children the story of Ruth, her thoughts persisted in straying from that Eastern cornfield and wandered away with her into the cold, crisp meadows outside. The decorous rows of well-scrubbed, apple-cheeked little girls and boys began to fidget. There was a sound of whispering, the toe of a stubby boot kicked against a pew, and Peggy saw her father glance in her direction with a faint reproving shake of his head. This would never do. She, the minister's daughter, was supposed to be a shining example to the others. She pulled herself together, and for the remainder of the time devoted her attention to the class, to such good effect that there was a sigh of disappointment when it ended, and children and teachers were free to go out into the churchyard until the bell summoned them back for morning service.

Ronald Graham, the organist, who came several miles on a bicycle to preside over the harmonium every Sunday, was waiting patiently at the Manse gate. He, and several of the Sabbath School teachers, were always taken in at this chilly season, and stayed with glasses of hot milk, plates of rich tea biscuits. Peggy made a vain attempt to appear deep in conversation with little Miss Webster, who taught the class senior to her own, but this did not deter Ronald Graham. He walked firmly on her other side, darting such bitter looks at Miss Webster that she seized on the first available opportunity of leaving Peggy to him.

Then he said quickly, accusingly: "It seems an awfully long time since I saw you."

"Thursday evening, at the choir practice," Peggy pointed out briskly. "That's only about two days ago. Come in and have your hot milk. The bell will be ringing in a minute."

He snatched at her ungloved hand as they went into the dark hall, and Peggy, hating the feel of his hot yet clammy touch, pulled her fingers away. "Please don't be so silly, Ronald," she said. "And do be careful where you're going—there! You've tripped over the step again! You always do."

In spite of the shining brass edge of the single step leading up into the inner hall of the Manse, Ronald Graham had not seen it, and stumbled, as he seldom failed to do, often as he entered this hospitable house.

"What's happening out there?" called the minister, glancing back from the open doorway of the dining-room. "Someone slipped?"

"Only Ronald!" Peggy called back in clear, unkind tones.

"Ronald? You're always falling over that step, my boy," said the minister, joining them to his daughter's visible relief and the organist's helpless rage. "We'll need to have it removed, for we can't risk anyone as valuable to us as you hurting yourself." He laid a friendly hand on the young man's shoulder, smiling at his own well-worn joke;

but Ronald Graham's answering smile was a wry one and summoned to his lips with an effort.

Peggy thankfully busied herself with handing round the plate of biscuits. She was glad to have escaped fairly easily from Ronald, who openly showed a liking for her which she by no means returned. Everything about him offended and irritated her: his clumsiness, his sullen temper alternating with bursts of much-too-noisy gaiety; the ill-breeding which an expensive education failed to disguise at times, and the fact that he traded on his standing as organist to pester her with his unwanted attentions. "Just because he's the only young man I ever meet," she thought resentfully, "he needn't behave as though I ought to be thanking heaven fasting for him. His horrible red hands, like bits of raw beef. Ugh!"

Catching his eye across the room, she gave him a cold look. However necessary Ronald Graham might be to her father, for he had trained the village choir to something approaching excellence, and loved his work, she refused to be more than polite to him—and not always even that, as she admitted to herself truthfully....

The bell began to ring; Mr. Cunningham and the organist set off to the church, followed more slowly by Peggy and her mother, the latter still deep in talk with the Sunday School teachers.

The Manse pew was at the back of one of the transepts, under the northern window, and commanded very restricted view of the church. Across an empty floor-space the choir occupied the first three rows of the south transept, and Peggy found that one of her reasons for liking to be among the young men and maidens who led the singing was that she could see more of the church. True, Ronald Graham's hateful, sleek head was close in front of her; she could not escape the constant sight of his profile as he sat at the harmonium at right angles to the choir; but by glancing discreetly sideways she managed to have a very fair idea of who were present. This morning, as usual, she watched them filing soberly in. Farmers with their wives, ploughmen and hinds with their families, the village, people; the three Miss Pringles, the most notable gossips in the neighbourhood; old Lady Brakespear, erect and eagle-eyed for all her eighty-four years, who only emerged from her nun-like seclusion to attend church; a sprinkling of "county" from the big houses. The Reiverslaw pew was empty, and Peggy missed Jed Armstrong when he was not there to give her a covert smile as he took his place. Suddenly her eyes opened wide: two persons were being shown into the Easter Hartrigg pew by Robert Elder, the beadle. The man, limping slightly, and wearing the church-going expression of devout misery common to normal men, was Commander Parsons. The tall woman in tawny tweeds, who carried her head high, and whose glance seemed to sweep the whole church in a second, must be his sister. She smiled at him as they sat down, and Peggy thought with young enthusiasm, "I like her! Oh, I do hope she'll like *me*!"

Then Robert Elder, the long tails of his Sunday black coat flapping down to his calves, carried the big Bible up into the pulpit, and while the harmonium began a wheezy voluntary, retired, only to make a second appearance, ushering in the minister from the vestry, in his black gown and snowy bands.

"Let us prepare to worship God by singing to His praise part of the forty-sixth psalm. Psalm forty-six, verses one to five. 'God is our refuge and our strength.' The tune is Stroudwater, number one hundred and twenty-eight. . . ."

Peggy, singing with the unselfconsciousness of a thrush, still looked from time to time towards Miss Parsons. There was something about her—not beauty, for she was not beautiful—that made you look, and look again. "She's like a person out of a book," thought Peggy, unable to describe Susan's curious appeal even to herself.

After church, standing shyly behind her mother while Oliver Parsons made introductions, Peggy was at last able to see her at close quarters. Very tall, with an out-of-date stateliness which seemed natural to her, Susan Parsons yet had a gracefulness that made every movement lovely to watch. Her hazel eyes, shining below black brows like her brother's, could flash with sudden gaiety and humour, yet seemed more often to contradict than to agree with the curves of her mouth with its deeply indented corners. A dimple which made its brief appearance when she smiled, and dark curling hair, lent an air of youthfulness to her face. "Susan belongs to the court of Charles I. She is out of place in this century," a discerning acquaintance once said of her, and Peggy recognized this, though she could not put a name to it.

Now she was being introduced. "My daughter Peggy, Miss Parsons." And with a shyness which she hated, but was unable to overcome, she murmured, "How d'you do?" Conscious of Oliver's dark gaze, she coloured hotly and, looking up, saw that Ronald Graham, who stood apart waiting to go over to the Manse for dinner, was watching her. Anger and a hint of fear brought more colour to her cheeks, for she knew that after the meal, when Mr. and Mrs. Cunningham had disappeared to rest for an hour, she would be taken to task by Ronald. It was none of his business, of course, but that would not stop him, and the thought of this unpleasant *tête-à-tête* filled her with dismay.

Susan's voice, inviting her to walk up to Easter Hartrigg and have luncheon with them, sounded like that of a rescuing angel.

"Oh, Mother, may I? I'm not wanted for anything, am I?"

Mrs. Cunningham hesitated. Sunday was a day to be spent between church and home; then she saw Peggy's imploring look, remembered how young she was, and nodded with a smile.

"You'll not forget, though, Peggy, that this is a Newtown night," said her father.

"No, no, Father. I won't forget," said Peggy joyfully.

Susan asked with interest, "What is a 'Newtown night,' Mr. Cunningham? I'm strange to the country, so please enlighten me."

The minister explained, with additions thrown in by Mrs. Cunningham, that on alternate Sundays he held an evening service at Newtown-of-Muirfoot, a few scattered cottages about two miles away, where a handful of the faithful gathered in a draughty tin hall to hear him preach. It was too much for his wife to trudge there and back in all weathers, so Peggy represented her.

"I see," said Susan. "Then may she stay to tea, and we'll see that she leaves in good time for the service."

"Who's the surly-looking bloke lurking among the tombstones?" asked Oliver as the three walked up the village.

Peggy gasped, but recovered herself. "He's our organist," she said. "Didn't you see him in church?"

"All I could see was that his hair had been mastered by Anzora, same like the advertisements," said Oliver. "So that's the organist, is it?"

"Yes. His father is Graham's Cough Mixture. A Cure in Every Dose," said Peggy. "He's—" she broke off, biting her lip.

"He's what?" Oliver asked, heedless of Susan's frown.

But Peggy had her temper in hand again. "He's a very good organist," she said demurely. "I'm sure I don't know what we'd do without him."

They turned into a grassy track, a short cut which led up out of the hollow to the Hartrigg ridge. High hawthorn hedges sheltered them from the piercing wind which sang through the bare, gnarled branches, black against a sky of keen blue. The distant woods were misty with an exquisite umber bloom, like nothing so much as the bloom on a grape, fields showed bright-green where young grass was springing, or dark-red of ploughland gleamed in the sun.

It was a stiff climb, but Oliver Parsons, in spite of his lame leg, went up it at a great pace, forcing himself on as if it gave him a queer pleasure to struggle against his disability. Peggy saw that his sister cast him a frequent anxious look without appearing to do so. She said nothing until they had covered half the ascent, and then begged for a halt. "Or at least, my dear, have mercy on us," she said. "I don't know about Miss Cunningham, but this pace is killing me." He glanced from her to Peggy suspiciously, but they were obviously tired and out of breath, and he slackened speed.

"That's better," said Susan contentedly. Peggy knew that her small sigh of relief was for her brother, not herself.

"How well she manages him," thought the younger girl, whose own impulse had been to beg him to spare himself. "And how he hates to limp, poor man!"

She looked at Oliver quickly, almost guiltily, in case he should catch her in the act. Instinctively she knew that he would resent pity most bitterly. But she understood now why he gave a petulant flick at his offending leg with the gloves he carried, why he drove himself as cruelly as if he spurred a done horse, why his cheeks were hollow and his eyes angry.

When, at the top of the hill, he turned to speak to her, the shadows had gone and he sounded cheerful, almost gay. It might have been a different person, Peggy thought wonderingly, as she tried to make amusing answer to his sallies.

An enormous black dog met them on the threshold of Easter Hartrigg, and nearly knocked them down in the exuberance of his welcome to Susan.

"Down, Tara, down!" she cried. And to Peggy: "This is the latest addition to the family. Poor boy, his people moved into town from the country, and as we had become country-dwellers ourselves, and he is obviously the wrong size for a small flat, they bequeathed him to us."

"He's lovely," said Peggy, laying a hand on the broad black head. ". . . Oh, and a cat too!"

"Yes. This is MacDaisy, rat-catcher-in-chief to the house of Easter Hartrigg," said Oliver, picking up the cat, black also, but adorned with four white socks and white whiskers of superb length.

"MacDaisy?" said Peggy, wishing she did not always sound so surprised at the remarks of these pleasant English persons.

Susan laughed. "Isn't it absurd? But his mother's name is Daisy, and Oliver insisted that a Scottish cat should have a 'Mac' about him. We got him from the grieve's wife at Reiverslaw."

Luncheon was a delightful meal to Peggy. She did not mind the fact that the wallpaper was faded, and in one place hanging from the wall, or that a leg of her chair caught on a hole in the carpet and nearly capsized her into a bowl of daffodils on the table. Here she had found the congenial society for which she pined, and if her tongue said little, her blue eyes spoke eloquently, telling Susan all her pleasure.

"A charming child," said Susan after she had left them to walk to Newtown-of-Muirfoot. "There's something so fresh and simple about her—"

"What you mean," growled Oliver, whose leg was paining him after his exertions, "is that she hangs on your words, my girl, as if you were a blooming oracle. Simple? Oh, yes; she's simple, all right. So's the village idiot. And of the two, I think he's the more enlivening. You can keep her."

"Liver," murmured Susan provokingly, "or spleen, because she likes me better than you, darling. I'll have my nice little Peggy—at least she's easy to look at—and you can enjoy your hulking Armstrong. Good night."

2

"You ask me whether I am not bored to tears. My dear," wrote Susan, "boredom and I are total strangers, and have been since I came here. You see, to be bored implies unlimited leisure, and of that I have little or none. When I shut my eyes and think back over the four months since I came, I can remember a period of ceaseless turmoil, a nightmare war waged against rats, damp, servants, local workmen, and the incursions of cattle on the wilderness which was once a garden, and which I have vowed will blossom again as the rose. Oliver poisoned the rats, and they avenged themselves hideously by returning to die under the floors. No sooner did we trace one leak to its source and stop it than another mysteriously took its place. A succession of domestics, their utter incompetence as incredible as the wages they demanded (and, perforce, got), has ruled in turn over the kitchen. Plumbers and strange artisans called in this country 'slaters' and 'joiners', have pervaded the house in muddy hobnailed boots, and sung, whistled, smoked, and bawled injunctions to one another as though miles instead of yards divided them. If the infinitely slow pursuit of their labours did not please us—miserably counting up the hours for which we'd have to pay them—at least the reigning staff were well entertained, to judge by the skirls of shrill merriment proceeding from the kitchen premises. As for the fences, hastily mended against invading bullocks which jump like stags or hunters, they are constantly requiring fresh repairs. There have been times, Charles, when only hysterical laughter has kept me from either sitting down to weep, or packing my belongings and fleeing to take shelter in an hotel; but of course I've weathered it, and the difference these months have made to Oliver is worth anything."

She laid down her pen and, setting both elbows on the bureau, rested her chin in her hands and stared out of the window. What she had said to Charles about the difficulties she had faced was quite true, but there had certainly been compensations. If confusion had held sway within the house, outside the slow days marched by in a painted procession of changeful beauty, the still nights throbbed with a myriad stars. Sunlight and cloud-shadow patched the long line of distant hills, and the singing of small birds made music. It was a kindly countryside in summer weather, of rich pasture and arable land, of deep old woods, of hills that melted roundly into the skyline and did not pierce it with jagged peaks. When, in a fury of revolt against the domestic cares with which she, an unwilling Martha, was cumbered, Susan rushed out of doors, or even thrust her head out of a wide-flung window, a deep peace instantly fell on her, and she returned soothed and refreshed.

And as the house itself gradually assumed its rightful air of ordered calm, as walls bloomed in clean new distemper, and chairs and sofas were clad in flowery cretonne covers which Susan made herself; as the effluvium of rat slowly faded, giving place to the pleasant smell of furniture polish and the scent of flowers; as the small army of workmen regretfully took their leave, she found herself not only able to bear Easter Hartrigg, but fond of it with the unreasoning, possessive affection reserved for what is one's own. No doubt about it, the country and the plain-faced house had a ridiculously strong hold upon her by this time.

"We now have a local girl as cook, a perfect treasure, who rejoices in the improbable name of Donaldina Sprot. There should be another, of course, but we simply can't afford it, and we had to have someone for outside work. Again the finances wouldn't run to a full-grown man, but we have engaged a taciturn boy, commonly known as 'Jems' to clean boots and things and to help in the garden. His official title here is 'orra-man.' In plain English, odd-job-man. And you mustn't imagine that all this time we have been neglected by our neighbours. Far from it. The Cunninghams are old friends of ours by now, and Oliver seems to find a constant delight in the society of Jed Armstrong, of whom I've written to you already. Personally, as you have gathered, I don't find Mr. Armstrong congenial, but I welcome him gladly for Oliver's sake, and he is a well-meaning clod." Susan paused, and then, rather ashamed of herself, scratched out the word "clod" and substituted "creature."

"Apart from these, it seems that almost daily I was summoned from battling with the workmen, the cook, or the furniture, and dirty and dishevelled, had to receive callers with a pleasant smile in one of the two half-finished sitting-rooms. If Oliver appeared at all, it would be looking more like a stowaway on board a tramp steamer than a retired Lieutenant-Commander of the King's Navee. And we would sit uneasily on cushionless—and often coverless—chairs, making polite conversation while the visitors kept their eyes discreetly turned from the more obvious traces of disorder. Oliver and I striving with idiot laughter and not daring to look at each other. Probably everyone thinks we are quite mad.

"Lately an epidemic of tennis-parties has broken out, and we have sallied forth in pure white raiment, Oliver to cover himself with glory in spite of his game leg, and I with disgrace. You know how useless I am on a tennis-court, or indeed, in any place where games are played. Our own court having been allowed by the tenants to go wild, now bears a fine crop of hay, and even Oliver's optimistic eye cannot see it as anything except a grass field.

"When are you coming to see us, Charles? All you do is to write disapproving notes—for they aren't long enough to be dignified by the name of letters. You know how we'd love to have you, and perhaps a sight of us will make you less gloomy about our future. In the meantime I must stop this haver (as you see, I am learning Scots) and go to tea at the Manse of Muirfoot."

Taking her letter, Susan set out with Tara, soberly gay, running ahead of her. It was a day on which the old gods might have chosen to leave their own mountain-tops for the golden haze of the Border hills. The lovely smell of new-cut hay and drying white clover filled the air, brambles were set with clusters of white blossom among their prickly leaves at the side of the old cart-road down which she walked. Tall hedges of hawthorn, the haws already beginning to show the faintest tinge of red, made a shaggy border to it on either side, and below them the flowers of late summer were blooming: sweet-scented feathery Queen-of-the-meadow, campions rose and white, St. John's wort and knapweed and willow-herb, with long sprays of honeysuckle and blue tufted vetch lifting their heads above this tangled riot of sweetness. Tara, sniffing luxuriously, ran from side to side in distracted attempts to miss none of the alluring smells which seemed to abound there. Susan found the walk all too short, and sighed a little when she came out into the road near Muirfoot, where the village War Memorial stood, a cairn of the local stone topped by a tiny lion, which was all that funds could run to in the shape of sculpture. Many people laughed at it, and said the memorial would look better without it, but Susan liked the little lion standing defiantly on his cairn, and gave him a nod of greeting as she passed.

On her left rose the walls of the Manse steading, the old slates of the roofs gilded with lichen, the iron weathercock dated 1780 swinging in the light wind high over them all. What a lot the cock must have seen since he was first erected on the older church, Susan thought. She turned into the post office to see Mrs. Davidson, a local character who never failed to amuse her.

After serving her with the stamps she asked for, the postmistress said: "Yer paircel hasna come yet frae Lunnon, Miss Parsons. They're awfu' slow at thae English shopes. I'm sure it's five days sin' ye postcarded them."

Swallowing the astonishment which was still liable to overcome her at such proofs of Mrs. Davidson's omniscience, Susan assured her that it was not an important parcel, nodded good day, and prepared to cross the road.

"Ye're for the Manse? Ay, I kent they was expeckin' fowk tae tea, for Mistress Cunningham was bakin' the day. When the wind's in this airt I can smell her girdle scones as fresh as if I stood by her kitchen fire."

"Yes," said Susan, "I've been asked to tea, especially to meet the little grandchildren."

"Ay. Bonnie bairns baith, an' the wee laddie as like his mither, puir Miss Elspeth that was! They've another wi' them this year," went on Mrs. Davidson relentlessly. "A lassie, a kizzen on the faither's side, so I hear. An' that flee-awa' lassie Jo-an Robertson frae Reiverslaw actin' nursemaid tae them. Her! I doot she needs a nurse at her ain heels tae mind her! Weel, they ha'e their tea on the chap o' hauf-past fower at the Manse, so ye'd better awa' ower the road."

Thus dismissed, Susan opened the Manse gate and went in. She found the minister, bare-headed and in a kind of clerical undress uniform, mowing the lawn. On seeing her approach, he stopped and frankly mopped his brow, further untidying his silver hair.

"Well, well," he said in his hearty Scots voice, "so you've walked down from Easter Hartrigg, then, Miss Parsons? You and the doggie with you—"

They shook hands, while Tara, no great admirer of the clergy, whom he lumped with dislikeable persons such as postmen and policemen, allowed himself to be patted on the wrong place, on his head, with a courteous but aloof air, for he justly resented being alluded to as "the doggie."

Susan herself always experienced a feeling of wariness on meeting any clergyman, and greatly preferred to see them only in church; but to this rule Mr. Cunningham had proved a shining exception from their first encounter. Even if he had not been what he was, a genial, kindly, broad-minded and upright man, of surprisingly wide interests, his passionate love of flowers would have endeared him to anyone who cared for a garden. The most rare and delicate plants flourished bravely for him, and repaid his tender care by making the Manse garden one of the sights of the neighbourhood from spring to late autumn.

That honest old-fashioned pleasance did not disdain to grow vegetables, modestly screened from the walks by glowing flower borders. Gooseberry and currant bushes offered their harvest freely, fruit-trees stood with gnarled trunks deep in blossoms. Nowhere else did sweet-pea hedges grow to such a height, or bloom with so lovely a profusion of exquisite clear colourings and fragile perfume. The long bed of Columbines fluttered their softly-tinted frilled petals in every slightest breeze like an elfin ballet, delphiniums backed the herbaceous border in massed spires of blue in every tone from grave to gay. Mrs. Cunningham could have supplied every linenpress in the county with lavender bags from the two great bushes flanking the garden door: the whole house was sweetened by its prim clean fragrance when it was gathered and laid on trays to dry in the sun. Silvery-pink peonies looked all the cooler beside their flaunting crimson sisters, lupins drew the bees with warm honied scent. The Manse garden held out its sweets to every sense as soon as the door leading into its walled beauty was opened.

A pomander of lovely odours for the princess of some fairy-tale could not have smelled more delicious, the colour dazzled and yet soothed the eyes, velvet or fine damask was never so soft as the grass walks underfoot or the brush of rose-petals against the cheek in passing under some laden arch. Fruit melted like gold sunshine in the mouth or tickled the palate with pleasant tartness, and birds added a song, bees a murmurous undercurrent of praise to hymn this simple paradise.

To think of the Manse of Muirfoot was to think of its garden; to think of the garden instantly called up a picture of its roses. They grew regally in a small garden of their own close to the house, backed by a tall yew hedge of great age, which made a perfect foil for them. Here were all varieties, old favourites for their dark sweet scent, newer treasures for beauty of form and hue, all in small beds carpeted with blue clouds of forget-me-not. Susan felt that she had never known, until she saw them in the Cunninghams' garden, how superbly lovely roses could be. They demanded and received their rightful tribute of silent admiration from all who came to look at them. Some of his parishioners whispered that Mr. Cunningham would have been better advised to spend less on the garden and more on the furnishing and decoration of the Manse itself. Certainly the rooms were plain enough, empty of almost everything but the bare necessities of furniture, with flowers their only adornment. Susan, thinking of the riches out of doors, considered the Cunninghams wise. She knew that a country minister, unless he has private means, is a poor man, and the amount of money laid out on their darling garden could never have given them an equivalent result if spent on interior decoration. If young Jim was at Cambridge, it was because he had won a scholarship, and his parents had pinched and saved to lay aside the remainder of the money necessary. Peggy, though always neat, was plainly dressed, as was her mother; and while the family lived so simply as to be almost frugally, their gracious hospitality might have given points to many a wealthier host and hostess.

Susan, therefore, approaching them cautiously, liked them at once, and was pleased to find that they liked Oliver and herself in return. The liking increased as they came to know each other better. Familiarity did not breed contempt in this case, for real goodness, especially when salted by a sense of humour, excites respect wherever it is found. The minister's solid virtues were never obtrusive, Mrs. Cunningham's gentle blue eyes had a merry glint in them which had carried her triumphantly through many a parish squabble. Jim and Peggy—the latter in particular—had an innocent gaiety which was most refreshing. It only remained for Susan to see what the beloved grandchildren, all they had left of their elder daughter, were like.

"I hope I'll see the children," she said, as they walked up the drive.

"Surely, surely. They're with Peggy in the rose-garden just now. It's a sheltered spot and they get all the afternoon sun. We'll just go quietly up and take a peep at them through the yew hedge, and you'll see them at their best, Miss Parsons. Pity that a child's lack of self-consciousness lasts such a short time."

Holding Tara by the scruff of his indignant neck, Susan followed the minister over the turf in conspiratorial silence towards the opening cut in the high dark wall of the yew hedge. A sound of voices came from behind it, and she peeped cautiously as commanded.

Peggy was sitting on the dry grass, her white cotton frock, sprigged with pink and blue flowers, spreading out round her, the sun shining down on her bare golden head. A small boy, with hair of the same bright gold, was carefully crowning her with a daisy wreath as she read from a book in her lap to two little girls who sprawled beside her, their four brown legs waving in the air. The ceaseless chatter of Colin seemed to disturb the party as little as the sleepy cooing of wood pigeons in the beeches beyond the yew hedge.

"Pitty Peg! Pitty Peg!" said the small boy.

> And when he came at London's court,
> He fell down on his knee.
> "Thou art welcome, Lockesley," said the Queen,
> "And all thy good yeomandree,"

read Peggy to her breathlessly attentive audience.

Mr. Cunningham interrupted them. "I've brought you a visitor—" and they all jumped up.

"Two visitors, Grandaddy," said one of the little girls reprovingly, and stroked Tara's head.

"Is that your dog?" asked the other, a small witch with silvery curls and dark eyes.

"Yes. Do you like him?"

"All but his tongue. He wants to wass my face with it," she said, avoiding a moist pink kiss with difficulty, for Tara's face and her own were on a level.

"It needs to be washed anyway, Cilly," said Peggy laughing, "before tea."

"I'm sorry to have disturbed you, Peggy," Susan said. "You all looked so happy without us."

"It's a good thing you did. I was getting hoarse, and we were coming towards the end of Robin Hood, and I didn't know what we were going to do about it. Death-bed scenes always make Cilly cry!"

"Is Cilly your niece, or the 'wee kizzen' Mrs. Davidson has already told me about?" asked Susan.

"Cilly is the 'wee kizzen.' Our two are much plainer, I'm afraid. Bun, Colin, come and shake hands—if you aren't too dirty——"

"I'm not ezackly scooplusly clean," said Bun advancing politely and extending a grubby paw. "But Colin's dirtier, far," she added cheerfully.

Colin, hearing his name, came no nearer, but burst into a roar of laughter, astonishingly loud for so small a person.

"What a terrible laugh," Peggy said. "It's quite new. I never heard it before this summer."

"He learnt it from a wee boy next door at Granny Richardson's," said Bun calmly.

She might not have her cousin's elfin prettiness, but her broad brow, her serious, wide-set eyes and clear colouring, were very attractive. An unusual-looking child, with straight thick dark hair tied back into two funny little pig-tails, with beautiful sturdy legs and upright carriage, there was something haunting about her. Charming creature though Cilly was and always would be, Susan felt that Bun was the one who would remain longest in the memory. As for Colin, he was the delightful mixture of rogue and cherub which goes to the make-up of every nice small boy, and his conversation consisted generally of parrot-like imitation of his elders' remarks.

"Here's Jo-an come for you, to make you tidy for tea," said Peggy.

A pretty red-haired girl in blue print dress and white apron stood hesitating at the far end of the rose-garden. The children went to her, Colin running ahead of the others, and clutching her round the knees.

"My nice Jo!" he shouted joyfully.

"How pretty Jo-an looks," murmured Peggy. "I'd like to take a photograph of her with Colin."

Susan nodded, but something about the girl, her small, still, secret face, troubled her. This was Mrs. Robertson's "flee-awa' lassie." Surely no child was ever less like her parents; this looked more like a fairy's changeling than the daughter of those two hard-faced Borderers, the grieve at Reiverslaw and his wife. She answered Peggy respectfully enough, but unsmiling, and her glance passed quickly over the children as swift and unheeding as a bird in flight. Only when Colin said again: "Nice Jo! Take me up!" her frozen expression melted to human warmth, a smile curved her small red mouth. She stooped with the same bird-like swiftness, lifted the little boy in strong arms, and followed by Cilly and Bun, went away to the house.

"A difficult lassie," said Mr. Cunningham. "Her parents find it hard to keep her contented at home, and she won't stay in a place. I don't know what's to come of her."

"But father! She likes being here," Peggy said eagerly. "And you can see she's really fond of Colin. I'm sure she'll go to the Richardsons when it's their turn to have the Infantry, and—oh, she'll settle down. After all, she isn't any older than I am, and she'll marry someone—"

Privately, Susan wondered if she would. Jo-an Robertson did not look cut out to be a ploughman's or shepherd's wife; but: "Now you're being fanciful," she told herself sternly. "The girl is just the same as others, except that she looks moire discontented." Aloud she only commented on the name "Jo-an," pronounced with two syllables in the old Scottish fashion.

Mrs. Cunningham met them at the door, and greeted Susan with the unfeigned pleasure which made it a delight to visit the Manse.

"Come away in," she said in her gentle lilting voice. "Yes, of course, the doggie can come too. He won't touch pussy, I know."

"No, he won't," Susan assured her, for Tara's calm ignoring of the very fact that such an animal as the cat existed or was ever created, would have been ludicrous if he had not managed to make it impressive.

Tea was delicious, with newly baked scones light and fluffy as feathers, dark heather-honey, and blackcurrant jam still tasting sunnily of the ripe luscious berries which had gone to its making, and yellow butter like solidified cream.

"I always mean to give up tea," Susan said pensively, "but somehow I can't bear to. I put it off from day to day, and then at last an afternoon comes when I've really made up my mind very firmly only to drink a cup of tea and eat nothing. And then of course I find that Donaldina has made some particular bun or cake, and I have to eat it or she'd be hurt. Rather than run the risk of hurting Donaldina's feelings I'd get as fat as any pig."

The Cunninghams all laughed, even the children. It was one of their charms as a family that they were so ready to enjoy anything that could possibly be taken for a joke. They greeted it not with polite unamused smiles, but honest and appreciative laughter.

"There's not much danger of anyone as active as you getting fat," said Mr. Cunningham.

"I know it's unfashionable, but I do like a good tea," said his wife. "Are you not for another cup, James? You've not had your second—"

"Gardening is drouthy work," said the minister, and passed her his bowl-like cup with the stock remark, quoted from one of his old parishioners. "'A cup o' tea's rale refreshin'.' Thank you, my dear."

Cilly, who had been allowed to leave the table after a hastily muttered grace, and was now perched on a chair in the window, said: "Here's Davie with the letters."

"How do you know?" asked Bun, looking up from her mug of milk. "You can't see the door from there, Cilly. You know you can't—"

"Yes. Can," retorted Cilly instantly.

"But it's round the corner."

"My eyes can see round corners," said Cilly blandly.

"Oh! That's not a truth, unless you've got a squint, and you haven't."

"Yes. Have. A wee teenty one, dus' enough to see round the corner."

"Cilly, dearie, you mustn't talk rubbish, and you're not to tell untruths," murmured Mrs. Cunningham.

Bun slid from her chair. "I'll go and see if Davie's brought the letters, and *then* we'll know," she said darkly, and left the room. On her return about two minutes later she eyed her cousin with a mixture of awe and frank disbelief, while handing a letter to the minister.

"On the contrary, he *had* come," she said.

Cilly bounced up and down on her chair until her silver-gilt curls danced. "I sawed him! I sawed him!" she squeaked triumphantly.

"I've got two dear little squinting eyes what can see round corners. I sawed him!"

"Peggy," said Bun softly, tugging at her aunt's dress. "Did she really? Was it a truth after all?"

Her father and mother were also looking to Peggy to settle this question. Susan, half amused, half admiring, heard her say as sternly as she could: "I think the less said about it the better. Cilly, do those dear little eyes of yours see as far as the toys and things you left on the study floor? Because it's high time you picked them all up."

Cilly opened her mouth to disclaim her squint, no longer useful, and always fictitious, caught sight of Bun's sceptical face, and decided that she did see the study floor. Followed by her cousin, she trotted away more seriously than usual.

"Most refreshing," said Susan. "And I do admire you as the kind young aunt, Peggy. It's very effective."

"Something has to be done to counteract the spoiling of the Infantry by two sets of doting grandparents," Peggy said, as they wandered out into the sunny garden. "They would be 'neither tae haud nor tae bind' if left to father and mother. And the Richardsons, I imagine, are every bit as bad."

"Well, can you leave your auntly duties for a day next week? Oliver and I are having a picnic to the sea, and we want you and your brother to come."

"A picnic! Bathing!" cried Peggy, no longer a Kind Young Aunt but a child little older than Bun or Cilly. "Oh, I'd adore it, and so would Jim. Thank you most awfully—"

"Don't thank me until you see what the weather is going to be like. If it pours, think how horrible everthing will be—"

"It won't," said Peggy with the calm confidence of youth. "It will be a lovely day."

CHAPTER FOUR

1

PEGGY was right in her weather forecast, and it was on a glorious morning of late July, when a haze promising heat veiled the hills, that Susan took her way to the kitchen to view the picnic preparations being made by Donaldina.

Her voice could be heard raised in lamentation all along the passage. "The gingerbreid's fine, an' the scones, an' the rock cakes, an' a' the lonch, but ma Mydeary cake's sat doon on me."

"Tchk, tchk," came the sympathetic clicking of someone's tongue in reply, and Susan recognized it as belonging to Mrs. Robertson, come down to help for the day.

"What the mistress'll say, dear kens. She was that set on me trying' the Mydeary cake." Then, a tone of thunderous command: "Jems! Awa' you oot tae the gairden an' get me the cress for the sangwidges, an' dinna staun' grinnin' there, ye muckle gowk!"

Susan trod with ostentatious heaviness down the passage, and smiled to hear hasty sounds of departure. When she entered the kitchen it was empty of occupants save Donaldina's demure small person, enveloped in an apron several sizes too large for her, and looking like a rueful dove.

"Well, Donaldina, it's a pity about the Madeira cake, and I'm sorry you were disappointed over it, but after all, there are lots of other things to eat. Your gingerbread looks even better than usual—"

Donaldina cast a baleful glance at the Madeira cake on the table, and sniffed contemptuously. "It's aye the way," she said gloomily. "I took as muckle trouble wi' yon Mydeary cake as wi' a' the lave o' them thegither. And ye see, mem, whit like it is. For a' the warld like the big drum efter a donkey's pit his fit through it."

Struck by this picturesque comparison, Susan also looked reproachfully at the erring cake, which certainly had a considerable concavity of outline where it should have been convex.

"Can we use it? Or will you give it to James to take home?" she asked.

"Is it gi'e it tae Jems?" on a rising note of incredulous indignation. "Na, na, mem. It'll mak' a fine trifle for the denner an' the Commander, ye ken, aye fancies a trifle . . . Was ye wantin' thae eggs champit for sangwidges?"

Susan could never keep her countenance for long with Donaldina, though she felt that such inability to restrain untimely mirth rendered her unfit to command a household. Perhaps it was Donaldina's Scotticisms, still amusing to southern ears, or perhaps it was the contrast between her demure face and mild blue eyes, and her extremely truculent manner on occasions; whatever the cause, there came a moment when Susan knew that she must retreat at once or be disgraced. Murmuring that she could leave everything to her cook, she now fled, and on reaching the sitting-room, collapsed on the sofa in a fit of laughter which her brother's disapproving eye, raised from the map he was studying, failed to quell.

"By the way," he said presently, and with a fine air of carelessness which did not deceive Susan in the least, "I thought I'd better take Shena Graham in the Squib. All right by you?"

"All right by me," said Susan; and as far as travelling in Oliver's car was concerned, she meant it. The Squib was an antiquated Morris two-seater with a dickey, which he had bought for fifteen pounds, and it had the alarming habit of backfiring when least expected, with sounds reminiscent of dark street corners on the night of November the fifth.

The name of his passenger, however, interested her. Shena Graham, sister of Muirfoot's gloomy organist, daughter of the famous Cough Mixture, studied art in London, but had come to spend her summer holiday with her people in Abbeyshiels. She was a pretty, feather-headed little creature with an infectious giggle, and Susan was privately convinced that the art to which she applied most study was that of make-up.

"Of course Oliver's heart is like a sponge, it's so absorbent," thought his sister with brutal candour. "But this is the first symptom of girl-friend-itis I've seen since his smash. He must be getting better. Pity he always selects such impossibly stupid young women!"

Aloud she said mildly: "D'you mind telling me what arrangements have been made for the rest of the party?"

"Well, the Scotts have their own car, and Peggy Cunningham will go in her brother's sidecar, I suppose—unless you'd like him to take you?"

"Perish the thought! I like Jim Cunningham. Off that motor-bike he's a nice boy, but on it he's merely a speed-maniac, and I have no desire to be suddenly and unpleasantly done to death. Let Peggy risk it. She's his sister, and young enough to enjoy it."

"I thought you'd feel like that. Then will you go with Jed?"

"Is *he* coming?" Susan asked in open amazement.

"Why not?"

"No reason at all. Only I can't picture him at a picnic, somehow. I think I'll go with the Scotts. Don't glare like that, Oliver. I haven't said anything even remotely unkind."

"Jed happens to be rather keen on picnics," said Oliver stiffly. "And I tell you what it is, Susan. You aren't fair to Jed. You haven't been from the start."

Susan was troubled by this accusation, for though she had nothing in common with Jed Armstrong, the fact that he was Oliver's friend counted for a good deal with her.

"I'm always nice to him when we meet," she protested.

"Oh, *nice!*" said Oliver in tones of disgust. "You treat him to your best society manners always, if you call that being nice. And with people like—well, Charles, for example, you might be a different person."

"Charles is an old friend of yours as well as mine," said Susan, a slight flush creeping into her cheeks. "I'm at home with him, so of course I seem different—"

The sitting-room door opened, and Donaldina, bearing a salver at arm's-length as though the orange envelope lying on it were a venomous serpent, entered.

"If ye please, mem," she gasped excitedly, "a tallygram. The boy's waitin' ootbye, but he says tae tell ye frae the postmistress that she didna think there'd be ony answer."

Months of country life had accustomed Susan and Oliver to the lively personal interest taken by Mrs. Davidson in all correspondence, particularly such as could be read: Susan, indeed, was certain that those eagle eyes could almost pierce through a mere envelope to the letter inside. Therefore this message, strange as it might have sounded to them a year ago, was now taken as a matter of course.

Stretching out a hand for the telegram, she said: "Will you give Donaldina threepence for the boy, Oliver?"

Donaldina reluctantly left the room with three pennies jingling in her hand, unwilling to miss the opportunity of hearing what the telegram contained, for she had all the delight in possible bad news common to her kind. Susan tore open the envelope, stared at the pencilled message in complete mystification, and handed it over to her brother.

He read it aloud slowly. "Arriving Abbeyshiels 6.30 p.m. please meet MacIlwaine."

"And who," he asked with interest, "may 'MacIlwaine' be?"

Susan shook her head. "Don't ask me. I haven't the vaguest idea."

"'Arriving Abbeyshiels 6.30'," quoted Oliver speculatively. "Do you suppose it's coming to stay?"

"It must be some ridiculous mistake," Susan said. "I don't know anyone called MacIlwaine. Do you?"

"Not guilty, m'lud."

"What are we going to do about it?"

"What can we do but go for our picnic and let it alone? I hear some of the people coming now—"

"But what about this person arriving at Abbeyshiels and expecting to be met?"

"There's a taxi. MacIlwaine can hire it," said her brother callously, and went out to greet the vanguard of the picnic party.

2

The somnolence born of comfortable repletion, fresh air and a warm sun had descended upon the picnickers where they lay at ease on the sands of Sunburgh bay. Before luncheon the scene had been lively enough, when those who felt so disposed had bathed, and their laughter and shouting had rung loud in the stillness as they ran, a living frieze of dark figures against the sunlight, into the blue water that broke in a thousand golden ripples where they disturbed it. Now no one wished to stir, except Oliver and Shena Graham, who could be seen rapidly decreasing in size as they neared the farther end of the wide bay. Even the murmur of conversation, drowsy-sounding as the noise of pigeons in a dovecote, had died away, and the deep silence was broken only by the busy waves which lapped unceasingly at the edge of the beach.

Jim Cunningham and the two Scott boys, still in bathing things, lay prone on their faces, more than half asleep. The Scott parents had frankly succumbed to the insidious spell of slumber, and Susan watched them, idly wondering how it was that so many people fell asleep with their mouths open. Presently Peggy rose and wandered inland over the shimmering grey-green dunes. Ronald Graham sat and fidgeted for some minutes, and then followed her, leaving Susan thinking that it was a pity a young man so lanky should elect to wear a kilt, below the edge of which his knees, as thin and pink as sticks of early spring rhubarb, were mercilessly disclosed.

Alone of the party she remained seated and awake. She suddenly wished that there was someone like Charles to keep her company. Dear Charles, who liked the things she liked, and who was such a good friend. . . . She got up and walked down to the water. The sea stretched empty before her, without a ship or even a smudge of smoke to break the line of blue which blended mistily into the sky at a distance immeasurably far. On the left lay the long ribbon of tawny sand, and to the right, crowning a low green hill, the gaunt ruin of Sunburgh Castle rose defiantly into the air. There was not a soul in sight, except the picnic party, silent behind her. A little wind ran rustling through the dry, sharp dune grasses and sank again.

Suddenly a voice spoke close to her. "Would you like to walk up to the castle?" it said.

Susan knew without turning to look that it was Jed Armstrong. No one else had such a rumbling bass voice, so pronounced a Scots accent.

"Yes," she said, remembering that her treatment of him worried Oliver, and determined to be more friendly. "I think I should."

Together they took a narrow path made by the busy feet of many sheep, and went towards the ruin. One thing pleased Susan about her silent companion: she need not try to make conversation, which was perhaps as well, for she had nothing to say. Small talk always seemed to die in his presence, she thought a little irritably, and glanced at him. His rugged brows were knit above his curiously intent dark-blue eyes. Maliciously she wondered whether he could be as bovine as he looked, and if he were thinking of sheep or cattle, or both.

Neither, it seemed, for as they gained the crest of the hill and stood under the high wall, broken by an archway long since doorless, he said: "A place like this makes me think, somehow, of an old dog that has lost all his teeth, but who'll still growl at a stranger."

Susan gasped aloud. "You feel like that? *You?*" she asked incredulously, her manners entirely forgotten.

He nodded unsmilingly. "Yes, I do. It seems to surprise you a bit?"

"Of course it surprises me. I thought you only thought about bullocks and things."

"Bullocks," he said seriously, "aren't as uninteresting as you might think."

"I'm willing to take your word for it," said Susan lightly, but her lips curved in a faint unbelieving smile as she walked past him under the archway and into the oblong of sheep-bitten turf which had once been the courtyard of the castle. At once she paused.

"Oh, there's someone else here," she exclaimed with a small gesture of annoyance.

Two figures, deep in conversation which did not sound too amiable, stood in the shadow of the wall at the far side of the court. They had not noticed the presence of Susan and Jed.

"It's Peggy," said he. "Who's with her?"

"Mr. Graham," Susan answered.

"H'm. Well, do we leave them, or will we interrupt them?"

"I think Peggy would welcome an interruption," said Susan gravely. Then, meeting Jed Armstrong's blue gaze more frankly than ever before, she added: "I don't care for that young man. Do you?"

"I do not," said Jed with emphasis. He raised his voice in a hail that set echoes ringing all round the walls.

3

Peggy, wandering happily in the castle courtyard, and pretending that she was one of the ladies who had lived there in troublous times long ago, was both startled and indignant to find Ronald Graham, rather out of breath, by her side.

"You followed me!" she said accusingly.

"Yes, I did. I wanted to speak to you, and you never give me a chance," he complained.

"Why should I? What have you got to say to me that you couldn't say down on the beach?"

"You know very well what I want to say to you, Peggy—"

"Well, if I do," countered Peggy with spirit, "I don't want to hear it."

"But you've got to," he insisted. "You've treated me dashed badly, and I won't stand any more of it."

"Treated you badly?" Peggy was almost incoherent with anger and a little fear; he looked so wild, and they were quite alone, out of sight or hail of the others. "How can you say such a thing? I've always been as nice to you as I could—"

He broke in, muttering something that sounded like "leading me on—"

Peggy stamped her foot on the short grass. "That's a lie! I never did anything of the kind!"

"Oh, I know how it is with you. You're so taken up with that damned Englishman at Easter Hartrigg, who's busy fooling with Shena, that you can't look at your old friends. You let me kiss you—and, anyway, he's only half a man with that limp of his!"

"Stop!" said Peggy, white with rage. Her incoherence had fled now. "You're a cad to remind me of that time you kissed me, and even though it was under the mistletoe, I felt dirty for days afterwards! As for Commander Parsons, it would take more than a limp to make him anything but a man. If he were a helpless cripple he'd still be a man—which you aren't, and never will be!"

For answer, 'Ronald Graham seized her in his arms. The look of passion in his eyes, so ugly to her, since she did not return it, the feel of his hot hands on her bare arms, of his breath on her neck, filled Peggy with sick horror.

"Let me go!" she said, struggling.

His hold tightened; then, at the sound of a loud, deep-voiced "Hallo!" he loosed her so suddenly that she had to lean back against the wall for support.

"Uncle Jed!" called Peggy, a world of relief in her shaking voice.

Ronald Graham gave her a glance that made her tremble in spite of her contempt. "You'll be sorry," he said. "Whatever I do, you'll be responsible for. Don't say I didn't warn you!"

He turned and stumbled away out of sight behind a mound of broken masonry.

Peggy, with a gallant effort to appear unconcerned, went to meet Susan and Jed.

"The—the beer must have gone to Ronald's head, I think," she said with a very creditable laugh. "He was—was being quite melodramatic!"

"How thrilling for you," said Susan lightly, but she put her hand through the younger girl's arm. "We won't hurry back, it's too hot. Mr. Armstrong, you don't seem to feel the heat. Would you mind going on and getting the boys to start a fire for tea?"

Jed Armstrong nodded and left them to follow slowly down the hill.

"Susan," said Peggy rather piteously, "why are men such beasts?" She was still trembling.

"Oh, darling!" Susan laughed, but her hand closed on Peggy's arm protectingly. "You don't call Ronald Graham a good specimen of man, I hope?"

"He—he said such horrible things—"

"It was the beer, I expect," said Susan. She knew that the girl had been shocked and frightened, but to take the matter seriously would only make Peggy cry. "Don't think any more about it, my dear. One has to make allowances for the creatures, and I do think that it isn't fair to judge the rest by the one rather unfortunate example—"

Peggy gave a long shuddering sigh and rubbed her eyes with the back of her hand, like a small boy.

"Better now?" said Susan.

"Yes, thank you. Only I do wish I didn't ever have to see him again."

"Can't your father get another organist?"

"Oh no! I wouldn't tell father or mother anything about it. And, you see, Ronald doesn't do it for money; and besides, he's really good at it. No; I'll just have to keep out of his way as much as I can," said Peggy resignedly.

Susan changed the subject, and by the time they had rejoined the party on the shore, Peggy was quite cheerful again.

The boys, boy-like, were as wolfishly hungry for tea as if they had not eaten any luncheon, but the others were only thirsty, and sat about toying with sandwiches generously sprinkled with sand, and gulping down cups of rather smoky tea. Shena Graham wore the expression of a cat which had recently lapped a saucer of rich cream, and Oliver smiled fatuously whenever he met her large, empty-looking brown eyes. Susan, irritated and slightly disgusted, could not make up her mind which of the Grahams she disliked more—brother or sister.

She turned away and spoke to Peggy, now amicably, squabbling with the Scott boys beside her.

"Did your mother give you any message about the woman who is coming to lecture on jam-making to her Women's Guild, Peggy?" she asked. "She wanted to know if I could provide a meal for the lecturer, and, of course, I shall be delighted, but I haven't heard yet which day she is coming."

Peggy, with a large piece of gingerbread half-way to her mouth, stared at her with blue eyes of concern.

"Good heavens!" she said. "*You're* feeding her? Mother must be mad. Didn't she let you know? It's this evening—"

A dreadful thought occurred to Susan.

"'MacIlwaine!'" she said faintly. "'Arriving Abbeyshiels six-thirty. Please meet'."

4

"Damnation!" muttered Jed Armstrong, drawing in to the side of the narrow road and stopping his car.

Susan said nothing, but in her heart she echoed his words. Since he had whirled her away from Sunburgh at her urgent request, before any of the others were ready to leave, misfortune had dogged them relentlessly. This was their second puncture, and as they had left the main road for various rambling byways which Jed had vowed were short cuts, there was no hope of assistance from passing cars. The rest of the picnic party would not come this way, and the spare wheel had already been substituted for the tyre which had punctured first. The precious moments were flying past, and the train bearing the jam-making expert whom Susan had promised to meet and feed before handing her over to the Muirfoot Women's Guild at seven-thirty drew steadily nearer Abbeyshiels. Meantime, an inner-tube had to be repaired. . . .

They disembarked, and Jed Armstrong, kicking moodily at a tyre as flat as one of Donaldina's pancakes, uttered curses not loud but deep, like Macbeth, while Susan looked forlornly up and down the stretch of road which mocked her by its emptiness. They were alone in a silent land of broad meadows and waving, sun-browned corn. Jed glanced at his companion, and a slow, rueful smile overspread his countenance.

Against her will, against her better judgment, for she felt that she ought to be exceedingly angry with him, Susan began to smile also, and in a second they were both laughing helplessly and heartily.

"I doubt," he said at last, "that Miss MacIlwaine—if she is a Miss—will have a long wait at Abbeyshiels." His tone was grave, even penitent, but a devil of amusement leapt in his eyes.

He took off his coat to start repairing the tube, in which a large nail had made what dentists call with gloomy zest "a serious cavity." After a time, during which he wrestled alone in a cloud of sulphurous language, Susan offered her unskilled assistance, and they wrought together, getting hotter and dirtier with each passing minute. Any idea of meeting Miss (or Mrs.) MacIlwaine had long since vanished by the time they were under way once more, and Susan's hopes were now fixed on reaching home before darkness overtook them, which seemed, in her pessimistic frame of mind, highly improbable.

"We must stop at the first post office we come to and send a telegram," she said. "Mrs. Cunningham will have to make apologies for me, though I don't envy her the task."

"Oh, that'll be all right," Jed assured her easily. "She'll just put all the blame on you."

"That," said Susan with some bitterness, "will be so nice for me, won't it?"

"Well, you can always shift the blame on to me," he retorted, maddeningly good-humoured. "*I* don't mind."

"I daresay you don't!" cried Susan angrily. "But it would only be fair if you did take a share of the blame. Whose fault was it that we left the proper road and got all those punctures?"

"Well," he began with the air of one weighing the matter judicially, "you might call it the fault of whoever left those nails in the road for the car to pick up. Or it might be just the inscrutable workings of Providence old Cunningham is always talking about. Or—"

Here Susan uttered an indignant noise, suspiciously like a snort.

"Come, now," he said, still amiably, while the car tooled along at a pace which in a horse would have been best described as a leisurely amble. "Come, now, there's no use flying into a rage. The thing's done, and if they can't have their jam, I've no doubt they'll manage to amuse themselves some other way. That's the worst of you folk who're used to town life: you can't leave things be. You—"

"Would you mind hurrying a little?" asked Susan bleakly, his reasonableness only having the not uncommon effect of making her more unreasonably angry. With a sidelong glance at her, which she intercepted in the windscreen, he obeyed, sending his old car banging and bumping over the stony surface until her teeth chattered. At last, as they came to the straggling fringes of a small village, she cried, "Stop, please!"

He slowed down. "Bumping too much for you?" he asked with a smile for which Susan could cheerfully have killed him. "I thought you'd have to give in, though you're as obstinate as a mule."

"And you," said Susan, "are as rude as—as a Scotsman. I can't think of anything worse. No, I have *not* given in. I want to send off that telegram."

A small, dilapidated cottage with three unsavoury bottles of sweets in one fly-blown window had the welcome words "Post Office" on a board above the door. Susan descended from the car and marched up the path. The door resisted her efforts to open it, and after she had knocked until her knuckles were sore and her small remaining stock of patience exhausted, a woman emerged from a neighbouring cottage.

"Ye needna' keep chap-chappin' awa' there," she said sourly. "Can ye no' see the p'stoffice is shut? It's the hauf day, an' he's awa' aff tae see his guid-sister."

"But I want to send a telegram—" Susan began.

"Weel, ye canna'. If ye like tae come back the morn's mornin', ye'll can get sendin' it then."

A burst of laughter from the shameless Jed answered this suggestion. Susan paid no attention to him. "I'm afraid to-morrow won't do," she said. "Is there nowhere I could telephone from? No house near?"

The woman pondered for a while. "A hoose?" she muttered in tones of amazement. "A hoose?" And then suddenly: "Ou, ay. There's Kelpieha'. They've the telephone there."

"How do we get to it?" asked Susan quickly.

There followed a string of instructions which were as Greek to her, though her companion in misfortune appeared to understand the injunctions to "haud awa' by," and "tak' the turn ye'll see at the hinner end o' the wood ablow the hill."

"Right," he said briskly. "Many thanks. Come on, Miss Parsons."

They roared off down a long hill with a sharp bend in it; up the farther side the road could be seen again, climbing towards a line of beeches which looked as if they might shelter a house.

"We'll need to put on speed if the old car's to get up that," said Jed Armstrong, nodding his head at the hill opposite. He set his large foot firmly on the accelerator, and they fled down, taking the corner with a perilous lurch. Below them, in the hollow, was the gleam of water, but no bridge. With a tremendous splashing they rushed at what Susan took to be a ford; the wheels went round bravely, the water rose about them, and finally, with a sigh, the engine expired, leaving them in the middle of the river.

"It's a pity," said Jed mildly, "that she didn't think to tell us about the ford."

5

There are some situations for which no language, however strong, is adequate. In silence they abandoned the car after several futile attempts to make it move and, wading through the shallows beyond, walked with wet squelchings up the hill, their shoes bubbling as the water oozed out of them. The thought that another half-yard would have seen them past the deepest part did not make the mishap any less infuriating. Susan hoped that in other circumstances she would have taken this series of accidents with philosophic calm; but as, wet of foot and in oil-stained garments, she trudged gloomily beside Jed Armstrong, she was haunted by the pale, accusing image of the unknown MacIlwaine, left to languish at Abbeyshiels railway station. Her one desire was to reach a telephone and communicate the news to the minister's wife, via Mrs. Davidson, and the "mile and a bit" which they had been told lay between the village and Kelpieha' house seemed, like a piece of elastic, to have stretched into leagues.

On gaining the top of the hill they were confronted by a meeting of four ways without any guiding signpost.

"It can't be far now," said Jed. "We've come a good mile, I should think."

But the crossroads stared inexorably, and there was not a symptom of human habitation in sight. Spurning the absurd suggestion that she should "toss for it," Susan exclaimed eagerly, "There's an old man. Ask him."

A venerable figure, white-bearded, bending under a load of sticks, was approaching at a snail's pace, and Jed hailed him forthwith.

"Eh?" said the aged man, eyeing them suspiciously. "I didna' hear ye. Ye'll need tae speak a wee thing looder. I've been deif this twal'month syne."

Jed Armstrong drew a deep breath and then, in a bellow which made the surrounding country ring, enunciated the one word: "KELPIEHA'!"

"Nae need tae roar on me, man. Ye've a voice like a bull! Haud on tae yer left, an' ye'll see the back-entrance on yer richt," said the old man peevishly.

"The back entrance? Is that the quickest way to the house?"

Again the old eyes travelled slowly over them from head to foot. "Ye'll gang in the back gate," he said firmly and finally, and hobbled on his way.

The thought of her appearance had not been included in Susan's anxieties, but now, with this insistence on the "back entrance," she began to wonder whether it was possible to arrive at a strange house in her present state of dirt, dishevelment and damp, and demand to use the telephone. A glance at Jed confirmed her fears as to what she must look like herself, and though she walked on at his side, she decided meanly that he would have to go up to the house alone, while she lurked under cover somewhere to await his return.

In a tone which forbade argument she told him so; and, rather to her surprise, he merely nodded and said, "All right."

A gate broke the long line of trees just ahead, and buildings could be seen looming behind it.

"Here we are," said Jed.

He advanced boldly, while Susan prepared to efface herself in a modest manner behind a convenient clump of rhododendrons. As he neared the gate, and before she could hide, there came a joyous soprano cry of: "Here they are!" and a bevy of young men and maidens, variously attired in day and evening dress, rushed out into the road.

"I say, you're awfully late, you know," said a tall young man in plus-fours of the most exotic pattern, and a cut more nearly resembling a Turkish woman's trousers than any male garments Susan had ever seen. He spoke reproachfully. "Have you had a breakdown?"

"Yes, we have," said Jed bluntly. "The car's still in the ford, and it'll take a couple of horses to pull her out."

"Well, it can't be helped, and, anyhow, you're here at last. The fiddler's been doing his damnedest, but it's pretty poor without the piano—"

"You've made a mistake. I haven't got your piano. I want to use your telephone for a minute, and—"

"Yes, yes, of course. Only come on. It's not the piano we want, but the pianist. You *are* the pianist from Abbeyshiels, I suppose?" said the young man, addressing Susan. A note of doubt had crept into his voice.

Susan had been standing mute, wondering vaguely if she were in Bedlam, and, now she shook her head. "I'm sorry—" she began.

"Why, good Lord, it's Armstrong of Reiverslaw!" broke in another voice, and a new young man, wearing a dinner-jacket, who had added himself to the party, bounded forward and smote Susan's companion on the back. "Jed, you old ruffian, what are *you* doing so far from home?"

A perfect babel of explanation and inquiry burst forth, in the course of which Susan gathered that Kelpieha' was holding a tenants' and employees' dance in honour of the son of the house, whose twenty-first birthday it was; that though the hired fiddler had arrived, the pianist engaged to share his labours had failed to put in an appearance; and that the dance looked like being a dismal frost in consequence.

"We've kept 'em fairly happy up to date," said the plus-foured one. "But now. . . ." He made a gesture of despair. "The thing's turning into a rough-and-tumble. Half of us haven't been able to get away to dress yet."

"If you'll let Miss Parsons here use your telephone, and give her a change of shoes and stockings, she'll play the piano for you."

This egregious suggestion was made by Jed Armstrong, and before Susan could even open her mouth to protest she was whirled away in the direction of the house by a loudly chattering group of young women.

While the daughter of Kelpieha' swept her up to a bedroom and literally flung the contents of her wardrobe at Susan's wet feet, someone else rang up Muirfoot and brought the welcome tidings that Miss MacIlwaine had arrived safely, and was even then making plum jam in front of the admiring eyes of the Women's Guild.

A few minutes more, and after performing a hasty toilet and "changing her feet," Susan was hurried down to a large, gloomy dining-room, where a meal had been assembled. Here she found Mr. Armstrong solemnly waiting for her, and solacing himself with whisky-and-soda. They ate, hastily and uncomfortably, the chill remnants of what had been a hot dinner, embarrassed by the continual entrances and exits of members of the house-party, whose eagerness to carry them to the scene of action was barely tempered by politeness.

"I've never felt so acutely that appetite was a crime," murmured Susan plaintively when, for a few seconds, she was alone with Jed, "or that hunger was a vulgar failing! I *was* hungry when I sat down, but eating under the calculating eyes of those young things, who keep glancing from my plate to the clock and back again, is too much for me. Another bite and I shall choke!"

Jed quite evidently harboured no such feelings. He cut himself a liberal helping of cold beef, and assured Susan that if she had to thump a piano half the night she would need nourishment, and placidly continued to eat. But she was not sufficiently impervious to the prevailing impatience to profit by his good advice, and presently, amid audible murmurs of thanksgiving, announced that she had finished, and was hustled from the room, leaving him seriously attacking a second portion of cold meat and salad.

The barn, in which the dance was taking place, was lighted by many oil lamps, whose feeble flickering was still mocked by the long rays of the sinking sun. At the far end of the building the fiddler, perspiring freely, had sunk on a bench, exhausted by his efforts to produce unaided a volume of sound which could contend successfully with the clamour of tongues. A knot of ploughmen and herds in their stiff Sunday clothes hung about the doorway, eyeing the girls who clustered, giggling, at one side of the improvised ball-room and exchanged highly flavoured personalities with their neighbours.

Pressing through the crowd, Susan was at last brought face to face with the battered piano which stood across one corner.

"I suppose you realize," she said desperately, "that I don't know any of the music?"

This objection was airily waved away. "It's noise they want," said the young host reassuringly. "Just thump on, and never mind about wrong notes."

"Ay, ay, Maister Wat," chimed in a burly farmer. And to Susan: "Gie's the auld dances, lassie, the Circassian Circle and Petronella. Nane o' yer frog's-trots nor foxes'-walks *here!*"

Thus encouraged, Susan took her seat and, obeying the injunctions to thump, pounded at the keys, a large proportion of which were broken, with hearty good will. The fiddler, enlivened by support and refreshed with whisky, sawed away beside her, breathing hotly down the back of her neck. The dancers, red-faced and serious, stamped their way through dance after unfamiliar country dance until her fingers were numb and her arms ached.

During an interval in which Susan leant thankfully against the hard back of her chair, she watched the interchange of courtesies between the girls and their attendant swains. These, to a man, dropped their partners like hot potatoes at the end of each dance, and retired to the doorway to smoke. Sitting-out, so important a part of dances as she knew them, was unknown here, where the girls all ranged themselves in a serried rank along the benches lining the walls, and there made necessary repairs to their finery, or shrieked replies to such, of the men as were bold enough to attempt badinage. The decorum prevailing at the beginning of the evening had vanished, and merriment, untrammelled, had its way.

"Well, what d'you think of it?" asked Jed, who unnoticed by Susan, had come to stand at her side.

"It's rather amusing," Susan screamed back at him above the tumult.

"Have you been dancing at all?"

"Dancing? I've never stopped hitting this wretched piano!" said Susan, indicating the time-worn instrument with its two candles guttering one on either side of the ragged and dirty country dance music.

"We'll soon see about that!" he exclaimed and, turning, seized by the arm one of the house-party, a languid and exquisite creature who, with a cigarette between lips ruddier than the cherry, was superciliously surveying the crowd, an attention which they returned with interest. "Here," said Mr. Armstrong, unabashed by her stare, "can one of you not play a bit and let Miss Parsons dance?"

"Dance?" drawled she. "But do you really want to dance? With that zoo? How too marvellous of you!"

Until she spoke, Susan had no faintest intention of dancing, but now the demon of perversity entered into her, urging her to declare that nothing would please her more. Whereupon, with a faint lift of well-plucked eyebrows, the other murmured that possibly she might be able to play "one or two of those utterly weird tunes," and took Susan's place at the piano.

The dance was that exciting and exhausting measure known variously as "Strip the Willow" or "Draps o' Brandy." Susan's acquaintance with country dances being limited to Sir Roger de Coverley, performed in far-off days at children's parties, she would have fared badly but for the tireless good nature of her neighbours. Aided by their instructions hissed in her ears, she was prodded, pushed and dragged through the dance, in jig-time, handed like any parcel from arm to arm of the grinning young men who formed the opposite line, and returned to her partner, "Maister Wat," of Kelpieha', with the breathless remark: "Here y'are! Tak' her!"

Slightly weary, and in wild disarray, Susan finally sank to rest on a hard bench between two buxom country girls, who alternately assured her that she had "done fine," and reviled the clumsiness of their men-folk.

"They'd tear the dress aff ye!" one asserted, and the other, agreeing, passionately added that "afore she'd tak' the floor wi' yon pig-man frae Kelpieha' Mains again she'd need tae get a new pair o' shoon."

"Shoon, did ye say? A new pair o' feet's what ye're needin'!" cried number one.

" 'Deed, ay!" chorused several others in shrill-voiced accord and skirls of wild laughter.

Towards midnight, when the company repaired to a smaller barn, there to partake of a lavish meal, at which tea and whisky flowed in almost equal quantities, a man with a melodeon made his appearance, and bashfully announced his readiness to accompany the fiddler.

"You'll be wanting to get home now, likely?" asked Jed Armstrong, and Susan was surprised to find herself quite reluctant to leave the revels. Their host and hostess—whose name to the end she never discovered—thanked them for their help ("Hers, you mean; I didn't do anything," growled Jed) and a vote of thanks was proposed, to Susan's great embarrassment, and responded to with vociferous cheering. Perhaps the most touching farewell was the fiddler's, who, weeping maudlin tears begotten of much whisky, shook her warmly by the hand, assured her that he was her friend for life, and hoped soon to play again with her. The last they saw of the Kelpieha' tenants' dance was his figure, propped against the doorway, while he waved a large red handkerchief after them.

The car had long since been hauled out of the ford, the damage assessed by the Kelpieha' chauffeur as nothing worse than lack of petrol, and now, filled up, was ready for the road once more. They travelled peacefully homewards through the sleeping countryside, the noise of the dance fading behind them, and nothing but the wind's sigh or the chuckle of a burn to break the silence.

Jed did not speak until they came to the gate of Easter Hartrigg. Then he said, "You've had a pretty long day of it."

"Do you know, I rather enjoyed it," Susan confessed honestly.

He laughed. "You weren't so keen when we had those punctures and got stuck in the ford," he said.

And before Susan could explain that her annoyance had been caused by the thought of Miss MacIlwaine and not her own discomfort, he added unexpectedly: "I rather like to make you angry. You look so handsome in a rage.... But I must say you stood it all very well."

From Oliver, being a brother, she neither expected nor received even this slight approbation.

"Nothing like it," he grunted the next morning at breakfast. "Leaving the Women's Guilders in the lurch while you went careering all over the place with Jed. I thought yon didn't like his society—"

"I hadn't much choice," Susan pointed out mildly.

"Well, you'll have to pay for your fun. Miss MacIlwaine's left a bill for her taxi, and her address for you to send on the cash!"

Miss MacIlwaine had. On the sheet of notepaper which Oliver handed to his sister were two items, written in a neat, clerkly hand:

> To hire of taxi from Abbeyshiels to Muirfoot .. 5s. 6d.
> To high tea at Kirkhouse Inn, Muirfoot .. 3s. 5d.
> Total .. 8s. 11d.

CHAPTER FIVE

1

A HEAVY after-luncheon somnolence had fallen over Easter Hartrigg, which the distant clatter of dishes and the voice of Donaldina drawling a gloomy Calvinistic hymn only served to intensify.

Presently, however, the silence of the sitting-room was broken by Donaldina herself, who entered with the Sunday paper, brought by Jems from Abbeyshiels. While Oliver, roused to semi-activity, seized it and prepared to wallow in lurid descriptions of the latest murder trial, she hovered in the doorway, quite obviously bursting with news.

"Yes, Donaldina, what is it?" asked Susan resignedly. It would have been sheer cruelty to dismiss her before she had unburdened herself of her load of local gossip, whatever it might be.

"Eh, mem," she began eagerly, "d'ye mind yon Bairniss Bald? Her wi' the mither that drinks, that was here a while back?"

"I remember her well," said Susan with feeling. "What about her?"

"She's mairret on yon Wullie Blair, him that used tae drive the baker's van."

"Dear me," said Susan, while Oliver lowered the paper to listen. "That won't please Mrs. Bald. I fancy she had other views for Bernice than marriage with a mere baker's boy."

"'Deed, an' Mistress Bald's as prood's a dug wi' twa tails, then. She didna' fancy Wullie when he was gettin' auchteen shullin' a week wi' the baker, mem, but noo that he's mairret an' drawin' the dole, d'ye see, they've twenty-sax shullin' a week—"

"But can't the boy find something to do? Why did he leave the baker?" Thus Oliver.

Donaldina, with a glance of pity for his innocence, enlightened him. "The baker gi'ed him the sack, sir, these twa-three months syne," she said. "An' there's no' anither body wad hae Wullie Blair in their employ. Wullie's a wee thing saft, ye see, sir"—thus delicately did Donaldina indicate a certain mental deficiency which Susan had long since suspected in the ex-baker's boy—". . . but he's canny eneuch tae ken that he'll get mair on the burroo than wi' honest wark. Though he'd need tae be gey an' saft ere he mairret on yon Bairniss Bald!" she added.

"So they've married quite happily, and no doubt intend to start a family on the dole—as long as it lasts," Susan said. The point of view prevalent among the idle that it was not only justifiable, but the height of common sense, to marry on the dole and, regarding children as a profitable investment, to increase the population almost as rapidly and prolifically as rabbits, was well known to her by this time. She still found it lamentable, but it amazed her no longer.

"Ma sister was in Kaleford yesterday," Donaldina went on, not to be diverted from her narrative by side issues, "an' sic a weddin', she said, she never seen. There was Mistress Bald in a new dress an' an awfu' nice hat she got at the last Jumbo Sale, an' Bairniss wi' a veil an' a', grinnin' awa' frae ear tae lug, an' fit tae Inirrst wi' pride because she'd got a man. An' Wullie, he had a flooer in his coat, a muckle great rose. . . . An' the cawr frae Muirfoot wi' Gibbie Johnston drivin' it, tae tak' them aff on their honeymoon, nae less, to some hottle I canna' mind the name o'. But ma sister says it'll need tae be a queer like hottle that wad tak' in two tinkler-lookin' bodies like yon, wi' their luggage a' done up in broon-paper paircels. The cawr was fu' o' them. I doot it wad be the puirs-hoose they'd look like mair nor ony hottle. Ay; they're gaun tee live in Kaleford wi' Mistress Bald, so ma sister heard tell, an' they havena' a stick o' furnitcher but juist three crystal bowls—frae Woolworth's—they got in waddin' presents."

Here Oliver uttered a choking sound and hurriedly retreated behind the paper, and Susan, retaining her self-control with difficulty, for Donaldina in the character of raconteuse was irresistibly comic, murmured that she hoped the newly married couple would be happy.

"Raither them nor me!" was Donaldina's comment. She set the empty coffee-cups on their tray, took it up, and prepared to depart. "Ye'll be oot for yer teas, mem?" she asked at the door.

"Yes, Donaldina," said her mistress with gravity. "We shall be out."

2

When Oliver had sufficiently recovered from the paroxysm of laughter into which the tale of Bernice's romantic marriage had hurled him, Susan put on a shady hat, and the two left the house. It was a brilliant Sunday afternoon of early September, and they were going to walk over to Reiverslaw to have tea with Jed Armstrong.

"I'm so glad he has summoned up enough courage to ask me at last," said Susan. "I've been curious to see how a descendant of Border reivers famed in foray lives—"

Her brother growled, "If you hadn't been so deuced stand-off with him he'd have asked you months ago."

"I know, I know. Don't start all that over again," implored Susan. "You can't say we don't get on well now, Oliver."

"After your midnight motor-trip with him, you ought to get on," was Oliver's reply.

Susan made a hideous face at him, and they proceeded in friendly silence.

The corn had been cut, and the fields on either side of the road they followed, shaded as usual by high hawthorn hedges, were filled with the rows of cunningly-built stooks, standing like small golden tents in the blonde stubble, over which they cast shadows of softest, deepest blue. As they mounted higher, the whole country lay spread out before them, walled in on one hand by the far purple line of the Lammermuirs, on the other by the dim, grey-green Cheviots. Between, the land rose in waves to the long ridges so characteristic a part of the view, and sank again in patched fields of green and gold, of woods sombrely clothed in their late summer foliage, to the hollows where burns ran unseen. On the top of one of these ridges stood Reiverslaw: house, farm-steading and cottages, a midget school, and a tiny ancient church which boasted in its quiet kirkyard the mouldering grave of a knight who fell on Flodden Field. Across the road, and hardly more than a stone's throw from the solid, unassuming house built on the site of the old reivers' fortalice, a little loch, fringed with brown rushes, rippled in the soft breeze. A deep Sabbath stillness brooded over all.

"Unless Jed's having a caulk in the house, I expect he'll be somewhere about the farm," said Oliver. "Which shall we try first?"

Susan, knowing that when her brother was disturbed in the afternoon nap by which most sailors seem to set such store he was like a lioness robbed of her whelps, had no difficulty in picturing Jed Armstrong in like circumstances, and decided on the farm. They turned aside from the white gates leading to the house, and made their way past a long cart shed, the red pantiles of its roof mellowed by age into a sunny rose, towards a stackyard in the rear. Fowls clucked about their feet in the soft carpet of straw and husks, pigeons rose with a storm of white and coloured wings and circled round the old buildings of the steading. From various sheds came the lowing of cattle, the ringing stamp of the resting cart horses' iron-shod hooves. All human activity, all the bustle which during the week makes a farm hum like a huge hive, was in abeyance. Even the dogs were nowhere to be seen, and the skulking cats had retired to their secret lairs until evening brought them out to hunt.

Presently, as they stood uncertain where to go next, the huge figure of Jed Armstrong made its appearance round the end of a stack, pastorally attended by a large and evil-smelling goat.

"Hullo!" he said, the greeting, in his tremendous voice, echoing like a view-hallo across the yard. The goat promptly rose to its hind feet, and lowering a pair of unpleasantly sharp horns, advanced nimbly. Susan hastily retired behind her brother and took her nose between finger and thumb.

"Please call off your goat," she said in muffled accents. "I don't care for it."

"Feardy! Feardy!" jeered Mr. Armstrong with his schoolboy grin and at least seven r's reverberating in each word. "I believe you're scared of him. Scared of a billy-goat!"

"I am," said Susan with shameless frankness. "I am terrified of it, and I've only one hand to ward it off, because I need the other to hold my nose. So please take it away."

"Poor old Captain Kidd. He wouldn't hurt a fly," said his owner, fearlessly seizing the evil beast by a horn and dragging it away.

"No. I should imagine he'd be more likely to fancy something a bit larger," said Oliver as the goat took a reluctant departure behind some pig styes.

"The Cunninghams are coming to tea," said their host, rejoining them with a powerful odour of goat clinging to him. "We'd better be getting back to the house, I suppose."

As they neared the white gate once more, a figure on a bicycle came into sight, whirling down the road towards them. It resolved itself into Peggy Cunningham, who flung herself off her machine almost into Oliver's arms.

"Uncle Jed!" she panted. "The Miss Pringles are on their way here. I passed them a little ago, all three of them, in the donkey carriage!"

Her cheeks were flushed to carnation brilliance, her blue eyes were dark with haste and excitement, she had never looked prettier. Susan wished, not for the first time by any means, that her brother's taste in young women was not confined to fashionable creatures of whippet-like attenuation of form, one adjective—the over-worked "marvellous"—and no brains to speak of. Now, someone like Peggy. . . .

She was speaking again. "It's no use hiding. They knew I was coming here—Oh, and by the way, father has had to take a funeral in Abbeyshiels, so he's gone with Jim on the motor-bike, and mother had a bad headache, so I'm the only one who was able to come. . . . Thank you so much—" This last, with a rather shy smile, to Oliver, who had relieved her of her bicycle.

"I'll not have those three old harridans in the house," growled Peggy's uncle by adoption. "They'll stay on and on till supper-time—"

"But what can you *do*, Uncle Jed?"

"Are these Miss Pringles really so very terrible?" asked Susan.

"D'you mean to say you've never met them yet?"

Susan shook her head. "Not so far. They called, and I was out, and I returned the call, but *they* were out. And that's the sum-total of our acquaintance."

"Never met Cissie, Jelly and Bell!" gasped Peggy, blue eyes wide. "You don't know what you've escaped."

"I like their names," said Oliver. "But are they real? I mean, Cissie and Bell are possible, but—Jelly?"

Peggy gurgled delightedly. "Oh, yes, they're *all* real. Jelly is short for Geraldine I believe—Uncle Jed! Here they come!"

A small governess-cart had come into sight over the nearest rise, drawn by a donkey which appeared to have some difficulty in keeping its fore-feet on the ground.

"They'll have that miserable brute going on two legs soon," growled Mr. Armstrong. "And it wouldn't look as much of a donkey as they do, anyway."

Eager cries rose from the occupants of the governess-cart, there were flutterings of hands and scarves, and a parasol, hastily furled, was seen rising and falling in ceaseless flagellation of the donkey's flanks, with sounds as of carpet-beating. At last, and in their steed's own time, the three Misses Pringle reached the group which stood by the gate. Seated, they were a dazzling spectacle, arrayed in flowery voiles and large shady hats, hung with chains of beads, clinking with bangles. But as they began to descend, unwillingly assisted by Jed, glimpses of stout and rather shapeless brogues, of dark, wrinkled cashmere stockings, detracted considerably from the first effect of their upper portions. They greeted Peggy with a kindly condescension which Susan at once recognized as infuriating: and being introduced, shook hands with Susan and her brother in a gracious manner plainly intended to convey their own high degree and the unworthiness of the recipients.

Cissie, evidently the youngest, became rather painfully skittish at once, and made allusions to the Navy, and Susan saw Oliver wince as she uttered the loathsome word "middy."

"And what boats were you on?" she continued. Oliver replied that he had served in several ships; and then Susan's own turn came.

Miss Bell Pringle, the eldest and the blue-stocking of the remarkable sisters, opened fire. "I hear that you *write*, Miss Parsons. Are you the author of 'Partners for the Lancers'? Such a *pretty* story." Susan did not at all dislike being asked about her book, for it was pleasing to discover that anyone had heard of it; but the question when accompanied by the dreadful expression "a pretty story," was more annoying than flattering. Even as she acknowledged the novel to be hers, she could guess what was coming.

"We have a cousin who writes, you know. Such a *gifted* woman. Of course, not novels"—this in a tone which relegated novels and their miserable authors to some lower plane of intelligence—"articles for really *good* periodicals. The *Scrutator* and so on. I always feel *I* could write a book myself if I had time."

Susan bit back the retort: "Try it, and see if it's as easy as you seem to think!" and smiling wanly, murmured a more suitable reply.

"You *must* join our Literary Club this winter," said Miss Pringle more graciously than ever. "We meet at a different member's house each fortnight, to read our own compositions, and we have a little friendly criticism—so *helpful*, we all find it—and tea. I feel sure you would enjoy it, Miss Parsons and find it useful to you in your work."

Susan felt perfectly certain that she would not, and registered a mental vow that nothing short of brute force would drag her to the meetings where tea and criticism were so freely mingled. But by this time they had reached the door of Reiverslaw, and even horror at the prospect of a winter spent in dodging Miss Pringle's invitations had to yield to curiosity as they entered the house.

Susan's anticipations of Jed Armstrong's abode had prepared her for one of two alternatives. Either it would be full of heavy Victorian furniture, stuffy hangings, and quantities of ugly valueless trifles left in their places because his mother had put them there; or it would be bare and comfortless, a dwelling used only as a shelter for sleeping and eating.

Her lively imagination had misled her, for the reality was like neither of these pictures. Reiverslaw was furnished in a completely harmonious fashion which made it difficult to pick out details, the general effect being entirely satisfactory and pleasing to the eyes. Tea was ready in the dining-room, comfortably set out on the table. The room was small. Coloured prints, a series of hunting recollections by Aiken, hung on the walls, and there was a set of fine Hepplewhite chairs. The silver was old and well-cared for, the china of good design. There were sandwiches as well as the large scones and solid cakes which Susan had expected, and China tea. It was all quite unlike Jed Armstrong as she knew him, and she had the irritating feeling that she was mistaken in her judgment of this big bluff man with his sneaking fondness for practical jokes.

The sitting-room, to which they wandered after tea, was another surprise. Walls, curtains and chair-covers were all in autumn colourings of brown and buff, with an occasional hint of soft orange or blue, yet nothing about it bore the obvious stamp of the professional interior decorator. Low book-cases were filled with heavy old calf-bound Volumes, gazetteers, works on farriery, and the like, long out of date. Probably they were never opened now, and had hardly been looked at for generations but they added a last touch of mellow colour to the room. There was a high oak dresser on which were ranged a few bits of good china, a handsome Toby jug among them, and two beautiful little pieces of lustre-ware; but that it was no show apartment, used only when visitors were there, could be seen from the large wireless set lurking in a corner, the deep, rather worn arm-chairs, the pipes and tobacco-jar on a small table, and the atmosphere which hangs about a frequently occupied room.

"Do you like it?" asked her host.

Afraid that her wandering eyes had betrayed more astonishment than was altogether polite, Susan said that she found it delightful.

He nodded. "I rather like it myself," he said. "Not that it was all my idea. It was really partly—"

The high imperious voice of a Miss Pringle broke in, piercingly shrill: "And what news have you of Mrs. Holden?"

3

Susan, turning from a closer inspection of the lustre jugs, saw that Peggy Cunningham's sensitive face had clouded a little, and that she darted an indignant look at the questioner. Astonished, she glanced at Jed, but he was answering with absolute composure.

"She was quite well when I last heard from her," he said.

And Peggy, who had been listening with forced politeness to a long monologue by the eldest Miss Pringle, now said in her clear tones, evidently determined to change the subject.

"But if you believe in spirits, Miss Pringle, why not in the fairies too?"

"Yes," chimed in Oliver. "Spare us the fairies! This country is so full of stories about them that it would be ungrateful to deny their existence."

"Conan Doyle said—" began Peggy, only to be cut short by a maddeningly indulgent smile, a bony hand playfully raised.

"Dear little Peggy! Always so enthusiastic! But I'm afraid your zeal carries you away, my dear. And I do not altogether agree with Conan Doyle," said Miss Pringle. "In fact, I think I may say that I have gone *farther* in my experiences than Conan Doyle."

She looked round the room as if defying anyone to contradict her, but her statement passed unchallenged, since none of her audience could know exactly how far these mysterious experiences had gone.

"But—fairies—" said poor Peggy, still clinging to her belief in what had been a living delight of her not far distant childhood.

"I believe in them firmly, Peggy," Susan said, boldly entering the lists under Miss Pringle's supercilious stare. "Nothing would persuade me to do anything to annoy them. I never touch their trees—"

Miss Pringle uttered the high, unamused cackle of laughter which she used to indicate boredom or displeasure. "How charmingly naive of you, Miss Parsons. Do you mean to tell me that you never pick hawthorn?"

"Never," Susan said firmly. And spurred by the joyful thought that if Miss Pringle continued to disapprove of her she might cease to be considered eligible for the Literary Club, she added: "I never pick hawthorn, or blackthorn, or rowan. I don't even like to pick broom since I read the ballad of Young Tamlane, when the queen of the fairies spoke 'out o' a bush o' broom'."

"Really!" ejaculated Miss Pringle. "Now *I* make a point of filling the house with hawthorn and blackthorn blossom as long as they are in season, and I never even *heard* that about broom."

"How strong-minded," murmured Susan, and though she hoped she sounded polite, she could see by Oliver's strained expression that he, at least, realized that politeness was not altogether her intention.

Jed Armstrong, who had listened to this crossing of swords in silent appreciation, now came to the rescue of his fellow-man, and suggested a move.

"What about going to see the steading?" he asked, and immediately there was a flutter of girlish ecstasy among the three sisters. As he led the way across his narrow cream-walled hall, Susan could hear the eldest Miss Pringle telling him how *devoted* they all were to animals of every kind. "Neddy—our dear little donkey, you know—is such a pet with us. And whenever I am in Edinburgh I make a *point* of visiting the Zoo—"

Strange, thought Susan, that such an ardent animal-lover should care to gloat over wild creatures in captivity, even such luxurious captivity as the beasts at Corstorphine enjoy.

Her arm was clutched by Peggy. "Every time I see them I make up my mind not to let them annoy me," she hissed in Susan's ear. "And every time they infuriate me to the verge of screaming. I—I hope the fairies will pay Bell out for what she said about them!"

Susan rather hoped so too, for she also had found the intense self-satisfaction of Miss Pringle exasperating, and her temper was ruffled.

"I'm afraid," Oliver said, joining them in time to hear Peggy's remark, "that I'd rather have some speedier vengeance than the fairies'!"

They visited the long cattle-shed, where phlegmatic bullocks standing deep in clean straw, blew out their wide black nostrils suspiciously and backed away from everyone except their owner, of whom they seemed to have no fear. The dim place was fragrant with their sweet breath, the air was filled with the placid crunching of their meditative jaws. The stables housed eight pairs of stalwart cart-horses, glossy as newly fallen chestnuts, but Susan did not linger there, for a couple of ploughmen had come in to visit and make much of their own particular teams, and horses and men alike made her feel an intruder. As soon as she could, she went out, to find that Jed Armstrong had followed her.

"You're surely not afraid of the horses?" he asked. He sounded aggrieved.

"No," said Susan. "But it seemed such a pity for us to disturb the men when they had come to see them." He opened his mouth as if to say something, and then shut it again without having spoken. They were standing on the cobbles in the warm sunshine, watching two kittens play at tigers-in-the-jungle among some long grass.

"Have you seen the barn yet?" he asked suddenly. Susan awoke to the fact that the others had not joined them.

"They'll come after us," he said carelessly, reading her look. "Unless you want to wait for them?"

"No, I don't," Susan answered truthfully. A very little more of Cissie, Jelly and Bell might have made her forget the courtesy due to them as fellow-guests.

It was very quiet in the great barn, empty save for a pile of grain in one corner. Jed saw Susan glance at it, and shrugged his massive shoulders. "Can't get any price for it with all this foreign stuff coming in," he said. "This is good, too."

He let a golden handful trickle through his fingers, and Susan did the same, liking the cool hard feel of it, almost like a handful of uncut gems.

"It'll lie there till it rots, likely," he ended. "Unless we feed hens on it. I'll need to turn grazier in another year or two if things don't get better."

He took her up an unrailed wooden stairway to another barn above, low-roofed, lighted by sky-light windows, immensely long, running away, at right-angles from the one below it, to a shadowy dimness at the farther end. Here was more grain, and several small plundering birds, disturbed by their entry, flew twittering close over their heads, finally making their escape with considerable noise by a broken pane of glass.

"All this—does it bore you?"

"Far from it," Susan assured him. "Though if anyone had told me a year ago that I should enjoy seeing over a farm, I'd have laughed at them. I never knew, you see, how interesting it would be." He kicked idly at a knot in the floor-boarding. "You ought to see the big Ram Fair at Abbeyshiels," he said after a pause. "It's rather a sight. Ten rings, and ten auctioneers, or more, all selling at once. I'll be going there to buy a ram. Like to come?"

"Yes, I should like to, if it isn't going to be a nuisance to you to take me—"

"I'll see that it's not," he replied at once, and Susan's faint surprise at his politeness vanished. Evidently it was purely temporary, and she wondered why he had troubled to invite her. . . .

4

"Let's escape," murmured Oliver in an undertone. He touched Peggy's arm, nodded towards the Misses Pringle, who were admiring a small brown and white calf fenced off in a hay-carpeted corner, and glanced meaningly at the open doorway.

Peggy said nothing, but when he edged cautiously in the direction of the door, she went with him. Once outside he seized her by the hand. "The hay-loft. Come on!" he whispered, and the two raced across the cobble-stones of the yard, dodged round a corner, and in at an entry where a steep ladder led to the loft above. It was as Oliver hoisted himself up rather painfully after her that Peggy remembered his limp.

"Oh!" she cried in dismay. "Your leg! You shouldn't have run like that!"

She regretted her impulsive words as soon as they were spoken, and reproached herself bitterly. She should have remembered that he hated any reminder of his infirmity. Though his limp was never very noticeable except when he was tired or when, as on this occasion, he had used his leg more violently than usual, he was morbidly sensitive about it. Always an active man, he loathed the necessity for having to take care of himself. And now, striking almost unconsciously at the offending limb in his nervous fashion, he met her penitent look, which he fancied to be one of pity. For the moment he hated her. How dare she, or anyone, look at him like that? Following on this sudden flare of rage and humiliation came the sullen desire to show her that, lame or not, he was a man still. The air in the dusty, sweet-smelling hay-loft was heavy with uncomfortable emotions. Peggy was miserably aware of having spoilt this escapade for both of them. She longed to tell him she was sorry, but had sufficient wisdom to say no more. Only when the silence had become unbearable to her, she rose from a heap of hay and walked to the ladder.

"Let's go," she said rather shakily. "I'm sure the others will be wondering what's happened to us."

Oliver laughed savagely. "Aren't you going to offer to carry me down the ladder?" he jeered. "Or at least give me your arm? Remember what a crock I am!"

He was behaving abominably, and he knew it, but half-ashamed of his childishness, he persisted in it. The fault was the girl's after all. He had been feeling particularly fit that afternoon, more like himself as he had been before his accident, and even the ridiculous escape at full speed from the Misses Pringle had done him very little harm.

True, there had been a twinge or two in his game leg, and climbing the ladder had not been easy but that would have been nothing if she had not pitied him, reminding him that however well he might feel, he must still seem a semi-cripple to others like her. Even now, when his jeering tone brought the blood to her cheeks, and he thought she was going to give him the indignant answer he deserved, he saw her head droop again.

"Please don't," he heard her say in a low voice, and panic seized him.

"My God!" he thought. "She's going to apologize for hurting my feelings!"

That would be the last straw. Rising quickly, though the sudden movement jarred his leg, he limped across to her. "Don't say any more. It doesn't matter," he began, awkwardly, abruptly. "I'm afraid I made rather an ass of myself."

His voice was still angry, his words could hardly be construed as an apology for his outburst, but Peggy's tender heart reproached her still and told her that it was really her fault. It did not occur to her that it would have relieved the situation if she had taken him to task, and in any case she was too young and inexperienced to do so effectively.

Instead, she looked at him appealingly, and he saw that her thick lashes were stuck together in little black points by the tears she had kept back with difficulty. Oliver laughed again, but this time there was a note of triumph in his voice. She might pity him, but she was a little afraid of him too. Without stopping to think, he put his arm round her, felt her stiffen, then relax. As his lips met hers in a long, hard kiss, and she, at first holding back, finally yielded, even seemed to return it, he knew that somehow, even by these unfair means, he had proved his manhood to her. He was no longer to be pitied by Peggy, at least. . . .

He let her go at last, and stood looking at her. His dark eyes were bright, the lips that had been pressed so passionately to hers were curved in a smile. Peggy stared at him silently. She was still dazed by the sudden strange feeling which had made her, instead of repulsing him, return his kiss. Could this be love, of which she had read so much, which she had never yet experienced? All she knew was that she had hated to have Ronald Graham's arms about her, but . . . she had not hated Oliver's. Her mouth still burned from the pressure of his, and she was trembling a little. His first words, carelessly spoken, were like a sudden splash of ice-cold water in her face.

"Well," he said, still smiling, "we'd better go and hunt up the rest of the gang, hadn't we?"

Plainly the kiss, so shattering to her, meant nothing to him; and something in his voice or his look, or her own intuition, told Peggy with brutal clearness that he had only been taking his revenge for her unfortunate remark. She was hot with rage and shame: his kiss was an insult, far more so than Ronald Graham's abhorrent clumsy embrace, for he at least was in earnest, much as she disliked him. In that one moment Peggy lost some of her childishness, and it was a woman's pride that raged against this man who had treated her so lightly. He must never know what it had meant to her, never.

"Never! Never!" Vowed Peggy to herself. And she answered him lightly, the effort bringing a rush of colour to her cheeks. "Yes, we really must. They'll think we are lost."

And: "Brute! Beast! Cad!" she stormed inwardly, following him down the ladder so recklessly that she almost missed her footing and had to be steadied by him. It might have comforted her sore heart to know that Oliver by this time was thoroughly ashamed of himself, and was applying her very words to his conduct. But his manner gave no sign of what he felt, and he whistled with what seemed to Peggy odious gaiety as they crossed the stackyard.

His voice rose in a stentorian bellow to Susan and her host from the lower barn. "Ahoy, aloft there! Come down out o' that, Jed! Do you think I'm going to do all your entertaining for you? The Pringles are in the pig-sty for the moment, but Lord knows how long they'll stay there."

"What have you been doing to Peggy?" demanded Jed, when he and Susan had obediently come down, to find Peggy quite speechless with laughter on the bottom step of the stairs.

Susan, knowing her brother's ways with young women, fixed him with a stern glance, which he met with one of firm innocence. "Nothing," he answered.

"Then what's she giggling about?"

"It's only that the Pringles make me hysterical after a bit," explained Peggy. "And—and he will keep calling them idiotic names like Blinderslosh!"

Susan felt that this mirth was excessive, and Oliver's joke of the feeblest, but she held her peace, only resolving to get some explanation from him later.

Her chance was at hand. Jed Armstrong took Peggy by the arm, and saying, "You wait here. Peggy and I'll go and get them," left brother and sister alone.

5

For a short time there was silence, broken only by Oliver's whistling. He looked so cheerful and innocent that Susan found it difficult to be severe.

"Not quite fair of you, Noll," she said, during a pause in the whistling.

"What d'you mean?"

"You know quite well. Peggy isn't fair game for you, my dear."

"Peggy? Pooh—she's only a baby. I've no interest in her whatever."

"As long as she hasn't any interest in you—" began Susan slowly.

"Can I help it if she has?"

"Yes, I think you probably can." Susan's hazel eyes, always so much more serious than her laughing mouth, met her brother's darker gaze, and read a certain shame in it. Answering his look she said: "Don't do it, Noll."

"All right, all right. I'm not going to," he cried, turning away and hunching his shoulders irritably.

Susan, guessing that she had won, said no more, and sounds of approaching voices brought them out from the cool twilight of the barn into sunshine that dazzled their eyes at first. They found the Misses Pringle being made much of by Jed, who had suddenly become amiably talkative. Though this seemed a sinister symptom to Susan, the three sisters, particularly the skittish Cissie, were more than content to take it as a tribute to their charms.

"Come on, and I'll show you something worth seeing!" he was shouting genially. "Never mind the others, they don't know a good beast when they see one. I've a prize bull here I want you to look at."

Waving the rest back with one gigantic hand, he led the Pringles, torn between wholesome fear of the bull and delight that they should have been chosen to view it, across the yard.

"What's he up to?" muttered Oliver. "I wish I knew—"

So far as they could see, Mr. Armstrong was "up to" nothing. He opened the gate of an enclosed pen backed by a shed and walked fearlessly in. The Misses Pringle, clucking like agitated hens, gathered timorously about the entrance, afraid to venture farther.

It was Peggy who first caught sight of Captain Kidd.

As the goat came mincing round the corner of the courtyard, his yellow eyes gleaming malevolently, his mephistophelian countenance turning from side to side in search of prey, she and Susan, followed more slowly by Oliver, took refuge in the barn, from which point of vantage they awaited events.

These were not slow in following. Captain Kidd caught sight of the three elderly ladies, and reared up on his hind-feet. In this heraldic attitude he advanced towards them, tossing his beard viciously. The two younger Miss Pringles, with a long and tremulous yell, darted into the bull's enclosure and slammed the gate behind them, leaving their strong-minded sister to face the foe as best she could. She did so for the space of perhaps five seconds, while the onlookers in the barn watched his stately progress with misgiving, Peggy audibly wondering why "Uncle Jed" did not "do something."

"Good boy!" cried Miss Pringle in trembling accents. "Good Billy, nice beastie, then. . . . *Oh!*"

The last exclamation was a high shriek, for Captain Kidd, enraged either by her appearance, which except for the beard and horns was not unlike his own, or her temerity in thus addressing him, made a lunge at her.

"Oliver!" cried Susan, "that brute is dangerous, I'm sure of it! You *must* rescue the poor old thing somehow!"

As Oliver left the barn, Miss Pringle's nerve finally gave way and she fled, shrieking, towards the house, pursued hotly by Captain Kidd. In an instant Jed Armstrong and the two younger sisters emerged from the pen, and while they clung together, crying that poor Bell would be killed, he and Oliver joined in the chase.

Susan and Peggy, following more cautiously, were in time to see the final tableau of Oliver supporting the eldest Miss Pringle, her stately condescension vanished, her scanty grey locks streaming, while Captain Kidd and his owner strove for possession of her red straw hat. Something had to give way, and as neither Mr. Armstrong nor his goat would yield an inch, it was the hat which at last disintegrated.

Captain Kidd bounded off with the larger portion, which he proceeded to eat, savagely and voraciously, before the fascinated eyes of the entire tea-party, and Jed triumphantly proffered the mangled remains to the now speechless Miss Pringle.

Long after the sisters, only slightly pacified, had taken a hasty departure in the donkey-drawn governess-cart, Oliver continued to laugh helplessly at intervals, and to mutter: "I'll never forget that goat eating the Blinderslosh hat, never, as long as I live. Poor old Belly, or was it Jell? I don't know t'other from which—with her venerable locks flowing—"

"It really was rather a shame," said Peggy.

"What I can't understand," said Susan, "is how Captain Kidd came to appear just then? I thought you said you'd had him safely shut up—"

Jed returned her suspicious look with one absolutely expressionless. "So I did," he said. And added thoughtfully, after a pause, "I think the *fairies* must have let him out."

CHAPTER SIX

1

"I HAD a dream last night," said Cilly importantly.

"Did ye? Well, staun' still while I do your hair, see, or ye'll get it tugged." Jo-an's voice was listless, and she plied the hair-brush in a half-hearted fashion as she brushed Cilly's silvery curls.

Bun looked up from the floor where she sat with a sock half-way over one foot. "What was it about?" she asked.

"About me. I was a dear wee eagle, layin' a egg up a tree."

"But you couldn't of got up the tree," objected Bun. "You can't climb trees."

"Can, in d'eams," said Cilly firmly. Peeping out from under her veil of curls she saw that Peggy had added herself to the audience in the nursery, and continued with redoubled vigour. "There was a tiger up the tree, gerrowlin' at me!"

Bun stared at her cousin with solemn dark eyes. "And *then* what happened?" she asked.

"I woke up," answered Cilly.

"But where was the egg?"

"The tiger ate it!"

"Tigers don't eat eggs, do they, Peggy?" Bun appealed to her aunt, who was assisting Colin into his minute trousers.

"Not that I know of!" said Peggy with her gay laugh.

"This tiger did," said Cilly. "It was *my* tiger, an' *my* egg, an' my d'eam—"

Released from Jo-an's ministrations, she jumped about the floor in high feather.

"Come, noo, Bun, an' let me see to that hair o' yours," said Jo-an.

A shower of thick, dark locks, straight as if soaked by rain, fell about Bun's shoulders. She tossed it back and cried: "You're a funny wee dreamer, anyway!"

"Funny wee d'eamer!" echoed Colin, and gave one of his shouts of laughter as if delighted by his own cleverness.

"Colin, my man, if you won't stand still, how am I to get these breeks of yours on? One foot at a time, now—" said Peggy.

"Colin's b'eeks!" said her nephew joyously, and laughed again.

"Jo-an says if you laugh before breakfast you cry before night," observed Bun.

"Dear me, I hope not, or we'll all be in tears to-day," Peggy said, and pulled a jersey over Colin's primrose-coloured head.

"Jo-an won't. She isn't laughing," said Bun, who had twisted her head round far enough to catch sight of Jo-an's unsmiling face.

Jo-an only said, "There, noo, that's enough." But Peggy was suddenly aware that the young nurse was unusually silent this morning.

"Yesterday was your day out, wasn't it, Jo-an?" she said. "I hope you enjoyed it."

Jo-an started, the colour flooded her cheeks and then drained away, leaving her curiously pale. "Oh, it was a' right, Miss Peggy," she said in a stifled voice. "See an' not lose yer ribbons to-day, Bun. They're new ones."

"It was such a fine day," Peggy went on. "The walk up to Reiverslaw must have been lovely."

"It was a bonny day," was all Jo-an said, and her small rosy mouth shut tightly as if on some close secret.

The breakfast gong boomed downstairs, and Cilly cried excitedly, "I'm goin' to have a egg for brekfuss'! A dear wee brown tiger's egg—"

"Such nonsense," said Jo-an. "Another word and you'll not get an egg at all!"

This sharpness on her part was most unusual, and Cilly murmured in a very subdued manner: "I'm goin to have a dear wee *hen's* egg for brekfuss'."

"I should hope so, indeed," said Jo-an.

Peggy went down to the dining-room rather thoughtfully. She hoped that Jo-an was not going to give notice, but it looked very much as if she might. No place suited her restless temperament for more than a month or two, and she had been at the Manse longer than anywhere. Her parents were beginning to congratulate themselves that Jo-an had "settled doun," and Mr. Cunningham also had commented on it. . . . But now. . . . Peggy shook her head. "I'll wait a day or two, and then if she isn't happier, I'll have to tell Mother," she decided. "Perhaps if she spoke to Jo-an it might steady her."

Then she forgot all about Jo-an, for Jim, bounding into the room, seized her round the waist and whirled her about until her head swam.

"It's the Ram Fair to-day!" he said, releasing her. "Want to go, Peg?"

"Oh, Jim, how lovely!" Peggy cried breathlessly. "Of course I want to go—"

"You shall, then, and I'll pay your entry money," said her brother, rattling some silver opulently in his trousers-pocket.

When they started out in Jim's motor bicycle and sidecar, a few hours later, a red head was pressed to one of the upper windows, watching them, a pair of dark, rebellious eyes saw them go; but Peggy did not look up. For the time being Jo-an had no place in her thoughts.

2

"By the way, Donaldina," said Susan, pausing as she was about to leave the kitchen after her morning interview with the cook, "why can't we have soup to-night? There's a large, handsome bone in the larder—"

Donaldina replied in shocked tones: "If ye please, mem, yon bone's promised tae Taura, an' if we bile a' the guid oot o't afore he gets it, he'll no' be pleased."

Susan had become accustomed to the respect, verging on reverence, with which her large black dog was regarded in the kitchen, and she suspected that, willing in their service though Donaldina was, she would let them go hungry rather than forget "Taura's" supper.

"Oh, of course, if Tara is to have it, that's a different matter," she said, and returned to the sitting-room smiling a little.

Neither she nor Oliver had realized when they rather dubiously accepted this offspring of a Labrador who had contracted a *mésalliance* with a neighbouring Newfoundland, what a powerful personality they were introducing to their household; but they had never regretted it. Tara, large, handsome, in a coat of glossy, curly black tipped with bronze where the sun caught it, combined the Labrador's pleasant temper and intelligence with the Newfoundland's faithfulness to a small circle of intimates, and a somewhat sombre air when depressed. His manners, except when on rare occasions he unbent so far as to frolic in a stately fashion, were so correct that his owners were sometimes abashed by his look of grave disapproval when Oliver played the fool. He did not beg; to steal he was ashamed; nor did he ever make meals uncomfortable as some dogs will by watching with a grudging eye each bite that went into a human mouth.

"I'm afraid," Susan said guiltily, as Donaldina brought in the coffee after dinner, and Tara, spruce and debonair, bustled in after her, sure of a welcome, "that we won't be able to take him to Abbeyshiels with us to-morrow, Oliver."

"No," said Oliver, and shook hands with Tara, who offered first his right and then his left paw solemnly. "The Ram Fair isn't for you, old man. You'll have to stay at home to-morrow and look after the house."

Tara looked at them, his ears and tail drooping, but apparently he accepted the decision, for as they set out for the Ram Fair on the following morning he saw them off with an air of manly resignation, and presently retired within doors again.

"Well, here we are!" shouted Oliver in self-congratulatory tones, as the Squib, after a succession of ear- and nerve-shattering reports, finally came to rest at the roadside in a cloud of odorous blue smoke.

Susan never set foot in her brother's car without the confident expectation that disaster would overtake them before their journey's end, and her murmured "Thank God!" as she got out was piously fervent.

Oliver did not share either her fears or her relief. "She's brought us in very nicely," he observed with simple pride, patting the Squib's dusty red bonnet affectionately.

"She has certainly heralded our arrival very effectually," said Susan. "We might as well have been attended by a brass band in full blast."

There was no false modesty about the Squib and her blatant progress. A small but interested group of loafers, sprung as if by magic from the ground, had gathered about the car and proceeded to exchange animated comments, the reverse of complimentary, on her general appearance.

"I suppose she'll be safe enough if we leave her here?" said Oliver, surveying the Squib with the doting pride usually shown by a young mother exhibiting her first baby.

"Safe?" Susan echoed faintly. "My dear Oliver, do you imagine that anyone in his senses would *want* to run away with the Squib?"

This remark was greeted with smothered guffaws and grins by the audience, and by Oliver with the scowl reserved by brothers for their sisters.

"Don't make such a fool of yourself!" was his low-voiced but heated request, interrupted by Gibbie Johnston, owner-driver of Muirfoot's sole taxi, who had strolled up.

"Weel, sir," he said with a genial smile and a finger to his cap for Susan's benefit—a signal honour, as she realized, for in this independent country such courtesies were only observed where liking went with them—"weel, sir, I see ye still have the auld bag o' nuts on the road! Ye've never needed to borry the Miss Pringles' wee cuddy yet to drag it hame for ye?"

If this opprobrious suggestion had been made by Susan, the vials of Oliver's wrath would have been poured on her devoted head; but from Gibbie, as a fellow-man, he took it almost blandly.

"Come, now, Gibbie," he said. "I bet you'd be pleased enough to have my engine inside your own old bone-shaker of a barouche!"

"Aweel," said Gibbie with the air of one making a handsome concession, "I'll no' go sae far as to say the en-*gine*'s hopeless a'thegither. But the boady! Are ye no' feart it'll rattle to bits an' leave ye sittin' amang the wheels?"

As further pleasantries of this nature seemed to be forthcoming, Susan left them to it, and walked slowly on through the goods station towards the park where the Ram Fair was being held. The railway yard, where empty trucks were awaiting their freight of rams, was choked with cars, which had also overflowed into the field beyond. A dull noise that from the road had sounded like the sea beating on a rocky coast now began to resolve itself into its component parts: the deep-toned buzz of many men's voices, the shrill yapping of collies, the continuous roar proceeding from the brassy throats of eleven auctioneers, and, above all, the ceaseless hoarse crying of the rams themselves. There were upwards of three thousand of them, and in their imperious belling the dominant male note resounded, fearless and challenging, utterly unlike the plaintive bleat which was the only sound Susan had associated with sheep hitherto.

She paid her entrance money at the gate and joined the crowd in the park, which doped gently away down towards the roaring rings. Everywhere on the poached and trampled grass men stood in quiet, serious groups, or laughed loudly at some joke, and slapped the jester on the hack with hands as large as hams, as hard as their own shoe-leather. Strong tobacco and the pungent smell of sheep and sheep-dip tainted the clean air with whiffs of the tweed in which almost everyone was clad. There were shepherds, their far-seeing eyes knowledgeably appraising this beast or that, their wistful, ivory-toothed dogs clinging like burrs to their heels; there were men in riding-breeches and leggings, men in inch-thick suits obviously made by their local tailor, and other men whose tweeds as obviously had been cut by a master-hand. The comradeship of mutual interest bound them together in a solemn temporary equality, even seemed to make them look alike, so that out of the mass of lean, hard-bitten, blue-eyed, brown faces it was next to impossible to distinguish friend from stranger.

It took Susan less than half a minute to realize that it was hopeless to look for Jed Armstrong, or any other acquaintance, in such a crowd. Big man though he was, there were others present of the same magnificent build towering among their fellows, where most were of good height, and even the smallest appeared either stocky or wirily strong. Susan wished that she could have had with her one of those gloomy spirits who shake their heads in dismal gloating over the decadence of the race, for here they might have seen what would have helped to give the lie to their prophecies. Here, bred on the land and for it, sprung of sturdy stock, was the very antithesis of the effeminate youth that lisps pornographic verse in so-called Bohemian surroundings to others of like kind. Perhaps the men here were narrow-minded, thinking of little beyond their crops or their beasts; perhaps coarse-fibred, too reminiscent of the strong earth by which they lived, to please the idealist. But at least their vices and failings were those of men, they knew nothing of the lust which seeks an outlet in perversion. It seemed to Susan, as she stood absorbed in watching, that they were akin to men of Oliver's stamp, those clean-run sailors who always bear with them the freshness of salt water.

A slender young man, wearing plus-fours and a brilliant canary-yellow waistcoat, went past, herding with a stick three large rams which had been dipped a glowing orange to show off the depth of their fleeces, he glanced at Susan, and she half-thought she recognized him. Then, leaving his contingent to the care of an elderly shepherd, he came over to her.

"Hullo!" he said. "How d'you do? I'm Wat Hepburn of Kelpieha', in case you've forgotten—"

Mendaciously Susan assured him that she had not. He went on at once: "You're looking for Jed, I suppose?"

"Why should you suppose so?" asked Susan with a smile and a faint lifting of fine black brows. This calm assumption that Jed

Armstrong should be her sole natural protector amused her. "As a matter of fact, I came with my brother."

"Oh, I say! Have I said the wrong thing? Have I put my foot in it?" he stammered, blushing like a girl of more ingenuous days. "You see, you came with him to Kelpieha' that evening in summer, and my sister thought—we all supposed—"

What they had all supposed was so patent that he might have shouted it aloud, and Susan, for all her amusement, did not quite know what to say. She had got as far as, "A natural mistake, perhaps, but a mistake—" when she was interrupted by the eager voice of young Jim Cunningham.

"Here you are!" he cried. "Hullo, Wat! Peggy's over at Number One ring, Miss Parsons. Won't you come along there? You'll see the pick of the rams and Jed said you oughtn't to miss them."

"More Jed!" thought Susan. "Why, the man's ubiquitous! Even his name seems always to be cropping up."

"Is Mr. Armstrong," she said, slightly stressing the name, "with Peggy?"

"No; we just saw him for a minute, and he told us to keep a lookout for you," said Jim Cunningham, and added in a tone almost of apology, "He's busy, you see."

"Well, let's all go over," said young Hepburn with some eagerness. "I've sold my rams. And I haven't seen Peggy for ages."

They made their way slowly through the crowd, which grew thicker as they neared the rings. In pens on every side the rams bawled their defiance to the world at large: huge, Scriptural-looking animals with blank agate eyes, long legs, and flopping ears. They had been dipped every conceivable shade of fawn and brown, yellow and cream and orange, and as they shouldered each other emulously, their fleeces glowed warm in the sun. One thing puzzled Susan, and that was their lack of horns. Her idea of what a ram should look like was based on a childish memory of a Bible picture in which Abraham, armed with a business-like knife, was about to sacrifice an animal whose horns curled like twin cornucopias, while Isaac looked on in smug relief at his own narrow escape. She said this to her escort, and Jim Cunningham laughed heartily.

Young Hepburn, looking half-shocked, half-amused by such abysmal ignorance, explained in a hasty undertone, "These are Border Leicesters, and half-breds, and crosses, and Oxford Downs, Miss Parsons. I don't suppose there's a single ram here with a horn to its head."

Jim, thrusting his way between two burly men who had evidently been celebrating a sale in strong liquor, made a path for Susan, and presently her arm was clutched by Peggy, who pulled her close to the ringside. Over the shoulders of large men, intent on their business, she caught a momentary glimpse of a round purple face, a hat pushed back from a streaming forehead, a mouth, opened to its fullest extent, from which issued a brazen bellow: "Now, gentlemen! Lot fourteen, number two . . ."

A primrose-coloured ram bounded into the ring and glared about it, uncowed by the press or the din. Arms were stretched over the palings, hands felt the thick fleece wisely, there were mutters of cautious praise.

Susan gazed, fascinated, as lot after lot was loosed into the ring, put up and knocked down after brisk bidding at prices which made her gasp, for these were pedigreed animals of well-known strains. Becoming bolder, and urged on by Jim Cunningham, she ventured to sink her own hand deep into the living wool on one broad tawny back, wool softer and springier and warmer than she had ever felt before.

Suddenly an elbow was dug into her ribs and, turning, she found a red-faced farmer, breathing fumes of stale whisky, leering at her. As she shrank back, "There's somebody wants ye, lassie!" he said with a sickening ogle. Susan peered past him and saw Jed Armstrong making unmistakable signs that she was to join him on the outskirts of the crowd. He was quite capable of roaring at her if she ignored this summons, she knew, for neither time, place, nor the presence of multitudes abashed him. Susan would have preferred to turn her back and remain where she was, but fearful of being made conspicuous, she nodded grudgingly. So dense was the throng that even the slight movement entailed by turning had placed a barrier of human bodies between her and her companions by the ring. Peggy, flushed and laughing, was talking to Wat Hepburn of Kelpieha', and her brother was nowhere to be seen.

With difficulty Susan struggled through towards the place where she had seen Jed, only to find, when she reached a clearer piece of the ground, that he was no longer visible. Hot with futile indignation, she was about to battle her way ringwards again when a large black object, which at first she took to be an enraged escaped ram, bounded at her, and in an ecstasy of untimely affection, put a paw on each shoulder and wetly licked her face.

"Tara!" cried Susan incredulously.

Tara it was, dusty, collarless, leadless, but beaming with delight at having found her. Before she had time to recover from the shock of this discovery, a hand seized her arm, and Oliver's voice, hoarse with fury, announced savagely, "Someone's pinched the Squib!"

3

"Someone's—pinched the Squib?" Susan echoed stupidly. "What on earth do you mean?"

"I mean," he repeated with grim patience, "that some swine has stolen MY CAR!"

Susan shook her head, unable to credit anyone with such sheer crass folly as the abduction of such a vehicle as the Squib.

"Have you seen Jed anywhere?" was Oliver's next remark.

"Yes, he was somewhere near here a few minutes ago, but he seems to have gone. And, anyhow, why Mr. Armstrong? Why not the police?"

Oliver laughed bitterly. "Every policeman in Abbeyshiels is on duty here to-day, except for one in the police station. . . . Ah!" He broke off suddenly, and dashed away with Tara, who evidently considered this a joke on the grand scale, leaping joyfully about him. In a few seconds he was back, hauling Jed Armstrong with him. From the latter's eye Susan guessed that he was of much the same opinion as Tara, and prepared to treat the whole affair as a huge jest.

"It'll be one of these lads that's taken a dram too many, likely," he was saying placidly as they rejoined Susan.

"I don't care if it's the devil himself," retorted Oliver, quite pale with passion. "He's not going to get away with MY CAR!"

"Better go up to the road," suggested Jed, "and see if anybody's noticed the car. I'll come with you. I've finished here."

He thrust the bulky paper-covered volume which catalogued the bewildering details of the rams' pedigrees into a capacious pocket, and led the way from the fair at a brisk pace.

Not one of the many loungers who still supported the fence by the roadside could give any assistance. When the obvious absence of the car was pointed out to them they expressed amazement, but apart from further enraging Oliver by the suggestion that he had perhaps forgotten exactly where he had left the Squib, they had nothing to offer except useless advice, of which they were lavish.

"Well, I don't know what's to be done just yet," began Mr. Armstrong as he meditatively stuffed tobacco into his pipe. "Of course, you'll get it back, all right. The police will trace it by the number-plate. Likely enough we'll find it in the ditch on the way home."

The mere thought of his beloved Squib, the apple of his eye, lying forsaken in a ditch, was sufficient to reduce Oliver to merciful speechlessness. Susan trembled with laughter which she dared not let loose lest she should be stricken by one look from her brother.

Fortunately, at this pregnant moment a very dirty small boy whose nose urgently required the application of a handkerchief was shoved forward by one of the onlookers.

"This wee laddie's sayin' he seen yer cawr," volunteered a bold spirit. And to the urchin, who showed no desire to approach the fuming Oliver: "Speak up, Tammie, and dinna' be feared. The gentleman'll no' hurt ye."

Thus encouraged, the small boy announced in a tremulous adenoidal pipe: "Ah seen a wee rid cawr gaun up the rod wi' twa men in't."

"Which way?" barked Oliver in a quarter-deck manner calculated to alarm the most intrepid, said which instantly reduced his informant to loud sobs.

"Come on, lad," said Mr. Armstrong, his voice more gentle than Susan would have believed possible, "and tell us which way the car went?"

The small boy sniffed, wiped his snub nose on his cuff, and pointed a wavering grimy finger in the direction of Muirfoot. On being asked how long ago this had happened, however, he once more burst into tears, and blandishments, even when further sweetened by a sixpence, could elicit nothing more than that it was "a wee whiley syne."

"You'd better go after it," said Jed. "Wait! Here's young Jim Cunningham. He'll take you on the back of his motor bike."

Jim, delighted at the prospect of adventure, instantly agreed, and with Peggy, who was to be set down as near the Manse of Muirfoot as possible, in the sidecar, they roared off. Susan was left standing, deserted, holding Tara by a most inadequate lead composed of her scarf tied about his neck, which his proud spirit bitterly resented; and with no apparent means of getting home except walking seven miles. She had entirely forgotten Jed Armstrong, and started when he addressed her.

"It's two o'clock," he said. "We'd better go to the police station about the car, and then have some lunch."

For a moment, remembering young Hepburn's half-spoken suggestion, Susan hesitated on the brink of refusal. Then Jed's composed, matter-of-fact manner, his clear and steady blue gaze, made her ashamed of attaching any importance to an idea so absurd. "Lunch," she said with the hungry wistfulness of one who had breakfasted early and was conscious of an aching void within, "sounds very nice indeed, thank you."

"Come on, then. The police station first," he said, and they walked down the hill into Abbeyshiels, crossing the river, running low between its pleasant green banks and trailing willows, passing the crumbling remains of the proud abbey which had given the town its name, and following the narrow streets towards the police station.

In the stuffy little office that smelt of hot navy-blue serge, a fat policeman, comfortably unbuttoned against the heat of the day, roused himself from torpor to assure them in a windy voice that they would have the cur restored quite soon. Like a large blue-bottle buzzing indoors on an unusually mild winter's day, he entered the Squib's description in a book, the tip of his tongue protruding as he laboriously traced the words with a scratching pen and a good deal of loud panting.

"Ou, ay," was his parting remark. "You'll can leave it tae me, Maister Armstrong. Ah'll see that ye get the cawr returned withoot a scratch on the pent."

"He'll be clever if he can do that," observed Jed as they emerged into the street again. "For that machine of Oliver's looks as if it had been clawed by angry wild-cats!"

Abbeyshiels was teeming with hungry men all hurrying to seek a meal, and the two hotels, beside every available public house, were doing a roaring trade.

"We'll go in here," said Jed, diving in at an open doorway whence blasts of hot air laden with the smell of cooking rushed to meet them. Following meekly, with Tara in tow, Susan found herself in a small baker's shop filled to the doors with others as hungry as they. A stair at the back led to unseen regions where, overhead, fortunate earlier arrivals were already feeding, for there was a ceaseless clatter of cutlery and china, a padding of swift yet heavy footsteps above, and ever and anon shrill cries of: "Twa steak-an'-kidney, wi' biled pitawties!" "Roast gigot for Mr. Black, an' look shairp, Beenie!" "Aipple tart, double portion!" . . . "Can ye no' haste wi' yon lentil soup, Beenie?"

To this last exhortation came a reply, screeched in the high-pitched tones of overwrought anger. "Is it haste, ye said? An' me near deid wi' the heat an' hurry! The lentil soup's feenished. If there's ony mair for soup, they'll need tae tak' Bov*rile*!"

Despite her hunger, Susan laughed, and Jed, it seemed, heard her. Glancing down, he grinned amiably at her. "Come on," he said suddenly. "I'll find you a corner up there, if it's only on the windowsill!" Seizing her by the arm, he whirled her towards the stairs, the crowd falling back on either side of him as earth from the ploughshare. Half-way up a door was flung open and a crimson-faced Amazon appeared.

"Here, Beenie!" cried Jed. "This young lady's dying of hunger. Is there not a place she can have up there?"

"'Deed, Maister Armstrang, they're *that* throng there's nae room for a moose!" screeched the cook heatedly. To a scurrying waitress, who bawled an order at her as if miles of stormy seas divided them, she answered in a voice of equal volume and far greater fury.

Susan, appalled, gave back a step, expecting bloodshed, but the Amazonian cook, ignoring all else, turned to Jed, evidently a privileged person, and said with ferocious amiability, "Ye can come ben the kitchen, if the leddy disna' mind."

They entered with gratitude a cavern hot as a boiler-room, and Susan sank on a chair in as remote a corner as she could find, while Jed, fearlessly snatching a plate, proceeded to dish a generous helping of roast meat and vegetables.

"Here you are," he said, thrusting the plate into her unready hands and, heedless of her nervous whisper that the cook might not like it. "Oh, she'll not mind," he said easily. "Here, Beenie, where d'you keep your knives and forks? We can't eat with our fingers!"

It was a truly amazing but excellent meal, eaten in haste, in a miniature inferno of heat and din. Under the kitchen table Tara devoured an enormous bone, gifted to him by the Amazon, and growled joyously. Jed Armstrong, quite at home, carved joints for the overworked Beenie with infinite neatness and despatch, and raided the shop below, returning in triumph with cheese-cakes for Susan. Finally, after gulping down cups of scalding black coffee, which Beenie picturesquely described as "het as Hielan' love," they went out into the sunlit street like wanderers returning from another world.

"I feel," said Susan with a sigh, breathing in the warm fresh air, "as if I'd been lunching in the crater of a volcano!"

4

"Well, I suppose I'll need to take you home to Easter Hartrigg now," said Mr. Armstrong with such a marked lack of enthusiasm that Susan felt constrained to apologize for the necessity.

"Oh, it's not that *I* mind," he said handsomely, "but there's two rams and a barrel of beer for the harvesters to go as well."

As the alternative to driving in this mixed company was a seven-mile walk along a dusty road, Susan bowed to the inevitable. The buff-coloured rams, handed over to their purchaser by a shepherd whose friends rightly described him as "roarin' fou," took their places beside the beer-barrel in the back of the car with calm dignity, and Tara, with the gnawed remnants of his bone, was bundled in on top of his mistress beside Jed Armstrong. They started with a lurch which caused the beer-barrel to bounce, and one of the rams fell forward heavily on to his Roman nose against Susan, knocking her hat over her eyes.

"We're off!" shouted Jed, and sped on their way by gales of loud laughter and derisive cheers from a small mob of spectators, they drove away from Abbeyshiels.

Though the unmoved decorum of the rams was admirable, Susan could not help feeling that their presence and that of the beer-barrel did not add to the dignity of their appearance. Everyone they met, and the road was busy, stared at them as at a travelling-circus, and usually paid them the tribute of a cheer or some shouted comment which, perhaps fortunately, was swept from their ears on the wind as they fled by.

As they neared the crossing where they turned off for Easter Hartrigg, a small car darted out from a side-road on the right and stormed off along the road they were about to take, through a belt of trees. A sudden loud report followed by several others, a glimpse of a battered red bonnet in a cloud of dust, and Susan cried loudly: "That's the Squib!"

"What? Oliver's car? Are you sure?" demanded Jed Armstrong, and trod heavily on the accelerator.

"Certain!" shrieked Susan. "I'd know that noise anywhere."

"Gone awa-ay!" bellowed Mr. Armstrong as they whirled to the left and banged along in pursuit of the cloud of dust, now fast diminishing before them. They roared past a farm, narrowly avoiding a number of hens, which, squawking their dismay, scattered in all directions. One, landing on the bonnet in a frenzied leap from death, went with them, an unwilling mascot, for several yards until, shedding feathers like autumn leaves, it fell off into safety in the ditch. The barrel bumped, the rams, at last losing their stately composure, began to utter hoarse protests, and Tara faced about to growl defiance at them.

"They'll turn off down the Kaleford road! Watch out!" shouted Jed, but they reached the turning, and still the red car was ahead of them and going straight for Easter Hartrigg.

"I never thought the Squib could travel so fast!" gasped Susan between bumps as Jed, with a splendid disregard for his springs, hurled his car and its loudly lamenting load over ruts and round corners.

"We're bound to overtake 'em in the long run!" was the grim reply. "Can you see how many there are in the car?"

"Two—a most awful-looking desperado without a hat driving," Susan told him as the car in front lost ground a little and they drew closer. "I'm sure I've seen him before somewhere!"

Jed Armstrong merely grunted. "He'll be damned sorry he's ever seen me, or that car, when I make up on him! Is it another man with him, or a woman?"

She had no time to answer. The Squib rocketed round a double bend, and Jed's car, taking the first turn, almost came to grief in the ditch. Tara, landing heavily in Susan's lap with his forequarters, took the opportunity to lick her face fondly, with a horribly moist and meaty tongue.

"Wonder where he thinks he's going? We'll be at Easter Hartrigg in a minute," muttered Jed. "If he's mistaken the road, and goes in there, we'll have him! Pity Oliver's not here—he'd enjoy this!"

In front of them the Squib, like a homing pigeon swooped between the gate-posts of Easter Hartrigg and disappeared among the trees fringing the drive. Jed, sounding his horn like one possessed, plunged his car, all in a second, into the shade of the same trees. Gravel flew aside like water as, with rams giving tongue, Tara barking, the horn tooting, Jed roaring, and Susan, regrettably, screaming like a sea-gull, they tore up to the house. In front of the doorway stood the Squib, as usual enveloped in blue vapour and, bending solicitously over her was the "awful-looking desperado without a hat"—Lieutenant-Commander Parsons himself. . . .

"What the devil—?" he and Jed Armstrong exclaimed loudly and simultaneously as the big car with its patriarchal freight drew up close to the Squib. Oliver had lost his hat, his suit was stained with mud and oil, he had a very spectacular black eye, and the knuckles of his left hand were bleeding profusely. The other occupant of his car, who was sitting on the step trying, with a most inadequate handkerchief, to remove the dust from her face, was Peggy Cunningham.

"You?" said Susan wildly. "Why—why didn't you stop when you saw us behind you?"

"Not on your life," said Oliver. "We'd given up the chase, and Jim dropped us at the crossroads to wait while he went to Kaleford to tell the police there. We walked on, and then—it was Peggy who saw them first—we found the Squib parked under a hedge with another car close by, and the beauties who'd pinched her picnicking off whisky in a field. So we hopped into the Squib, started her up, and roared off. Of course, we thought you were the blokes coming after us in the other car. Peggy kept looking back and telling me you were a pretty tough-looking lot. And so you are!" he ended, with a disparaging glance at his sister.

"Not half so villainous as you, my dear," Susan said. "How on earth did you come by that black eye?"

"Oh," he said carelessly, wiping his knuckles with a gory handkerchief, "we had a bit of a dust-up before we could get away. I've knocked one fellow's teeth down his throat. Hope they choke him!"

"You look," said Susan, eyeing him dispassionately, "as though you'd been brawling in a low pub."

"Well, what does it matter? We've got the Squib back again, and there's no one to see us," said Oliver placidly. "Let's go and have tea."

Susan became aware of Donaldina hovering on the doorstep, her open mouth and wide eyes indicative of unwelcome tidings. "If ye please, mem," she said in a hoarse whisper, "the Miss Pringles are in the wee sitting-room at the back. I tellt them ye were oot, but they said they'd juist wait on ye. I doot," she added with dismal relish, "they'll be wantin' their tea."

A stricken silence fell like a pall, only broken by an indignant bleat from one of the rams, which had become plaintive. As they stared at each other, Susan realized that Tara's attentions had left large dusty streaks on her suit, that her hat had long since been trampled underfoot by the rams and was beyond redemption, that she was scarlet in the face, her hair like a bird's nest. The others were not in much better case, and there was little to choose between any of them, though possibly Oliver was the most ruffianly of the quartette.

"We must creep in," she said desperately, "and try to make ourselves look a little more respectable. Peggy, come with me—"

"I wish you'd gag those brutes of yours," growled Oliver as the rams once more raised lamentable voices.

"Too late," said Peggy with the calm of despair. "There they are."

Donaldina, melting unobtrusively into the background, left them to face the Misses Pringle, who, arrayed in the chaste splendour of their calling coats and skirts, with hints of Jaeger underwear peering coyly above lace-trimmed blouses, now came forth in a body.

"Ah, the wanderers returned!" cried Miss Pringle with truly dreadful playfulness. "You *naughty* people! *Quite* like the Elusive Pimpernel, we began to think you had forgotten *all* about us!"

In spite of her apparent *bonhomie*, there was an angry glitter in her eye, and Susan, though she could not imagine what this greeting meant, murmured feebly: "Oh no, not—not at all! Not in the least, I assure you—"

"Didn't you *get* our postcard?" asked Miss Jelly in more trenchant tones.

"It's such an *age*, dear Miss Parsons, since we saw you," chimed in Miss Cissie girlishly, "that I said yesterday that we really *must* look you up, or you would be thinking we'd forgotten you altogether. I'm 'fraid we're very, very bad about our calls in the tennis season, and we felt so *guilty* about you! So I said—"

"I think, dear Cissie, that the suggestion was *mine*," said Miss Pringle with a dangerous suavity which caused Miss Cissie to wilt. "I sent a postcard, Miss Parsons, suggesting that we might come to-day, but when we arrived—"

"The birds were flown!" chirped Miss Cissie in a valiant attempt to hold her own.

"Well, the birds are back again," said Oliver abruptly and with a marked lack of enthusiasm. "Let's go and have *tea*."

Susan had been nourishing a secret hope that their appearance was not so tramp-like as she herself had supposed, but this was doomed to disappointment.

"Have you had an *accident*?" cried Miss Jelly eagerly, stretching a lean and scraggy neck towards the cars in a manner horribly reminiscent of a vulture's. "You all look so untidy, so upset!"

"Not a bit of it. We've been at the Ram Sales," said Jed Armstrong stolidly. "And you know it's a rough sort of show. Oliver's been fighting—"

"Fighting?" cried the two younger Misses Pringle in tones of delighted horror. "Oh, Commander *Parsons!*"

"I do not consider the Ram Fair at all a suitable place for *ladies*," said Miss Pringle, her look apprising Susan and Peggy that she did not include them in this category. "So rough, so much inebriety. Disgusting. I never go myself, nor do I permit the girls to attend—"

"Quite right; quite right," quoth Jed perfidiously, but with a devilish glint in his blue eyes. "See what's come of it. Peggy and Miss Parsons looking like tinkers' wives, and Oliver here with a black eye. I wouldn't go near the place myself if I hadn't to buy rams."

"I do think, my dear Peggy, that you are really too *old* now to mix with that sort of crowd," pronounced Miss Pringle. "Look at Cissie—she *never* goes. I shall drop a hint to your mother. No doubt she doesn't *quite* realize that you are no longer a child, and cannot go tearing about the country in this fashion!"

Peggy, who bitterly resented being placed on an equal footing with the simpering Cissie, opened her mouth to make an angry retort, her cheeks burning; but Donaldina announcing that tea was ready, Susan led the way into the house in haste.

It was a crestfallen party, with the exception of Jed Armstrong, who continued to agree so slavishly with the Misses Pringle that Susan became vaguely uneasy. Tea dragged on miserably. Tara at one point tried a little light relief when, in response to Miss Jelly's invitation to "Come here, then, good, sweet doggie," he approached and laid in her lap the gruesome fragment of his luncheon bone.

"Will you put Tara out, please?" said Susan with commendable self-control, glancing at her brother He, however, was sitting in morose silence between Miss Pringle and Peggy, his scowl accentuated by his rapidly blackening eye. It was Jed who rose with suspicious alacrity and led Tara from the room.

As Susan turned her attention to her unwelcome guests in an effort to be brightly hospitable, she heard him say in the hall, "There you are, then, lad. Be off outside with it."

"Kind of him to give Tara back his bone," she thought.

5

"Your boa, Miss Pringle? Are you sure you brought it? I don't remember seeing you wearing it," Susan said with weary politeness.

Time seemed to have stood still during the visitation of the three ladies, but at last she was speeding the parting guests in the hall, and trying not to look overcome with joy. The guests, however, refused to be sped without Miss Pringle's feather boa, which she was certain she had laid down on entering the house.

Jed Armstrong had wandered out to look at his rams, but Susan and Peggy, sullenly assisted by Oliver, searched in every likely and unlikely corner of the hall, vainly moving chairs and the table, and even the oak chest in which the travelling rugs were kept. Donaldina was summoned and her face, on her being questioned, instantly assumed the well-known expression of one unjustly accused of theft. Her replies were noteworthy for their obstructive stupidity, and would have reduced opposing counsel to a state of dumb frenzy had she been in court.

"A tie made o' feathers? Na, mem. Na, Miss Pringle. A' the feathers I seen ben the hoose was the feather duster."

Only the reminder, timidly made by Miss Cissie, that they were dining out and would have to go home at once unless they wished to be late, eventually prevailed on Miss Pringle to take her leave without the boa. Her farewells to her host and hostess were fraught with suspicion and disapproval; but she said good-bye to Mr. Armstrong outside with a cordiality rendered doubly impressive by contrast.

"They were surely an awful time getting away?" asked Jed placidly. "The rams have settled down in the car now as cosy as if it was a pen—"

Sounds of violent sneezing could be heard from the dining-room, and they trooped there in a body to discover the cause. At the door they met Tara, unmistakable feathers sticking to his muzzle and chest. As he saw his mistress he sneezed again with vigour. Overcome by a dreadful foreboding, Susan stooped and looked under the dining-table.

The carpet was covered with feathers, damp and bedraggled, and with shreds of what had once been the grey silk lining of a boa.

Peggy, after one long look, collapsed on a chair in helpless laughter, and Oliver promptly followed suit.

Susan fixed Jed Armstrong with a steady stare. "Do *you* know how Tara got Miss Pringle's feather boa?" she asked.

"I saw him with something," he said, meeting her look guilelessly. "I thought it was a dead hen. So that's what they call a boa, is it?"

Tara, re-entering, dived below the table and, coming out with a mouthful of feathers, laid it faithfully at Susan's feet.

6

Peggy was still in high spirits when, having refused the offers of Jed and Oliver to drive her home, she walked down the long hill towards Muirfoot. It was a most lovely evening, and it had been a good day, both amusing and exciting. Though she had not wanted to be left alone with Oliver Parsons, for the memory of that afternoon at Reiverslaw still made her burn with shame and indignation, she was glad now that she had not gone back to the Manse with Jim. She was far from forgiving Oliver, yet she had admired him tremendously when he had knocked down the fighting-drunk man by the roadside, so coolly, so carelessly, almost with an air of enjoyment. Besides, as he had told his sister and Jed, she had made the discovery of the Squib, half-hidden under a hedge along a deserted cart-track. But for her he would still be mourning the loss of his precious car. This was a bond between them, which had been further strengthened by their wild outburst of laughter over the fate of Miss Pringle's boa. "Somehow," she thought, "once you've shared a joke with anyone, once you've laughed together, it makes you feel friendly to him."

She knew now, instinctively, without being able to explain it, that Oliver would never insult her again as he had. She had neither forgotten nor forgiven that kiss, but still she could not help liking him in spite of it. Perhaps if she had not previously had an unfortunate experience with Ronald Graham she would not have felt so strongly about it, but Ronald had shocked and frightened her as only a very young girl can be shocked. . . . At least, however, she had been spared a repetition of that unpleasant scene; no longer did the organist seek her out. He avoided her as much as possible, never spoke to her unless it was absolutely necessary, and scowled like a thundercloud if his eyes chanced to meet hers. Peggy felt that she could endure to be scowled at by him. She asked nothing more than to be left alone, and rejoiced in her escape from his unwanted affection.

Life was very much as it should be, and the bright September evening was in tune with her mood. The grassy road was soft beneath her feet, the sun, striking between the leaves of the tall hawthorn hedge, swam in patches on the ground like small golden fish in a bowl. White blossoms still flowered on the brambles, but the fruit was faintly tinged with pink, and some of the leaves on the prickle-set red stems already wore their brilliant autumn colours. On either side of the road lay the pale stubble fields, bathed in clear light, where cock-pheasants strutted gorgeously, careless of their approaching doom. Down in the hollow, hiding the village from their sight, rose a small wood of tall old trees, beech and larch and spruce, a wood which, according to local tradition, was haunted. None of the village girls would venture into it even in broad daylight, nor would they so much as pass it after dark. Peggy always found herself unconsciously hurrying along the stretch of road which flanked it. Now, looking at it, she was astonished to see a girl's figure approaching the belt of trees, stealthily, as if afraid of being seen.

It seemed to Peggy that she plunged in among them with relief, and the westering sun, as she crossed a patch of light between two great trunks, fell on a head of dark-red hair and turned it to flaming gold. Peggy stopped dead, for she knew that hair. No one in the whole neighbourhood but Jo-an Robertson could own it, but what was Jo-an doing, Jo-an who should have been sitting in the Manse kitchen at this hour? And Jo-an, of all people, entering the haunted wood in a manner which showed that it was not for the first time. ... Strange, almost uncanny girl, so different from the rest of her kind. ... "Perhaps she's in love," thought Peggy, "and that's what made her so queer this morning. But she can't be going to meet anyone there, surely. No one would ever choose the wood; even the men are afraid of it, though they pretend it's all nonsense!"

She passed the wood even more quickly than usual, for this evening it really did harbour a mystery. Ought she to mention this to her mother? It would distress Mrs. Cunningham to know that Jo-an had gone out secretly like that. The girl might be dismissed on the head of it, and Peggy felt certain that she would be better at the Manse than at home, where she had more time for getting into mischief if she wanted to.

Deep in troubled thought, she turned the corner into the village, and almost ran into a young man. As she avoided him with a murmured "I'm sorry," she saw that it was Ronald Graham, walking fast, his soft hat pulled down over his eyes. He made no reply, but, hurrying on, disappeared up the road down which she had just come.

A strange and most unwelcome thought occurred to Peggy. Could he be going to the haunted wood also? Then she shook it from her. "What nonsense!" she said aloud. "I must have a nasty, suspicious mind. It's all imagination, really, I expect."

She walked on toward the Manse briskly, trying to think of other things. But still the remembrance of Jo-an's furtive look back as she entered the wood returned again and again.

CHAPTER SEVEN

1

SUSAN stretched her long arms above her head and sighed wearily. Before her the big writing-desk was littered with household bills, the total of which appalled her.

"What a hideous and exhausting way of spending an evening!" she thought disgustedly.

She rose and went over to the fire, burning with soft comfortable sounds behind its bars. The gentle light of two oil lamps filled the pleasant room and made her rose-coloured dress glow vividly. Opening a silver box, she took a cigarette, lighted it, and smoked meditatively for a few moments, the toe of one shining shoe poised on the old brass fender; Finally she glanced over her shoulder with exasperated distaste at the papers on the desk.

What a profitless business it was, when demand outran supply, as she could tell from her accounts. She and Oliver lived simply enough, Donaldina was that treasure almost beyond price, a really thrifty cook, and yet their income did not quite stretch far enough to cover outlay. Susan could not see where she could cut down expenses. Ends very nearly met, but she wanted them to overlap sufficiently to give her an easier mind about money.

"A laird and twenty pence, pronounc'd with noise," she had called her brother in fun but, unfortunately, it was true. Perhaps if they could do without Donaldina? But she was sure that she herself would be more extravagant as a cook, and in any case Oliver had to be properly fed or he would go sick. Then James. He might be dismissed, of course, and the place could run wild, and return to the neglected state in which they had found it. No; one owed a duty to the land; and no tenant, if they had to let Easter Hartrigg, would take it in a ruinous condition. Letting the house was a last resort, and even as Susan thought of it she knew that it must not come to that. Somehow or other they must contrive to stay here, where Oliver had in a great measure recovered his health, where he had found interests and friends. For herself it did not matter so much, though she had come to love this country as she had never loved anywhere else. She had no interests outside Oliver; she was settling down very comfortably into the beginnings of placid spinsterhood. To Susan Parsons at thirty-three life had become a game at which she looked on. She was content that it should be so; indeed, she had deliberately set for herself the part of onlooker. Amused, sorry, or interested, she watched other people's more active share in love, in pleasure, in money-making, in any of the businesses which they pursued with such feverish intensity. Of pleasant acquaintances she had many, of friends few, since friendship, like love, exacted a heavy price for its favours. Charles said she was the most restful woman he knew, and the best fellow, and that satisfied her.

Her cigarette had burned down to within an inch of its end. She threw it into the fire, wished that she could get rid of the bills by bundling them after it, and turned back to her task. It was growing late, and Oliver, who had been dining at Reiverslaw with Jed Armstrong, would soon be back. She did not want him to find her struggling with ways and means, did not want to see the old strained look on his face again.

He came on her unexpectedly, having entered by the back door, and she had barely time to shut the desk on its hateful contents before he burst into the room.

"Susan! Fine! I was afraid you might have gone to bed—"

"What is it? Nothing wrong?" she asked, seeing his excited face.

"I've got a job—a fizzer. Or, rather, Jed's got it for me. Old Elliot up at Wanside is getting too gouty to see to things for himself, and wants a part-time factor—"

"But do you know anything about factoring?" asked Susan, hating to damp his ardour, yet afraid to let him involve himself in a job he might not be fit to undertake.

"More than you'd think., I've learnt a lot from going about this place and Reiverslaw with Jed, and if the Service did nothing else, it taught me to handle men, Gawd bless it! And that's what's wanted at Wanside. Someone to see that the work's being done, and everyone isn't swinging the lead. Old Elliot will tell me what to do, and I'll see that it gets done."

He was marching up and down the room, his limp barely noticeable to-night, as if on a quarter-deck. From his open pleasure and relief Susan could gauge that his own anxiety about the ways and means problem had been as acute as hers.

"This will just make all the difference between cheeseparing and moderate ease," he went on. "We'll be able to have people here now and then, to stay, and there'll be some cash going spare for a few extra furbelows for you. . . . It's been worrying me, Susan, you know—"

"So it has me," said his sister with a glance at the writing-desk. "And I'm overjoyed, my dear—so long as you are quite sure you can do it, and are fit enough for it."

"Do it? My dear old thing, of course I can do it!" he answered. "I could do it on my head—and I will, if my damned leg gives out. It was most uncommonly decent of Jed to suggest me to old Elliot. Lots of fellows would never have thought of it, but it seems that he'd spoken about me to the old man, and that was why he had me up to dinner. Old Elliot was there, too, gout and all, and we got on well together. In fact, the thing's more or less settled, or will be tomorrow. Jed's what I call a real friend—"

With this Susan agreed heartily, but later, in the solitude of her bedroom, where candle-light strove with the creeping shadows, she wondered whether Jed Armstrong's friendship had outrun his discretion. Feeling much too wideawake to go to bed, though she had mechanically made her preparations for doing so, she went to the window and, pulling up the blind which Donaldina always modestly drew down, sat down with her arms on the sill.

The moon, which had risen a luminous primrose-yellow disc, had now swung into sight above the tops of the trees, its broad, innocent face shining with the dull lustre of old pewter. Stars, paling before it, had yielded the night sky to its sovereignty and the world on which Susan looked out was sharply defined black and cold white, a ghost of a world. There was not a single cloud to break the deep indigo-blue overhead, the trees stood motionless, dark, enchanted bastions of heavy foliage. Far before her, beyond the ridge on which Reiverslaw was perched, the Cheviots lay like some gigantic beast chained in slumber. The cool air breathed of cut corn, of dew, of late roses, even of distant heather, and Susan was glad that she would not have to leave Easter Hartrigg.

Then an owl, shattering the stillness with a loud melancholy hoot, roused her. She nodded towards Reiverslaw. "Even if Oliver can't manage this job, I'll never forget that you helped him," she said and, turning away from the window, crept into bed.

2

Although the one post of the day never arrived until well on in the forenoon, it always seemed impossible to settle down to anything until it had been. On the morning after Susan's battle with the bills the letters came while she was still in conference with Donaldina.

On the kitchen-table, scrubbed to snowy whiteness, was a dish which Susan had learned to call an "ashet," and on this ashet lay the remains of a roast leg of mutton.

"I don't see how it can possibly be made to do for another meal, Donaldina," said Susan sadly.

"It was a wee gigot," the cook agreed. "But I think I could mak' dae wi't—if ye can eat rissles again, mem?"

"Post, Susan!" cried Oliver from the end of the passage.

Susan quickly said that rissoles would be very nice and hastened to join her brother in the sitting-room.

"Is there anything very thrilling?" she asked, finding him removing the *Scotsman* from its wrappings. "Because if there are only bills, I shall swoon."

"Then swoons is off for the day. There's a letter for you from Charles, and a type-written thing—"

"Is *that* all?" Susan said ungratefully, and tore open the "type-written thing."

"Well," said Oliver at last, throwing aside the paper, "has someone died and left you a fortune?"

"Not exactly, but it's from that weekly paper I used to write for, asking if I'll do a set of articles of the semi-historical, folk-lore description—six articles, and they'll give me five guineas for each."

"Good work! I suppose you'll take it on?"

"Of course I will. Am I going to lose thirty guineas? Besides, it's time I did a little work." Susan spoke vaguely, her eyes had a far-away look which Oliver knew well.

"As long as it isn't another book—" he began uneasily, for he was remembering Susan's exceedingly variable temper when her last novel had been on the stocks and its feverish conclusion had coincided with his leave.

Susan remembered it, too, and laughed rather guiltily. "No, it won't be as bad as a book, my poor old Noll," she said. "And now I'd better see what Charles has to say for himself."

"By Jove, yes; I'd forgotten about Charles—"

After reading the three pages covered with small, distinctive handwriting, Susan gave the letter to Oliver. "I say," he said, "isn't this luck? If I hadn't got this Wanside job, I don't see how we'd have been able to put him up, but now—And so he's on unemployed time, is he? Of course you'll write and tell him to come here on his way north, or south, is it? Let's have another dekko at his letter . . . and stay as long as he likes?"

"I don't know that I shall," Susan began rebelliously. "I've got these articles to do, and lots of reading up for them, and I don't see how I can possibly with people staying—"

"Charles isn't people," said Oliver. "And you know you like him. Dash it, it's *you* he comes to see—"

"Yes, I know; that's the trouble. He'll take up such a lot of my time—"

Oliver was not listening. "Look here, the races are the week after next. Tell him to come in time for them, and we'll all go."

"Races? What races? I'm not going to *any* races," said Susan. "I tell you I am going to WORK."

"But listen, honey. We don't need the money as much as all that. Haven't I just told you that we'll have some cash going spare after this?" he argued. "Tell the editor to get someone else to write his articles for him."

"The spare cash ought to be kept for a rainy day," Susan said, "and not all spent in—"

"My dear girl, if we have any rainier days we won't need to bother at all. We'll simply be washed away by the flood."

Susan gave in, with the mental reservation that she would devote all her time to writing until Charles Crawley came. "All right," she said recklessly. "We'll ask Charles to stay. We'll fling money about. We'll go to the races. And very probably I shall take myself to Edinburgh for the day and buy a new hat."

"Splendid—You'd really *like* to have Charles here now wouldn't you?"

"Of course I should. Isn't he your oldest friend? Didn't you share your last shirt-tail in Gun-room days when your handkerchiefs gave out, you disgusting little brutes? Besides, I'd really like to have him to stay, myself. I am very fond of Charles."

"H'm, yes. And he doesn't seem to regard you with loathing exactly," said Oliver. " 'Lots of love, yours ever, C.' What?"

"Oh, my dear Oliver!" Susan protested, laughing at the suspicious look he gave her. "You ought to know by this time that Charles says that sort of thing. It means nothing."

"H'm," said Oliver again. "Well, I must be off. I promised Jed I'd lunch with him and go up afterwards to Wanside. Don't tell me, now it's too late, that I'll miss one of Donaldina's more dressy luncheons?"

3

Far from objecting to a solitary luncheon, Susan liked it, for it gave her an excuse for taking a book to table with her, and she loved reading during her meals. To-day her rissoles were shared with the Newcomes; and parting reluctantly from these old friends just as the inimitable F. B. called on the Colonel in Mr. Honeyman's rooms, she betook herself to the spare-bedroom most remote from the front door, determined to write without interruption.

Already she was shaping the first article in her mind, and she was not to be turned from her purpose by Oliver's arguments, the more so as the day had broken down, and clouds lying heavy on Cheviot had sent a scurry of rain beating briskly on the window-panes. There was nothing to lure her out. She pulled a large solid table into the best light, established Tara on a rug, and sat down before a pile of virgin paper as yet unsullied by ink . . . .

She plunged joyously at her task, and in the first frenzy of composition time slid by unnoticed. Even the pleasure derived from reading cannot begin to compare with the half-painful delight of writing, or trying to, though the results may be but poor reflections of the thoughts that inspire them. Susan in her eager pursuit of an idea, of the exact words in which to give it form, forgot that she was no longer a free agent, but a domesticated person in charge of a household.

Her reception of Donaldina, whose entrance was the first interruption of the afternoon, was as amiable as that of a lion disturbed during his meal. "What is it?" she said. "If someone has called, I am not at home."

"It's the fish-man, mem," said Donaldina with a small offended sniff. "He has some fine fresh herrin', an' I was wantin' tae ken wad ye like me to tak' some, an' ye could hae them potted for the breakfast?"

"Yes, yes. Do what you like," said Susan. "Buy what you like as long as I am left alone."

Donaldina, awed by this unusual crustiness, for normally Susan was extremely good-tempered; withdrew on tip-toe, closing the door behind her with a slow exaggerated caution infinitely more distracting than a hasty bang. For some time after she had creaked away, still ostentatiously on tip-toe, Susan sat nibbling the end of her pen, and trying to recapture a particular train of thought which, now that it had eluded her, seemed of unusual value and beauty. Tara rose, stretched himself, and uttering a loud melodious yawn indicative of boredom, approached delicately like Agag, only to be commanded with brutal brevity to lie down. He did so, sighing, but immediately began an exhaustive toilet of his person, a process which entailed long, slow luxurious lickings varied by the noise known to his owners as "gruffling." This, peculiarly irritating to listen to at any time, caused Susan to rise on the present occasion and smack him. Possibly the violent activity stimulated a somewhat sluggish brain, for she sat down again, and instantly a new paragraph began to shape itself out of a welter of ideas. Absorbed and happy, she wrote busily. . . .

There was a timid knock, and Donaldina once more entered, with the air of a virgin martyr being led to the stake.

"I thought I said—" began Susan in an awful voice.

"Oh, if ye please, mem, I couldna help it! There an awfu' wild-lookin' man at the door sellin' wee books, an' wadna gang withoot I'd askit ye tae buy—"

Plainly resignation was all that was left to the writer. "What sort of books?" asked Susan.

Donaldina produced a small volume, hideously bound in paper of a bilious yellow tinge, on which Susan's incredulous eyes beheld these words:

"HOW I ESCAPED, HOW I ESCAPED AWAY OUT OF HELL."

In smaller characters below this arresting title was printed:

"An Account Of My Escape From A Lunatic Asylum."

"Good Heavens, Donaldina!" said Susan. "*Is* he an escaped lunatic?"

"He micht be onything," said Donaldina, charmed by the shock she had succeeded in giving her mistress. "I wadna pit it past him, mem, tae be a murderer!"

With tremendous gusto she rolled out the last word, giving the "murrderrerr" as many R's as the teeth of a saw.

"Where did you leave him, Donaldina?" Susan asked rather nervously, and with a horrid foreboding that the maniac might be slinking about the darker corners of the house by this time.

"He's plapped himsel' doon on the front-door step, mem, an' he says he'll stir for neither Goad nor man afore he's sellt a book."

"I'll go down and see him myself," Susan decided, and not without an inward tremor, descended, purse in hand, to the hall.

The door, even on that dreary afternoon, stood confidingly open, country-fashion, as it did from morning to night during summer and autumn. Not the weather, but the seasons, decided whether it should be open or shut, and this always struck Susan as being not only characteristically Scottish but positively biblical. There was a hint of the stern Mosaic law about it, and she had waived her foolish English desire to have the front door shut on a wet day in June, or open to admit a flood of March sunshine, since she had realized that such waywardness provoked Donaldina's silent but withering contempt. On the step before the open door was seated a gaunt and prophetical figure, gloomily austere as Elijah under his juniper tree. He rose as Susan advanced, an old, grey-bearded man whose tattered appearance more than justified Tara's low growl of distrust. But as Susan's one wish was to placate this unnerving visitor, she would have preferred Tara to reserve his watch-dog manner for some less awe-inspiring tramp.

"Madam," began Elijah grandly, fixing her with an insane and fiery eye, "have ye glanced at ma book?"

"Indeed I have," Susan said with specious cordiality. "It seems a—a very interesting book, and—"

"It's the tale," said he, "o' ma ain pairsecution in Hell—though they ca'ed it the Loo-*natick* Asylum; an' ma escape there-froam. ... *A penny!*" he added so ferociously that Susan started back, and Donaldina from the hall behind her uttered a faint squeak of terror. "D'ye quarrel wi' the price? It's cheap, dirrt cheap, at a penny!"

"Indeed," Susan hastened to agree, "it's very cheap, absurdly cheap, and I will give you sixpence for a copy."

"A penny's ma price, nae mair, nae less. Wull ye tak' it or leave it?" he roared.

"Eh, mem! Tak' it, tak' it, for peety's sake!" wailed the voice of Donaldina.

With trembling fingers Susan opened her purse, pressed a penny into his horny hand, and fled in, shutting the door behind her. This time, she noticed, Donaldina made no protest about it. Evidently there were still some few occasions on which one might shut one's door during the day, even as early as September.

"I'll no' close an e'e this nicht," Donaldina said with what her mistress could not help thinking misplaced pride. "For fear o' being *murderred*! Would I no' be better tae bar the door, mem?"

"Certainly not. The poor old man has gone," said Susan, already ashamed of her moment of sheer cowardly panic. "You can open the door again presently."

Deaf to her muttered "I'd be feared! I'm no' wantin' tae loss ma life!" Susan returned, though rather hopelessly, to her writing upstairs. As she had feared, it was a mere waste of time, but she sat idly at the table drawing stupid little designs with her pen on a blank sheet of paper.

The sound of the front-door bell, jerked by an impetuous hand which had set it jangling like a tocsin through the whole house, came almost as a relief, and she had left her lair before Donaldina had time to summon her.

"It's Miss Peggy, mem!" she panted, reaching the top of the stairs—Donaldina invariably rushed up like a charge of horse and arrived so breathless that she could hardly utter an intelligible word—"I pit her in the droyn-room—"

4

Peggy seemed oddly ill-at-ease. She fidgeted with her gloves, which she had taken off, accepted a cigarette and forgot to light it, blushed violently when this was pointed out to her, and finally plunged into fitful conversation quite unlike her usual spontaneous chatter, with an almost desperate air.

"You'll stay to tea, won't you?" Susan asked at last, when the weather as a topic had been discarded. "Oliver will be back, I expect, and probably Mr. Armstrong."

Her ingenuous face showed nothing but dismay. "Oh, will he? Are they?" she said incoherently. "I hoped, I mean I thought—I met old Mr. Elliot and he said they'd be at Wanside—and I *did* think—"

"Take a long breath and begin again."

"You must think I'm quite mad," said Peggy, flushing scarlet.

"Not a bit, but you seem a little distraught. What's the matter, Peggy? Anything you can tell me?"

"Yes, oh, yes. I came here to tell you," she said.

"It was those horrible Pringles. It would be rather funny if it weren't so annoying."

"A good many things about the Miss Pringles would be funny if they weren't annoying!"

"Perhaps I'm only being interfering, but I didn't want them to come and tell you, and watch like three elderly vultures to see how you'd take it—"

"Take what?" Susan asked in some bewilderment.

"Well—" Peggy drew a deep breath. "Have you ever heard of Mrs. Holden?"

Susan frowned a little, thinking. "I seem to have heard the name," she said, "but it doesn't mean anything to me. Who is this Mrs. Holden?"

"She's—well, Uncle Jed and she were once engaged, ages ago, or they had an understanding, whatever that may be. It's the sort of thing that never *is* understood, isn't it? Anyhow, she married a Mr. Holden instead, and he has been an invalid for years—Miss Pringle told mother that he can't possibly live much longer. Some friend who must be as great a gossip as Bell herself, told *her*. . . . Anyhow, Mrs. Holden comes and stays at Reiverslaw every now and then, with an ancient deaf cousin as a chaperone. They're to be here for the Races—this is Miss Pringle again. Uncle Jed has never looked at another woman, and now Miss Pringle is sure that Mr. Holden will soon die, and she—Mrs. Holden, I mean, will marry Uncle Jed at last, and he'll live happily ever after, etcetera."

"I see. Well, it's all very romantic, though perhaps a little premature on Miss Pringle's part, to say nothing of the cold-bloodedness of arranging a second marriage for a woman before she is a widow," said Susan dryly. "What I *don't* see, Peggy, is where I am concerned in this."

"This is the difficult part. I hope you'll laugh at it," Peggy said a little apprehensively. "You see, Miss Pringle thinks that you are getting too fond of Uncle Jed, seeing such a lot of him, and that you ought to be told there's no hope for you!"

There was a silence, and then Susan laughed with such wholehearted merriment that Peggy gave a sigh of relief.

"Oh, Peggy, Peggy! What an exquisite joke! I'm so glad you summoned up your courage and told me! Does Miss Pringle *really* think that because I've been involved in two or three perfectly ridiculous escapades by the man that I've fallen in love with him? I couldn't have believed that credulity could possibly go to such lengths!"

"She does indeed," said Peggy with conviction. "Of course this is funny—but Susan, I do think; she's a dangerous woman. I do really."

"I rather agree with you, but fortunately in this case she can't do much harm, can she? Now let's talk of something pleasanter. Tell me what Mr. Armstrong's Mrs. Holden is like. Is she a very attractive person? Is she nice?"

"She's awfully attractive," said Peggy slowly. "But I don't care for her, somehow. Perhaps you'll like her. . . . And, of course, she isn't nearly good enough for Uncle Jed."

"Ah, but would you think anyone good enough for him?" asked Susan lightly, and before Peggy could reply she went on: "You are prejudiced in his favour, like Mrs. Robertson, his grieve's wife, who thinks there is 'naebody like the maister.' She sang his praises so loudly the other day when I went up to Reiverslaw to see her, that I could hardly get a word in edgeways. And talking of Mrs. Robertson reminds me that I saw Jo-an the other day, out walking. I love that girl's name, like an old song. How is she getting on as nursemaid to your Infantry?"

"Jo-an," said Peggy, and her blue eyes were troubled, "Jo-an has given a month's notice. She's leaving at the end of October."

"The silly girl! I wonder what her parents will say. I know that Mrs. Robertson is delighted that she should be at the Manse. What reason does she give for leaving, Peggy?"

"Only that she's tired of service and wants a change. I'm worried about her. I thought she had settled down with us, and would go south with the Infantry to the Richardsons. She is fond of them, especially Colin."

"She is a strange girl," Susan said thoughtfully. "I never saw such a secret face as hers. But it's no use your worrying about her, Peggy, for she will never stay long in any one place, even her own home. She is restless by nature, I fancy."

Peggy stirred uneasily in her chair. "There's something about Jo-an that frightens me," she said suddenly. "As if she weren't quite—quite human, Susan."

Susan nodded. "A changeling? Yes. She made me think of that the first time I saw her. But I think we're both being rather fanciful. Probably it's just the restlessness and discontent of the age, and die is a normal young woman really. If she is at home after she leaves the Manse, I'll have her down here instead of her mother to help Donaldina once or twice a week. Would that relieve your mind at all?"

"Yes, thank you," said Peggy like a polite child. She was not yet easy in her mind, but she had found it impossible to tell Susan any more. To speak of Jo-an visiting the haunted wood was merely being more fanciful than ever. . . .

"We'll have tea. I hear the men coming," and Susan rang the bell.

Oliver, calling loudly for hot scones, tramped in with Jed Armstrong. Their cheeks were wind-reddened, their shoes muddy, and with their arrival came a robust air of common sense, before which fancies fled away like cobwebs blown by a strong wind.

Looking at Jed as he ate and drank with serious zest, or rumbled out his few remarks in a good-natured growl, Susan found it very hard to believe that he was the victim of an unhappy love-affair; but then, of course, most people wore masks in self-defence, when all was said. She herself . . . "but that was over, long ago. It's finished, done with. I don't need the mask now, it's just habit to wear it," she told herself. Aloud she said:

"Are you going to the Races, Peggy?"

"No, I'm not allowed to. You see, being a minister's daughter makes it a bit difficult," explained Peggy, blushing under Oliver's gaze of interest and astonishment. She held her head up in spite of the shyness which always embarrassed her now in his presence, and returning his look with her own candid glance, continued bravely: "As mother won't even allow a cushion or a cake to be raffled at the Guild Sale in case it encourages gambling, I could hardly be seen at the Races by members of the congregation, could I?"

"Hardly," Oliver agreed quite gravely, for which she could have thanked him. "Never mind, we can do lots of other things just as amusing. We've got a man coming to stay, an old shipmate of mine, and a boyfriend of Susan's into the bargain, and we'll make whoopee together. Won't we, Susan?"

"I haven't a doubt that when you and Charles once get together, we shall," said Susan, laughing.

Not the flicker of an eyelid betrayed that she had anything but a friendly interest in this unknown Charles to whom her brother alluded so easily as her "boyfriend." Peggy thought that Jo-an was not the only person she knew who had a secret face. There was a difference, and she puzzled it out to her own satisfaction while the talk went on round her at the tea-table. Certainly there was a difference. Even if Jo-an had nothing behind that face except a mind empty of thought, she would still look secret as the Sphinx: Susan's habitual expression of tolerant amusement was the result of years of practice; she wore it for protection.

"Peggy's miles away!" Oliver was saying, and she came to herself with a start, blinking like a baby owl.

"I'm sorry. I was thinking," she said.

"I know. It takes me like that too, sometimes. But you should be careful, you know. Fearful strain on the mind, thinking," said Oliver, with every appearance of kindly sympathy.

"Pay no attention to him, Peggy," advised Susan. "He's only trying to be funny."

Peggy's blush had faded by this time. "I thought he was," she answered demurely.

Everyone laughed, but Oliver's eyes had a look of respect mingled with the amusement, and Peggy left Easter Hartrigg feeling that she had made a small start towards levelling the score between them. In fact, she was beginning to know how to deal with men.

CHAPTER EIGHT

1

"It really is terribly nice to see you again, Charles," said Susan, breaking in upon the Service gossip which had kept both men talking hard since the beginning of dinner.

Charles Crawley turned his head quickly to look at her, saw the open affection and pleasure in her eyes, and answered in his soft voice: "Thank you, darling. That's very sweet of you."

His glance travelled round the room, skimmed over Oliver, seated alert and cheerful at the head of the table, and returned to Susan's face. "I like your house," he said.

"'Umble but 'omely, Mr. Crawley, sir," said Oliver. "We like it too. Don't we, Susan?"

"We do," answered Susan. "We love the whole place." This time her eyes, as they met Charles's, held a look of challenge, as if daring him to disagree or disbelieve.

Dinner was over, but the three still lingered at table in the soft light shed by four green candles in tall silver sticks. A bowl of apples, another of green grapes, glowed brilliant as jewels above the dark surface of the polished wood, which faithfully reflected their rounded contours. Susan sat in a high-backed chair with arms, her dress of darkest green velvet shining where the light was spilled over it, her soft hair pushed back behind her ears and curling at the nape of her white neck. She felt happy, and her eyes had lost their gravity and smiled with her lips. It was good to see Oliver in such spirits, for she had been half-afraid that seeing Charles again might bring back too poignant memories of the life which he no longer shared with his best friend. That it had not was plain to see, for his dark face was alight, his eyes sparkled, and he spoke without a trace of regret of old days. . . . It was good, too, to have Charles at Easter Hartrigg, handsome Charles, the exact opposite of Oliver in looks, with his fair hair, his long blue eyes, and the absurd youthfulness of appearance which often misled strangers into thinking him a very junior officer indeed, instead of a Lieutenant Commander. He was her own kind, she could talk to him, and she only realized now how much she had missed him during the months which had slipped away since their last meeting.

"Are you awfully huntin'—shootin'—fishin' nowadays?" asked Charles later, when they were gathered close to a companionable fire of logs in the sitting-room.

Susan laughed. "I'm not, anyhow. Oliver does a little desultory shooting, but that's about as far as it goes. The best people, of course—or so Miss Pringle assured me, go in for all three, but we certainly couldn't afford to hunt even if we knew how."

"Jed Armstrong, our nearest neighbour, wants us to go and shoot with him one day," said Oliver, stirring the fire until a shower of golden sparks flew up the chimney. "You'll like him."

Charles Crawley once more looked at Susan, and it was to her that he spoke. "You've mentioned him in your letters several times, haven't you?"

"Probably I have," Susan answered tranquilly. "We see a good deal of him. He is a great friend of Oliver's."

"We haven't seen much of him lately," Oliver reminded her. "I've been kept pretty busy at Wanside, and then he's got this Mrs. Holden staying with him—"

Susan's expressive face lighted with interest. "Have you seen her, Oliver? What is she like?"

"No, I haven't seen her, but she'll be at the Races, of course. Judging from the fact that our Miss Pringle doesn't approve of her, I should say she'd be pretty good value."

"I wish you'd tell me who these mysterious females are!" Charles sounded plaintive, but there was a look of relief in his eyes. "This Mrs. Holden, for instance. Is she a girlfriend of your Armstrong, Noll?"

"More or less," said Oliver taking a cigarette and pushing the box towards his guest. "At least, rumour says she used to be. Married some other fellow, name of Holden, who's been in a looney-bin of sorts for years, and isn't expected to last much longer."

"And local public opinion—in other words, the Pringles—is that when her husband dies she'll return to her first love and become Mrs. Armstrong."

"So they've got it all taped before the poor devil of a husband is even dead," said Charles. "Seems a bit previous, doesn't it?"

"Oh, my dear!" Susan laughed. "Every neighbourhood contains a few industrious persons, highly skilled in the art of making bricks without straw or any other material, and ours is no exception to the rule."

"In this case, there actually happens to be a little straw," Oliver conceded handsomely. "I mean, old Jed was honestly keen on Mrs. Holden—"

"Well, here's luck to him, anyhow!" said Charles, so fervently that Susan, who had been going to ask Oliver the reason of his certainty about Jed's feelings, looked at him in astonishment.

"Have a drink?" suggested Oliver, and rising, limped over to a small table behind them.

"Thanks, Noll," said Charles, and then, meeting Susan's eyes, added quietly: "Don't you wish him luck too?"

"Of course I do. But—you haven't even seen him yet," she said.

"It's me kind 'eart, duckie. I've been in love meself!"

"'All the world loves a lover—'" began Olive sententiously, and Susan rose with her quick yet graceful movement.

"Oliver dear, if you've reached the stage of producing antiquated quotations, I'm going to bed. Good night," she said lightly, and left them.

2

"I'm afraid Miss Pringle isn't pleased with me," murmured Susan, as that lady greeted them with a bow of extreme hauteur on their arrival at the race-course.

"What have you been doing?" asked her brother.

"Well, she sent a postcard inviting herself and the other two to tea, and I sent back a polite telegram full of regrets by James. It was only curiosity. She wanted to see Charles before anyone else did."

"My head is bloody but unbowed," said Oliver cheerfully. "What's your fancy for the first race?"

Susan, who had never pretended to any knowledge of the Sport of Kings, would have spent the afternoon quite happily without putting a penny on anything, if it had not been for Oliver's shocked remonstrances.

"What on earth's the good of coming if you aren't going to back a single horse?" was the conclusion of his somewhat heated harangue, delivered in an undertone in the paddock.

"I enjoy watching it all," Susan replied quite unchastened; whereupon her brother groaned aloud and washed his hands of her.

"After all," she said to Charles, "I derive just as much pleasure out of a day's racing as those people who knit their brows over their cards, and confer so importantly with their favourite bookies, or rush frenziedly to and from the tote!"

The whole countryside had gathered there, from the unemployed of Abbeyshiels and neighbouring towns to that select few known as "the County." Smart tweeds, fur coats, bowlers, field-glasses hung across immaculate suitings, collected and dispersed in ever-changing groups. The scent of good tobacco from cigar or cigarette mingled with delicate whiffs of French perfumes, and strove with the smell of wet trodden grass. There was a sudden splash of colour as rainbow-tinted jockeys sidled past on horses as sleek, as sinuous, as well-groomed as any fashionable debutante, with the muscles making moving shadows and highlights shimmer on their polished skins.

It was a day of fight winds which harried the clouds fast across blue sky, of fitful sunshine enamelling the grass, brilliant after a night's rain. Wherever the humbler enthusiasts had not clustered, the white-painted palings marking the course gleamed against the green. Tears of excitement and pure pleasure filled Susan's eyes as the horses thundered by to finish the first race. They came, passed, and were gone in a second; flash of colour, dazzling, confused, dizzying; the sound of hard breathing from flaring nostrils, and that dull, hollow thud of hoofs which, with distant drums, is surely the most heart-stirring in all the world. Deserted long before, at her own request, by Oliver and Charles, Susan remained in one of the stands, entirely content, careless as to the result, since she had nothing to win or lose.

"Hullo!" Jed Armstrong loomed beside her, field-glasses hanging like an out-sized pendant round his neck. To her astonishment, for she had pictured him in his usual costume of riding-breeches and tweed jacket, he was attired with conventional correctness in a suit, a navy-blue overcoat and a bowler set on at a rakish angle. More surprisingly, these garments did not look in the least incongruous on him.

"Where's Oliver? Left you in the lurch?"

Susan hastened to clear her brother of this charge. "I am hopeless at this sort of thing," she said. "I don't even *want* to bet, and Oliver is indignant and says it's a sheer waste of money for me to have come at all!"

"H'm," he growled. "A pity everyone hadn't as much sense; I know some people who've lost a packet over the last race. But you'll have to have a little on Dauntless in the next, you know. He's a local horse, owned and bred by Hepburn of Kelpieha', and young Wat is riding—"

"It isn't a bit of good. I don't know how," said Susan. "And the bookies rather terrify me. I'm sure I should pick out a welsher or something, and Oliver would never let me hear the end of it."

"You come with me," said he. "I'll look after you." Susan hesitated. She had come to the Races with two men perfectly capable of "looking after" her; and surely Mr. Armstrong ought to be in attendance on his guest, Mrs. Holden. He seemed so unaware that his proper place was not here that she said at last: "What about—Mrs. Holden? Won't she be wondering where you are?"

"Not she. She's with a pack of friends. We lunched with them, and I'm sick of hearing them all squawk."

"And I am the lesser of two evils?" said Susan, unable to restrain her laughter, which seemed to puzzle Jed. But she could not very well explain that her amusement was partly due to the construction which the Misses Pringle would undoubtedly place on his kindly intention.

"What a good thing it is," she thought, as she followed him through the crowd in the direction of the bawling bookies, "that I've reached an age when I can laugh at these ridiculous insinuations. If I were a young thing like Peggy, I'd be miserable, and refuse to have anything to do with him simply because those three wretches have made up their minds that I have a tendresse for him!"

Suddenly she caught sight of them steaming in what Oliver would have called "line ahead" towards the totalisator. Miss Pringle herself led the way, bowing and smiling with insufferable graciousness on all her acquaintances. Miss Jelly and Miss Cissie followed in her wake, less majestic, but sufficiently striking in their home-made hats to justify the stares which were levelled at them. It seemed impossible that they should be able to pick out individuals among such a throng, but Susan had forgotten her escort's conspicuous size, and under-estimated the lynx-keenness of the sisters' eyes. Miss Jelly sighted them first, drew Miss Cissie's attention to the pair, then passed on the information to Miss Pringle. Instantly six gimlet eyes swivelled round, the better to observe them, three heads in feather-trimmed hats strangely reminiscent of an Alpine guide's were bent together in conclave; then the gambling spirit presumably over-powered both curiosity and disapproval for the time being. The sisters hastened on their way to the tote; and Jed Armstrong chuckled sardonically. Evidently he was quite alive to the interest he and Susan had aroused.

"They'll be busy picking us to pieces now," he said. "Your reputation will just be a ruckle of bare bones when those old hoodie-crows have done with it!"

"I don't see why," Susan protested with spirit.

"No?" he said, in a gently inquiring tone which made her want to stamp. "I like you in that red hat."

Susan had not recovered from the shock occasioned by this remark when he made their bets with the bookie, who loudly lamented the grievous loss caused to him and his fraternity by "them blistering totes".

Dauntless won. With the help of Jed Armstrong's glasses Susan saw the brown horse carrying their colours, red and gold, slide past the favourite to win by a length.

"Pretty good," said her companion contentedly. "I put ten bob on for you, didn't I? You should have let me make it more. At eight to one. You get four pounds. I like to see a horse I know do well."

"So do I," said Susan with shameless greediness. "When I make money by it." .

Returning from collecting their winnings, Susan with four dirty pound notes making a pleasant bulge in her usually empty notecase, they came upon her brother and Charles Crawley. The two might have been posing for companion pictures of Joy and Grief, for while Oliver's face radiated satisfaction, that of Charles was exceeding downcast. He had, it presently appeared, indulged a mistaken fancy for a complete outsider which had finished fifth. Oliver, on the other hand, had profited by Jed's good advice and put no less than five pounds on Dauntless.

"Forty quid, thanks to you, Jed!" he exclaimed. "I feel like a blinking capitalist!"

"You ought to feel like an extravagant, reckless idiot," Susan cried, aghast at his having risked a sum which would have made a considerable hole in their finances if he had lost. "I wish you'd remember, Oliver, that you are a laird with twenty pence!"

"No, my love. A laird with forty beautiful paper quidlets," he retorted gaily. "You're jealous, you are!"

"I made four pounds myself," said Susan with dignity. "Didn't I?" But Jed Armstrong was not listening.

"Here come some more losers," he announced with a broad grin. "Cissie, Jelly and Bell have backed the wrong horse, I doubt."

Charles had wandered away, but Oliver and Susan turned to see the Misses Pringle approaching like a little band of mourners. Loss was written large on their grieving countenances, the very plumes of the jaunty hats drooped dismally over their wearers' rather pink noses.

"Poor old things!" said Oliver with the generous commiseration of one who had been winning. "They oughtn't to be allowed out alone to a place like this."

"Backed a wrong 'un?" asked Jed with callous geniality as the sisters joined them.

"Certainly *not*!" said Miss Pringle, rearing up her long neck and giving him a Medusa-look, which entirely failed in its object of freezing him.

"Sorry, I thought you'd gone down over the favourite," he said. "You all look as if you'd lost money—"

"Oh, Mr. Armstrong, so we *have*!" cried Miss Cissie in wailing accents. "That wicked man in the totalisator has—"

"I have been *grossly* defrauded," said Miss Pringle, as usual cutting her youngest sister's remark in two. "And I shall write to the papers about it, about the *disgraceful* mismanagement of the totalisator, and the impertinence of the operators. I have never cared to deal with a bookmaker, such a low class of man! But the totalisator is *equally* as dishonest!"

"Poor Bell put two shillings on Mr. Hepburn's horse Dauntless," Miss Cissie burst out again in Miss Pringle's pause for much-needed breath. "It was such a *pretty* horse, wasn't it? And we *all* thought the jockey's colours *most* artistic—and she got a ticket for her money at the little window, so like a railway booking-office, and when she took the ticket back again after the race, the man, such a *rude*, horrid person—said it was the wrong number!"

"He had the impertinence to refer me to the notice printed above the windows," said Miss Pringle, "and accused me—*me* of carelessness, in not examining my ticket sooner! 'My good man,' I said to him reasonably, 'surely that is *your* business, not mine.' But I shall demand compensation—"

"We *trusted* him, and he has cheated poor Bell!" cried Miss Cissie.

"I always understood that the tote was fool-proof," murmured Oliver.

"Thirteen-and-twopence lost," added Miss Jelly in sepulchral tones. "I must say that the dishonesty, practised by these persons has *ruined* my afternoon!"

". . . actually told *Bell* that she was old enough to take care of herself!" concluded Miss Cissie.

"Well, well,", said Miss Pringle rather hastily, "don't let *our* misfortunes spoil the pleasure of others. *We* saw you, Miss Parsons, and no doubt Mr. Armstrong was able to help *you* to back a winner."

"Mr. Armstrong," said Susan sedately, "has been most kind."

"But what will Mrs. Holden say to this *desertion* of her?" cried Miss Pringle, who was plainly bursting with spleen and more than ready to vent her own disappointment on all within reach. "I am sure she must have been *relying* on you—"

"Primrose is all right," responded Jed Armstrong with unmoved stolidity. "She's with friends of her own."

"In-*deed*. Delightful for her.... Er, Miss Parsons, I wonder if you could *spare* me a *moment* or two?" said Miss Pringle, almost every other word in italics. Susan could see from her glittering eye that she was about to impart, doubtless in "*strict* confidence, dear Miss Parsons," the knowledge which she charitably hoped would prove completely shattering, not realizing that this project had already been rendered harmless by Peggy Cunningham's confidence.

Obediently Susan turned, prepared to receive the news that Mr. Armstrong's affections were engaged otherwise, with an assumption of entire surprise, when there came an interruption.

"I say, Sue darling!" said Charles in his soft voice, which yet was distinctly audible to the whole party. "I suppose you haven't a cigarette on you? I've run out of them."

The effect of this endearment, uttered in public with the ease of long practice, was like an electric shock to the Misses Pringle. They wilted instantly and visibly and when, on Susan's handing over her cigarette-case to Charles, he said cheerfully: "Thank you, my sweet," their discomfiture was complete.

Susan knew at once that any danger of hearing about Jed Armstrong's private and personal affairs from Miss Pringle was now averted, since in her experience no man addressed a young woman in such terms unless he was engaged to her. But a little demon of amused malice prompted her to say sweetly: "Yes, Miss Pringle? There was something you minded to say to me, I think, wasn't there?"

Miss Pringle's confusion would have been pitiful to witness in anyone less deserving of being routed. "No—no, my dear Miss

Parsons—*nothing* of importance. I can let you know by post—" And almost without farewells she and her satellite sisters hurried away.

"Hullo!" exclaimed Charles, who was not accustomed to seeing females of any age flee him as the plague. "Have I frightened your friends the Miss Pinpricks away?"

"Looks like it," said Oliver. "They never run from *me*."

Jed Armstrong uttered a short laugh. "They're off!" he said. "Gone to spread the news that you and Miss Parsons are engaged likely."

"Good luck to them," said Charles equably. "I'm all for it. Nothing I should like better. What d'you say, Susan?"

"I say," said Susan, in the same light tone, but avoiding his eyes, "that you are talking absolute nonsense, and that the Miss Pringles are dangerous old harpies and ought to be put down."

"Put down? Do you mean something in the Liverpool Virus line? All same rats?" asked Oliver. "Sound scheme. Whose is to be the hand that does the fell deed?"

"The discovery that Charles and I are *not* engaged will be quite sufficiently dampening, I expect," said Susan firmly. "Let's talk about something interesting—making some money, for instance—"

"I knew Susan would take to racing as soon as she'd won something," said Oliver. "Just like a woman. Now, my dear, you trot off and put all you've got on some unlikely horse with a pretty name, at nice long odds, for the next race, and in a few minutes you'll find yourself reduced to your original ten bob. That's how it goes!"

"That is not how mine goes," said Susan. "I'm going to keep what I've won—or rather, what Mr. Armstrong won for me. I shall buy a new hat with it."

3

"Have you any interest in the last race?" asked Jed later in the afternoon. "Because if you've not, come and have some tea."

Oliver and Charles, intent on taking advantage of a remarkably sound tip which they had been given, had gone off together in sweet accord. Confident that even Miss Pringle would not say very much now, Susan accepted the offer; and presently they were seated at a small table companionably drinking very dark brown tea.

"You've been most uncommonly kind," Susan said, taking a cigarette from the case which he offered to her. "I only hope Mrs. Holden won't feel proportionately neglected! But you've made the day profitable as well as amusing for me, and I'm afraid I have been a good deal of trouble."

"No trouble at all," he said surprisingly.

"I sometimes wonder," said Susan idly, as much for the pleasure of hearing her own voice as anything else, "what you did before we came to live at Easter Hartrigg. I mean, on whom did you exercise all this benevolence?"

"I can't make head or tail of what you're driving at when you use those lang-nebbit words," said Jed Armstrong, but his weather-beaten cheek assumed a darker shade of brick-red, and his eye did not meet Susan's. It did not require any very great degree of acuteness to gather that formerly his benevolent instincts must have lain fallow.

"You know perfectly well what I mean," she told him calmly. "(Are you going to eat that rather enticing chocolate cake? Because if not, I will . . . oh, thank you.) Ever since we came to this place you have kept a friendly eye on Oliver and me. Particularly Oliver. I do thank you for that. He'd have been lonely and miserable and missed the Service far more if it hadn't been for you."

"I like him," interposed Jed grudgingly, as if almost ashamed of the fact. "I was damned dull up at Reiverslaw all by myself until you—meaning Oliver, of course—came—"

"Passing over your rather unkind omission of myself," said Susan, "I am glad you and Oliver are friends. But there's just one thing I would like to ask you. This job at Wanside. It's a real Godsend to Oliver, but—did you recommend him to old Mr. Elliot out of pure friendship, or because you really do think he is the man for the job?"

"What d'you take me for?" growled Jed Armstrong. He seemed indignant and Susan realized for the first time that this good-natured giant might be a formidable person when angered. "Of course he's fit for the job. I wouldn't recommend my own brother if I had one, unless I thought he could do it properly. That's not my idea of friendship—nor any man's!"

"I'm sorry," murmured Susan. She sounded contrite, but mirth flickered in her grave hazel eyes. "Of course I am a mere woman, and probably lacking in these finer sensibilities. I *might* have done what you say you never would, you see. You must make allowances for me."

"Now you're laughing at me," he said.

Susan suddenly felt a little ashamed, for after all he had been very good to Oliver, who liked him so much. . . . "I'm not really; and it was rather horrid of me," she said. "Because of course I know you are quite right."

"Laugh away," he invited. "I rather like it."

But Susan rose and said that it must be time to go home, and she ought to look for Oliver and Charles. "And you must find Mrs. Holden," she reminded him, since he seemed to have forgotten this necessity.

4

They reached Easter Hartrigg in time to avoid a savage shower of rain, and Tara welcomed them to the sitting-room, which a leaping fire made doubly inviting by contrast with the sudden bleakness outside. Oliver, opening the baize swing door leading to the kitchen, shouted plaintively:—"May we have some tea, Donaldina? We're starving!"

A faintly heard affirmative answer came back, and Oliver joined his sister and Charles at the sitting-room fire.

"I saw a woman at the Races," said Charles meditatively, "I've seen her somewhere before, but I can't for the life of me remember where."

"Stranger things have happened," murmured Oliver.

"Don't try to be clever. It doesn't suit your style," Charles besought him.

Oliver rose and placed a cushion on his guest's head. The guest, struggling out from under it, fell on him, and in a second the peaceful room was in a turmoil.

"Stop it!" cried Susan, hurriedly moving a table on which preparations for tea had been set out by the faithful Donaldina. "What a pair of babies you are!"

"Ouch!" and "Ah, *would* you?" grunted the combatants, battling to and fro, breathless with wild laughter. A ring at the front-door bell was unheeded by them, and Susan's commands that they should cease instantly had no effect. Donaldina opened the sitting-room door on this scene of confusion, and ushered in, to Susan's relief, no one more formidable than Peggy Cunningham, holding by the hand Cilly and Bun.

"I'm so sorry, Peggy!" cried Susan above the din. "I've done my best to make them stop, but it is quite useless." And to Donaldina, who stood gaping by the door, she added: "Please bring some more cups and things, Donaldina."

The astonished handmaiden withdrew, and Tara, emerging from the corner to which he had retired in disgust, offered a large black paw to Bun.

"Ooh! Aren't they *naughties*?" squeaked Cilly in great delight. "Will you send them to bed without their suppers?"

"I wish I could, Cilly, but they're too big. Charles, if Oliver won't pay any attention to me, I think you might at least!"

With a final effort the two regained their feet, and stood, rumpled and untidy, facing the company.

"Hullo!" said Oliver, unperturbed by the fact that his hair was on end and his tie under one ear. "What are you doing here?"

"We've been picking brambles," Peggy explained, after Charles had been introduced. "And it was so fearfully wet that I thought you wouldn't mind if we came here to shelter till the rain goes off. And Bun fell and cut her knee, and—"

"Poor old lady," said Oliver, lifting Bun on to his own knee. "How did that happen?"

"I fell," said Bun, whose eyelashes were still wet with recent tears, "an' cut myself on a stone. It *wasn't* very talented of me, was it?"

"Not very. But accidents happen, you know," Oliver said. "Let's have a look at your wounds." He untied the handkerchief which had been hastily fastened over her chubby knee. "It's a bit dirty, isn't it?" he said to Peggy. "What about some iodine?"

Bun wriggled uneasily. "I don't much care for iodine," she murmured. "It nips."

"It won't nip for more than a minute, Bun darling," said Peggy. "And you want it to get better quick, don't you?"

"Y-yes," said Bun dubiously.

When Susan and Peggy were about to take her away to wash the cut and apply the iodine, however, Bun remained firmly on Oliver's knee. "You come, too," she said. "*You* put on the iodine."

"All right." Oliver set her down, and limped to the door with her.

"You've got a sore leg, too!" cried Bun delightedly. Peggy, horror-stricken, realized that it was too late to intervene. To say anything now would only make matters worse; and Susan, though her brows drew together for an instant, did not speak. It was left to Oliver to break the uncomfortable silence.

"So I have!" he exclaimed in tones of cheerful surprise. "And now there's two of us with sore legs!" said Bun.

"Now there are two of us," Oliver agreed, and with Bun's hand in his, they limped carefully from the room after Susan and Peggy. Half-way upstairs, Bun dragged at his hand to stop him.

"Did they put iodine on your leg, too?" she asked.

Oliver's smile was a little grim. "They did things to it that hurt more than iodine, old lady."

"Oh! But it's getting more better now, isn't it?"

"Yes, Bun, as a matter of fact, it is," he said.

Charles, left in the sitting-room, muttered: "Well, I'm damned!" quite forgetful of the presence of Cilly. He was reminded of it by a voice of extreme severity.

"You should say 'beg my pardon' when you say a naughty word," she said.

He looked down at the small person who stood shaking her silver-gilt curls at him disapprovingly.

"I beg your pardon," he said obediently. "I quite forgot there was a lady present."

Cilly was gracious. "I expeck I'm such a wee lady you didn't see me," she said, and smiled bewitchingly at him.

Charles fell a victim to her at once, and when the others returned they found him giving a spirited impersonation of a very wild beast to the great detriment of his best trousers.

"Now be the lion-an'-the-unicorn!" Cilly was saying, when tea arrived in the nick of time to spare Charles this difficult task.

"I'll take you back in the Squib," Oliver said when tea was over and Peggy had announced that they must go home at once.

They were on the point of departure when a large closed car drew up in front of the house, and Oliver, going out to discover whose it was, came back almost immediately with the news that he was wanted at Wanside.

"Old Elliot's sent for me. I'll have to go in the car," he said briefly. And to Peggy: "I'm awfully sorry, Peggy, but you understand that I can't get out of it."

"Of course," said Peggy. "We can walk home perfectly well."

"Certainly not," said Oliver. "Charles will drive you in the Squib. Good-bye for now. Good-bye, Cilly. Good-bye, Bun. You must have that leg well by the next time I see you. No more limps!" He was gone, and the Wanside car could be heard purring off along the road until its discreet engine was drowned by the noise of the Squib starting.

"Can you manage with one on your knee and one in between us?" asked Charles. "It's too cold in the dickey."

They all packed themselves in, and the Squib, letting off several sharp reports, took the Muirfoot road. For a little they drove in silence, for the children were sleepy, Peggy rather shy of Charles, and Charles himself fully occupied in mastering the Squib's tricky ways. He spoke first.

"Amazing how much less sensitive old Oliver's got about his game leg," he said suddenly. "There was a time when it was as much as your life was worth to mention it to him, poor chap. But, of course, he's better. He hardly limps at all now except when he's tired."

"I know," Peggy said. "I—it was awful when Bun spoke about it before tea. I didn't know what to do—"

"I'm not sure it wasn't a jolly good thing, do you know. She was so natural about it, and I think it may shake him up a bit. He'd got morbid over the thing. Did you ever hear how it happened?"

"No," said Peggy. "Susan never speaks of it, and, of course, *he* doesn't."

"It hit Susan pretty hard, Oliver's having to leave the Service," Charles said. "She's devoted to him, and I think for a bit she was afraid he wouldn't get better. For ages he didn't want to live. It's a damned shame, of course, Noll was absolutely made for his job, and going ahead at a rate of knots. Somehow I can't fit him in yet with a job on the beach."

"But don't you think he's settled down here, and happy?" asked Peggy rather wistfully. "He seems to like the life, and I know Susan does."

"H'm. I wouldn't bet on Susan's being so keen on it. Probably that's partly eye-wash for Oliver's sake," said Charles, and there was a note almost of satisfaction in his voice which puzzled Peggy. "But I was going to tell you how Oliver damaged himself."

"It was an accident, wasn't it? A smash with a car? I'd heard that."

"Yes," said Charles grimly. "It was a smash with a car—a car driven by a damn' fool who'd had just one too many and wouldn't let Oliver take the wheel. They went over a bank and were thrown out, and the car went on down a cliff and was made into matchwood. Oliver was chucked clear, and barring a knock on the head was all right. But the other chap wasn't so lucky. He went half-way down the cliff and got caught by a sapling on a ledge. If Oliver had left him and gone for help he'd be in the Service to-day. . . . But Br—I mean, the fellow on the ledge was damaged, and Oliver was afraid that when he came round he'd roll off, so he decided to go after him. A man on a push-bike came past, and went to get help and a rope, and Oliver went down the cliff. The ledge was a tight fit for one, but he managed to find a footing on it, and to hold on to the other until some men arrived. They lowered a rope, Oliver hitched it round—well, I don't want to mention his name, you know—and he was hauled up all safe. Then, before they could let the rope down again, the ledge gave way under poor old Noll, and—well, that's the lot. They got him at the bottom, badly smashed up, but it's a wonder he escaped with his life. I've told you all this, Miss Cunningham, because I've seen you looking sideways at Oliver, as if you thought he was a surly devil. So he is at times, but can you wonder?"

"No," said Peggy. Her voice shook a little. "Thank you for telling me. Not that I've ever thought he was a surly d-devil," she stumbled over a word which she had never pronounced before except when it occurred in passages of Scripture. "But I *have* been rather frightened of him sometimes."

"Well, you know now why."

"Yes. I used to be sorry for him, but now—I shall always remember that he was hurt saving his friend. It would be—rather cheek to pity him now that I know."

They had reached the Manse gates. Peggy roused the drowsy children, and they all got out of the Squib.

"Good night," said Peggy. "It was very kind of you to bring us home. And—thank you."

Charles knew that she was thanking him for more than the drive, and he wondered why she should be so interested in Oliver's story. "Another of them?" he thought as he turned the Squib's blunt nose towards Easter Hartrigg. "Poor kid! Still, Oliver doesn't seem to be treating her as he does most of 'em. I wonder... and if it *is* so, if he's serious, I wonder what sort of a chance I'll have...?"

CHAPTER NINE

1

"I LIKE the Scottish verb 'to postcard,'" Susan said. "There's an economy of words about it that would have appealed to the old Romans. They were always so averse to the use of an unnecessary word in spite of their rolling Latin phrases."

"Now, if the lecture's finished," said Oliver, tearing up his own correspondence and throwing it into the waste-paper basket, "perhaps you'll let us know who has been 'postcarding' you and calling forth this flow of eloquence?"

"Let's have three guesses," suggested Charles idly.

"No need. I know the answer already," said Oliver, lighting his pipe with the unbearably superior air of a Sherlock Holmes.

"Then why ask?" said Susan.

"A purely rhetorical question, my dear Susan. There's really not the slightest need to exert the brain over this problem, Watson—I mean, Charles. The person who does her utmost to keep Susan's pet verb in constant use in this part of the country is our energetic friend, Miss Pringle. Not Belly. Jell. The eldest, you know, the one with the face like a camel which has just seen the last straw and found it unclean."

"Susan, darling," said Charles patiently. "Am I? Or is he? I mean, these Scottish names are so difficult to master—"

"Nothing difficult about Belly, surely?" began Oliver.

"Be quiet," Susan said to him. "It's all right, Charles. You know what he is. I have been postcarded by Miss Pringle to the effect that the Literary Club will hold its first meet of the season at her house, and will I bring some little thing of mine for reading and criticism."

"No suggestion that you may possibly refuse, you'll notice," said Oliver. "I like old Belly, upon my word I do. A rare woman, one who knows her own mind, and everyone else's into the bargain."

"I shall not go," said Susan firmly.

"If you don't, you needn't expect to have your unwillingness put down to modesty," Oliver pointed out. "It will only be supposed that your literary efforts are so poor that you daren't give them to the world of Muirfoot and Kaleford. Aha, you blush, woman! I've touched you on a tender spot!"

"I never heard such a base libel in my life," said his sister indignantly. "And if you are so interested in Miss Pringle's literary society, why don't you attend the meeting at Kaleside yourself?"

"Done with you!" he cried to Susan's open dismay. "I will. And what's more, I'll read something to them—a masterpiece, one of those little gems that they'll never forget."

"Do you mean," asked Charles with interest, "one of the famous songs you used to compose and sing on Saturday nights on board?"

Oliver threw him a withering glance. "I shall compose something suitable to the occasion," he said loftily. "An ode after the style of Pindar, or a tender little lyric to my mistress's—"

"I didn't know you *had* any," murmured Charles, and then, meeting Susan's stern look, added hurriedly: "If it's anything like the compositions of yours that I've heard already, you'll have to leave the neighbourhood. After all, what sounds pretty good after a fair number of gins is liable to be misunderstood when only diluted with tea."

"I don't think either of you should go," said Susan. Nevertheless, her resigned acceptance of Miss Pringle's command—for the postcard hardly came under the heading of a mere invitation—included the request that her brother and his friend Charles Crawley might come with her. This bore immediate fruit in the shape of a rapturous postcard in Miss Cissie's gushing hand, from which, reading between the underlinings, Susan gathered that "the menfolk" would be more than welcome at this feast of reason and flow of soul.

The days that followed were made hideous for both Susan and Charles by Oliver's poetic inspirations. From the disjointed scraps of verse which were found littering every writing-desk and table in the house, and which Susan hastily burned lest Donaldina's innocent eyes should be offended by reading them, she augured the worst.

"Oliver," she said one evening, after consigning to the flames of the sitting-room fire a fragment headed "Ode to the Alimentary Canal", "if you can't avoid these subjects you will have to give it up. I wish you had as much sense as Charles. *He* hasn't tried to write anything—"

"I did try once. I made a dashed good limerick. I forget the beginning and the end," said Charles regretfully, "but it was about a rough Channel crossing, and the middle went:

> "He staggered to leeward
> And called for the stoo-ard—"

"Ah, Charles, my lad, the divine spark does not glow in your heart," said Oliver, rising and strolling across to the fire. "Now, I've written a lyric, a sweet thing, 'To Muriel's Adenoids,' but I think perhaps it's a trifle impassioned for Miss Pringle's maiden ears. It might make Jelly boil—I mean blush. So I am going to content myself with a pastoral poem in the Doric, as a compliment to our neighbours."

"Well," said Susan with relief, "at least it can't possibly be as indecent as some of the bits I burned."

"Susan, my poor girl," said her brother in gently pitying tones, "I fear you have no soul for poetry."

"For your kind, none whatever."

"Come, now, Charles, show your mettle," urged Oliver. "Are you, an Englishman, going to be dumb before a pack of northern females? Surely you can troll out a roundelay, a seaman's ditty, something on the lines of that charming song we used to render with such feeling when tight—"

And with intense pathos he sang dolorously:

> "My byby 'as gorn dahn thuh pur-lug 'ole!
> My byby 'as gorn dahn the plug!
> Pore little thing, she was so slim an' so—"

Here the entrance of Donaldina, round-eyed, with a tray bearing liquid refreshment, cut him short. In face of such complete and open amazement even Oliver was unable to continue. When she had gone, "I'm afraid not," said Charles simply. "All the songs I know are unprintable after the first verse, and if I gave a—a purified rendering there'd be more gaps than words."

2

Beset as she was by the fear of Oliver's almost certain misbehaviour, Susan felt that the drive to Kaleside would have been unpleasant enough without further trials, but these were not wanting to fill her cup to the brim. The Squib, always malevolent, chose this particular day to display her worst qualities. Three times in the space of fifteen minutes she gave one of her better imitations of a machine-gun in action, following on which the engine stopped. As the party was all packed in front under the doubtful shelter of the hood, as closely as sardines in a tin, even oil not lacking to make the simile perfect, this necessitated their getting out on each occasion. Three times, in a smouldering silence, they climbed down into the muddy road in their best clothes. The Squib added to her charms by having no self-starter, so Oliver and Charles in turn swung the handle with a passionate verve unsurpassed by the most temperamental organ-grinder. Susan stood miserably in the mud, umbrella-less, waterproof-less, by Oliver's advice—"what on earth d'you want an umbrella in the car for?"

The rain, descending impartially on the just and the unjust, played havoc alike with her new hat and her temper. Even the poor refuge of the car was denied her, for the floor had been torn up, and Oliver was probing in the interior as absorbedly as a dentist at work.

They were sunk in sodden gloom when they finally got under way once more, and pursued their journey through a countryside in tune with their mood. The hills were blotted out by a curtain of grey mist, the empty fields were pearled with rain, from every weeping tree heavy drops and brown or yellow leaves fell sadly to the ground. With heartfelt longing Susan thought of her own fireside, a warm cardigan, and an amusing book; and, "Oh, why left I my hame?" said Oliver, as he turned the Squib in at the narrow entrance to Kaleside, avoiding the nearer gate-post by a miracle.

"Oh, why left I my waterproof at hame?" Susan retorted peevishly; and Charles, between whom and Oliver she was wedged in a now steamy proximity, began to shake with laughter.

"I'm glad you find it amusing," said Susan with concentrated venom. "Oh, and would you mind not laughing quite so heartily? It gives me less room to breathe. . . . Of course, I suppose it *is* funny to you and Oliver. *You* aren't wearing an absolutely new and wickedly expensive hat bought with your own winnings."

"Darling," protested Charles, taking advantage of the fact that his arm was along the back of the seat to put it round her neck. "Have a heart. I'm sorry about your hat, though it looks to me as good as new, but what price my one and only shore-going suit? I can feel the sleeves creeping up my arms and the legs shrinking to leave my ankles well in view, an' I haven't paid Gieve for it yet!"

"Well, here we are," announced Oliver, and drew up before the gaunt, bare-faced house. Several other cars occupied the gravel sweep, which was of that nobbly variety so excruciatingly unsympathetic to feet clad in thin shoes. They crunched painfully over it towards the doorway, a somewhat damp and crumpled trio. The whining of a violin execrably played assaulted their unwilling ears as they stood on the step awaiting an answer to Oliver's ring.

"No one who is not a first-class player ought to be allowed to *touch* a violin," Susan said crossly, and shivered. Oliver answered only with a grunt, Charles with a sudden passion of sneezing. The bell was not answered at all, the door remained shut.

"Ring again," suggested Susan. "My teeth are beginning to chatter."

Oliver pulled violently at the bell, and at last, losing all patience, set his foot against the side of the house and hauled as if taking part in a tug-of-war. A faint but furious jangling was the result, but quite a foot of bell-wire protruded from its brass setting in the stonework, and they were still engaged in frantic, futile efforts to induce it to go in again when the door opened and a maid faced them. In her cold and cod-like eye they read surprise and disapproval, but she said nothing, and they followed her into a hall draped with the waterproofs of more provident persons. The violin had ceased, and a tepid round of applause, and a sudden buzz of conversation, from behind a closed door on the right, told them where the Literary Club was already in full cry. When Oliver and Charles had deposited their hats on top of a mound of mackintoshes, they were not ushered in on the meeting, but marshalled into a small, empty room to the left of the hall, smelling faintly but unpleasantly of cage-birds and mice.

"Thank God for a moment's respite!" ejaculated Charles after the maid had withdrawn, and cast himself thankfully on a sofa. This instantly subsided, precipitating him in an indignant heap at Susan's feet.

"We've made a promising start, I must say," said Oliver. "I've bust their bell, and you've broken a sofa. Your turn now, Susan."

"I hope I shan't disgrace meself," said Susan. "I'm not quite so violent as you two."

At that, without any warning, the chair in which she was warily leaning back lurched, and in a wild attempt to save herself, she clutched at a tall and peculiarly hideous vase filled with dusty pampas grass which stood on the floor close by. In a second she was staring horror-stricken at the handle which, to use the housemaid's classic phrase, had "come away in her hand."

Upon the dismayed silence broke a loud, raucous chuckle, and a phonographic voice said threateningly: "I'll tell the mistress on ye!"

The shock to their overwrought nerves was such that all three leapt like mountain goats. Coming to earth again they looked timidly round for the owner of the voice. It was Charles who made the discovery that in a large and musty cage set in a dark corner perched a grey parrot of evil aspect and moth-eaten plumage.

"Hullo, Polly! Pretty Poll, then!" wheedled Oliver.

The parrot merely fixed him with a baleful and unwinking stare. "Ye'll catch it!" it said, and chuckled sardonically.

"Charming bird," Oliver murmured, turning away.

"How can we hide the traces of our crimes?" was Charles's practical inquiry. "We can't do anything about the bell, but they may think someone else pulled it out by the roots—"

"A book under that sofa-leg—" Oliver said, and while they hurriedly pushed a fat volume of Browning's *Complete Works* into place as a castor, Susan turned the vase round so that the lack of its handle was concealed from the casual glance.

"Judging by the dust, this place is merely a dump for aged furniture, and nothing will be discovered before next spring-cleaning," she said, and cheerfully dropped the handle in among the pampas grass.

These guilty alterations were hardly carried out before the ⌐ opened and Miss Pringle, resplendent in royal purple velveteϲ entered sweepingly, astonishingly like the Spirit of Poetry Calling Burns from the Plough in an engraving above the fireplace. "Ah! At last! I am so glad to see you!" she exclaimed, her manner that of a queen condescending to lackeys. "And you have brought your men-folk with you too. *So* pleased—"

Oliver, who strenuously objected to the term "men-folk," muttered a greeting with an expression of stifled fury. Charles, whose manner on such occasions was so languidly exquisite as to be overpowering, murmured "How-d'you-do?" with distant sweetness.

"I *hope* you've brought your little contributions to read?" continued Miss Pringle in a slightly less exalted voice. Even on her Charles's prince-in-exile courtesy had its effect.

Oliver brightened at once. "*I* have," he said eagerly. "But you'll have to excuse Charles. You see, all his articles are so frightfully technical and highbrow that they are only intelligible to the—well, to the intelligentsia, in fact."

"*Really?*" breathed Miss Pringle, plainly supposing that she was entertaining Genius, and casting a respectful glance at Charles. He, though hard put to it not to laugh, passed a hand wearily over his noble brow and frowned sternly into vacancy. After a suitable pause he said in a faint, tired voice: "I'm afraid that my work would hardly be interesting to your little gathering, Miss Pin—Pringle."

Susan turned a laugh in quite a creditable cough, and the three moved in their hostess's majestic wake across the hall and into the room beyond.

3

The collection of drooping women seated in a semi-circle about the edge of a mustard-coloured carpet seemed to revive a little on beholding two men. But Miss Pringle was not going to encourage any frivolity. Before greetings could be exchanged or introductions made she said graciously: "I am sure, Miss Parsons, that you won't want to interrupt Cissie's little song recital. All her own composition, and we are so *eager* to hear the last one of the cycle. So shall we just find chairs and *listen?*"

Susan crept to a vacant seat next to Peggy Cunningham, behind whom, on a comfortless wooden settle, was perched a small, smart, fair woman with her back to the light. She was in the act of yawning dismally but prettily, as some fortunate women of the kitten type can.

Miss Jelly Pringle was seated at the upright piano, and by her, also arrayed in a flowing velveteen robe of extreme shapelessness, stood Miss Cissie, her hands clasped on her stomach, in an attitude of rapt meditation. After several discords, struck in a commanding fashion by the pianist, she warbled a song about fading lilies in a faint flat voice admirably suited to the theme.

Polite hand-clapping and murmurs of "'Wonderful!" "so *gifted*!" "a real treat," followed this last number of the "song-recital," and Susan heard the pretty fluffy creature behind yawn again.

Peggy was about to speak when the unknown leaned forward and whispered exhaustedly: "Peggy! how long will this perfectly terrible entertainment last?"

"Ages." Peggy was quite certain on that point. "Oh, do you know Miss Parsons? Have you met? Mrs. Holden—"

"How do you do?" began Susan and Mrs. Holden in chorus, and broke off to laugh.

"Isn't this too, too appalling?" said Mrs. Holden, bending confidentially towards Susan and sweetening the rather stuffy atmosphere with lily-of-the-valley. "I came to be amused, but I've had to creep out of sight because I'm yawning so terribly. It's lack of air as well as boredom, of course."

Susan, interested in meeting the object of Jed Armstrong's alleged affections, was surprised to find her a woman of this particular type. She had expected someone more open-air, more straightforward, and certainly older, though to be sure it was difficult even to guess at Mrs. Holden's age. She had a neat little turned-up nose, a lovely fair complexion, possibly supplied by Elizabeth Arden but none the less effective, an air of entire self-possession, and a pair of those eyes which wander at once in the direction of a man. She had also the faculty of making every other woman in her presence feel hot, clumsy and ill-dressed, and correspondingly irritated or amused according to their natures. Susan was amused. "A man-eater," she thought. "Amusing for short periods at a stretch, but fatal for anyone as simple as poor, dear Jed. This woman could do what she liked with him—and no doubt she's going to!"

Aloud she said in a cautious undertone: "Has Miss Pringle performed yet?"

"Oh, dear me, yes." It was Peggy who replied while Mrs. Holden hid another dainty yawn with an exquisitely gloved small hand. "She opened the ball. Don't ask me what it was all about, for I'm sure no one knew. But it was very mystical and allegorical and bursting with split infinitives. 'He bent to tenderly gaze'—you know—"

"Mrs. Williamson is going to read us a poem," announced Miss Pringle with a reproving glance towards Peggy's corner of the room.

Mrs. Williamson, a stout woman, purple in the face with heat, pride and embarrassment, rose and took her place in the centre of the carpet. Her hands, tightly gloved, clutched a sheet of paper, from which she now proceeded to read in a voice broken by frequent gasps. "Blackthorn Blossom," she began, and gasped.

> "Fair harbinger of the summer day,
> You gladden us with the promise of May,
> And your snowy crown
> Which the wind blows down,
> Is beautiful (gasp) but you cannot stay.
>
> Ah, shed no tear for the flowers that fall.
> For heaven is watching o'er them all.
> And another year
> They will all appear,
> And your eyes with beauty again enthral."

"Well, it rhymes," said Mrs. Holden thoughtfully, "so I suppose it is a poem? Somehow, I have always hated poetry."

Miss Pringle then opened fire with a "little *friendly* criticism, dear Mrs. Williamson," in the course of which purely destructive work she pulled the luckless "poem" to shreds and succeeded in wiping the pleased smirk entirely from its poor author's round, fat face When she had finished, Mrs. Williamson looked as though she might burst into tears at any moment, and only the entrance of the maid with a tea-tray cheered her.

It was strange to see how every face brightened at sight of the massive Victorian teapot, and Susan could only conclude that the feast of poesy had not been sufficiently satisfying to fill those whose thoughts strayed lovingly towards scones and cakes.

"If we can only escape without one of Miss Pringle's own poems," murmured Peggy. "I can bear anything."

Oliver, who had moved closer to them, at once said loudly, ignoring Peggy's angry glances: "By the way, Miss Pringle, aren't we going to hear one of *your* poems? You know, we missed your reading—"

Miss Pringle, nothing loath, beamed on him. "Mine are simple little verses," she began, almost coyly. "Let me see, I wonder if I can remember anything. . . . Ah, yes! I have some lines inspired by meeting a poor little orphan one day on the road. I will recite them—and of course," she added generously, "I shall expect *criticism*."

"As if she didn't know that everyone's afraid to criticize her!" grumbled the mutinous Peggy.

"Little lad with the golden hair," began Miss Pringle in an assumed babyish lisp which Susan found peculiarly revolting:

> "Little lad with the golden hair,
> And the wistful, wondering, blue-eyed stare—
> 'Where is your mother, dear?' said I,
> And you said: 'Muwer's up wiv Gawd in the sky!
>
> Up above where the angels are,
> Where the skies are bwight wiv many a star—'"

"Oh, God!" said Charles violently in Susan's ear. "I'm going to be sick—I want to creep under a sofa and howl!"

Susan missed the remainder of the orphan's touching references to his "muvver," but the poem contained the name of the Deity, always pronounced in a reverent hushed tone, repeated an incredible number of times. There was, of course, no criticism. The poem received its meed of sycophantic applause from the Literary Club's members, while the few Philistines present sat in a dazed silence until roused to partake of tea.

"And *now*," said Miss Pringle when the repast was all too speedily over, "we have a *great* treat in store to finish off this pleasant afternoon. Commander Parsons has very kindly composed a poem, which he will now read to us."

At this last moment Susan seized her brother by the sleeve. "Oliver," she whispered desperately, "*don't* you think you'd better not?"

It was in vain. He shook off her hand and stalked to the middle of the room, where he took a small note-book from his pocket, and clearing his throat impressively, flapped over the pages.

"Charles!" said Susan. "Can't you do anything to stop him?"

"It's all right," said Charles consolingly. "I don't believe a soul will understand it."

Oliver was speaking in a modest manner to Miss Pringle. ". . . Oh, yes. I carry this little book and jot down any ideas as they occur to me. Of course, they are crude, unpolished, but I know you will be lenient. We rough sailors, you know . . ."

Susan found herself clasping Peggy's hand and praying that he had at least refrained from the too blatantly vulgar, but as she had not been allowed to censor the masterpiece, she did not know what might be about to be read aloud.

"Stray Stanzas," said Oliver pompously, "in the Doric. Ahem." Once more he cleared his throat, and then, in a broad accent obviously acquired from studying the almost unintelligible speech of Jems, he delivered himself of his effusion.

> "Oh, crappit heids are a' perjink,
> The apple-ringie's jimp an' sma',
> Frae ilka airt the hoodies blink,
> An' whaups gang wheeplin' i' the snaw.
>
> Ayont the law the yowes are sweir,
> The gowans wimple tirra-vee:
> The wullie-waught's ta'en a' his gear,
> An' aiblins he's gane aft agley.
>
> Wae's me yon waefu' wullie-waught
> That's rived the baudrons frae the ha',
> Sair was the collie-shangie wraught,
> But fient a haet said he ava'.
>
> Gae steik the yett wi' caller oo,
> An' gar the boatie row fu' weel:

Yon crimson-tippit beastie's fu',
For Bauldie is a stieve dour chiel."

To say that this farrago of nonsense was received in respectful silence would give a poor idea of the breathless hush which fell over the drawing-room of Kaleside when his voice died away. Of all his audience apart from Susan and Charles, Peggy Cunningham was the only one acute enough to gather the truth, and she, with shaking shoulders, had buried her face in her handkerchief. Susan and Charles thought it wiser to avoid one another's eyes. They did not want to break down altogether and give the graceless poet away.

"I find," said Oliver gravely, in reply to his hostess's somewhat dazed thanks, "that I can express myself so much more vividly in Scots. Ah, Miss Pringle, What a wealth of beautiful words the Doric contains. But—you haven't given me any helpful criticism on my little attempt to capture the spirit of this wonderful countryside."

Never in her wildest imaginings had Susan pictured herself feeling sympathy with Miss Pringle. Whatever the circumstances, but impaled on the horns of the present dilemma, she knew a momentary pity for the august poetess. To admit ignorance of her native tongue was obviously not to be thought of by a professed admirer of Burns: to criticize the incomprehensible was not possible. And when, with a gracious smile, she said that any criticism of such a—such a charming piece would be impertinence, and she felt *sure* every member agreed with her, Susan almost clapped her for her adroitness. The members, thankful that nothing more difficult than appreciation was called for, all cordially assented.

"I thought," said Mrs. Holden plaintively, "that you and your brother were English, Miss Parsons?"

Susan noticed that she said "I fought" and "your bruwer," for among other pretty little affectations she evidently numbered an inability to pronounce the letters "th," which men at least probably found appealing.

"So we are," said Susan; and unwilling to give Oliver away, richly though he deserved it, added: "But I think he has been studying the local dialect ever since we came to Easter Hartrigg. We love Scotland and all things Scottish."

"Do you really? How wonderful of you!" said Mrs. Holden. "Now *I* simply loave it all. Why hasn't Jed asked you to Reiverslaw while we are there? I'm *so* bored with everyone!"

"As a matter of fact, we are coming to dinner in a few days." Susan told her.

"How *divine*! Your bruvver too, of course? And your friend?" Her eyes wandered towards Oliver and Charles, and Susan with an inward feeling that was not all amusement, beckoned to them. Even as she was making the necessary introductions, she could not help wondering if this pretty, feather-headed little creature would ever settle down with honest Jed and live his country life with him. A charming animation had taken the place of Mrs. Holden's former bored languor, and in a second she had absorbed both men as a sponge mops up water.

Besides a faint misgiving on Jed Armstrong's behalf, Susan felt a pang as she caught sight of Peggy's rather wistful face. Poor child, she could not hope to compete with this little grass-widow any more than I could, thought Susan; but I don't mind in the least, she evidently does.

Peggy's vague envy was dispersed by an unwelcome interruption in Miss Pringle's most rallying tones.

"Surely you were out on a *very* wet afternoon the last time I saw you, Peggy?" she asked meaningly. Her voice was loud, and the attention of everyone near was instantly attracted. Peggy's smooth young face remained blankly polite as she answered: "What day was it, Miss Pringle? I don't remember having been out in any bad weather lately."

"But *yes*, dear child. We all three saw you, we were driving in the donkey-carriage, and you were just coming out of that wood near Muirfoot," the inquisitor persisted. "Perhaps, though," with a dreadful archness, "you were too much *occupied* to notice *us*! We saw that you were with young Graham—"

"I think you must have made a mistake, Miss Pringle. I haven't seen Ronald Graham except in church for months," said Peggy quietly. She held her head up, but the tell-tale flush rose to her cheeks in a rich tide of colour, and Susan saw that her frank eyes were troubled.

Miss Pringle never took a contradiction kindly, perhaps because she herself was in the habit of contradicting others, and Susan was thankful when Oliver suddenly turned and said, loudly and clearly:

"Well, we'll have to push off, Miss Pringle. Thank you for a delightful afternoon."

Other people began to make drifting movements towards the door, and Peggy seized the opportunity to leave, after being bidden farewell by her hostess with marked coldness.

"I am so sorry we had no time to hear *you*, Miss Parsons," said Miss Pringle. "But at our next meeting you *must* come earlier and let us have the pleasure—"

Mentally resolving to shun the next meeting and all those which succeeded it, Susan replied with a smile and a vague polite murmur; and catching Charles's eye, moved out into the hall. The three hostesses, lovingly intertwined, stood on their step, an imposing group upholstered in velveteen, and waved as the Squib bucketed off along their drive.

"That little woman you introduced me to, Susan," said Charles suddenly. "She was the one I saw at the Races. You remember? I was sure I'd seen her before somewhere, but I still can't place her, and she flatly denied it. Who is she, anyhow? Mrs. Someone? Not a wife, I should say, by the look of her. A widow, probably, either merry or grass."

"Neither," said Susan. "Though her husband isn't supposed to be going to live long. That was Mrs. Holden. I'm sure I said her name quite distinctly."

"No, darling. You mumbled 'Lieutenant Commander Um, Mrs. Er-hur' in such a county voice that I couldn't make out my own name, let alone hers," answered Charles. "But look here, that isn't the girlfriend of your pal, Oliver? The fella with a voice like heavy firing practice and a figure to match—is it?"

Oliver chuckled. "That's her," he said briefly and ungrammatically.

"Well, well. And what does our gifted novelist think of her? She's a regular sprig o' fashion, isn't she, Sue? Too much scent for my simple taste, though."

"I think she's probably amusing when she takes the trouble not to be bored," said Susan. "And certainly most beautifully dressed, and easy to look at. But I don't know her any better than you do."

"I thought you authors could spot characters at a glance. Another illusion shattered," said Charles.

The Squib, now behaving with lamb-like meekness, was' bearing them homewards swiftly; the narrow road ran before them into a stormy sunset where jagged peaks of dark purple cloud strove with a sea of gold. The long rays fell slanting over the drenched woods and fields, touching them to splendid deep colour, but the hills still sulked behind a bank of mist, which drove across their humped shoulders, heavy with rain yet to come. "Jed would say that the packman's on Cheviot," said Oliver, nodding his head at the half-seen line of hills. "There's going to be rough weather."

They turned into the familiar road, lined with giant willows which had been planted generations before as stakes of a fence but had taken root in that kindly soil and burgeoned like Joseph of Arimathea's famous staff. The pale yellow leaves were drifting to the ground, and had already covered the road with a thick soft carpet, over which the Squib slithered almost without sound.

"How nice it is to be home!" Susan said as they went into the house, and Tara came to meet them in the hall, his whole body agitated by the furious waving of his welcoming tail.

"I say, Oliver," asked Charles with respectful curiosity, when they had congregated close to the fire, "how did you manage to make up that poem of yours? It was a bounce, of course, I mean, stuff that sounds such utter gibberish couldn't make sense even in Scots—but how?"

"It was really extraordinarily simple," said Oliver. "I borrowed a few lines at random from one Mr. Burns of honoured memory, and picked out the weirdest words that would rhyme, from the Scottish Dictionary, and the thing was done. There were some other words I'd have liked to put in, but either they were too long, or I didn't dare to take the risk of using them or reading them aloud, so I had to drop them. They were beauties, too. It was a pity," he added in a tone of gentle regret.

"I think you did pretty well," said Susan drily. "And I wonder that even you didn't blush when you saw all those poor dupes sitting round you and listening to that balderdash!"

"Blush? Why should I? A set of frauds, pretending to drink it all in and understand it!" cried Oliver.

"Hear, hear!" Charles agreed heartily. "You deserved to win, if only for the sake of pulling the leg of old Miss Pringle—the high-priestess, I mean, the one who looked like a sofa on its beam-ends."

Oliver closed his eyes and shuddered. "I beg," he said brokenly, "that you will refrain from even suggesting such a very indelicate act on my part. I wouldn't touch Miss Pringle's limb with a pitch-fork!"

"No. Perhaps you're right there," Charles said, after a moment's careful consideration of the question.

"Well, there's one thing certain," said Oliver, slapping his sister resoundingly oh her shrinking shoulder. "And that is, you'll have hard work to live up to the standard I've set for the family, Susan, my girl, novelist or not!"

"I shall not try," retorted Susan. "And, anyhow Peggy wasn't taken in by your ridiculous poem. She had more sense."

"Peggy!" Oliver suddenly became serious, even gloomy, and started to prowl up and down the room, a sure sign that he was either worried or restless. "Why did Peggy contradict Miss Pringle like that, do you suppose? About the time they saw her with Ronald Graham, I mean."

Susan and Charles stared at him in open astonishment, and Charles murmured that personally he would swear black was white if he thought that it would annoy Miss Pringle.

"I expect that was how Peggy felt," said Susan. "You know what prying old busybodies the Miss Pringles are. It's nothing to do with them if she chooses to go out on a wet afternoon and meet Ronald Graham."

"Has it occurred to you—" Oliver turned on her quite savagely, "that these same prying old busybodies could do quite a lot of mischief—and will, too, if that little fool of a girl isn't more careful."

"But, Oliver, my *dear*—" began Susan, at a loss.

Charles spoke for her. "As far as I remember, Noll, Miss Cunningham said she had not been out on that particular afternoon, so the old sharks must have made a mistake."

"That's just what they didn't do," muttered Oliver, ashamed of his outburst, but doggedly sticking to the subject. "Peggy *was* out, and with that sulky brute Graham, for I saw her myself."

Charles pursed his lips and whistled softly. "Oh, like that, is it?" he said. Then, in a soothing voice: "But even so, Noll, I think she was justified in refusing to gratify the old ladies' kindly curiosity, though she chose rather a stupid way of doing same. It was absolutely none of their damned business if she wanted to have a quiet walk with her young man and nothing said."

"They'll make it their business, curse them!" said Oliver, with bitterness. "It's all they live for, and a thing like that spread about in a small place, as they'll spread it, can be quite damaging enough. If she hadn't lied about it—"

"I don't believe Peggy did tell a lie," said Susan very firmly. "What a range of mountains you're making out of a molehill that isn't even there! The Misses Pringle—yes, and you too, Oliver—must have mistaken someone else for Peggy. You saw her at some little distance, I suppose?"

Oliver nodded.

"Well, then! Lots of girls are small and fair and wear a blue coat and a red beret. It was probably some village lovely—Ronald Graham is just the type to cut a dash with them and enjoy his conquest."

"I recognized him all right," muttered Oliver.

"He's pretty easily recognized, isn't he?" said his sister. "Those long knock-kneed legs of his and that bouncing heather-step of a walk could hardly belong to anyone else."

"No. All the same—"

"It's perfectly ridiculous, particularly as Peggy can't bear the creature. Now do stop being stupid, Oliver."

Susan's common-sense view seemed to carry the day; and she retired to dress for dinner smiling a little over the everlasting childishness of men. "Charles fussing because he imagines he has met Mrs. Holden somewhere before, and can't bear to be proved in the wrong. And Oliver, poor pet, in a flap because he thinks Peggy has told a lie. I believe he's beginning to be jealous about her," she thought. "Dear me. I think they 'have their troubles to seek,' as Donaldina says!"

CHAPTER TEN

1

"Just a moment," said Oliver, interrupting his sister's conversation with Charles. "Did I understand you to say that you promised the Cunninghams we'd give them a lift to Reiverslaw this evening?"

"You did," said Susan.

"And how do you propose to cram six persons, none of them small except Peggy, into the Muirfoot taxi, plus the driver?"

"Five of us should be able to get inside with a squeeze," said Susan. "And one must sit in front with Gibbie Johnston, of course."

"I see. Perfectly simple. 'One must sit in front'," said Oliver with a hollow laugh. "I—I suppose that will be me? But how cleverly you've arranged it, haven't you?" He walked to the window and, twitching aside a curtain, stared out bleakly into the gathering night.

In the light that streamed out over the gravel from the bright room, the teeming rain could be seen falling in straight, relentless shafts. Even without this visible evidence, the noise of full water-pipes, gurgling melodiously, the continuous purring patter of the steady drops would have spoken plainly to the state of the weather.

"'Kiss me, Hardy,'" murmured Oliver faintly, letting the curtain fall back into place, and putting a hand over his eyes. "I do wish, Susan dear, that when you want to do a kindness to anyone it needn't always be at some other hapless creature's expense. Usually mine. Charity begins at home, and—"

"I think you're making a fuss about nothing," said Susan. "After all, it's a closed car."

Oliver groaned. "The back's closed all right, hermetically sealed, in fact, but Gibbie doesn't approve of these new-fangled notions in the front seat. There's no glass at the sides, and I might as well run behind the car with an umbrella, or have a shower-bath, before starting, in all my clothes—"

"Don't be absurd," said his sister heartlessly. "If your miserable Squib had not chosen to fall to bits you could have gone in her. And besides, you can wear a waterproof."

"Do you hear the woman, Charles? I can wear a waterproof, she says. What I really need, of course, is a deep-sea diver's outfit, or a mackintosh dinner-jacket and under-fugs."

"Tough luck, old boy," said Charles, lighting a cigarette. "Can I lend you a pair of goloshes, or would you rather have a tot of cough mixture? You will have my thoughts and sympathy every inch of the way."

With an awful look Oliver left the room.

"He's great fun, isn't he?" said Charles. "Quite got back to his old form. You and this place between you have done wonders, Susan. When I saw him in hospital after the crash I thought that if he didn't pass out he'd be like old King Whatsisname, the one who never smiled again."

"Then you do think he's all right now? Of course he'll never be quite as fit as he used to be. That leg will always be a bother to him. But you *do* think he's better? You know him so well, Charles—ever since Osborne—"

"Yes. But he ought to marry," said Charles bluntly.

Susan laughed. "He's so dreadfully large-hearted! I can't quite see him settling down with one wife. A harem would be more in his line."

"That's all very fine and large." Charles remained obstinately serious. "But what happens to him when *you* marry?"

This time her laugh was a trifle forced. "Dear me, Charles! You aren't suggesting that I should get married, my dear? I'm a born old maid, and I rather like it, if the truth be told."

"Now you're talking bunk. You could marry to-morrow, if you liked," said Charles. "Oh, yes, I know you're both very happy as you are, an' all that . . . in the meantime. But one of those days one or other of you is bound to marry. Oliver's just about done with the frittering stage, and once he finds his girl it'll be haste to the wedding. And you wouldn't want him to stay single because of you, Susan?" Charles very seldom dropped his normal tone of pleasant banter for earnestness. When he did, he talked with brutal candour and sound sense which commanded attention. At the thought of Oliver's possible marriage, which suddenly sounded inevitable, Susan was conscious of a purely selfish pang. But she answered at once: "Of course I shouldn't."

"And you wouldn't want to stay on here as second fiddle, however well you liked his wife. It doesn't do, you know, a triangular establishment like that. Not fair on any of the three."

"No," Susan said, promptly and decidedly.

"Then—what about you? Do you want to be just 'Auntie Susan' to the end of the chapter? You aren't cut out for this bachelor-woman business, my sweet. You like a man to look after. Can't you see that you're bound to marry?"

"I *wish* you wouldn't, Charles!" Distress rang in Susan's voice. "I don't want to marry, I don't even want to discuss such a possibility. I've put all that away long ago. I've been through it once—oh, I don't mean I've been actually married, you needn't look so startled! Nor have I been living in sin, as they say! But I was in love, badly in love, and he—well, he let me down. And as I'd put all my eggs of that particular kind into one basket, there was—rather a wholesale smash. I learnt my lesson by heart, Charles. I'm very trusting until I've been fooled. After that, I can't be taken in again. Marriage without love has always struck me as being rather a poor show, so marriage doesn't appeal to me any longer."

"Because one bounder treated you badly, are you going to distrust all men?"

"I don't know. I don't know. Perhaps not. But—I'm a burnt child, Charles. Can you blame me if I dread the fire?"

"Yes," he said, "I can. You aren't a coward, and that's a coward's argument. No good using it on me. You see, I know you, Susan."

"I wonder."

"I don't. Unless you still care for this—this man, you wouldn't shirk marriage for a reason like that. Do you still care for him?"

Susan shook her head. She had quite lost her air of faint, detached amusement, and looked, though piteously troubled, much younger.

"Do you distrust—me, Susan?"

"No. You're my friend. 'Faithful and just to me,' Charles."

"I'd like to be more."

"I'm sorry. I'm so sorry. I wish you hadn't said any of this. I'm so fond of you—"

"It had to be said, sometime. So you're fond of me, are you?"

They were both standing by now, and Susan was shivering in spite of the fire close beside her. He took her hands in his.

"Look at me," he said, "and tell me straight that you don't care for me."

Susan's eyes, black with distress, met the long blue ones, usually so gay and careless, now stern and almost threatening.

"Yes, I care for you," she said. "But not enough!"

He nodded as if he had heard what he expected, dropped her hands, and stepped back. "I thought so. Well, it will do for a start, and I won't bother you again just now. But when Oliver gets engaged to be married, will you be engaged to me?"

"I—I'll think about it," said Susan.

"That's a promise," he said quietly. "I'd like you to think about it, to get used to the idea."

The sound of a car drawing up outside the door broke the tension, to Susan's heartfelt relief.

"What-ho, Oliver! The carriage waits!" cried Charles, going to the foot of the stairs and shouting in stentorian tones so like his everyday call that Susan began to wonder if she had not dreamed the whole of the past twenty minutes.

His warning cry was seconded by the ringing of the bell. After a silence, the bell rang again. Susan awoke with a start to the fact that Donaldina had been given leave of absence to attend a "kirn" or harvest-home dance near Kaleford, for which festivity, undeterred by the weather, she must already have departed "Charles," said Susan, joining him in the hall and speaking with a determined effort to be natural, "please open the door for Gibbie and tell him that we're just coming. And we'll have to bolt all the windows because there's no one in the house to-night except Tara."

"Bolt? Did I hear you use the English word 'bolt,' my girl?" said the voice of Oliver from aloft, as Charles opened the front door to admit a rush of cold, wet air and the leather-coated form of Gibbie Johnston. "Surely you know," continued the master of the house, unseen but very far from unheard, "that in Scotland windows are snibbed, and never bolted?"

"Come and snib them, then. And hurry, or we'll be late. Don't forget to lock the front door after we're out, and put the key in your pocket. Donaldina has the back-door key with her."

Susan went through the baize door and along the passage to make certain that all was fast there. The kitchen was bathed in a warm red glow from the banked-up fire, and before it lay Tara, gloomy and dull. He knew that his family was dining out, and hated it.

Susan knelt down beside him and put her hand on his broad black forehead. Two brown eyes looked at her, the feathery tail beat a tattoo on the hearth-rug. He turned over and took her hand in his mouth, so gently that it might have been engulfed in a velvet bag.

"Lovely," said his mistress, "I'll tell you a secret. You are the only man I love."

She was feeling hurt and bewildered. To rake up her miserable love-affair, hidden in decent obscurity for years, and resolutely put aside except in rare moments of weakness, had been a very painful business. It was not really Charles's fault that the bare bones had been disinterred, but it had been ghastly, and now the bones refused to allow themselves to be buried again. Instead, they grinned at her like a pirate's flag wherever she looked: would even strength of mind make it possible for her to shut her eyes to them after this? That last scene in the hotel bedroom, after she had run away to join him, and his wife had come, to find her waiting for him, already regretting the step she had taken, but too proud, too obstinate, to give in. . . . Susan shuddered. Again she could hear that other woman's voice in pity: "You poor child! Did he tell you that I wouldn't divorce him? It's he who doesn't want it, he's afraid of endangering his position, losing his job" . . . and then her own precipitate flight, a nightmare of escape. . . . Every piece of furniture, hideous, bulky, in that room, was still familiar to her shrinking memory, the double bed occupying a blatantly large amount of floor-space, the mirror which reflected her pale, shocked face, even the wall-paper, gross purple roses straggling over an ugly neutral-tinted background. . . . What a sordid, wretched ending to her brave, idiotic dream of defying the world's disapproval by his side! "A romantic fool, that's all I was," thought this older, wiser Susan drearily. "And now, there's Charles. I want to be friends with him. I've never really thought of him in any other way, attractive though he is; could we still be friends if we were married?" That would certainly put a different complexion on the matter. She knew Charles so well, saw him without any veil of illusion, trusted him. Perhaps, after all, sometime, it might work out happily that way. . . .

"Susan! *Susan!* Come on, for the love of Mike! D'you want to arrive and find them halfway through dinner?"

Susan dropped a kiss in the dusky hollow between Tara's steadfast eyes, and a little comforted, hurried back to the hall.

Her face wore its look of amused tolerance as she came upon Charles, expostulating heatedly with Oliver.

"You can't possibly go looking like that. It's not decent. It's an outrage," he was saying.

After one look at Oliver, Susan sank on the nearest chair in a fit of helpless laughter.

He was wearing fisherman's waders with snow-boots crammed on above them, and a waterproof. Round his neck was a large bath-towel arranged as a scarf, and on his head he had a sponge-bag pulled well down over his ears. He carried a red golfing umbrella in one hand, and in the other an enormous silk handkerchief.

"But why not?" he said blandly. "Am I to catch my death of cold and sow the seeds of rheumatism merely to satisfy your sense of what is fitting? I maintain that I am suitably clad for the inclement weather. If my friends don't like to take me as they find me, they can do the other thing."

There was a choking sound from the darker end of the hall and Susan was aware of Gibbie Johnston struggling with some ungovernable emotion. Suddenly he gave up the attempt, and rushing towards the door-way, bolted through it. Immediately after, loud and prolonged guffaws from outside filled the air.

By the time they had argued, persuaded, and scolded themselves hoarse, and had finally prevailed upon Oliver to divest himself of the greater part of his wrappings, Susan and Charles had lost any constraint which they might have felt, and were back on the old safe footing, temporarily at least. They set out to pick up the patiently waiting Cunninghams, exactly ten minutes before the hour at which they were expected at Reiverslaw.

2

Thanks to the terrifying speed to which Gibbie Johnston urged his old car over the country roads, its occupants were only a few minutes late in arriving. Mrs. Holden, acting as hostess, received them radiantly, her greetings quite overshadowing those of the host himself, who seemed content to lurk in the background. The "old cousin," Mrs. Holden's official chaperon, was nowhere to be seen. Evidently she was one of those convenient old ladies who could be relied on to retire early and spend the greater part of the evening in bed.

Before Susan could begin apologies and explanations for their lateness, Oliver had stepped forward and was halfway through a long and garbled story, chiefly conspicuous for its shameless lack of truth.

"I must apologize, Mrs. Holden, for our unpunctuality, which I beg of you to believe is no fault of mine, or the Cunningham family. The woman, my sister, prinking before her glass until the last moment—" He threw out a hand dramatically, and a storm of protest was changed to laughter. Dangling by an emerald-green cord from his wrist was a black-and-white check sponge-bag.

"My little reticule amuses you?" Oliver said in gently chiding tones. "But where else would you have me carry my handkerchief and the latch-key of Easter Hartrigg?"

He dived his hand into the bag, and with the air of a conjuror producing a totally unexpected white rabbit from a hat, drew out the massive iron key which locked the front door of his establishment.

"Dear me, Miss Parsons!" said Mr. Cunningham, wiping his tears of honest merriment from his eyes. "Your brother is what we call a real divert!"

If Oliver had first struck the note of hilarity and set the pace of the party at a gay gallop, it was Mrs. Holden who saw that it was maintained in her own neighbourhood at least.

The round dining-table, a shining dark pool under shaded lighting, in itself encouraged a pleasant sense of intimacy never so easy of achievement at an oblong board, where the corners conspire to act as barriers, and host and hostess face each other in splendid isolation from either end.

"This is an informal party," announced the hostess with her dazzling smile, "so I shall have Commander Parsons and Commander Crawley one on either side of me."

The chosen ones leapt with pleased alacrity to their places, and Susan, glancing about her, thought with some amusement that Mrs. Holden had done the arranging with considerable skill. Not only had she secured both the younger men for herself, but she had managed to escape the pitfall of putting two members of one family together so cleverly that only Peggy and her father were side by side. Susan had ample opportunity for playing her favourite onlooker's part, for of the two men between whom she was seated, Mr. Cunningham believed that good food, like all gifts of providence, was not to be taken lightly, but enjoyed with quiet pleasure; while her host appeared to have been stricken dumb, and if he spoke at all, merely uttered monosyllabic grunts. Mrs. Cunningham, having given up her attempt to converse with him also, was placidly eating filleted sole. Beyond her, Charles threw an occasional remark across the table to Peggy, who gratefully returned the ball when it was not intercepted by Mrs. Holden on the way. She, though to all appearances absorbed in Oliver, was yet alert to break in on Peggy and Charles with airy composure and delicate grace. Poor Peggy.

Though she had Oliver on her left, he was devoting his entire attention to his hostess. It was hard, thought Susan, for a very young girl who was feeling callow and badly-dressed, to have the conversation swept from her, and never to be permitted to take any real part in it. . . . Too bad of Mrs. Holden. Her pretty little ways were quite charming, or would be in a woman ten years younger, but there was too much of the pussy-cat about her for Susan's taste. Sometimes those little dabs that she made were made with unsheathed claws. . . .

While Susan was thinking this, her eyes met Charles's roving glance. He twinkled, raised one eyebrow comically, twisted his mouth into a soundless mew, and by these slight indications gave her clearly to understand that his opinion of Mrs. Holden was much the same as her own. The excellent dinner progressed, the talk and laughter about the other side of the table continued to make up for the comparative silence in Susan's neighbourhood, but she realized that everyone was not so pleased and contented with the party as the acting hostess. Peggy, for instance, smiling bravely and holding her head up, was having a poor time, and Jed . . . What was the matter with Jed? Perhaps he hated to see Mrs. Holden sitting there as if she were his wife when she was not. It must be rather a trying situation for any man who loved a woman. . . .

"You're very quiet to-night. What's come over you?" demanded the subject of her last thoughts so suddenly that she started and let her fork drop with a tiny clatter on her plate. Amazed and a trifle indignant, Susan stared at his weather-beaten face rising uncomfortably above the stiff collar, at his blue eyes fixed on her with mischievous intentness.

"Very quiet?" she repeated. "I've made three separate attempts to talk to you, and you have said 'No,' 'Yes,' and 'Umph.' In fact, I think a Trappist monk would have been a more cheerful companion! And you have the audacity to accuse me of being very quiet."

As always, this slight and very natural display of temper by the equable Susan restored his own good spirits at once, and he loosed one of the tremendous laughs which made the glasses ring.

"What's the joke, Jed?" cried Oliver, rather too eagerly. For Mrs. Holden, perhaps annoyed that his attention should have been distracted from her, said with a small tart smile:

"Dear Jed, must you *roar* so? It simply goes frough and frough my head."

Peggy turned very pink, and darted an angry look at her. In a second her zeal to champion "Uncle Jed" might have led her to rush in where any angel of discretion would have feared to tip-toe; but she was saved by Charles, who murmured in his most languid manner: "I likes a good 'earty laugh meself, sir."

The contrast between his gentle, pensive look and the assumed lower-deck accents in which his remark was voiced provoked an outburst of mirth, and poor Jed's spontaneous roar and his love's remonstrance were alike glossed over. He relapsed into his former silence, however, and Susan found herself disliking Mrs. Holden. The little Persian cat did not mind whom she scratched, it seemed.

When, leaving the men to their port, the four women retired to the drawing-room, all their gaiety of the dinner-table fell from them like a discarded cloak, and conversation languished. Mrs. Holden was not going to trouble to sparkle when only her own sex was present. The sight of two tables set ready for bridge did nothing to raise Susan's spirits, and Peggy positively blenched as she looked at them.

"Susan," she whispered aside, while her mother was trying to interest Mrs. Holden in harmless local gossip with little success. "This *is* a horrid evening! And I can't bear it if I have to play bridge. I'm so awfully bad. I'm sure to revoke or do something terrible!"

"Nonsense, my dear," said Susan. "You won't do anything of the kind. Just keep your head, and—"

"But that's what I can't do. I'll feel exactly like a nice fat rabbit sitting with three starving stoats," she said dismally.

"Be comforted. They won't be able to have two tables, because Oliver doesn't play, and you can be unselfish and sit out."

Later, as Susan sat down with her host as partner, to play against Mrs. Holden and Mr. Cunningham, she envied Peggy. The other four—Mrs. Cunningham as eager to escape as her daughter—withdrew to a far corner, where some childish card game which occasioned a good deal of talk and laughing argument was soon in full swing. Meantime Susan made the comforting discovery that if Jed Armstrong played with a recklessness probably inherited from generations of mosstrooping ancestors, which added considerably to the hazards of an otherwise dull game, he was also possessed of skill and more than his share of good luck. All the finesse of Mrs. Holden, all the minister's sound, conventional tactics availed them little. After three rubbers, during which Susan seemed to have taken little part except as dummy, the other two professed themselves tired, and announced that they had had enough.

"Well, well," said Mr. Cunningham, his cheerfulness standing him in good stead in this hour of utter defeat. "We haven't had much of a chance to-night, partner. They held all the cards. Still, you know, Jed, there's an old proverb that says 'lucky at cards, unlucky in love,' remember!"

"I'll remember," said Jed, his face expressionless, and Susan thought that the minister had not been too happy in his choice of proverbs.

Mrs. Holden merely uttered a small, irritated laugh, and begged Jed to remove his foot from the hem of her dress. She was not a good loser.

3

It was difficult afterwards to decide who had first suggested that the party should return to Easter Hartrigg, where there was a drawing-room floor covered only with easily-removed rugs, and end the evening in dancing. Susan suspected Oliver, who swore that the idea had been Charles's; and he in his turn held that Mrs. Holden had been responsible.

Be that as it might, Mr. and Mrs. Cunningham were dispatched to their Manse in the hired car at the respectable hour of half-past ten, while the rest, loud in promises of seeing that Peggy would be sent home safely, bestowed themselves in Jed Armstrong's large and draughty vehicle and presently were jolting over the rough roads towards the Parsons' house.

The rain had ceased, but the air was damp and chill, and smelled deliciously of wet earth and fallen leaves. From every puddle in the road drowned images of the stars winked feebly, pale travesties of their originals overhead. Ghostly hares, leaping from the hedgerows, loped before them in the glare of the lights until overtaken, or swerved recklessly across the car's path, almost under the wheels, yet always escaping by some miracle. The trees, hung with raindrops brighter than any diamonds, flashed into momentary splendour as they passed, and driving up to Easter Hartrigg the black windows gave back the reflection of the car's lamps so faithfully that the whole house seemed illuminated in honour of its owners' return.

"Now, then, Oliver, look sharp with that key. It's cold," said Charles, as they disembarked and gathered round the front door.

"Key?" Oliver's voice sounded blank. "It's in the sponge-bag, isn't it?"

"It may be," said Charles. "But I haven't got the sponge-bag."

Oliver proceeded to turn out the capacious pockets of his Burberry, and after a few seconds fraught with anxiety, produced the bag. "Here we are . . . ! I say . . . the darned thing's *empty*!"

"I'm *so* cold," murmured Mrs. Holden plaintively.

Peggy began to laugh.

"Rot, my dear fella. You must have it. This is no time for practical jokes," said Charles, and was acidly requested by Oliver not to make a fool of himself.

Jed Armstrong joined Peggy in her now unrestrained mirth, and the fair Primrose murmured again:

"I'm so *cold!*"

"God knows where it is. I don't," said Oliver finally, after a further desperate search which proved unavailing.

He was assailed with a chorus of questions, as futile as those usually put on such occasions. Had he dropped it in the car? Had he left it at Reiverslaw? Was he quite, *quite* sure it wasn't in another of his pockets? (This was contributed by Mrs. Holden.) Could it possibly have fallen on the gravel? Above all, why had he been such an ass as to put it in the sponge-bag at all, and after doing so, to take it out again?

"Oh, my nose was bleeding, an' I've shoved it down my back!" Oliver retorted savagely. "Perhaps you'd like me to undress and have a look? Or would someone care to search me?"

On this Peggy broke down and fairly cried with laughter, in spite of his murderous glare, and Susan, who had concealed her own amusement out of politeness for Mrs. Holden, cast self-control to the winds and laughed also.

Mrs. Holden said she fought she'd raver sit in the car, and retreated there shivering ostentatiously.

"It's a good thing the rain's off," said Jed philosophically. His Primrose's discomfort did not appear to prevent him from enjoying the contretemps immensely.

"There's nothing for it but to try the windows," said Charles, and they began to make an exhaustive but fruitless survey of every window within reach. When they had roamed round the house rattling the sashes, to the intense indignation of Tara, who from inside, and in spite of their reassurances, never ceased to bay untiringly, they met once more at the front door.

"How long d'you think it'll be before Donaldina comes back?" asked Oliver.

"Hours," said Susan helpfully. "Their dance won't stop until three at the very earliest—"

He groaned. "It's only just after eleven!"

"Well, look here." This was the resourceful Charles once more. "Are none of the upstairs windows open? If they are, we might run a ladder up, and—"

"But what a brain, Charles!" said Susan. "Of course, some of them are sure to be."

"Let's look." Peggy, still enthusiastic, began peering upwards.

All their prowling and craning like demented star-gazers, however, only revealed the sinister fact that as far as could be seen the faithful retainer had closed every window above stairs as well as on the ground floor. With a sinking heart Susan remembered that a house not far away had been broken into recently, which accounted for this excessive caution. More, Donaldina had assured her mistress before she left that ony burrglarr wad hae his wark afore him if he thocht to break intil Easter Hartrigg. . . .

"Hi!" bawled Jed Armstrong from the back of the house. "I've found one. It's pretty high, and pretty small, but it might be managed."

With the exception of Mrs. Holden, who preferred to remain sulking in the car, they hastened round to him. It was true. The bathroom window, the top portion of which opened inwards by a rope and pulley, showed a welcome aperture.

"The damn' thing will have to be unshipped before anyone can get in that way," said Oliver gloomily. "However—where's the ladder?"

Charles emerged from an outhouse with one, which he set up against the wall.

"Now, Oliver, my lad," he said, "it's a bit on the short side, but we'll do it all right. Show a leg I Which of us is going up?"

"I am," said Oliver.

"Oh, but—" began Peggy, but was nudged into silence by Charles. "Let him alone," he muttered.

Grimly Oliver looked at the ladder. "It's good-bye to these trousers," said he, and sighed. "I suppose modesty forbids that I take 'em off? I thought so. Well, here goes—"

When he had got a little more than half-way up the rain began again.

"Would anyone like to fetch me an umbrella?" said Oliver resignedly.

"We'd better get under shelter," said Jed, ignoring him.

"But who's going to steady the ladder for him?" Peggy cried indignantly as they turned to seek cover, and she lingered, heedless of the rain.

"Go on, Peggy!" said Oliver from above, "you're the only one in the whole outfit with any heart, and I don't want you to die of damp. Stand from under, like a good girl. What if I fell on you?"

"Oh!" wailed Peggy, who had quite forgotten that she was afraid of him and had even disliked him heartily. "Don't fall! Please don't fall!"

"He won't fall. Climbs like a cat," said Jed callously.

"I'll be all right, Peggy!" cried the hero on the ladder in a manly voice. "Off you go!"

"He reminds me," said Charles in reminiscent tones, "of a bloke I once saw at a music-hall. The Loquacious Laddie on the Tottering Ladder. It was a good turn, but I'm not sure Oliver's isn't better. More romantic-like."

To seek shelter where she could watch him was one thing, to retire to the car out of sight was another. Further than the precarious haven offered by the back-door Peggy refused to stir, and they collected there while the drips from the ledge above fell coldly on their upturned faces or trickled down their necks.

"Here," exclaimed Jed suddenly, stripping off his overcoat and trying to envelop Susan in it. "Put this on!"

And as she protested: "Don't be a fool. Peggy's got on a thick coat, and that thing of yours is no good."

"But what about you?" asked Susan weakly, for her only evening coat, an old one, was certainly not intended to be worn for standing about in the rain.

"I'm all right. Never get cold," he said shortly and buttoned the enormous garment under her chin as if she had been a child.

"Thank you," said Susan with extreme meekness.

From where they stood they could see the road, up which a wavering light was now moving towards them, evidently attached to the bicycle of some returning reveller. As it drew abreast of the house there was a rending crash and the ladder fell to the ground, leaving Oliver clinging to the bathroom window like the ivy to the oak.

"Hell!" he ejaculated loudly.

Before anyone could move to go to his assistance the bicycle came to a stop, and a stalwart figure, bounding through the laurels and rhododendrons bawled: "Bide whaur ye are! I've got ye!"

"What on earth—" began Susan, only to have her arm seized in a vice-like grip by Jed Armstrong.

"Keep quiet," he muttered, "it's the policeman from Muirfoot. Now we'll see some fun!"

Charles, chuckling, restrained the indignant Peggy, and the limb of the law, standing below the window, addressed himself to Oliver.

"I chairge ye," he said, "wi' burrglarriously enterin', or attemp'in' tae enter, a hoose or dwaliing. Dae ye gi'e yersel' up?"

"Oh, don't be a damn' fool!" cried Oliver. His annoyance was natural, but the remark was hardly conciliatory, and did not meet with the policeman's approval.

"Wull ye come down?" he asked ominously. "Or wull I come up tae ye?"

"I strongly advise you to stay where you are on the good brown earth, as one of our poets so beautifully puts it. This ledge was never intended for anything larger than a thin cat."

"Ha'e ye ony accomplishes?" demanded the policeman.

"Trot along and see!" suggested Oliver pleasantly. The policeman ruminated for a few seconds, evidently decided that Oliver could not descend while the ladder lay on the ground, and tramped off round the corner of the house.

"Charles," said Susan, "he'll see the car, and perhaps frighten Mrs. Holden. Do go and—"

"Oh, no, Susan darling. She'll be all right. He'll know who she is, won't he, Armstrong?"

"Jed!" cried Susan, now agitated, and calling on Mr. Armstrong by his Christian name, which she was not in the habit of using. "*Do* go and—"

"Not I. It'll do Primrose good," said he heartlessly.

Peggy, who since Oliver's ascent had been very quiet, began to laugh softly.

"Hurrah!" shouted Oliver. "I'm in! I'm in! I'm—oh, Lord! There go the tooth-glasses!"

By this time Susan was running towards the front door. "Constable!" she called breathlessly as she sped. "Officer! It's a stupid mistake! There isn't any burglar!"

A piercing feminine shriek proclaimed that she was too late to save Mrs. Holden from the misguided policeman's sense of duty. In another lightning flash of memory she remembered that the real burglar's "accomplish" was presumed to be a woman....

"How dare you! Let me go at once!" cried Mrs. Holden as Susan came in sight. The zealous constable had haled her bodily from the car, and she now confronted him, her fur coat thrown open over her smart black gown, in a royal rage.

"It's all right, Smith. That's Mrs. Holden, a guest of mine, that you've got hold of," said Jed, who had followed close on Susan's flying heels. "You're on the wrong tack altogether, man. There's no burglar here or we'd have seen him."

The policeman, abashed and discomfited, fell back scratching his head. "I'm sure I'm verra sorry, mem," he began. "But I couldna ken wha ye micht be, an' there a pairson breakin' in at the back—"

"Take me home at once. At once, do you hear?" almost screamed the fair Primrose, turning her back on the unhappy Smith.

"I'm damped if we're going until we've had a drink, anyway," said Jed obstinately.

Lights had begun to flicker inside the house, and in a minute the door was flung hospitably open. Oliver, the complete laird, his appearance only marred by streaks of white on his trousers, stood on his steps inviting the party to enter.

"Do come in and get warm," Susan begged, but Mrs. Holden ignored her. It was only when Jed took her by the arm, and shaking her gently enough, adjured her not to make a fool of herself, that she condescended to go in, sweeping past as though they were all pariahs.

No further mention was made of dancing. There was a little subdued talk while the men, including the policeman, who badly needed it, swallowed their whiskies-and-soda. Then Mrs. Holden, with the air of one shaking the dust of Easter Hartrigg from off her golden shoes, sailed out to the car. Jed, giving the rest one last rueful grin, followed her.

"Well, well," said Oliver pensively, pouring out another round of drinks. "I can't say I'm sorry to see the last of her. A bit too temperamental for my simple taste, and a little disgusting, at her age. This has been some evening, has it not?"

"How is Peggy to get home?" Susan asked later, when P.C. Smith, restored and comforted though still apologetic, had taken his leave, and they were sitting close to the fire, by this time roused to a cheerful blaze.

"That's all right," said Oliver. "If you'll lend her some night-gear, Susan, she can stay here. I've sent a message to the Manse by the policeman—"

"Oh, Susan!" cried Peggy, her eyes big with delight, her round face deliciously pink. "How lovely! May I?"

Oliver smiled at her indulgently.

"Of course you may, you ridiculous child," said Susan. "I can lend you all you need."

"Except a tooth-brush. What am I to do about my teeth?"

Oliver coughed. "No one can brush his or her teeth," he said. "For one thing, I've stood on every tube of tooth-paste—"

"But there are brushes," began Susan.

Oliver raised his hand. "There *were* brushes," he corrected gently. "But they've—well, they've gone where they can never be recovered, short of calling in the plumbers. And I hardly think you'll want—"

Charles began to shake with silent laughter.

"Let's change the subject," said Oliver. "Did it never occur to any of you to wonder how I'd opened the front-door?"

The others stared at him in a wild surmise.

"Don't—don't tell me it was unlocked all the time?" Susan murmured faintly.

"Not so, sweeting. It was locked securely enough." He thrust a hand into a trousers-pocket and pulled out a large iron object which he laid reverently on a table. "After scaling that ladder at infinite risk to my neck, after unshipping a window which valiantly resisted my efforts, after being brutally accosted by the *polis* and in sheer terror getting into the bathroom, I skidded on the tooth-paste, and came down with a crash on something hard. Yes," he said brokenly, "you are quite right. It was the key. But finding it even in that painfully sudden manner proved that I was right."

"What do you mean, right?" they cried indignantly.

"I had a feeling, you know, that I hadn't really mislaid that key," he murmured.

CHAPTER ELEVEN

1

THANKS to Mrs. Cunningham's foresight, her daughter was able to appear at breakfast the next morning suitably clad, for "Jems" had been waylaid at the Manse gate on his way to Easter Hartrigg and given a change of clothes to convey to Peggy.

"Don't dash off immediately," said Oliver. "Stay and keep Susan company for a bit."

He and Charles were both on the point of starting for Wanside, where Mr. Elliot had arranged to have a day at his pheasants.

"I must," said Peggy. "It's Hallowe'en, you see, and the Infantry are having a small party, and I've got to make turnip lanterns and do all sorts of things."

"Tara and I will walk down with you, if you can wait until I've seen Donaldina," said Susan.

Frost had kissed the woods to burning splendour, and the air had a cold freshness that made them both want to sing or shout aloud when they went out. The barberry hedges had been stripped of their waxen red and orange fruit by hungry birds, and even the hawthorns were almost bare. Underfoot the fallen leaves rustled crisply, overhead the sky was a chill faint blue, and a field of turnips, where the sun fell on it, was vivid emerald green.

"That's the most brilliant green that Nature can show, I think," said Susan, pointing to the patch of exquisite clear colour.

"Lovely!" Peggy danced along as if the blood ran in her veins too fast for mere walking.

"I always think that round wood looks so mysterious," said Susan.

Peggy sobered at once. "It's—supposed to be haunted," she said, throwing a quick glance towards it as they approached. "No one in the village will pass it after dark."

"Won't they? I've always wanted to see what it was like, and I will, one day—"

"Oh, Susan, don't!"

"Why? Are you afraid of it too?"

"Yes, I am, rather," Peggy confessed. "I've never been into it beyond the first trees. I tried once, but I just had to turn back." She added with a rush, her colour heightening. "It was there that the Pringles thought they saw me. Remember?"

"Yes, I remember," said Susan. "I thought it a piece of unwarrantable impertinence on their part, but of course they're like that."

"Susan. It wasn't me they saw," said Peggy earnestly and ungrammatically. "But I wish they hadn't seen her, for all that."

"So you know who it was?"

"I can guess." Peggy looked troubled. "I hope I'm wrong, but I don't think I am. . . . How I hate Ronald Graham! He's the horridest person I know. But he's going away, to Manchester or somewhere. His father has found him a job."

"About time," was Susan's comment. "*Not* a nice young man."

"Horrible!" said Peggy fervently, and they turned into the village of Muirfoot.

Passing the post office they were hailed by the imperious voice of Mrs. Davidson, and resignedly turned aside into the dark stuffiness of her domain. "Ha'e ye heard?" was her dramatic greeting.

"No. What's happened?" asked Peggy quickly. "Yon Mistress Holden, her that's at Reiverslaw the noo, her husband's deid. Ay. M'phm. The tallygram cam' in a wee whiley syne, an' I've juist foamed them up. She'll be awa' by the neist train, nae doot. An' a guid riddings," ended Mrs. Davidson, while Susan and Peggy stared wordlessly at each other.

Somehow, although Mrs. Holden's invalid husband was only a shadowy figure even to Peggy, though his death was not unexpected, the news, received on such a morning, was a shock.

"Poor Mrs. Holden!" murmured Susan at last, to Peggy.

Mrs. Davidson answered her. "Nae need tae peety *her*, I'm thinkin'. We'll be seein' her back sune eneuch, the more's the peety. The pentit hizzy! A wumman o' her age suld think shame o' sic ongauns. It's puir Maister Armstrang *I'm* wae for." Folding her arms, she stared defiantly at her two startled hearers.

"But really, Mrs. Davidson, you oughtn't to say—" began Peggy, remembering that she must uphold her position of minister's daughter.

"Hoot awa', lassie! Wha's tae stop me? Ye ken fine that I'm richt, though ye maunna say it yersel'!"

"I think," said Susan with tact, "that I'll have to be going home, Peggy. I've left all my household duties undone."

"Yes, and I must fly too." Peggy seized on the chance of escape with relief. "Good morning, Mrs. Davidson, I'll have to—"

"Ay. It's the bairns' Hallowe'en, is it no'? I'll no' keep ye. Yon Jo-an's leavin' the morn, they're tellin' me?"

"Yes, I'm afraid she is. Now I simply *must* fly!"

Outside again, and beyond hearing of the post-mistress, Peggy said, "I like Mrs. Davidson, but she is a terror at times, isn't she? Good-bye, Susan, and thank you for my lovely time."

"Lovely time, my dear! Standing for hours in the cold because that lunatic Oliver thought he'd lost the key—"

"Well, it was *fun*. And I thought it was going to be such a dreary evening."

Susan, as she walked away at a brisk pace, found herself rather in agreement with Mrs. Davidson's outspoken sentiments regarding Mrs. Holden.

"Anyhow, she won't hear the true story of the key," thought Susan, and a smile tugged at the corners of her mouth. "Jed will think it a huge joke and roar, but I don't think Mrs. Holden's sense of humour is very robust. She wouldn't appreciate it at all."

And then she felt suddenly remorseful, remembering that Mrs. Holden would be going back to a house heavy with death. For, even if she had not loved her husband, and somehow, love and Mrs. Holden did not seem to go together very well, yet she had been bound to him by ties of intimacy, of years under the same roof, even of petty annoyances, which all go to make up marriage.

"Poor Mrs. Holden!" she said again.

2

Peggy, speeding up the well-raked drive towards the Manse, did not think of Mrs. Holden at all. Her mind was concentrated on Jo-an, about whom she was still troubled, for the girl's face looked as if she really had a secret, and a tragic one, when she fancied herself unobserved. Mrs. Davidson had reminded Peggy of the fact that Jo-an was leaving the Manse on the following day, and after that, what was going to become of her? Common sense assured Peggy that she was going home, to good if narrow-minded parents, and on the face of it anxiety seemed absurd; but Peggy had been brought up to a feeling of responsibility towards her father's parishioners. She could not add the vague burden of her fears to Mrs. Cunningham's cares, nor could she speak to Jo-an herself. Somehow Jo-an was quite unapproachable. Peggy, with a small shudder of distaste, was aware that her conscience told her she must tackle Ronald Graham. . . . However, as she realized thankfully, that could not be done to-day, she would have to wait until the next choir-practice. At present her business was to arrange the Infantry's Hallowe'en party.

Her mind was full of a jumble of apples, nuts and turnip-lanterns as she flew into the house, dashing over the slippery linoleum of the hall with the ease of long use, and called.

"Mother! Where are you, Mother?"

A voice from upstairs answered her. "In my room. And Peggy, if you're coming up, just bring Father's best boots with you. I want to pack them. They'll be in the Bootery."

"To pack—?" Then Peggy remembered that her parents were going away for the night to Mr. Cunningham's old parish to attend Hallowe'en festivities there.

"All right!" she called back. She opened the door of the Bootery, a small cupboard-like apartment off the hall, where the family's outdoor shoes stood tidily on shelves, and waterproofs and umbrellas hung on their appointed hooks. The household lamps were trimmed and filled here, and the little room smelt of boot-polish, mackintosh, and paraffin. It had been one of Peggy's pet refuges in childhood, and she still loved the strangely assorted odours for the memories they called up. This morning the Bootery was occupied by Bun, who sat curled up among the boots and shoes, a battered writing-pad on her knee, and a much-chewed yellow pencil clutched in her grubby right hand.

"Bun! It's much too cold for you in here!" said Peggy, even while she hunted for the minister's Sunday boots.

"It's peaceful," said Bun placidly. "An' I'm making a poetry. Would you like to see it?"

"Of course I would. I'd love to." Peggy dropped the boots and respectfully accepted a page, from the writing-pad on which was written in Bun's laborious script four lines of verse.

> The King has ridden away to Fife,
> Becos he Wants to save his lif.
> We all did see him Mount his Horse
> But he doth take it very corse.

"There's more to come. It's a ballid," Bun explained. "When I'm big I'm going to be a Littery Club like Miss Pringle."

Peggy laughed. "Your poetry seems to me a great deal better than Miss Pringle's," she said.

Bun was suitably gratified. "I'll write it out for you, one all to yourself."

Leaving her to her congenial task, Peggy took the large black boots, beaming with faithful polishing, up to her mother's room.

The well-known expanding suitcase of blue fibre stood on a chair, and Mrs. Cunningham was bending over it, stowing away sponge-bag, hair-brush and handkerchief sachet into vacant corners. Peggy knew that each shoe already packed held its neatly rolled pair of stockings, or the minister's socks, or some other small uncrushable article.

"Here are Father's boots, Mother," she said.

"Thank you, dear." Mrs. Cunningham planted a somewhat absent-minded kiss on her daughter's pink cheek. "I think he'd better wear them to travel in. Just put them down somewhere, so that he won't forget to put them on. Last time he went in his old pair with a great patch on one, and I was so ashamed. Now, where did I put my bottle of lavender water? Do you see it anywhere, Peggy? The little flat one. It will just go nicely into this corner."

Peggy sat down on the big bed and clasped her hands round one of the solid mahogany posts, watching her mother with mild interest.

"You always like to go back to Kirklaw, Mother, don't you?"

"Indeed I do, Peggy. They give us such a welcome even yet that it nearly makes me cry. They thought the world of your father, and they're more forthcoming in the West, less afraid of showing their feelings. You'll not remember Kirklaw, of course, for Elspeth was only Bun's age when we left, and Jim no bigger than Colin. . . ."

Peggy had heard this many times before, but though her parents' often-repeated stories occasionally made her irritated and impatient, she listened now with a new interest, vaguely conscious that there was something stable and comforting about her mother's gentle kindly reminiscing.

"You wouldn't like to leave here, though, and go back, would you?" she asked.

Mrs. Cunningham shook her neat grey head. "No. It's never the same, going back. We probably see it differently on a visit like this. Muirfoot is home to me now. You were born here, and we've been here longer than anywhere. . . . There, I think that's everything. Peggy, you're sure you can manage all right? Agnes is going out to-night, I promised her before I knew you would be alone; but you'll have Jo-an, of course, and we'll be back to-morrow."

The Manse was strangely quiet after they had gone, for Peggy sent the Infantry out for a walk in the frosty afternoon sun with Jo-an, while she made ready for the party. At first she felt lonely and oppressed, but she was too busy for this mood of faint self-pity to last. Agnes brought the big wooden tub, half-filled with water, to the dining-room, and stood it on the floor in the bay-window, behind the long red curtains, to be ready when the time came. Then there were the red apples to be polished until their dark skins had the rich satiny gloss of old furniture. A basket of these and a great dish of nuts were put on the hall table for the village children who would come "guizarding" later in the evening. Turnip lanterns had to be made, too, and Peggy gouged out their soft interiors with a sharp knife as she chattered to Agnes in the warm kitchen. She was a child again herself, sniffing the sharp, sweet smell of the turnip pulp, carving grotesque faces on the tough, well-scrubbed yellow skins.

The afternoon wore on, the lanterns were fitted with candles and hung in dining-room and hall. The Infantry returned from their outing with cold, rosy cheeks, and were led quickly upstairs by Jo-an, lest the temptation to take "just *one* peep" at the hidden delights in the dining-room should prove too much for them. Peggy was changing into the brown velvet dress which suited her soft colouring so well when she heard the front-door bell ring, and then a man's voice in the hall. Presently Agnes came to her, smiling broadly.

"It's Commander Parsons, Miss Peggy. He says he's a' alane at Easter Hartrigg, and I was tae ask ye can he come tae the pairty?"

"Oh!" Peggy's heart jumped absurdly. "Tell him of course he can, Agnes, and I'll be down in a minute." But she lingered, staring unseeingly at her reflection in her dressing-table mirror, her soft lips parted, her cheeks aflame, her breath coming fast. Oliver . . .

3

After it was all over, and the Infantry had gone to bed, taking their apples, from which they refused to be parted, with them, Peggy stood at the dining-room window and looked out. It was a wonderful evening, just right for Hallowe'en, with stars freckling the frosty sky, a smell of coming snow in the air, and mingled with it the harsh yet pleasant scent of a bonfire where someone in the village had been burning garden-rubbish. Peggy knew that the party had been a success. The Infantry had loved it, Oliver had enjoyed it openly, and she herself had felt that for her it had been the pinnacle towards which all the Hallowe'en parties she could remember from babyhood had been climbing. Oliver at her side, gay and friendly, his fingers touching hers as he gave her the silver fork when her turn came to spear an apple from the bobbing mass in the wooden tub. . . . Oliver playing with the children, helping her to hand out fruit and nuts and cake to the guizards who came shyly into the hall, their eyes shining horribly out of cork-blackened faces in the light. . . . Oliver carrying Bun and Cilly up to bed one under each arm, while the gurgling Colin was borne before them by Jo-an. . . . Oliver, finally, holding her hand when she said good night to him at the door, and telling her that it had been one of the best evenings he had ever known. They had crossed the boundary between acquaintanceship and friendship in those few hours, had advanced into a pleasant intimacy which was very sweet. Peggy, gazing at the sky trembling with stars, hoped passionately that they would never go back. To go on might mean something which she could not bring herself to hope even in her innermost thoughts, since she felt childishly that to do so would break a spell; but the possibility was there, she knew, as sure as the seven stars of the Plough overhead.

At last she turned to go back to the warm little study, where the firelight played on the sober bindings of her father's theological books and made the dulled gold lettering of their titles bright. She was sitting there, making a pretence of knitting a bed-jacket for the Women's Guild, when Jo-an came and stood in the doorway.

"I'm for my bed, Miss Peggy," she said in the muted voice which always sounded as if a more passionate note was throbbing behind it. "The bairns are a' fast asleep."

"All right, Jo-an. Did you leave the back-door unlocked for Agnes?"

"Yes, Miss Peggy."

"Didn't you want to go out yourself?" asked Peggy on a sudden impulse. "When it's Hallowe'en?"

Jo-an shook her head. "Na, Miss Peggy. I'd suner be wi' the bairns."

"And yet—you're leaving them to-morrow?"

A sort of spasm twisted the small secret face. "Ay."

"Wouldn't you—" Peggy had summoned up all her courage. "Wouldn't you change your mind and stay, Jo-an? I know Mrs. Cunningham would be glad—"

Again the girl shook her head. "I canna, Miss Peggy. Oh, dinna say ony mair! But I'll need tae gang."

"Oh, well!" Peggy sighed. It was useless to go on. "I'm sorry. Good night, Jo-an."

The door shut quietly, and she was alone again, but the glow which had wanned her thoughts had lost something of its first splendour.

Jo-an went slowly upstairs to her little room opening off a larger one where the children slept. She passed quickly through without a glance at the two small beds or Colin's crib, and shut herself into her own room. The blind was up and a late-rising moon shone coldly in. On the chest-of-drawers was an apple which Bun had pressed into her hand, a spot of glowing colour on the coarse crochet mat. Jo-an looked at it, then at her mirror, and a faint derisive smile curved her small set mouth. Eating apples before the glass was not for her; it was a childish ploy at best, and she had no longer any heart for that sort of thing. And yet she hesitated, and even while she began slowly to untie the strings of her white apron, she looked at the apple again. After all, it was an old custom, and even if there was nothing in it, where was the harm?

She threw her apron on to the bed, picked up the apple, and holding it in her hand, went towards the mirror. The sight of her pale reflection, dimly seen by the light of one candle and the moonbeams, seemed to mock her superstition. Defiantly she began to eat the apple, her strong teeth biting through red skin and crisp white flesh, her eyes fixed on the glass. The room was cold, and she shivered as she ate: it was growing darker, too, for her image seemed fainter. Something was coming into sight in the dim glass, something long and black and sinister, growing more distinct with each second that crawled by. At first she could barely see what it was, but now it was quite plain. What was it? What was it? Jo-an gave a strangled cry, and as the apple fell from her shaking hand, she slid to the floor and lay there quite still.

Peggy heard the cry from the study below, and ran upstairs, her feet winged by a strange fear.

"Jo-an!" she called softly as she ran. "Jo-an!"

There was no answer. She saw at once that the children were still sleeping soundly, and opened the door of the inner room.

Faint yellow flickering of a single candle striving with the white light of the moon, showed her the crumpled figure on the floor. She did not lose her head. She seized a towel, wetted one end of it at the ewer on the wash-stand, and dabbed Jo-an's forehead, already damp with sweat. In a very short space of time, though to Peggy in her alarm it seemed ages, the unconscious girl shuddered and opened wild eyes.

"Na! Na!" she moaned. "I didna see it! I didna see *that*!"

"Hush, Jo-an. You'll waken Colin." It was all Peggy could think of to quiet her, and it had its effect. Almost at once Jo-an became mistress of herself, the terror was wiped from her face as if it had been removed by the towel still in Peggy's hand.

"What is it? Are you ill?" asked Peggy in a low voice.

Jo-an essayed a smile. "I doot I've had an ower guid Hallowe'en, Miss Peggy," she said in a whisper, and staggered to her feet. But she still looked ghastly, and catching sight of the mirror, began to shudder again.

"I'll make you some tea," said Peggy. "We'll both have a cup. Come down to the study where it's warm."

When a little colour had flowed back to Jo-an's cheeks and she had drunk two cups of strong hot tea, Peggy said to her quietly, but with a firmness that surprised herself, "You'd better tell me what's the matter. Even if I can't help it always does you good to tell, and nothing is as bad once you've spoken of it."

For a moment, meeting the other girl's eyes, she thought she had won, that Jo-an was about to unburden herself of her secret trouble. But the moment passed and nothing was said, and after a pause, when Jo-an spoke, it was only to say, with her gaze fixed obstinately on the floor as if studying the well-worn carpet, "It's naething, Miss Peggy. Dinna fash yersel'. I had a—a pain, nae mair. . . ."

It was hopeless. "I'm sorry," Peggy said. "I think you'd better sleep in the second bed in Agnes's room to-night. She won't mind."

A look of relief passed over Jo-an's face, and she made no demur. Long after she had fallen asleep, lulled by the placid and unsurprised company of Agnes, Peggy lay awake, startled and worried. Finally she got up, and putting on a dressing-gown and slippers, crept soft-footed to Jo-an's little room.

The blind was still undrawn, the moonlight still fell on a corner of the room as if unwilling to leave it. Peggy's foot touched something hard, which rolled off a rug and across the bare floor towards the dressing-table. She set down her candle and picked up the hard object: it was an apple, half-eaten. Puzzled, she looked at it. Jo-an must have been eating it when she fainted. But why should an apple cause such a thing? Suddenly she found herself staring at the mirror, which stared back at her, blank save for her own reflection. Peggy felt as if an ice-cold hand had been laid on the nape of her neck. Hallowe'en, the apple, Jo-an's terror, the now sinister looking-glass. . . . Could the girl have imagined she had seen something, a thing so appalling that she had fallen where she stood? It was ridiculous to suppose it in the nineteen-thirties; and yet—strange things happened on Hallowe'en. . . . People had seen dreadful portents in their mirrors.

... For the first time Peggy felt almost relieved to think that Jo-an was going away. She was uncanny, not like other people ...

There was snow during the night, and they awoke to a wintry grey and white world. Jo-an, insisting that she was quite well, left early, walking away down the drive in a soft flurry of flakes. She did not look back once. Peggy knew that though before last night she had not wanted to go, now she was glad to be leaving the Manse. She would never have slept in her little room off the nursery again.

CHAPTER TWELVE

1

WINTER came in with November, bringing a shrewish nip to the air, wreathing Cheviots and Lammermuirs deep in snow, and sending rude winds to bang at doors and windows, or howl desolately down the chimneys. Wonderful sunsets of angry red and purple set the skies ablaze behind the black leafless trees every evening, lamps were lighted and curtains drawn by tea-time. The hawthorn hedges were gay with their rich crimson fruit which the birds, looking chill and pinched, ate thankfully; among the glossy leaves of the hollies the berries were already glowing in preparation for Christmas. The world outside the immediate neighbourhood seemed to have receded to a great distance, which newspapers, the daily post, and the wireless only served to intensify. In its winter isolation the countryside did not go to sleep, like a squirrel or hedgehog, only to rouse itself when spring came round again. As if everyone had drawn closer to a cheerful fee, this rural life was only enriched by the narrowing of its boundaries.

Deprived of the amusements which during the longer, finer days took people so much farther afield, the villages of Muirfoot and Kaleford, the little town of Abbeyshiels, seemed to become one large family, busied with local entertainments and activities. This was the season when Boy Scout troops and Girl Guide companies flourished, and the roads were apt to be dangerously thronged by infant girls in brown, hopping like wrens towards their Brownie meetings. This was the season when Miss Pringle's Literary Club was galvanized into a frenzied outpouring of works more or less inspired, when concerts in aid of various deserving objects were organized. Mr. Cunningham's Guild for the young men of his parish met weekly in a disused cottage, to debate solemnly on topics of international importance with all the Scots fondness for intellectual argument which has not yet died out in spite of the influence of the cinema. Once a week, too, the Women's Guild sat in the Manse drawing-room, plying needles and tongues with equal industry under the direction of Peggy and her cheerfully indefatigable mother.

Nor were more ambitious efforts wanting, in Abbeyshiels at least, where the Dramatic Club were reported to be rehearsing a three-act play, and where the strains of Gilbert and Sullivan, issuing from a church hall, proclaimed that the Amateur Operatic Society was hard at work on *Patience*.

Finally, there was a mysterious institution known as The Looral, of which Mrs. Davidson the postmistress was a pillar. For some time Susan did not dare to expose her ignorance by asking what the name meant, in case it might be some dark masonic sisterhood which scorned to reveal its secrets to the uninitiated. But on discovering that Donaldina was a member of the Muirfoot branch, the same over which Mrs. Davidson presided, she braved ridicule one morning, and said:

"Donaldina, what exactly *is* 'The Looral?'"

As she had feared, Donaldina looked faintly astonished, but replied politely, "It's whit they ca' the Weemen's Looral Institute, mem."

"Oh!" said Susan, a great light breaking upon her. Once she had heard the translation, she wondered how she had been so dense as not to guess it before. She felt that she ought to have been prepared for any little idiosyncrasy on the part of a people who, while never dropping an H, yet invariably rendered "Helen" as "Ellen," and talked cheerfully about a Jumbo Sale without any ironic reference to the possible white elephants they might buy at it. . . . Whatever its name, The Looral had a fine following in the district, and its douce meetings were always well attended by the wives of lonely herds and ploughmen in the more remote places of the neighbourhood.

Topics of conversation narrowed with the interests, and also tended to come nearer home. Mrs. Cunningham's hens and their prodigious laying capacities, the Miss Pringles' progress in home crafts—for they had taken to leather-work and pen-painting—Susan's literary efforts, were freely discussed in one circle. In another, village tongues clacked of Mrs. Davidson-at-the-post-office's new teeth, which gleamed like Oriental pearls, a really startling display in her brown nut-cracker face; of the arrival of a ninth lusty infant at Buckhaugh Mains, and of other matters of note. Above all, the matrimonial prospects, real or rumoured, of every single young woman, every eligible man, formed by far the most engrossing subject wherever women neighbours met. The men had their own talk in smoking-room or bar, bothy or market-place: deep-voiced chat of the lately-gathered harvest, shooting, hunting, poaching, the price of beasts at this sale or that, the lambing outlook for the coming season. But no woman supposed for a moment that these could be so all-absorbing as their own questions.

Muirfoot gossip did not lack material near at hand, for Peggy Cunningham's name was cropping up rather frequently at any gathering from which she and her mother were absent. At first it was all very good-natured, but presently a more malicious tone began to be noticeable, particularly when Miss Pringle was about. Vague rumours floated through the district, rumours which Miss Pringle and her immediate circle of cronies piously hoped would never come to the ears of Peggy's parents, while they lost no opportunity of spreading them by portentous head-shakes, sighs, and sentences left tantalizingly unfinished. Peggy had been seen with that rather ne'er-do-well young Graham at odd hours and in lonely places, obviously meeting him without her parents' knowledge or consent. True, Ronald Graham had now left Abbeyshiels for Manchester, but Miss Pringle was afraid that the mischief had been done. Had no one noticed how Commander Parsons had given up going to the Manse? No doubt he had heard *something*. Of course Peggy was now much to be seen with a dashing young surgeon, fresh from one of the big London hospitals, who had come as partner and assistant to his uncle, old Doctor Scott at Kaleford; but that would not last. When Hugh Collier heard about young Graham, he would desert Peggy as suddenly as that delightful Commander Parsons had. "Poor Peggy. *Very* foolish of her, and such a pity!" the gossips would wind up, wagging their heads above their tea-cups.

Poor Peggy, indeed. She was going through a difficult time, nor could she remain unaware of the fact that her name was constantly on the lips of Miss Pringle and her intimates. It was quite true that Oliver, who had been an almost daily caller at the Manse for some weeks after the Hallowe'en party, was now seldom seen there.

Mr. Cunningham commented on this not once but many times. "He seemed to be taking such an interest in the Young Men's Guild," he lamented. "That was a fine talk he gave on 'Life in the Royal Navy.' And now he never comes near us. What can be the matter, do you think, Grace?"

"He's probably kept busy at Wanside, James," his wife would reply, and Peggy felt grateful for this plausible explanation. She was more than thankful that her father and mother had no suspicion as to the real cause of Oliver's absence, thankful that they heard nothing of the reports fostered by Miss Pringle; but she felt desperately alone. Had Susan been at hand she would probably have confided in her, but Susan was away in England, paying a round of visits. So Peggy hid her troubles, held her head high, and out of bravado encouraged the attentions of young Hugh Collier. And Oliver became more and more distant. He had retreated so far that their friendship, begun on the evening of Jed's dinner-party at Reiverslaw, might have been a figment of her own imagination.

Peggy sometimes even wondered if it had not. Then, as she recalled the reason for his withdrawal, she knew again that the friendship had existed, had begun to blossom into something rarer and more precious—until that last unfortunate encounter had killed it.

Not without misgiving had she decided upon speaking to Ronald Graham, about Jo-an, and not without difficulty had she arranged a meeting with him. For Ronald, once so eager to waylay her after choir-practice and on Sunday afternoons, now showed an elusiveness which she knew to be spiteful. Peggy had plenty of spirit, and the very fact that he avoided her made her the more determined to have it out with him. Finally he agreed to meet her, but at his own time, and in a place of his choosing.

"Very well," said Peggy, realizing that this was inevitable, that it was his nature to make it as difficult and unpleasant as possible for her.

"I'll be at the wood to-morrow at half-past four," he said.

Half-past four, he knew, was tea-time at the Manse, an hour when Peggy's absence would be noticed and would have to be accounted for. The wood as a meeting-place bore an evil reputation not only from his use of it. For an instant Peggy hesitated, realizing that it might be wiser to leave matters as they were. But his shrug, his sneer as he said, "Take it or leave it. *I* don't mind!" spurred her on against her better judgment.

"Very well. I'll be there," she said recklessly.

A dozen times between then and the appointed hour she repented her decision, the more so as it turned out a dreary afternoon of thin, mist-like rain, when it would be dark earlier than usual, and no person, meeting her, would suppose that she had gone out merely for a walk. Only her Calvinistic conscience drove her on. And the meeting fulfilled her expectations.

Alone with Ronald Graham among the dark trees of the haunted wood, where already it was almost night, she was so nervously anxious to get it over and be away from him and the place, that she could hardly manage, to put her questions.

"Well, what did you want me for?" he asked, coming much too close for her liking. "You've changed, surely! It's not so long since you thought I wasn't good enough to throw a civil word to."

"If you hadn't bothered me and forced yourself on me, and taken advantage of being useful to Father to annoy me, I should always have been polite to you," said Peggy angrily, her fear of him forgotten.

"You'd better be polite to me now, or I'll be off."

"I want to know what you've been doing to make Jo-an Robertson so restless and miserable," Peggy said, taking the bull by the horns without further ado.

"You've got a nerve, haven't you? What business is it of yours?" he asked.

"She was a maid in our house, and she's one of Father's parishioners. If you don't leave her alone I'll go to your father about it."

"You needn't bother. I've done with her," he said carelessly. "And anyway, I'm going away in a few days. I won't be seeing her again. Nothing suits me better than to leave her alone, so you might have spared yourself the trouble of interfering, my dear Peggy."

She could tell from his tone that he was speaking the truth, but something in his voice, a hint of relief mingled with satisfaction, roused her suspicions.

"If that's all you wanted, I'll push off," he added, and turned to go.

Peggy sprang forward and caught him by the sleeve. "No! Wait," she cried. In the faint remaining daylight which filtered in through the interlacing branches of the spruce-firs overhead, she peered at him, trying to read his face. "You've made her unhappy," she accused him. "Does she think you—you're in love with her?"

"Perhaps she did. People do make mistakes at times, don't they? And she's rather a sweet little thing—"

"You absolute cad and bounder!" Peggy was trembling with rage from head to foot. "So that's what it is! You led her to believe that you love her, the poor silly thing, and now you're through you're just throwing her over."

"Well, Good Lord! You don't expect me to marry the girl, do you?"

"I don't, but perhaps she did!"

"Nonsense. I've had my fun, and presumably she's had hers. Why, she's a servant, a grieve's daughter!"

"You make me feel sick," Peggy said. "I see that it was silly of me to speak to you at all. Please go away quickly, I really can't bear to be near you."

"Oh, can't you? That's a pity, because now I'm going to say a few things. I've listened to you. You can damn' well listen to me for a change."

He thrust his face, distorted with spite and passion, close to hers, and Peggy shrank back against the rough trunk of a fir. Seen in the shadowy dusk he looked barely human. The sombre stillness of the listening wood, where a withered leaf in falling made a noise startlingly loud, was a fit setting for him. It needed little imagination to picture a murder taking place in this secret spot, with Ronald Graham as the murderer.

He laughed harshly as he saw her slight movement of fright and aversion. "Yes, you're afraid of me now!" he said. "Well, you've made me what I am. If that girl is unhappy, it's your fault. *Yours*, do you hear?"

"I think you're mad," said Peggy, and slipping past him, made her way towards the edge of the wood.

He followed her, pouring out a flood of self-excuse, of wild accusations levelled at her.

"Mad? Very likely I am. And who made me mad? You. If you'd treated me better than you did, I wouldn't have looked at Jo-an. But now—whatever happens to her or to me, you can blame yourself for it, because it's all your fault!"

Beyond the last line of trees Peggy stopped, again to face him. She felt bewildered, battered, dirty, as if he had thrown mud at her instead of this torrent of words; but she spoke quite steadily.

"Good-bye, Ronald. When you come to your senses I hope you'll have the decency to be sorry for what you have said."

Then she forgot everything but her horror of him and of the wood, and ran as fast as she could across the open ground between her and the road. A faint afterglow still tinged the western sky, and compared with the wood it was light. As she came through a gap in the hedge, wrenching her clothes free of the thorns and twigs as if they had been Ronald Graham's hands on her, she found herself face to face with Oliver. There was no time to regain her composure, to think of something to say. Oliver, standing there glancing from her troubled face to Ronald Graham's retreating figure and back again to her, loomed large and menacing against the last of the sunset.

Peggy spoke first, making an unsuccessful effort to appear quite at ease. "I didn't expect to meet you," she said.

"No. I should imagine not," he answered with a coldness that dismayed her. "Isn't it—getting a bit late to meet anyone out of doors?"

Extreme weariness sounded in her voice as she said, "It's not so very late. Only just after tea-time."

"That isn't what I meant, and you know it, don't try to hedge," he said sharply. "Do your people know where you are, or—who you've been meeting?"

"No."

"That dirty hound!" he muttered just above his breath. "Why, I thought you hated the sight of him!"

Peggy was too tired to think before she spoke, too overcome by the misfortune of having been seen by Oliver of all people. "It isn't anything to do with you," she said.

"I suppose it isn't. But what about your people?"

"They won't know so long as you don't tell them," said Peggy wearily. "I hope you won't. It would only worry them." She was thinking of Jo-an and Ronald Graham and how the story would upset her parents, but as he had no clue to this it was natural that he should become even colder.

"I certainly shan't. But you'll have to give me your word that there'll be no more of this meeting in woods."

"You needn't bother. He's going away."

"Thank God for that," muttered Oliver.

"It's all very well for *you* to say 'thank God' when you don't know anything about it!" cried Peggy, at the end of her tether and now completely losing her temper. "If you did, you'd—"

"But, Peggy—Peggy!" began Oliver.

But Peggy had fled and was running home with hot tears scalding her cheeks and a hatred of all men burning in her sore heart.

Oliver did not attempt to follow her. "That's the end of that, I suppose," he said, and walked slowly up the road to Easter Hartrigg, his shoulders hunched against the thin rain, his limp more in evidence than it had been for months.

2

Cilly celebrated her sixth birthday in December, and having been rashly offered her own choice of entertainment, promptly demanded "a grown-up tea-party."

Susan, newly returned from her visits, was invited, and so was Oliver; but he would not have gone near the Manse if Cilly had not asked him "most par-tick-you-early" to be present.

As the Squib bore them jerkily over the frost-hardened ruts of the little road to Muirfoot, Oliver said crossly, "This is bound to be about the world's silliest show, Susan, and I don't know why on earth you ever let me in for it."

Though the remark seemed to her both unjust and absurd, Susan said nothing. Oliver in the frame of mind in which she had found him ever since she had come home, was not reasonable, and she only hoped that he would not cast a heavy blight over Cilly's "grown-up party."

"There's eggs for tea!" cried Bun, as the Squib, as unreasonable as her owner, deposited the Parsons early in front of the Manse door.

Peggy, who had come out to greet them, devoted herself to Susan after a cold and hurried "How-d'you-do" to Oliver. "You'll have to eat an egg, too," she said. "Mother told Cilly she could have anything she wanted in reason, and she insisted on the eggs, boiled and with faces drawn on them. She said she'd rather have them than a birthday cake."

"Well, I think I can manage to eat an *egg*," Susan promised. "What a good thing your hens are so well-behaved and obliging, Peggy."

They went into the drawing-room to find Cilly and Bun doing the honours to a group of amused grown-ups. Colin, gurgling with laughter but refusing, to utter a coherent word, flitted from one to another, intent on showing the pocket in his small shirt, a manly feature of which he was overweeningly proud.

Having already heard of the young doctor, Susan was interested to meet Hugh Collier, whom she at once set down as good-looking but somewhat too opinionated. At the moment he was trying to induce Bun to sit on his knee and see what he had in his pocket for her, but Bun would not have it.

"What's in your pocket *should* be for Cilly," she reminded him reprovingly; and as he loosed his hold of her on seeing Peggy, she wriggled away and escaped across the polished floor to Susan.

"Don't you like sitting on knees, Bun?" she asked, laughing a little at young Collier's disgruntled air.

Bun answered superbly: "I don't much care for that sort."

Susan would have liked to ask whether she objected to all knees on principle, but in a few minutes it became quite clear that Bun only disliked these particular knees, or their owner. For Oliver came into the room with Jim, and he had hardly presented Cilly with her gift, a large picture-book, before Bun flew to him and cast her arms about him.

"My dear wee Commander!" she cried loudly. "Sit down and I'll sit on *your* nice knees!"

Oliver rather sheepishly obeyed, and Bun, enthroned, gazed about the room with bland satisfaction.

"I say, Bun, that's a bit steep," said Hugh Collier. "You wouldn't sit on *my* knee."

"I *prefairr* the Commander's," she answered, adding lovingly as she stroked Oliver's tie, "I do like sailors, they're so neat."

"Don't mind Bun, she's only showing off," said Peggy to Hugh Collier. "She isn't old enough to know her own mind." This last with an unkind glance at Oliver, who appeared not to notice it.

It seemed to Susan that there was a certain tension in the atmosphere, and she was relieved when the young hostess said wistfully, "Isn't it nearly time for tea yet?"

The tea-table, hospitably laden with good things, with a comely brown egg, complete with features in Indian ink, at *every* place, reminded Susan of the picture of King Valoroso at breakfast in her old copy of "The Rose and the Ring." Even the noble birthday cake, its six pink and white candles all alight, which should have been the centre of attraction, sank into insignificance, even the festive crackers lost their charm, beside the array of boiled eggs which gave the individual touch to Cilly's party.

Peggy poured out tea at a side-table, assisted by Hugh Collier, whom she appeared to be encouraging as much as she frowned on Oliver. He, his offer to help having been refused, sat down between Bun and Cilly, his look expressing impolite relief, and beheaded their eggs for them.

"Cilly has a distinct flair for entertaining," Susan said to Mrs. Cunningham. "The eggs are a tremendous success."

"Bless their hearts," the fond grandmother replied, beaming on the flushed and somewhat eggy Infantry. "They were so set on having them. It's a mercy the hens are laying well."

Long after the guests had eaten to repletion the birthday cake still remained to be cut and tasted. It was hacked into alarmingly large jagged slices by Cilly, and carried round the table by the minister. No one was allowed to refuse it.

"It's most terribelly unlucky not to eat a bit," said Bun anxiously, watching.

"An' there's things *in* it!" squeaked Cilly. "I do hope I'll get the frippenny bit, I do!"

Susan found a tiny silver ring in her portion; Colin, to his grandmother's horror, almost choked on the "frippenny bit" and Hugh Collier, amid shouts of laughter, unfolded a small scrap of paper to disclose a minute donkey.

"That means you're silly, you know," explained Cilly kindly but unnecessarily.

"Well, you're Cilly too," he said, a little nettled by the renewed outburst of mirth which had greeted her remark.

"I amn't! I *amn't*! Am *not*!" shrieked Cilly furiously. "I'm a different kind of a silly. I'm a Cilly with a C!"

"Now, now." The minister's booming voice—what a blessing that he was accustomed to filling a church with its resonant tones, thought Susan—rose above the clamour of protest and explanation, rapidly approaching the inevitable climax of tears and disgrace. "What about all these crackers I see, eh? Or are they just for ornament and not for pulling at all?"

"Oh, Grandaddy, you *are* a funny one!" cried Bun. The minister and the crackers had saved the situation just in time.

When everyone had been adorned with bead necklaces and ruby glass hearts with brass pins, and grown-ups were peering shamefacedly at each other from below ridiculous hats, and the air was shrill with dreadful whistles, the party proceeded by slow degrees to return to the drawing-room, there to play ah the time-honoured exhausting games which belong to children's parties.

Mrs. Cunningham in her "Sunday dress" with its real lace collar, sat at the piano pounding out reels and jigs, while the guests circled warily round a long line of chairs. Susan was one of the first to fall out, and secretly thanking her lucky star that she had never been good at Musical Chairs, retired to a corner to look on. Presently she was joined by Peggy, who took off her pink paper sun-bonnet and fanned her flushed cheeks with it.

"My *goodness*!" she exclaimed. "Aren't parties tiring, Susan? Just look at those men. They are as much in earnest and as anxious to win as the Infantry—"

"More so," murmured Susan, watching her brother and Hugh Collier creeping round the one remaining chair like two hungry tigers, each with one eye on his rival and the other on the pianist. The music stopped unexpectedly, and Oliver, to the sound of rapturous applause from Bun, threw himself into the long-suffering chair just before the other could reach it.

"I hope it's a strong chair," said Susan.

"Yes. Oh, yes," said Peggy absently, smiling at the discomfited young doctor so sweetly as to make up for his defeat, as was plain from his recovered sprightliness and Oliver's corresponding gloom.

"I don't want to play Blind Man's Buff, I think," Susan said hastily, as an enormous silk handkerchief of rainbow hues was produced by Jim.

"Nor I," whispered Peggy, and they both stole meanly away to the untidy dining-room.

"Could you eat a sandwich, Susan?" she asked hopefully, eyeing the still heaped plates on the table among the wreckage of cracker-papers and crumbs and icing.

"Sorry, Peggy. No can do. But don't let me stop you," said Susan, as she sighed.

"Well, bar the egg and a bit of birthday cake, I didn't have anything, so if you don't mind watching me, I will." And she took three sandwiches of different kinds, put them together, and munched peacefully. Susan lighted a cigarette.

Silence fell, while Susan wondered what had happened to Peggy to lend her this new, rather unhappy assurance of manner, and Peggy tried not to remember the last party at the Manse, when everything had been so different, and she had been friends with Oliver.

"I went up to Reiverslaw to see Mrs. Robertson the day before yesterday," said Susan suddenly. "I was going to ask Jo-an if she would like to come and help Donaldina, as I promised you I would, you remember. Peggy, what has happened to that girl? She looked like a wraith."

All Peggy's artificial brightness fell from her. Her lip quivered childishly. "Oh, Susan, I'm afraid she's very miserable," she began piteously. "Oh, why must everything go wrong? I tried to make it better, and instead I've only muddled it all!"

Susan looked at her gravely. "Can't you untangle it?" she asked very kindly.

"I don't seem able to do anything but go on, and things get worse every day—"

"They'll come right if you give them time," said Susan. By now she was sure that Peggy and Oliver were in love, but she would not interfere. They would not thank her for it later. It would mean that some of the gilt had been taken off the gingerbread, and though the gingerbread was what really mattered, the gilt counted for a good deal, especially with anyone so young as Peggy.

"Don't lose heart, Peggy," she went on. "Have patience and try to be yourself again."

"I sometimes think that if you hadn't been away it would have been all right," said Peggy. "I could have told you. But now—"

"I can't work miracles," said Susan. "Even if I'd been here, do you think it would have made any real difference?"

Loud cries from the drawing-room proclaimed that their absence had been noticed, and they had to return. Susan hoped that Peggy might be a little less disagreeable to Oliver, but when she saw that Hugh Collier remained firmly at her side, while Oliver obstinately devoted himself to Bun and Cilly, she sighed inwardly. Truly, it was impossible to help any pair as difficult as these two.

3

"Old Elliot up at Wanside," Oliver's gout-stricken employer, had imported two experts from Leicestershire to trim his hawthorn hedges, this being an art whose cunning was apparently not properly understood by the native Borderers; and on her brother's invitation Susan walked out one frosty afternoon not long before Christmas to see them at work.

With Tara at her heels she went briskly along the ringing roads towards the march, and met Peggy, for once unaccompanied by her shadow, the young doctor, whose devotion to her must have laid the bulk of his professional duties on his uncle's shoulders.

"I thought I'd come and see you," she said, turning back with Susan. "It's ages since I was at Easter Hartrigg."

"When you have nothing better to do, in fact, you fall back on us," Susan said teasingly for the pleasure of seeing her vivid carnation blush. "You're getting quite terribly like the Miss Pringles, Peggy.

The last time they appeared for tea they took great care to tell me that they had only come because they had been disappointed by someone more exciting, and rather than stay at home they decided to drop in on me."

"A good long drop from Kaleside to Easter Hartrigg," was Peggy's comment. "But it's unfair to compare me with them. You were away for a long time, and I couldn't come then and—and, somehow, lately I seem to have had so little time and so much to do—Oh, there are the hedgers. And isn't that Uncle Jed talking to Oliver?"

She brought out the "Oliver" with a sort of desperate composure, and indeed, Peggy did feel desperate this afternoon. She had made up her mind to try to speak to him, to find out if he really believed that she was in the habit of meeting people like Ronald Graham secretly. If it could not be managed all at once, at least she was determined to pave the way for some future occasion.

Before the two the side of the long ridge beyond Reiverslaw, patterned by variegated fields of brown ploughland, tawny stubble, and the dull green of winter pasture, rose steeply from the march in the hollow, which they were approaching. Wanside, girdled by leafless trees, stood high above its surrounding lands, the Wan burn, pursued its devious course down the hillside and added itself, a natural boundary, to the fence dividing "old Elliot's" property from Reiverslaw. Pigmy figures about a high, overgrown hedge which ran like an enormous black hairy caterpillar up and over the crest of the ridge, spoke to Peggy's quickness of eye. Two stood apart looking on, two moved slowly and steadily along the side of the spreading thorns, their long-handled hedging knives cutting bright arcs through the air, the downward flash followed inevitably by the fall of another branch. Jed Armstrong came to meet them, walking with the short step which always struck Susan as curious in so big a man, and rolling very slightly in his gait, for he had that faint, stiff-legged, attractive swagger common to all men who ride a great deal. Oliver remained beside the hedge. Beyond lifting his disreputable old soft hat, he paid no heed to the new arrivals.

"Hullo, Uncle Jed!" sang out Peggy in her clear, carrying voice. Her eyes shone dangerously, her cheeks were very pink. "Why won't

Oliver deign to come and speak to us? Have you been quarrelling with him?"

It was plain that Oliver had heard, as he was meant to, but his very back, as he stood with shoulders obstinately hunched, and all his attention apparently riveted on the hedgers, spoke eloquently of his determination not to be drawn into conversation by this or any challenge.

"You leave Oliver alone," growled Jed. "He's looking after his own business."

As Peggy, unabashed, made a face at him, he turned to Susan.

"What d'you think of it?" he asked. "These fellows are wonderful at their job. It's a treat to watch them. I only wish our own men could learn it, but it seems to be handed down from generation to generation, and we haven't got the trick of it somehow."

"I know absolutely nothing about it," Susan said truthfully, "but I like to watch them."

There was a fascination about the movements of the two hedgers, so deliberate, so rhythmic in their slow, steady sweep, as the lopped branches fell to the shining blades, and were dragged aside without haste or waste of strength or time. Each man's right hand was protected by a long gauntleted glove of heavy leather against the vicious black spines; drab clothing blended with their surroundings, and a note of bright colour was added by a blue scarf which one wore about his neck. Slowly they moved up the line of shaggy bushes, bending the long, supple boughs as though they were weaving baskets, until the top of the trimmed hedge lay flat and smooth, a strong barrier against marauding cattle or fierce winds.

"That's the way it should be done," said Jed approvingly. Almost unconsciously he and Susan were following the hedgers, while Peggy, careless of his forbidding attitude, remained standing beside Oliver, her hands deep in the pockets of her big coat, chattering to him with apparent ease and friendliness. "They've left the young branches, d'you see, and they'll shoot," went on Jed. "The twigs will grow up straight, and in a few years' time this hedge will look just as it does now where they haven't cut it yet. If you look, you can see the line of the last trimming, down close to the ground."

Susan nodded, absorbed in watching these skilled craftsmen plying their old trade, as though the age of machinery were still a dream of the far future. The cold which nipped savagely at her finger-tips through her lined gloves, could not move her, nor could Tara, sitting patiently and delicately on his tail with the air of a martyr chilled to the bode, and yawning from time to time. The sun, a fiery orange ball, had begun to slip behind the black woods to westward, the sky in the east was turning a cold, clear, unearthly green, and still they looked and the hedgers worked.

"I don't know how I ever imagined the country could be dull," Susan said suddenly. "Town can't show you anything to match this hedging business. I've had the most interesting time of my life since we came here to live."

"Well, of course, there's always something happening. There's no close season in the country," said Jed in the slow, rumbling voice which sounded loud and gruff in a drawing-room, but was tuned to these outdoor scenes. "Ploughing and sowing and harrowing, and then reaping. . . . Beasts to look after, and all the wild life as well. If you care for that sort of thing. Of course, there's nothing like theatres, and so on. I dare say it's that that people miss when they're used to going out at nights."

"Theatres!" said Susan with lofty scorn. "The concerts at Muirfoot and Kaleford are far better fun than any first night I've been to. And as for going out at night, I can go out here, and see the moon and stars moving across the sky, and hear the owls—"

He laughed, though not at all derisively. "You haven't been a year away from town yet, lass. You haven't got over the novelty of all this. It's early days to say you like the country better."

"But *you* prefer it?"

"I was bred to this kind of life. You weren't."

Susan began eagerly to explain how she felt. "It isn't just novelty. Haven't you ever come to a place where you've never been before, and found that you belonged to it? That's what I feel about this part of the country. You know I've been staying with friends in England, ending up in London. I thought it would be heavenly to see Bond Street again, and the Park, the shops, the streets, the lights—everything. Theatres—because I'm not so silly as to suppose that I'd never miss them. Everyone wants bright lights and soft music now and then. I was half-afraid I'd hate to come away. . . . It *was* lovely, and I did enjoy it, for a few days. But something had changed. Not my friends, not town. Me. I couldn't sleep after the quiet nights at Easter Hartrigg; I felt dazed and bewildered. And I got so tired of having people sympathize with me over living buried in the country. I told them until I was hoarse that I loved it, and wasn't buried at all, and wouldn't live in town now for a fortune, but it was so obvious that they didn't believe me. . . . I knew they'd go away saying to each other how Susan Parsons was making the best of a bad job, poor dear, but *did* you see her clothes? And her face, quite weather-beaten. . . . It made me want to scream and throw china about. And then Oliver wrote and told me that the Muirfoot Boy Scouts were having a 'Grand Variety Entertainment.' I suddenly realized that I couldn't bear to miss it, and I packed in a hurry and came home the next day. They all thought I was mad, and I didn't care!"

As she paused, breathless, laughing a little at her own vehemence, Jed said slowly, "Of course, if you feel like that . . . I'm the same myself. In London, even in Edinburgh, I'm all wrong, out of place, boxed up among too many houses and people. But I didn't think it would affect you that way, after being used to it—"

"I suppose," said Susan rather resentfully, "you think I'm 'out of place' here, do you?"

He looked at her, liking the sparkle which the little spirt of temper lent to her gravity. It had always pleased him to be able to bring it into being. But he answered her question quite seriously. "No; you fit it like your hand into that glove of yours. You look like a country-bred woman, and it suits you. But—all your old friends live in town, don't they?"

"I thought so," said Susan. "But when I saw all the people I used to know again, I knew at once that none of them was more than an acquaintance, a nice, usually congenial acquaintance. The ones who came nearest being friends were those who lived in country places themselves and quite understood my longing to get home. And I find there are people here who are more real friends than any of those others. Friendship's a plant of slow growth, and needs country air to make it hardy, I fancy. Forced on too quickly, as it often is in town, it is a sickly hothouse thing, and a breath of cold wind kills it."

Jed, pondered over this excursion into metaphor with knitted brows. "I like that," he said at last. "It's very true. All the same, I would have thought that Crawley was a real friend of yours. You wouldn't call him just an acquaintance, would you?"

"Charles?" she said, and paused. "Charles is different. He's in a class by himself."

"I suppose you saw him in London?"

Susan nodded. "Yes; he's stationed at Chatham, so I saw quite a lot of him."

"He seems a very good fellow," said Jed rather heavily.

"He is. He's a perfect darling, and we've been friends for more years than I'd like to count. I can always talk to Charles—" Susan broke off, the rare flush rising to her face. Suddenly she realized that this afternoon she had been talking to Jed as freely, as easily, as she had ever talked to Charles.

"He's coming to us for Christmas leave," she ended with unusual confusion.

The hedgers had stopped pruning and were drawing the cut branches into a great pile, which they set alight. With a tremendous crackling the flames shot high, devouring the dry wood. Clouds of sparks rose golden against the sky, to die before they fell, and the sunset's conflagration, was put to shame by the glow of the bonfire.

"We'd better be getting back," said Jed slowly, as if he did not want to leave. "Oliver and Peggy have gone long ago."

With a start Susan looked round. The field was empty save for themselves and the two gnome-like figures busy about their blaze. It had turned very cold. An icy little wind was blowing straight from the snow-capped hills, making her shiver. Tara was nowhere to be seen.

"He's made tracks for home, sensible beast," Jed observed. "He knows there's going to be snow."

Even as he spoke, the first few flakes, came drifting eerily, soundlessly, out of a sky grown leaden. Against her will, Susan turned to go, since all her whistling did not bring the black dog bustling into sight. Silently she and Jed made their way across the fields to the road, silently they trudged along it. In a sheltered corner several stacks stood like high, pale, windowless houses, steep-roofed, and as they neared them, the sound of voices came to their ears.

"Who the devil—?" began Jed, taking a hasty stride towards them. Susan laid a hand on his arm, for she thought she recognized one of the voices.

"If it's some damned tramps smoking in among the stacks—" growled Jed, but she shook her head.

"I don't believe they are tramps."

As if to prove the truth of her words, one voice said quite clearly, "But why won't you come to the dance, Oliver? It's sure to be a good one, and you told me you loved dancing."

The deeper reply was lost, then suddenly Peggy said, "Oliver, *please* do. Don't be so—so unreasonable! Oh, well, if you're determined to be horrid—"

"Let's go, quickly," whispered Susan guiltily, and they stole past. From behind one of the stacks Tara appeared, looking utterly bored and disillusioned. On seeing Susan, he bounded joyfully to her side, showing a glint of ivory teeth in a doggish smile.

"H'm," muttered Jed. "I bet he could tell us a thing or two if we could speak the language!"

But as Tara not unnaturally kept his own counsel, they were none the wiser, and Oliver came home so grim and silent that even had she wished, Susan would hardly have dared to question him.

CHAPTER THIRTEEN

1

"Now tell me all the news," commanded Charles, stretching out his long legs towards the fire. "How are my friends, the scandal-mongers, the Misses Pringle?"

Susan was sitting on the window-seat, busily tying up Christmas presents with gay lengths of holly-patterned ribbon. At his question she looked up and laughed a little. "The Misses Pringle are not very pleased with me just now," she said. "In fact, we are hardly on speaking terms."

"That's interesting. Why?" asked Charles, and Oliver also raised his head from the book he was pretending to read.

"I refused to listen to some scandal," said Susan calmly. "And though I didn't tell them what I thought of them, I did just mention that it wasn't a habit of mine to discuss my friends in that fashion."

"Good for you. And is one permitted to ask who the friends in question are?"

"Peggy," answered Susan briefly, and addressed a parcel.

Oliver started, but neither of the others appeared to notice it, and presently Susan said with a sigh of relief, "There, that's all, thank goodness. Now I can settle down and talk with a dear conscience."

"I'm glad to hear it," murmured Charles. "I was beginning to wonder when I was going to get a little attention. Of all the lousy hosts and hostesses—"

"Ungrateful wretch! Aren't we going to take you to a ball-dance?"

"Ah, ha! *That's* better. Tell me about it."

"Well," said Susan, taking her seat on a long fender-stool and stirring the fire to a blaze, "everyone is thrilled about it, even the Pringles, and they have only one fault to find. They think it ought to be fancy dress—"

"My God!" breathed Oliver, roused at last. "The Pringles in fancy dress! Wouldn't you be willing to lay any money that they'd appear as Helen of Troy and Cleopatterer—"

"Complete with asp," added Charles.

"Madame Recamier would do nicely for Bell," said Susan cattily. "She has told me more than once that she'd have been in her element conducting a salon."

"I expect, you know, really, the old trout would have gone as the Three Graces." This was Charles.

Oliver groaned hollowly. "Well, you'll be spared that grisly spectacle, at least," he said.

"'You?'" the others both repeated. "Don't you mean 'we?'"

"Oh, no. I'm not going," he said airily. "Jed and I are going to have a quiet evening at Reiverslaw."

"Well," said Charles when he had recovered his breath, "little did I think that the day would dawn when *you'd* deliberately stay away from a dance, Noll."

"It's for a good cause, Oliver," urged his sister. "The Abbeyshiels Cottage Hospital extension. I do think you ought to patronize it, and you one of the local lairds too. Besides, I've bought your ticket, and everyone knows you're a dancing man."

"My dancing days are over," said Oliver, not without a certain gloomy pleasure.

"What a great pity we have no Marines here," sighed Charles.

"Marines?" echoed Susan.

"Yes; for Oliver to tell his pretty little fairy-tale to, my love," answered Charles.

He rose to his feet, strolled across the room, and sat down before the piano, where he proceeded to strike several chords with more vigour than precision. When he had finally disentangled those he required from the general tumult, he raised his voice, a pleasant though untrained baritone, and assuming a manly, square-shouldered attitude, sang.

> "Shall I, wasting in despair,
> Die because a woman's fair?
> Or make pale my cheeks with care
> Because another's ro-osy are?"

"You are the world's biggest fool, Charles," said Oliver, but he winced and coloured slightly in spite of his carefully dispassionate tone.

Charles, unheeding, finished the verse *con brio*.

Susan had half-expected something of this sort to happen, and Oliver's refusal to attend the charity dance in the Abbeyshiels Corn Exchange did not really surprise her. Peggy was going, Hugh Collier, of course, would be there; it seemed to his sister preferable that Oliver should invite comment by staying at home, rather than holding up the wall and looking daggers at Peggy while she danced, for all the local world to see.

But Charles did not share this opinion. "I never heard such tripe in my life, Susan darling," he said elegantly. "Of course Oliver must go, and dance with everyone."

Susan never knew, though she could guess, the arguments he used to persuade her brother, and on the evening of the dance Oliver duly appeared in tails and a white tie, looking handsome and gloomy, and overflowing at intervals with a haggard gaiety which she found rather distressing.

He did dance with everyone, with one notable exception—Peggy was never his partner. In spite of his lame leg and his total ignorance of the intricacies of the dance, he insisted on taking part in the Eightsome Reel.

"A scandalous performance, I call it," murmured Charles who, with Susan, had discreetly elected to look on. They gazed, appalled, at Oliver as he leapt and pranced like a mountain goat in the middle of the ring, his coat-tails flying. Miss Cissie Pringle, attired in a profusion of somewhat draggled tulle flounces in a girlish shade of blue, had taken the floor with him and was obviously entranced by his activity and verve.

Miss Pringle, herself temporarily partnerless, had come to sit beside Susan and Charles, and now said in her most condescending tones, "Of course, the Eightsome Reel is a mere *romp*."

"Have you ever," said Charles languidly, "been to any of the Northern Meeting balls, Miss Pringle? No? I can assure you that it is not looked upon as a mere romp in Inverness."

Routed, Miss Pringle took refuge in commenting unfavourably on the dresses and deportment of various dancers; but Susan was sure that she had stored up Charles's remark for future use, this being an annoying habit to which she was greatly addicted.

Later in the evening they were rewarded by hearing the well-known voice addressing Jim Cunningham as, flushed and breathless after a second reel, he paused close by her, his partner on his arm. "Of course, the reel is not *danced* here," Miss Pringle was saying. "Now, at the Northern Meeting balls, my dear Jim . . ."

Susan caught Charles's eye, and hurriedly murmuring, "I think I should like some coffee," led him away to a secluded corner where they could loose the demon of laughter which had attacked them both.

"The old girl's an absolute fizzer, isn't she?" said Charles with unfeigned admiration.

Though she spared time for a little silent sympathy for Oliver, forced to see Peggy dancing in the close embrace of young Collier, Susan found herself heartily enjoying the ball. Her fears that she might not know enough people were rendered groundless by the discovery of several friends, among them a rear-admiral, recently retired, whom she had known some years before as a captain, and his wife.

"You *know* the Heriots?" cried the second Miss Pringle, pouncing on her in the ladies' cloakroom, a drear apartment, sole haven of luckless wall-flowers, to which Susan had retired for the purpose of adding a few necessary repairs to her hair and complexion.

"Why, yes. We do."

"But he's Lord Soutra's brother, his *heir*!" she cried breathlessly.

"So I have heard."

"And his wife is a daughter of the Earl of Sark!"

"Is she? I'd forgotten," Susan said with truth.

"Why did you never tell us that you knew them?" This was uttered so accusingly that Susan felt she must defend herself.

"Really, Miss Jelly, I never thought about it. After all, they haven't been here until quite recently. In fact, it was only when I met them again to-night, and they told me they were coming to live near here, that I remembered their connection with Lord Soutra."

"Indeed?" she said in accents of outraged incredulity. "But perhaps you didn't know them so *very* well?"

"It depends on what you call 'very well,'" said Susan, losing patience. "I've stayed with Lady Evelyn at Wei-hai-wei, when Oliver was on the China station. Her husband was in command of the ship Oliver was in—"

"Oh, in *China*!" exclaimed Miss Jelly, as if any extraordinary happening might come to pass in the Far East. "Here, of course, they will be in the hunting set. Lord Soutra and all the County belong to it."

"Well, we can't afford to hunt even if we wanted to, and I am quite pleased with the 'set' we are in," said Susan shortly. "I think. I hear the next dance beginning. I must go."

"Are you *dancing*?" asked Miss Jelly with quite unwarrantable surprise. "Who is your partner?"

Susan felt that she deserved a stab, however tiny, and dealt it as they left the cloakroom.

"With Admiral Heriot," she said.

In the passage leading to the ballroom they—for Miss Jelly now clung to Susan like a burr—found a small group conversing with the animation of easy intimacy. Susan recognized the sparkle of Lady

Evelyn Heriot's diamonds, the gay and tuneful ring of her pretty voice. As always, she had several men about her, among them Oliver, Charles, and the Admiral, the last-named her most devoted admirer.

"Susan," she cried, "do come and reminisce with us. Your brother has just been reminding me of those days of the China station—"

"It's a far cry from Abbeyshiels to Hong-Kong and Wei-hai," said the Admiral. "But I seem to remember, young woman, that you were in the habit of keeping your partners waiting even then."

Behind her, Miss Jelly drew a breath of amazement so deep that it would not have surprised Susan had she been sucked up by it as by a vacuum-cleaner.

"I'm so sorry!" she said, laughing.

"Yes, be an angel and take Robbie away and dance with him," said Lady Evelyn. "You know how cross he is, poor darling, if he's done out of even a tiny bit of a dance with a partner he likes. But first—you know we're going to settle down at King's Inch? Robbie's brother is giving us the Dower House to live in, and we expect to be there for a good part of the year. Lovely for the children. I wanted to ask if you'll all three come to luncheon one day next week? Don't let us waste time in calling on each other like mere acquaintances—"

"Thank you," said Susan. "We'd all love to come."

The Admiral muttered impatiently, and his wife said at once, "You and Robbie go and dance. Oliver can fix a day with me, can't he?" Lady Evelyn waved them away. "I'm going to sit out with these nice people and hear all their news. You know how I adore young men."

Thus dismissed, "Robbie" and Susan obediently continued on their way towards the ballroom. As they swung into the dance: "Who was the old girl starin' at us as if she was a hungry cat and we were a bowl of goldfish?" demanded the Admiral. "Expected to hear her mew any minute, on my word I did!" Poor Miss Jelly. Even as they revolved rapidly, for it was a waltz and the Admiral believed in that particularly breathless but exhilarating form of it known to him as "the good old-fashioned valse," Susan could see her imparting her precious information to her eldest sister.

2

The crowd was beginning to thin, but among those who remained were the three Misses Pringle, whose custom it was to drink the cup of pleasure dry, and linger until the exhausted band had gratefully brayed out the last notes of "God Save the King."

"I say, our stock's soaring," said Oliver as brother and sister strolled up and down a dimly lighted passage between dances. "At least mine is. I don't know if you're forgiven yet, but old Belly has invited Charles and me—been most pressing about it—to shoot the rabbits at Kaleside, to come over for the day and not to bother to bring sandwiches, because they'll be delighted to give us lunch. What's the reason for this overwhelming hospitality all of a sudden-like?"

"Perhaps she thinks you'll do nicely for Cissie," Susan suggested lightly, and then bit her lip. Oliver was so composed, so like his usual self, that for the moment she had forgotten his feelings about Peggy, whose engagement to Hugh Collier was confidently expected by some people to come about by the time the dance ended.

Oliver took the remark very calmly. "Thanks awfully," he said, even more lightly. "Why not for Jelly, or even for herself? She can't be *more* than thirty years older than me—"

"One saucer of skim for the gentleman. Who said that women were the catty sex?"

"Well, hang it all, Sue, she'll never see sixty again, I'm sure—" he broke off with a guilty start as the subject, of his calculations spoke close behind him.

"Ah, *here* you are!" Miss Pringle spoke briskly, her hand resting fondly on Charles's arm, the rigidity of this member not repelling her in the least. Had not the hand of an Earl's daughter also lain there this evening? "Now, I've thought of such a dee-lightful plan, dear Miss Parsons. This will be your first New Year in Scotland, so let us make it a *really* Scottish one! You must all three come over to us at Kaleside on Hogmanay, and we'll see the New Year in together. Positively I *insist!*"

"Oh—oh, thank you so much," gasped Susan, feeling as though a pistol had been presented at her head, and quite unable to think up a respectable excuse for refusing. "I—we—that is—"

"Frightfully good of you, Miss Pringle," broke in Oliver with complete sang-froid. "And there's nothing we should have liked better, but we've already accepted an invitation for—Hogmanay, d'you call it?"

"Oh, what a pity! You naughty people are *always* engaged!" cried Miss Pringle with grim playfulness. "I suppose you are going to the Soutras, at King's Inch?"

"We don't know Lord Soutra," said Oliver blandly. "No; it's to Reiverslaw—"

"But you know Lord Soutra's brother, Admiral Heriot. *Such* a charming man. Such an asset to the neighbourhood, don't you think? His father, old Lord Soutra, and my own father, were great friends, real old cronies."

"What exactly is a crony?" asked Charles in his dove-like party voice, so different from the hearty bellow which he employed among his intimates. "It always sounds to me like a golf-club."

Nothing they could say or do annoyed Miss Pringle that evening. Susan supposed that they must shine with reflected glory shed by the Heriots on all their acquaintances; all offences of the past had been forgiven, if not forgotten, even her own quite recent refusal to listen to gossip about Peggy. For Miss Pringle now actually produced a sound approximating to a giggle as she replied. "How *very* amusing of you, Commander Crawley. I must tell Jelly and Cissie; they *will* enjoy that. And you know the Admiral, too, *don't* you?"

"An old shipmate of mine," said Charles carelessly. "He was our skipper in China."

Miss Cissie suddenly made a fluttering appearance, looking like a rather elderly butterfly. "Oh, Bell, I've lost my dear little evening-bag. That sweet gold bead one, you know. I've looked everywhere, except just behind that screen. Perhaps it's there—"

The screen to which she pointed concealed what Oliver had learned from Jim Cunningham to call a "sit-ootery," and was placed discreetly across a corner of the passage. Behind it, Susan knew, for she had spent a few cooling minutes there with Charles earlier in the evening, a large potted palm acted as chaperone to two well-cushioned chairs. It did not seem possible that any of Miss Cissie's partners would have led her to this secluded bower, but she ran girlishly towards it, pulled aside the screen, and exposed to the public gaze Peggy in the act of being well and truly kissed by young Hugh Collier.

While everyone paused, petrified, uncertain what to do or say, Miss Pringle, whose little gimlet eyes had not missed a detail of the scene, remarked acidly, "Dear me, Peggy. Surely I am not mistaken in supposing that this is an occasion for congratulations?"

"For God's sake let's get out of this!" said Oliver hoarsely in his sister's ear, and she turned away with him, sick at heart for his sake. Charles, whom Miss Pringle would have retained by her clutch on his arm, shook her off as though her fingers stung him, and raced after his friends.

"Strewth!" he ejaculated faintly as he reached Susan's side. "Talk about a close-up!"

Oliver merely uttered a savage laugh.

3

In his character of laird, Oliver had been eager ever since he came to Easter Hartrigg to give some sort of party to which all his neighbours could be invited; and though Susan, urged by prudence, had restrained any prodigal scattering of his "twenty pence," she agreed with him that Christmas ought not to pass without a celebration.

"They'll keep New Year for themselves," he had said. "It's their own day. But we, as poor ignorant English bodies, will be forgiven if we have our show at Christmas."

So it was arranged that there should be a dance two days before Christmas in the old barn, which had been empty for many years, while the youngest generation were to have a Christmas tree on the afternoon of Boxing Day.

"Charles dear," said Susan gratefully, "if it hadn't been for you and Mr. Woolworth I'd have given it all up. Oliver has been quite useless since the dance at Abbeyshiels, and apart from ordering drink for the men, has done nothing about the preparations. He seems to have lost all interest in his parties."

"It's hardly to be wondered at," said Charles. "Never mind, honey, we'll do it between us, and make a damn' good show of it too, see if we don't!"

Susan smiled down at him from the top of a step-ladder. There was something very heartening about Charles....

They were alone in the big barn, where the faint sweet smell of long-vanished hay still strove with the stronger resinous scent of fir branches. Paper and tinsel streamers, gaudy exotic flowers, were strung from the beams. The Christmas tree, a sturdy young spruce-fir, stood in a far corner, decked with enticing toys, balls of silver and gold and green glass, strings of glittering tinsel.

"What now?" asked Charles.

"Only the high leather screen to put round the tree to hide it," said Susan indistinctly, for she was wrestling with a refractory spray of holly, and held a piece of twine between her teeth.

"Good work. We're done, then. Come down off that ladder, Susan. I've got it all right."

Susan thankfully descended. "I feel that I deserve tea after this," she said.

"Tea? I want beer, buckets of beer—"

"Beer's fattening. You'd much better have tea."

"The British workman," said Charles firmly, "must have his beer. Or wot abaht a tot o' rum, duckie?"

"There's no rum. All there was has gone into the plum-puddings; but come along and you shall have your beer."

They lingered, however, in the doorway, to cast a last look of proud achievement over the decorated barn, transformed by the green of laurel and fir, the red of holly berries, the brilliant tinsel and paper flowers. Above the door hung an enormous bunch of mistletoe, and Charles, catching Susan round the waist as she stood unwarily below it, kissed her heartily, to the open delight of Jems, who happened to be passing on his homeward way.

"Charles! Aren't you ashamed of yourself?" asked Susan severely, disengaging herself with decision from his hold.

"Not a bit. Why should I be? It's a charming old custom, an' if you look at me like that I swear I'll do it again."

"Indeed you won't. Once is more than enough. As it is, I expect Jems has fled home at top speed to broadcast what he saw all over Muirfoot."

Charles sighed. "The worst disadvantage of the feudal life you're living, darling, is that all your affairs are of such overpowering interest to your neighbours. Now in town, if I'd kissed you in the middle of Oxford Street, do you suppose anyone'd have cared, if they'd even noticed it? Not a bit. At the worst they'd have thought we were acting for the talkies. And the moral of that is—"

"Reserve these evidences of your affection for Oxford Street!" Susan said laughing.

"No. Marry me and come back to your own sort of life!" he answered eagerly.

"What? And desert Oliver when he is so miserable, and leave him forlorn? It can't be done, Charles dear. You know I said that we couldn't even begin to discuss our own affair as long as he is dependent on me to look after him."

"But damn it all, Susan, this is fantastic. Am I not to be allowed to marry because Oliver doesn't want to?"

"Poor old boy," said Susan. "It *does* seem a shame!" Charles remained serious. "If Oliver fixes things up with Peggy, will you consider yourself engaged to me?" he demanded, and added, "It'll be a short engagement, too, if I've any say in the matter!"

"Well, yes. I will. . . . If you are quite sure you really want to marry me," said Susan. "Oh, I know you are fond of me, my dear! If it comes to that, I'm fond of you. But—somehow, I don't believe it will break your heart if you *don't* marry me."

"I never said it would. My heart's pretty tough. But you're so dashed cold-blooded about it all," he grumbled.

"It's because I've been caught once before," Susan said, serious herself now. "I don't want to make a mess of things this time, Charles."

"We won't make a mess of things, you'll see. We always get on well together. Why shouldn't we make a good show of marriage, Susan darling?"

"All right." Susan yielded suddenly and charmingly. "You're probably right. I leave it to you, partner—no, you are *not* to kiss me. We aren't engaged—yet!"

"I believe you're half afraid of being kissed!"

"I don't want to be swep' off me feet," said Susan. And in spite of his muttered, "That's what you need!" she remained firm on this point.

By the time they had reached the house, Charles was gay again, and full of plans for throwing Oliver and Peggy into each other's arms by main force if need be, at the dance in the barn the following evening.

A note lay on the oak chest in the hall, addressed to Susan. She tore it open and read it quickly.

"Bad luck, Charles," she said ruefully. "You won't be able to do any match-making to-morrow evening. This is from Peggy, to say she isn't feeling very fit, and won't be able to come to the dance. Poor Oliver!"

"Poor me!" was Charles's gloomy answer.

4

The dance at Easter Hartrigg was in full swing. An exceedingly refined young lady from Abbeyshiels presided at the piano, her abnormal agility of finger only equalled by the strenuous exertions of the dancers, whose feet twinkled like those of Squirrel Nutkin. Beside her a pale young man, introduced with a coy flourish as "my fee-*ong*-say" sawed perseveringly at his fiddle. Oliver and Charles were doing their duty nobly among the ploughmen's wives and daughters from Reiverslaw and Wanside, and skirls of delighted laughter rang from end to end of the barn, drowning even the stentorian bellow in which the Master of Ceremonies, a burly hind from Reiverslaw, announced the dances. Susan found it pleasant to watch the honest enjoyment of the guests, the hearty appetite with which they attacked the refreshments provided for them. Only the pianist asserted her gentility by sitting apart beside her "fee-*ong*-say" and drinking horribly strong tea with such an elegant quirking of fingers that it caused her hostess to marvel how she could hold her cup at all. She further showed her refinement by refusing almost all nourishment, and nibbling at what she did deign to accept with an air of faint distaste which enraged Donaldina.

"Eh, I could murrder yon Jessie Watson!" she hissed in Susan's ear, her cook's pride touched on a tender spot. "Luikin' at her guid food as if it wad pushion her!"

"I very much hope you won't, Donaldina," said Susan anxiously. "For she plays exceedingly well, and we can't do without her."

"Ou, I'll no' meddle her," she replied reassuringly. "I wadna touch her wi' the tongs. Thae Watsons are a' the same. There's her younger sister that's comin' oot as a dancin'-teacher, fancies hersel' a Paloovia, or ane o' them. She's aye flitterin' aboot on her taes. An' for Jessie, she'll mebbe can play the piano, but whit ca' has she tae be that proud? Her an' her fee-*ong*-say!"

During a set of Quadrilles, Susan wandered out by herself. The merry strains of the music, the tap and shuffle of dancing feet, broke the utter stillness of the frost-bound countryside. Out of a deep blue sky a wonderful bright star shone in the East to remind the world of an Eve when shepherds watched their flocks in other fields near Bethlehem.

"I wonder what Peggy's doing now?" thought Susan. "I wish she had come—"

Peggy, in her bedroom at the Manse, was wishing the same thing. Perhaps they would think that she was sulking, when her real reason for staying away was just that she couldn't bear to meet Oliver's cold and unfriendly eyes.

She sighed and turned restlessly in her small bed. It had been rather a disturbing evening, and not only because one half of her had wanted to go to Easter Hartrigg. While the Infantry had been going to bed, Bun had said suddenly, "Colin saw Jo-an to-night!"

"What do you mean, Bun?" Peggy was surprised. "Was she—was Jo-an here? I didn't know. Perhaps she came to see Agnes."

"No. She didn't come in. Colin saw her looking in at the window when we were playing in the study after tea."

"Do you think he really saw her, Bun dear? Colin isn't always very sure of what he's saying, he's so little—"

"Oh, yes. He saw Jo-an." Bun was calmly confident.

And Colin, bouncing up and down in his cot, primrose curls rampant above his rosy face, cried quite distinctly: "Jo! Jo! Wan' Jo!"

"Peggy," Bun said softly. "Why did Jo-an go away? Was she naughty? She cried so—"

Peggy's heart had smitten her. She had not seen Jo-an for weeks, had not even thought about her. Soberly she answered her niece. "No, Bun. Jo-an wasn't naughty. She went away of her own accord. I think perhaps she didn't know herself what she wanted."

"*I* know!" Cilly piped. "Like me when I'm bo'ed."

Turning about and trying to cool her hot cheeks on the pillow, Peggy decided that she must go up to Reiverslaw the next day and see Jo-an. Probably she was being ridiculous; probably Jo-an was dancing gaily in the barn at Easter Hartrigg even now, her dark red hair flaming, her small secret face alight; but all the same, for her own satisfaction, Peggy knew that she would have to see her.

5

"You don't know where she is?" Peggy faltered, her cheeks paling a little.

Mrs. Robertson shook her grey head. She was quite impassive, her lined brown face showed neither disquiet nor sorrow, but her hands plucked nervously at the apron of sacking which protected her black skirt.

"She went oot i' the efternune, an' never cam' hame," she said in a dull toneless voice. "Robertson's been seekin' her a' day."

"Do you know of anywhere she might go?" asked Peggy, who felt singularly helpless.

"Na, Miss Cunningham. There's nae place she wad gang. Puir lassie. She's licht like her mither was."

"Her mother—?"

"Ay. Did ye no'ken? Ye'd be ower young, maybe." Mrs. Robertson was mechanically smoothing her rough apron. "Jo-an's ma grand-dochter, ma puir Jean's lass. A love-bairn, as some wad say, though it's a queer kin' o' love, I'm thinkin', that . . . Aweel, dinna fash yersel', Miss Peggy. Ye've a kind hert, I ken, but ye canna bear ither fowks' troubles."

"I'll look for her, anyhow, Mrs. Robertson," said Peggy, her eyes filling. This uncomplaining grief caught at her throat. "You don't think we ought to tell the policeman?"

"I doot we'll need tae, if we get nae word or nicht. But—"

"We must try to find her ourselves without having a fuss," Peggy said quickly, understanding the gleam of fierce protective feeling which lighted a spark in the old woman's eyes. "Does Mr. Armstrong know?"

"Ay, the Maister kens. He's been seekin' her himsel'. He minds Jean, ye ken—"

"Then I'll go. We'll find her yet, Mrs. Robertson." Peggy spoke confidently, but she felt rather helpless and very much afraid. Unable to say more, she turned and walked quickly down the road which would take her to Muirfoot.

The afternoon was in time with her mood. Still, grey and cold, the country seemed so bound in frost that it could never quicken to life again. The fields were colourless, the woods bleakly dark. The woods ... Peggy drew a sharp breath, her eyes looked for that tangled mass of firs, beeches and oaks which lay like a blot along the bottom of the valley, the haunted wood. Suddenly she knew where to look for Jo-an, and her pace quickened until she was almost running. She passed the road leading to Easter Hartrigg without a glance or even a thought, and plunged into the grassy cart-track which was her quickest way to Muirfoot and skirted the haunted wood. The sound of a car approaching hardly roused her, though cars seldom used the rough road over which she was stumbling. Only when it stopped and a voice called to her by name did she stop and look up.

"Oliver!" she cried, forgetting everything except her immediate need. "Will you come with me? Will you help me?"

She did not know that her eyes blazed dark and wild out of her white face, nor how urgent her cry had been. Oliver was out of the Squib and beside her in an instant.

"Help you? Of course," he said simply. "I'll turn the car first—"

Peggy gulped down a sob as he managed to get the Squib round, heedless of scratches the thorn bushes made on his precious paintwork. A second sob caught her unawares as she took her place in the battered little car.

"Where to?" demanded Oliver, putting his foot on the accelerator.

"Stop beside the wood."

He shot her a quick glance, and then she noticed how haggard and care-worn he looked; but she could not say anything more. In silence they bumped down the steep hill, in silence Oliver stopped the car again when they reached the wood.

"Do—do you want me to come?" he muttered, as she sprang out. He had not moved from his seat, his hands were clenched on the wheel.

"Yes, of course—of course!" cried Peggy impatiently. Already she was half-way through a gap in the hedge, and by the time he had followed, was speeding over the narrow strip of open ground towards the trees.

Oliver asked no questions even of himself. Peggy was in trouble and needed him, that was enough. He set his teeth grimly as his lame leg resented the pace to which he forced it, and overtook her before she had gone more than fifty yards.

"We must look every inch," said Peggy in the low voice which the darkness of the solemn fir-trees seemed to make necessary. "If you'll go one way, I'll—"

"What are we looking for?" Oliver's own voice was sunk to a whisper.

"Jo-an, of course...."

It was Peggy who found her beneath a twisted beech. The cold earth on which she lay seemed hardly colder than her hand or her pallid face. Oliver, hastening up in answer to Peggy's cry, looked from the unconscious figure on the ground to the girl kneeling beside her. The navy-blue beret had fallen from Jo-an's flaming hair, but she still wore a dark blue coat like Peggy's; and a navy-blue beret covered Peggy's head. Oliver knew now, and cursed himself for having been a fool. Of course it had been the nurse he had seen: and if Peggy had been there that one time, she had probably good cause for meeting Ronald Graham. Men's gossip, always more direct than women's, had mentioned him in connection with pretty Jo-an, and Oliver felt bitterly that he ought to have known. No wonder Peggy had turned from him to that damned Collier.... Her cry of distress brought him back to the present.

"Oliver! Is she—is she *dead*?"

He lifted one of the limp hands, felt a very faint fluttering pulse, and said, "No. But she's pretty far gone. We'll have to get her to the car somehow, and take her home as fast as we can."

Small and slight though Jo-an was, her dead weight was no light burden, and Oliver sometimes wondered afterwards how, hampered by his leg, he had ever managed to struggle across from the wood to the road. Only stark necessity and Peggy's utter trust in his ability made him equal to it, and even so, he was hardly able to get the unconscious girl into the car.

"We ought to have rugs," he muttered, but Peggy was dragging off her heavy coat and wrapping it round Jo-an. When he would have protested: "Oh, never mind about me!" she cried. "It is Jo-an who matters now!"

"But I do mind about you," he retorted, and his tone, even at that moment, made Peggy's heart jump. "You'll put on my Burberry. Don't waste time in arguing, but put it on, and get in beside her. It'll be a tight fit, but you'll have to hold her steady."

The short winter day was over, the sun had sunk out of sight and a few stars were beginning to glimmer in the darkening sky as they drove up the hill to Reiverslaw. To Peggy, tired and overwrought, everything after that seemed to be happening in some sort of long-drawn out dream. She helped Mrs. Robertson to put Jo-an to bed while Oliver went to ring up the doctor. Ages passed, during which she sat beside the unconscious Jo-an, holding Mrs. Robertson's trembling hand in a warm clasp. Then the doctor—old Dr. Scott, not his nephew, arrived, and Oliver insisted that she must go home, she could do no more now, and he was waiting to drive her in the Squib.

Once out in the cold night things were better. Peggy was young enough to be confident that now Jo-an had been found and was safely at home with the doctor there, she was bound to be all right. Oliver, who had seen death often enough to recognize it, had no intention of disillusioning her. Poor child, she had gone through a good deal, and had held up bravely. No need to trouble her, she would hear soon enough about Jo-an if his fears were realized.

It was Christmas Eve, too, the season of peace and goodwill. . . .

Peggy, her eyes on the brilliant star now glowing in the east, wondering if in the well-filled cattle sheds the patient bullocks would speak with human tongues at midnight, as legend said they did, was startled by hearing him say:

"I—I've never congratulated you yet, Peggy. You must be thinking me a mannerless brute."

"Congratulated me? What about?"

"Well," Oliver floundered on. "I believe the proper thing to do is to wish *you* joy, and congratulate Hugh Collier. I do, with all my heart—"

They were almost at the Manse gate. "Do you mean," said Peggy rather breathlessly, "that because you saw Hugh kiss me, you think we're engaged?"

"Yes."

The Squib was slowing up. Peggy seized the door handle, ready to jump as soon as she had said what she wanted to.

"Does it always follow, Oliver, that if a man k-kisses a girl they're bound to be engaged?"

"It needn't," said Oliver hoarsely.

"Well, then—" Peggy sprang from the car and dashed for the gate. There she paused. "You—you kissed me yourself, once, Oliver. . . . Well, then—*silly* Oliver!"

She was gone. He could hear her running up the frosty drive and he knew it was useless to think of overtaking her. "Peggy! Peggy!" he called.

A faint laugh answered him, and for a second he could see her standing against the lighted oblong of the open door.

"Good night, Oliver! I'll see you to-morrow at church!"

The door banged. Oliver sat quite still for a little, then he solemnly took off his hat. "Here's a happy Christmas to us both!" he said.

CHAPTER FOURTEEN

1

ON CHRISTMAS morning the one bell above the little parish kirk of Muirfoot summoned the people to church, where they sang the old, well-known hymns with a heartiness which prevented them, for once, from seeming hackneyed; and Mr. Cunningham's short sermon on "Goodwill," spoken from his kindly heart in homely rugged accents, sent the congregation out into the clean cold air full of brotherly love. Greetings were exchanged in softened voices at the kirk-gate, with the green mounds and staggering headstones as a reminder of those others who in past years had spoken the same "Merry Christmas" to their friends now resting beside them. Even the noses of the three Misses Pringle seemed less inquisitive than usual, their eyes not quite so sharp. And Peggy, coming up to the Easter Hartrigg party, her rosy face smiling above the fur collar of her new winter coat, her cornflower blue eyes full of a new gravity, put her hand into Oliver's, silently, but with a look which said everything. There on the path, surrounded by the homeward-bound churchgoers, Peggy and Oliver plighted their troth without a spoken word, and Susan, with a pang which she could not suppress, guessed it. Rather soberly she and Charles walked towards the Squib. . . .

On reaching Easter Hartrigg, they found that the post had made a belated arrival, and took up their letters. Among the pile of Christmas cards from people to whom she had forgotten to send similar tokens of friendship, Susan discovered a note from Lady Evelyn Heriot and ripped it open.

"This is to remind us that we are to dine at the Dower House, and to ask us if the day after to-morrow will do," she said. "Will you find the telegraph forms, Oliver? I'll send a wire—"

Oliver, rummaging in the bureau pigeon-holes, was heard to mutter indistinctly that he might walk down to Muirfoot after luncheon and send it off. Susan opened her mouth to tell him that this would be unnecessary, since Jems could go on his bicycle, but fortunately remembered in time that Muirfoot held an attraction for her brother more potent than the ginger beer and kola with which Jems slaked his thirst whenever an errand took him to the post office.

"Thank you, Oliver," she said. "That will be kind of you. Oh, and by the way, while you're down there, you might call at the Manse and remind the Cunninghams to have the Infantry here at three o'clock to-morrow—for the Christmas tree, you know."

"I could do that, yes," said Oliver, quite as though he would not otherwise set foot within the Manse gate. Susan did not so much as smile, but Charles was not so considerate, and his peals of mirth rang through the sitting-room.

"Is there a joke?" asked Oliver in an austere and stately manner, at which the graceless Charles, incoherently mumbling something about ostriches and sand, once more gave himself up to noisy merriment.

The heavy midday meal of turkey and plum-pudding sacred to the day having been eaten, Oliver departed for Muirfoot, while Susan, determined to walk off the effects, took a stout stick, and with Tara beside her, left the house also. Charles, announcing that he felt like a boa-constrictor after its monthly feed, laid himself down full-length on a sofa, and all her blandishments did not avail to move him.

"Leave me," he said faintly. "I would be alone. Perchance slumber may restore me, but to walk would be fatal to one in my present delicate condition."

"A walk would do you all the good in the world," said Susan, and poked at him with her stick.

Tara, full of goodwill and turkey scraps, and seeing in the recumbent figure a fit object for affectionate demonstration, placed his large fore-paws firmly on Charles's defenceless body, and fell to licking his face lavishly.

"Ugh! Ugh!" gasped Charles, vainly trying to ward off these caresses. "Are you aware, Susan darling, that your mammoth is grinding my stomach to pulp? Call him off, or I won't be answerable for the consequences. Yes, Tara, old man, I know you mean well, and it's frightfully generous of you to give me a whiff of your turkey, but don't let me deprive you of it. I mean, I had turkey myself. You're standing on it now—"

Weak with laughter, Susan succeeded in hauling Tara off, and they went out together, leaving Charles to rearrange himself in a nest of cushions.

The air was sharp, but the sun shone with defiant splendour, as though to blazon the fact that the shortest day was past, and the season approaching when he would rule the heaven for about seventeen hours out of each twenty-four. The country was bathed in clear pale light, the hills under their cover of snow gleamed whitely, almost hurting the eyes by their chill purity; every distant cottage, every haystack, could be seen as distinctly as through a telescope. Trees, their exquisite outlines no longer hidden by disguising leaves, held out bare branches, each smallest twig etched in lovely perfection against the far cold blue; and rooks, cawing gravely, flapped their way, a sober frieze, across the open spaces of the sky, their black wings shimmering where they caught the light. A hardy starling, that nefarious but diverting mimic, perched high in an old ash-tree beside the road and amused himself by piping selections from an apparently inexhaustible repertoire. Curlew, plover, blackbird, he copied faultlessly, while Susan stood listening below. Then he gave an admirable imitation of a self-satisfied rooster hailing the dawn, and even a few bars of "Braw, braw lads," an air which he must often have heard some ploughman whistle as he turned up the rich red soil. At the end of the performance Susan could not resist clapping, whereupon, with a sudden affectation of startled modesty the small comedian flew away, leaving her laughing.

The sight of a stalwart figure striding over the bare fields towards Reiverslaw caught her eye. Unseen by him, Susan watched Jed Armstrong as he walked his land, or stood to let the black cattle gather about him unafraid, even shouldering each other aside in order to approach him. He was going back to his lonely house, to spend Christmas day with only a wireless set to keep him company. Susan shook the thought from her. After all, he would probably have Mrs. Holden with him by next Christmas, no longer Mrs. Holden, but Mrs. Armstrong. . . . As if she found the idea vaguely displeasing, Susan frowned, and turned towards Easter Hartrigg, where Charles, recovered, would be waiting for her.

2

"Never, again!" said Oliver with a gusty sigh of relief, as he tore off the red dressing-gown (borrowed from Mrs. Cunningham for the occasion) and the voluminous cotton-wool beard and mustachios in which he had enacted Santa Claus at the children's Christmas tree party. "Never again! For two blistering hours I've played the goat, made idiotic jokes, and handed out presents by the hundredweight. I calculate that I've swallowed quite half a pound of cotton-wool, which is now twined cosily round my most vital tubes, and I endured agonies of terror when that lighted candle fell off the tree on to my wig. And what is my reward? The thankless brats begin to snivel as soon as I appear, and run bawling to their mothers when I open my mouth to speak, while Charles merely gambols in, raises screams of laughter by uncomplimentary references to my personal appearance, and becomes the hero of the afternoon. Bring on the serpent's tooth. I'll hardly feel it!"

"Have a drink instead," suggested Charles.

"Poor old chap, were you hideously uncomfortable?" said Susan. "You did it so well, too. Everyone said so."

"Did they indeed?" retorted her brother. "The remarks *I* overheard were distinctly unfavourable. 'Come awa', then, hinny, an' we'll no' let yon ugly felly wi' the baird touch ye'! was about the pick of them."

"Think of the pleasure you gave them, even if some of the tiny ones *were* frightened at first."

"The thought of their pleasure doesn't make up for my damnable discomfort," said Oliver. "What I wanted was to see several she-bears enter the barn. Good old Elisha! I never really sympathized with him until to-day."

Charles having supplied him with a tankard of beer, his grumblings died away into a muttering reminiscent of the she-bears which he craved.

Susan was conscious of a vast relief that the party was successfully over. Some forty children, replete from a large and ornamental tea, sticky with sweets and oranges and laden with toys, had by this time reached their own homes, where it seemed probable that the after effects would amply avenge Oliver for their fear and freely expressed dislike of "Sandy Claws." The Christmas tree, denuded of all its trappings save a few tinsel ribbons and one star on its topmost twig and the burnt-out ends of many coloured candles, stood alone in its dark-green beauty in the disordered barn. To save it from the fate of Hans Andersen's Little Fir Tree, over which she had wept bitterly as a child, Susan had insisted on its being uprooted instead of cut down; the next day would see it replanted among its brethren in the strip of wood alongside the garden. There it could grow and flourish, and bore all the other trees through years to come with the oft-told tale of a day when it had blossomed unexpectedly with strange gay fruit and flowers.

"Where are you off to now, Susan?" asked Charles, seeing her in the hall in her hat and coat.

"I'm going to ask for Jo-an Robertson and take her a few little things. No, I'm not tired, Charles, really, and I don't want you to come. It isn't dark. Stay and minister to Oliver."

With Tara beside her she climbed up the steep side of the ridge to the grieve's house, glad to be alone after the heat and noise of the children's party. It was very quiet at Reiverslaw; so quiet that at first she imagined that the Robertsons must be out.

As she raised her hand to knock a second time the door was quietly opened, and the grieve's wife, her eyes sunken and red-rimmed with weeping, stood facing her.

"Jo-an?" asked Susan, but she knew what the answer would be.

"Ay, she's won awa', the puir wee lamb—"

It was difficult to know what to say, and Susan was not one of those to whom words of consolation came easily and glibly. She stood for a little looking down at the bunch of sweet smelling violets which she had put into a gilt basket for Jo-an, knowing her love of pretty, useless things, at the small trifles saved for her from the Christmas tree.

"These are for her," she said at last. "Please take—please take the flowers, anyhow, Mrs. Robertson." She put the frail basket into the old woman's gnarled hand, and with a broken, "I'm so sorry, so very sorry!" made more eloquent than she could guess by the rare tears in her hazel eyes, left the cottage door.

Stumbling a little as she went, for the road was rough and her sight blurred by the tears she had always found it difficult to shed, she started homewards, and rounding a corner with bent head, walked straight into Jed Armstrong.

"Steady, lass," he said, his deep voice kind, and before she could command her voice to speak, he went on: "I'll walk down to Easter Hartrigg with you." He turned and walked beside her. Susan, until she met him, had been thankful to be alone, but now she was aware of being less desolate in his company, strange though it seemed to her. There was a strength and comfort even in his silence, a silence which she had always imagined to be merely stolid, which she suddenly realized was sensitive and rather shy.

"I've been at the Robertsons'," she said, "and—and heard about Jo-an."

"They'll take it hard. Their kind does," he answered briefly. "And there's little you can do for them."

"It seems so dreadful, a young thing like Jo-an, who should have been happy!"

"There was nothing but grief before her," he said. "It's perhaps better the way it is. Life was too difficult for her, poor lass."

"But it shouldn't have been!" cried Susan. "I feel that we ought to have been able to do something for Jo-an!"

"You can't save some folk from themselves," he said, but quite gently. "No matter how you try."

Susan sighed. Presently she said: "I'm afraid Peggy will be distressed when she hears, and news like that is so much worse when it's broken with—with gusto by someone like Mrs. Davidson at the post office."

"That's what I thought myself. So I rang up the post office when I was pretty sure Peggy would be there for the evening paper, and told her—"

"That was like you, Jed!" Impulsively Susan put out her hand to him, and though it was almost dark, he saw it and took it into his warm, strong hold. "Anyone would have done it," he muttered.

"Very few people would even have thought of it," said Susan.

"Your hand's cold," he said, still holding it firmly. With a quick movement he drew her arm through his, and plunged the hand he held into the pocket of his raincoat. "Leave it there," as she made a tentative effort at withdrawal. "You're better like that. I can help you over the rough places."

And so, silently, linked together, they came to Easter Hartrigg gate, where he left her.

Susan stood for a little, her hand still warm from his clasp, conscious that she had not wanted to free herself. "But this is ridiculous!" she said aloud. "Utterly ridiculous!"

Jed, climbing back up the ridge, his own hand still half-shut as if to retain the feel of those cold, smooth long fingers, was saying the same thing in other words. "Don't be a damn' fool, man!" he adjured himself. "She was upset and tired, half-afraid of the dark. You needn't think it meant anything more." And still his heart kept saying: "but she left her hand in mine. She didn't want to take it away. I've held her hand in mine. . . ."

3

It was late. The candles in their old silver sticks on the dressing-table had burned low, and still Susan moved about her room restlessly, and still in the sitting-room beneath she could hear the deep voices of her brother and Charles steadily talking.

They had been dining with the Heriots, and though any entertainment given by Lady Evelyn, from tea after an uproarious mixed hockey-match to the stateliest of official parties, was always admirably arranged, the evening had seemed to Susan to drag interminably.

Oliver had grudged even a few hours spent away from Peggy, who, he knew, would be feeling low in her mind over the approaching departure of the Infantry for England; and Charles, who had started out in high spirits, had returned moody and silent. Perhaps it was only the usual effect of the aftermath of Christmas, which is never a really merry season except for children young enough to have no regrets for the past, no fears for the future. Still, it was not like Charles to be plunged in gloom, and he had been gay as ever when they arrived at the Dower House earlier in the evening.

Susan stopped beside the dressing-table, and gently drumming with her finger-tips on the polished surface, looked back on the dinner-party. Just one thing might possibly have accounted for Charles's sudden change, but it seemed so far-fetched, so improbable.... She frowned a little, remembering details, looks, scraps of conversation. The drawing-room at the Dower House was a long room, with two doorways at one end, the space between them occupied by a huge mirror which doubled the expanse of shining parquet floor, and reflected the groups of guests who stood about waiting for some late arrival. A soft clinking of sherry and cocktail glasses, a whisper of long skirts, voices and laughter, had supplied an undercurrent to Oliver's tale of his sufferings as Santa Claus, with which he was amusing his hostess, while Charles added a running commentary. Everything had been quite normal then. It was when Susan had turned to him with some careless remark that the change had come. Charles, usually so attentive to her, had not even heard what she was saying to him. He was staring down, the long room at a girl who had just come in, a tall, slim, brown girl with deer's eyes and a dainty head held high. At the moment her cheeks were almost as pale as the white satin dress she wore. She had seemed as startled by seeing Charles as any doe surprised in a woodland glade....

"Oh! Here is Daphne at last," said Lady Evelyn. "A first-cousin-once-removed of my husband's," she had added to Susan. "Haven't you met her? Daphne Fleming.... We had her out in Malta with us one winter a few years ago. Charles knows her, I think."

Obviously Charles had known her, thought Susan. Again she frowned. Oliver had said carelessly, when they came home, "I say, I thought that pretty young cousin of Robbie's was married, didn't you, Charles? She seemed headed that way when we saw her in Malta...."

And Charles had murmured, as if the subject did not interest him very much, "Er—yes, she did."

Then why, thought Susan, did they both look as if they had seen a ghost when they met? She shook her head, and began to make ready for bed.

4

A quick though heavy step on the gravel brought Susan's head up from the writing-pad over which it was bent as she sat in the window-seat. Looking out, she saw Jed Armstrong approaching the front door, a gun under his arm, a cartridge-bag slung over his shoulder. The formality of ringing the bell had long since been waived by him, and he tramped into the hall and presently appeared in the sitting-room doorway.

"What are you all fugging in here for?" he demanded. "It is a fine day."

"I *have* been out," said Susan righteously. "Before lunch, in the rain. It certainly wasn't fine then, whatever it may be now."

"Bring yourself to anchor, Jed," said Oliver in sleepy tones. "Charles and I were having a bit of shut-eye, an' you've gorn an' bin an' disturbed us, you blinkin' behemoth. If you want to prattle, do it in a whisper. I'm Sandy Claws, I am, enjoying a rest after playing at chimney-sweeps—"

"Well," said Jed, acknowledging with a nod the cigarettes which Susan pushed towards him. "I came to see if you'd like a shot at the duck, but seeing you're all so comfortable it's a pity I—"

"Duck?" Charles's eyes opened and he sat up with surprising alertness. "Where? When?"

"At the loch up at Reiverslaw. Now. They'll be flighting just before sunset, and we ought to be in our places in plenty of time."

"Come on, Oliver!" Charles rose and shook his somnolent host mercilessly. "Get your gun, my boy, and look sharp!"

"Not the proper season," Oliver, was heard to mumble. "Duck an' green peas—not till June—"

"Come on, you fool, or we'll be too late. Where's your gear?" said Charles.

Galvanized into activity, Oliver rose also and stretched himself, and with a good deal of noise and argument they made ready for the slaughter which appeals so strongly to almost all right-minded men.

"Would you like to come too?" asked Jed suddenly, addressing Susan. "The car's at the gate, and we'll run you up in no time."

"Yes, come on, Susan darling," cried Charles. "Leave those letters of thanks for all the presents you didn't want, and come on!"

Gladly, though rather guiltily, Susan left her half-finished letter, and hurried to put on thick shoes and a heavy coat.

"Are you warmly enough wrapped up?" asked Jed, as he turned his car into the narrow road that ran like a spinal column up the whole length of the ridge. "There's a cold wind blowing, and I think we'll have snow before night."

There was something rather touching about his solicitude for her, his constant absurd assumption that she was incapable of taking care of herself, which Charles also seemed to have adopted recently.

"Thank you, I'm quite warm," she assured Jed gravely.

He only grunted. "Warm enough just now, but how about after you've been waiting in the open for a bit?"

A wind whistled piercingly about their ears as they left the car at the highest point of the long ridge. There was no shelter up here on top. The little church stood bleakly by the road, and over the Flodden knight's forgotten grave the ancient yews of the kirk-yard stooped black and melancholy. They had been standing there long before his day; and now that he was dust and his good sword rust, as Sir Walter wrote of another knight, they still stood, seemingly ageless, sombre and unchanging. The loch was steel-grey, fretted into waves by the wind which ran among the rushes and sedge by the water's brink with a continuous dry hush-hushing. A well-filled stackyard at the nearer end of the loch looked homely and comfortable, speaking of harvest and prosperity. The sun, half sunk below the western horizon, was gilding the straw and giving the waves little crests of gold as Susan stood watching the day fade to the tune of the wind, while the men fussed with guns and bags.

Jed caught her by the arm. "You'll be best in the lee of one of the stacks," he said, hurrying her towards them. "And here's a coat to sit on. Wrap yourself in it, and don't make a sound, whatever you do."

Obediently Susan allowed herself to be established in what he called a "bield" behind a huge stack like a round tower. In a moment he was gone, and she remained alone, with the wind's sigh and the rustling of straw for company. Slowly the shadows lengthened, the air grew colder, the tops of the stacks, from being golden, turned greyish yellow, and the gold slid gradually down their rounded sides. There came a whistling of powerful wings overhead, and looking up, Susan saw the duck flying straight into the sunset and their deaths. They were big birds, even to her inexperienced eyes larger than mallard, and beyond the noise of their flight and an occasional "carrr-carrr," they came over the stackyard in silence, high and fast against the wind. The outstretched red-billed heads, the green-glossed backs, the strong wings beating the air so rhythmically, all were dark, but their breasts were flushed to an exquisite rose, as though the setting sun had dyed them. To watch them was like looking on a Japanese picture come to life, and for one wild second Susan longed to spring up, regardless of sport, and by alarming them, save them from destruction. In that second, however, they were over and out of her sight, and the next instant shots broke out, shattering the stillness.

The duck set up a lamentable quacking, and the dull thud of bodies falling to earth from a height told Susan that toll had been taken of their numbers. One bird, twisting and turning, came tumbling down not far from where she crouched. . . . Almost before the echoes of the shots had died, another flight appeared above the tree-tops, but these, warned by the clamour of their fellows, swerved, mounted, and passed far out of range. When the men came to pick up the spoil, there were six limp corpses which a few minutes earlier had been living embodiments of winged grace. Already as they were stowed on the floor of the car, the gloss was fading from the bright plumage, leaving it dull. Even those sunset-tinted breasts, though still flushed, were an uninteresting shade of pale salmon-pink.

"Goosanders," said Jed. "D'you want them?"

Oliver and Charles accepted them eagerly, but Susan thought she noticed a peculiar glint in Jed's blue eyes, and she wondered.

She had regretted the slaying of these birds, and Oliver and Charles were to share her regret when they tried to eat the one goosander they had kept after sending the others to various friends. Donaldina had cooked and sent it to table with considerable misgiving, which Susan fully appreciated on tasting her first—and last—mouthful. To eat it was merely to eat very tough, rather high, and intensely fishy fish.

Even Tara turned from it with undisguised loathing when Oliver, abandoning the attempt to eat it which pride had forced him to make, presented him with a generous portion.

5

"How did you enjoy your duck?" was Jed's greeting, as they arrived at Reiverslaw on New Year's Eve.

Susan looked coldly at him. "Even before I knew they were unfit for human food I said it was a shame to have shot them—"

He burst into a roar of laughter, and turned to Oliver. "I hope all the friends you sent them to will like them," he said agreeably.

Oliver's jaw dropped. "How the devil did you—" he began.

"Oh, I happened to meet the postman on his way back to Muirfoot. The poor lad's carrier was loaded with—game. Still and on, they're handsome birds, and if your friends write before they taste them they'll be grateful enough!"

Peggy, who was also dining with him, chuckled.

Champagne appeared at dinner, and Jed, perhaps in answer to his guests' interested glances, said: "It's not an ordinary occasion, you know. Hogmanay, for one thing. And for another, we've a special health to drink to-night." He rose, looming enormous in his small dining-room, and raised his newly filled glass. "I'd like to propose a toast. The newly engaged couple!"

For a second everyone looked bewildered. Then the scarlet confusion of Peggy, the half-smothered smiles of the discreet elderly parlour-maid and her younger satellite gave them a clue.

"The newly engaged couple!" was drunk with great good will.

"But—but nothing's settled yet! That is, I've never said I—Oliver!" cried Peggy.

Oliver, shamelessly holding her hand, said gaily: "Thank you, Jed! We were wondering how to announce it."

"What an exciting party," Susan observed when the exchange of congratulations and good wishes was over, and dinner proceeded. Charles shot her a quick look, and his face took on a determined expression, but Susan's eyes were on Peggy, who sat, shyly blissful, beside Oliver, and played with her food. Clearly happiness had deprived her of appetite.

"We'll have coffee in the sitting-room," said Jed. The parlourmaid, bringing it in, announced that there were some children in the kitchen "waiting to play Galashans."

"It's the children from the cottages," Jed explained. "They come round every year on Hogmanay and act this play of theirs. Galatians is its real name, I believe, but I can't tell you the origin of it."

"Oh, do let's have them in!" said Peggy eagerly, glad to have attention distracted from herself and Oliver.

The little group of children, blue-eyed, tow-haired, and apple-cheeked, wearing their parents' coats and armed with wooden swords, while one small boy was almost extinguished beneath an aged bowler hat green with age, came into the room with bashful giggles, pushing each other forward. After a number of false starts, and a sternly repressed tendency on the part of the youngest to burst into tears, they reeled off a patter of doggerel verse in broad Scots, impossible to follow. Finally one was slain with the wooden swords, and red with embarrassment and pleasure they retired, each clutching a sixpence, to be regaled with cake and tea in the kitchen.

"They're not so good as they used to be," Jed observed. "I remember when I was a boy they acted a lot better, and it was a much finer affair altogether—or seemed so to me. It's a long time ago, though."

"Galatians" paved the way for pleasant talk about old customs, old sayings, old songs.... Presently they gathered about the piano, where Susan played and the rest sang all the ditties beloved of Charles and Oliver. "Widdicombe Fair" was followed by "Spanish Ladies," "Rio Grande," "Sally Brown," until they were tired.

"Susan will sing us some English songs," said Charles suddenly. "She knows any number."

"Oh, Susan, do you sing? Why did you never tell us?" cried Peggy delightedly. "How lovely. I was wishing someone would sing!"

"Dash it, haven't we been bawling the place down?" Oliver wanted to know. Peggy smiled at him wickedly.

"I said 'sing'," she said. "Not bawl. Do sing, Susan!"

Susan, who had been thinking how much pleasanter it was without Mrs. Holden, and wondering if, when she reigned at Reiverslaw, Jed would ever have another party quite like this, was taken by surprise. "Absurd!" she said. "I've hardly any voice, and what there is of it is quite untrained."

But: "*Please*, Susan!" begged Peggy, like a child asking for a treat, and "I wish you would," muttered Jed.

"Of course she will," said Charles firmly.

Susan sat down at the old piano, the full skirts of her green dress spreading out round her feet. Her voice was certainly small, but it was true and sweet, and suited the songs. "High Germanie" she sang, and "The Crystal Spring," and "Searching for Lambs." . . .

"Sing 'Greensleeves,'" said Charles softly from where he sat.

> "Alas, my love, you do me wrong
> To cast me off discourteously;
> And I have loved thee so long
> Rejoicing in thy company.
>
> For, oh! Greensleeves was all my joy,
> And, ah! Greensleeves was my delight!
> And, oh! Greensleeves was my heart of goold,
> And who but my lady Greensleeves!"

The quaint old words, the minor air planing up and up, to drop at the end almost to a whisper, might have been composed especially for her. When she sang "Greensleeves" she lost her quiet, amused look: to Peggy, and to Jed, she suddenly was Greensleeves herself.

As she rose with a small deprecating smile, Charles seized her by the hand. A strange excitement seemed to possess him, for his eyes shone and the fingers that clasped Susan's were burning hot.

"Congratulate me, please, everyone," he said. "For Susan and I are also engaged!"

6

Certainly it was an exciting party, too exciting to be altogether a happy one. Susan, even as her astounded gaze left Charles's face, met a look from Jed that was sharp and sudden as a sword-thrust. It was gone in an instant, and he joined in the chorus of amazed delight which rose from Oliver and Peggy, but Susan knew she had not imagined it.

And: "Why? Why?" she thought. "What reason has he to look at me like that?"

She wished that Charles had chosen another time, a less dramatic manner, of announcing their engagement, particularly as his air suggested a rather desperate satisfaction, a there-I've-*done*-it, instead of the contented happiness shown by Oliver.

They stayed to see the New Year in, but the lightheartedness had gone from the party, though they sang "Auld Lang Syne" with vigour and clasped hands. Susan found herself wondering what sort of a New Year it would be for all of them. Joyful for Peggy and Oliver, and her generous heart rejoiced with them: but for Charles, for herself, for Jed? Impossible to tell yet.

CHAPTER FIFTEEN

1

The grey February afternoon was passing very slowly; even the steady clocks seemed to lag. Susan was alone at Easter Hartrigg, for Oliver had gone to Edinburgh with Peggy to stay the night with her only wealthy relative, an elderly spinster cousin, who wished to see him for herself before she gave the engagement her blessing.

Oliver, frankly nervous of the approaching ordeal, had gone off wearing a new suit and an expression of resolute cheerfulness. His last words had been: "I never envied Charles as much as I do to-day. Lucky beggar! *He* won't have to be vetted by any ancient and crusty relations, because you haven't any except me, and I know the worst about him already!"

When he had gone a deep silence settled down over the house. Only once was Susan's solitude disturbed, by a band of tinkers, the lordly males of which strutted up and down before the windows, like two rival gamecocks, playing the bagpipes, while their ladies conducted a loud and impassioned appeal for alms at the back door. Beginning with the customary modest request for "a piece," which was at once provided, their demands soared from "a pickle tea" through rags and rabbit-skins to garments. Having filched from Oliver's room a pair of his most ancient and adored grey flannel "bags" to furnish "a pair o' troosies for ma puir man," Susan felt that she had done well; but discovered that they were a mere drop in the bucket. "Buits for the bairns" were the next requirement, and Mrs. Tinker, her wealth of coarse dark auburn hair, which framed a handsome swarthy face, falling in disarray about her plaided shoulders, continued to plead for those necessities as though Susan had a heart of stone, in spite of repeated assurances that there were no children in the household. Finally, after presenting her with an old tweed skirt and a woollen sweater, Susan lost patience, and told Donaldina to let them know that as there was no more to give them they might as well depart. For some time the pipes wailed and droned on outside, and the non-playing members, ranging themselves in a reproachful row, stared in unblinkingly through the sitting-room windows. But as Susan remained blind and deaf to their presence they lost heart and tramped away, a healthy, dirty and good-looking set of vagabonds as might be seen anywhere.

"A guid riddance!" was Donaldina's comment as she carried in the tea-tray. "Thae thievin' tinklers wad hae the sark aff yer back, an' the bite oot yer mooth, an' *then* speir could ye no' gie them yer skin tae sell!"

With tea came an unexpected mail, brought up from Muirfoot by the baker's van, Mrs. Davidson having pressed the letters into his hand, announcing: "There's twa wi' the Lunnon post-mark an' penny-ha'penny stamps, an' nae doot Miss Parsons'll be glad o' them the nicht seein' the Commander's awa' tae Embro."

"How thoughtful of her," was Susan's comment, as Donaldina delivered letters and message without the flicker of an eyelash to denote that there was anything unusual in this procedure.

One of the letters, as Mrs. Davidson no doubt shrewdly surmised, was from Charles. Susan decided to pour out and drink a cup of tea before reading it. Somehow she had lost most of her pleasure in his letters. Since he had gone back to Chatham he had written faithfully, but without the easy, spontaneous friendliness which had always made him such an agreeable correspondent before their engagement.

The other envelope, a long, business-like one, was an offer of a post on his staff from an editor who had always liked her articles. It would entail living in London if she accepted it; it meant a new opening, a fresh outlook. Perhaps this was a way out, for Charles as well as herself. Susan's tea cooled beside her, scenting the warm air with delicate fragrance, while she thought deeply. Presently she picked up his letter, and taking several closely written sheets of notepaper from the envelope, began to read.

Her method was always the same. First she skimmed through his letters hurriedly, half-dreading, half-hoping to find some expression of a love and passion for which she had no real use, yet which would have made her feel that she was doing the right thing if she married him. Afterwards, when the absence of anything warmer than his usual affection had been ascertained, she read the whole thing carefully, noting what she would answer in her own letter back. It was during this preliminary glance that she found Mrs. Holden's name mentioned, and at once gave her full attention to the page that followed.

". . . You remember I was sure I'd seen her before somewhere? And you and Oliver laughed at me, because she obviously didn't recognize me? Well, I've placed it now, not that it matters much. It was a photograph of her I saw. The P.M.O. had it in his cabin, framed in silver, stuck on his table. I don't know him very well, and the other day, when I was in his cabin again it was only for the second time. Of course I said I'd met her, and he was thrilled to bits. Said he hoped to marry her one day, and all the rest. None of my business, but I can't help wondering how many men are hoping to marry her now that she's a widow? It seems a bit rough on Armstrong if he is really keen on her. He always struck me as the faithful sort of chap who'd prize faithfulness in others. This is between you and me, I needn't tell you . . .

Susan drank some tea, blinked, and read the paragraph again, in case she had made a mistake. But there it was, in Charles's clear small handwriting. . . . Peggy had said all along that she wasn't good enough for Jed. Still, if Mrs. Holden was the woman he wanted, it didn't much matter whether she was good enough or not. People were like that, and love could be very blind indeed where the loved one was concerned. Anyhow, it was no business of anyone's.

"I wish Charles hadn't told me," thought Susan. And then laughed a little. He was so determined to prove himself right, poor darling. . . . She read on.

"I stayed last week-end with the Flemings—you know, the girl was at the Dower House that night we dined there."

"Indeed I do know," thought Susan. "Poor child—and poor Charles. And perhaps poor me too? That settles it. I'll wait until later in the evening, and then I'll write," she said aloud. "Both these letters—to the nice editor man who thinks I'll be an addition to his staff—and to Charles—must be answered before I go to bed, and I'll sleep in peace with a quiet mind."

Tara, lying at her feet, thumped the rug with his tail.

2

The weather had changed, the piercing wind which had screamed round the house during the morning had died away, and a deathly hush had fallen over all the countryside. Heavy banks of cloud, rolling sullenly up from behind the Cheviots, and massing in huge pinnacles and towers across the sky, threatened snow before another night passed. In the early twilight the first large flakes began to fall, soundlessly and inexorably, from a dull sky so low that it seemed a hand stretched up must touch it. By the time Susan had dressed for dinner, the world on which she looked when she drew aside the curtains was white as though a great winding-sheet had been laid over it.

"Thank goodness Oliver and Peggy are staying in Edinburgh to-night," she thought.

A blazing log-fire, faithfully stoked by Donaldina, awaited her in the sitting-room after her lonely meal.

The sound of the wind, which had sunk for a time only to rise again with renewed strength, made the warm room doubly pleasant. Susan sat on the fender-stool, a writing-pad on her knee, and Tara, beside her, breathed deep and evenly, his black muzzle hidden by his fore-paws.

It was surprisingly easy to write, this letter to Charles which would break off their engagement, for Susan knew that though he might be sorry and hurt for a time, it would make for his happiness in the end. He would marry the slender nymph Daphne, Admiral Heriot's cousin, and then he would realize that Susan's place in his heart was a friend's, not a wife's. She pushed the sheet of notepaper into an envelope, addressed it, looked at it for a second with a little, rather wistful smile, laid it aside, and wrote to her pet editor accepting the post he offered. Now all that remained for her to do was to argue the matter out with Oliver, who was certain to want her to continue to live at Easter Hartrigg with him—and Peggy.

"But I won't. This job will make me independent, and even if I have to pretend that I'd rather live in town," thought Susan, "I'll convince him somehow."

She sat by the fire, hands clasped round her knees, her head a little bent, thinking over the months that had slipped past since, an unwilling pilgrim, she had forsaken her old life to come to Easter Hartrigg. Not quite a year ago she had hated the idea of it; and now she hated much more the thought that she must leave the place she had learned to love, her first settled home since early childhood. Looking back on it, she saw that it had been a good year in spite of difficulties. Oliver was better, when she had feared that a life of semi-invalidism lay before him; he was happy as a laird with twenty pence, even happier as Peggy Cunningham's future husband. For herself, Susan knew that she could never regret the change which their move had brought about, though she had not gained what her brother had. Love had passed her by, but there was friendship to remember: laughter and tears and pleasant days in plenty. Quiet afternoons at the Manse of Muirfoot, long walks with Tara in all kinds of weather, evenings spent beside the fire with favourite books, even the Miss Pringles' extraordinary tea-parties; picnics and tramps and talks with dear Charles, so much dearer now that she was not going to marry him. Amazing and ridiculous escapades in Jed Armstrong's company, which she had unexpectedly enjoyed and thought about with laughter afterwards.

Jed.... Somehow he had dominated the scene from the very beginning, when he had stepped in and routed Mrs. Bald, their first cook. Starting as Oliver's friend, suffered by Susan solely on that account, he had gradually come to have a place all his own in her life. It was not easy to decide exactly what she felt or thought about him, but she realized now with surprise that she would miss him more than anyone else when she went away. He had recognized at once that she was not the tolerant, unperturbable person she seemed. Even Charles had never thought her anything but serene.... Jed knew her as she was, without a word said on either side....

A log fell, and the flames soared, picking out ruddy lights in Susan's dark hair, gilding the long white arms linked about her knees. She rose and replenished the fire, though it was late, and she had heard Donaldina go up to bed some time ago.

"Ah, well, Tara," she said with a smile, poking the sleeping dog gently with the toe of her slipper, "it's a good thing I can always see the funny side of life. 'Werena my hert's licht I wad dee.'"

Tara yawned widely, a delicate reminder that it was time to retire; but seeing that Susan had sat down again with a book, he resigned himself to sleeping where he was.

The clock ticked placidly on, punctuated by the wind's voice shrieking down the chimney, by a sudden rattle of hail at the windows, by the soft sound made when the logs settled in the grate, and still Susan sat half-reading, half-dreaming.

It was after midnight when a sudden deep growl from Tara, startling her so that the book slipped to the floor, roused her to the fact that something other than hail was beating at the window. She sprang up, frightened for the moment. To hear a rapping on the pane at such an hour, when all the house was sleeping, was an eerie business, nor had she even been so reluctant to do anything as she was to cross the room now, and pulling back the curtain, peer out into the snow-laden darkness and see—what?

Even as she reminded herself that Tara, a stout protector, was with her, even as her unwilling feet carried her towards the shrouded windows, she was assailed by wild superstitious fears. Old stories of dead lovers or friends who returned to announce their passing by this means flashed through her mind, and it was with an effort that she put out a hand and drew the curtains aside.

At first she could see nothing save the black darkness and a flurry of snow-flakes on the glass; then a figure loomed gigantic, and biting back a cry of pure terror, she found herself staring at the dimly seen face of Jed Armstrong. Snow lay thick on his broad shoulders, wreathed his cap, clung to his eyebrows and short-clipped moustache. He motioned with his head towards the door. Without a word, moving as in a dream which clogs the feet, Susan went out to the cold hall, lighted by a lamp turned low, and unlocked the heavy front door. A rush of chill air blew past her, the lamp flared, a smother of snow lay white on the rug, to melt and make little wet patches where it had fallen.

Almost as soon as she had opened he was standing before her in the deep snow, holding by the rein a trembling, exhausted horse which puffed great breaths of vapour on the icy air.

"Come in," said Susan.

"I'll need to put this poor brute under cover somewhere first and give him a rub down, if you can let me have a light."

It was not until he spoke that she entirely believed that the real man, and no ghost, stood there. She turned, took a powerful electric torch from the oak chest in the hall, and put it into his hand, which was warm and living enough for conviction.

"The potting-shed is nearest," she said, "and there's room in it. Do you want a rug?"

He nodded, took the rug she handed to him, and trudged off round the house, the weary horse at his heels, the torch-light throwing a pale narrow beam on snow-laden bushes and walls. Susan waited, shivering a little, until presently he came back and followed her silently into the house.

"Would you like whisky-and-soda? Or tea? Or—what *would* you like?" Susan asked when, leaving coat and cap in the hall, he came into the sitting-room to be made much of by Tara.

"I'd sooner have tea than anything."

Still in the species of daze which Donaldina described as a "dwam," Susan fetched a kettle, still warm, from the kitchen where the range gaped black and empty; and while he set it on the fire, collected cups and saucers in the same numb, mechanical fashion.

"Weren't you surprised—frightened—when you saw me?" he asked. "I thought, of course, it would be Oliver up so late."

"Oliver's away for the night," said Susan. "I was frightened—until I saw you—"

"Not surprised?"

Susan shook her head. "I—don't—believe—I was," she said slowly, as though her own words astonished her.

She felt no surprise. It seemed the most natural thing in the world that this man, so like his foraying ancestors, should come to her at dead of night, in the dark of the moon, with his tired horse stumbling behind him. . . .

"It's a queer time to pay a call," he said, as Susan made tea. "But a woman up at Reiverslaw was taken ill, the telephone wires have been brought down by the wind and weight of snow, and the car's out of order. The doctor was needed badly, so I rode down to get him—"

"And haven't you succeeded? Wouldn't he go?" she asked. A fresh storm of wind brought snowflakes whirling down the wide chimney to die with a faint hissing in the red heart of the fire.

"Go? He'd have gone all right if he'd been in. But he had been called out already, Kelpieha' way, and I suppose he couldn't get back, though the snow isn't so bad down there. They'll send him up as soon as he goes home, poor devil—if he can make his way through the drifts. My beast's about done. I couldn't get him to go another step just now, and I saw your light—"

"And the woman?"

He shrugged his shoulders, and began to drink the tea she had poured out for him. "The other women'll have to look to her," he said. "It won't be the first time this has happened."

Susan fell silent, staring into the fire, thinking how light an impression civilization had made on these outlying places, where the elements in freakish mood could swing the cycle of years back to ruder times, and a woman must suffer the pangs of childbirth unaided save by her neighbours, as women had since the world began. A rough life, in spite of modern comforts, but a life which made for patience and endurance and deep-rooted kindliness.

"How's Oliver?" asked Jed suddenly. "I haven't seen much of him since New Year."

"I haven't seen very much of him myself," said Susan, smiling. "You must remember that he's an engaged man. Peggy occupies a good deal of his time, naturally."

"And what about you?" He shot her one of his direct, lance-thrust looks.

"Me?" Susan was hedging, and she knew it. A curious shyness had seized hold upon her.

"Yes. You're engaged too. Are you going to make a double wedding of it?"

"Well, no." She had risen and taken a cigarette, and now seemed to be engrossed in searching for matches to light it. "There's only going to be one wedding in our family, actually . . . where *can* I have put that box of matches?"

"Here. I'll give you a light," said Jed. Holding the match to the end of her cigarette, looking steadfastly into her eyes, he demanded: "Aren't you going to marry Crawley?"

"No," said Susan, rather relieved to have broken the news. "I'm not. I wrote to Charles this evening, breaking off our engagement. I am going to London as soon as Oliver is married, to a job on a paper which has been offered to me—"

He did not seem to have heard the last sentence.

"Do you change so quickly? I didn't think you would be that sort—"

"I haven't changed at all. That's the root of the trouble. I feel about Charles exactly as I have always felt. He is my very dear friend, no more. I ought never to have said I'd marry him. You needn't look at me like that, Jed. Charles doesn't love me that way, either. It was a mistake we both made, perhaps a natural one, because we're fond of each other."

Jed drew a deep breath. "Look at me," he said, almost roughly, and Susan looked long at his burning blue eyes. Then she remembered Mrs. Holden, and shook her head.

"Don't say it," she whispered.

"You can't care enough about me, either? Oh, well, why should you? I'm too old, too rough, for you. I—sort of expected that!"

This was more than Susan could stand. "Jed! It's not that. It's—aren't you going to marry Mrs. Holden?"

"Primrose?" he said incredulously. "Primrose? But what has she got to do with it? She's an old friend, she was a sort of pet of my mother's, and we've known each other since we were children, that's all there has ever been to it. Have those damned Pringles been putting ideas into *your* head? Good God, Susan, I thought you had more sense than to suppose Primrose was anything to me. She's not my kind—"

He was standing close to her, towering above her, tall though she was. "Didn't you guess how I've felt about you? Ah, you know it, lass, don't you? We belong to each other—"

"I think I did know, Jed. But—it's rather lovely to hear it—from you."

He drew her closer to him, and as his arm tightened about her, as his lips met hers, Susan knew that this moment was worth waiting a lifetime for. . . .

"Think what the Misses Pringle would say! You must go," said Susan, when they awoke to realization that he must go home.

"They'll say plenty, anyhow!" and Jed laughed. Then his eye lighted on the two envelopes propped against the clock on the mantelpiece. "One to Crawley—poor devil! He doesn't know what he's losing. One to—burn this, Susan. You'll need to write another letter to this editor of yours, telling him you've got a different job!"

"A masterful man," murmured Susan. Her lips curved in a wilful smile, but she took the letter, tore it into shreds, and dropped them on the fire.

"You've too much spirit yourself to want any other kind of man," he retorted. "And you know it."

"You've reived my heart from me. Don't leave me too long," she whispered, going with him to the door.

"What I'd like to do," he said wistfully, "would be to put you up in front of me and ride off with you now to Reiverslaw. But as I can't . . ." he took both her hands in his and kissed them very gently, as if they might melt under his touch. "Until to-morrow, my dear love."

The wind had died, and a great peace had fallen on the snow-smothered earth. High above in the dark bowl of the sky, stars swam like brilliant fish, the white ground sparkled back at them. Susan stood on the step, warmed by a fire which defied outer cold, and watched Jed ride away, the horse's hoofs crunching through the crust of snow which frost was beginning to harden. He was going back to Reiverslaw, but very soon there would come the day when he did not have to go alone.... "In such a night...." What mattered it that winter bound the country in an iron grip, that the sunset wind which sang to Jessica and young Lorenzo was hushed, that the patines of bright gold were chill points of twinkling steel? In such a night love had come to two people, when Susan, her fear of it all forgotten, had put her hand joyfully into Jed's stronghold.

THE END

FURROWED MIDDLEBROW

FM1. *A Footman for the Peacock* (1940) . . . . RACHEL FERGUSON
FM2. *Evenfield* (1942) . . . . RACHEL FERGUSON
FM3. *A Harp in Lowndes Square* (1936) . . . . RACHEL FERGUSON
FM4. *A Chelsea Concerto* (1959) . . . . FRANCES FAVIELL
FM5. *The Dancing Bear* (1954) . . . . FRANCES FAVIELL
FM6. *A House on the Rhine* (1955) . . . . FRANCES FAVIELL
FM7. *Thalia* (1957) . . . . FRANCES FAVIELL
FM8. *The Fledgeling* (1958) . . . . FRANCES FAVIELL
FM9. *Bewildering Cares* (1940) . . . . WINIFRED PECK
FM10. *Tom Tiddler's Ground* (1941) . . . . URSULA ORANGE
FM11. *Begin Again* (1936) . . . . URSULA ORANGE
FM12. *Company in the Evening* (1944) . . . . URSULA ORANGE
FM13. *The Late Mrs. Prioleau* (1946) . . . . MONICA TINDALL
FM14. *Bramton Wick* (1952) . . . . ELIZABETH FAIR
FM15. *Landscape in Sunlight* (1953) . . . . ELIZABETH FAIR
FM16. *The Native Heath* (1954) . . . . ELIZABETH FAIR
FM17. *Seaview House* (1955) . . . . ELIZABETH FAIR
FM18. *A Winter Away* (1957) . . . . ELIZABETH FAIR
FM19. *The Mingham Air* (1960) . . . . ELIZABETH FAIR
FM20. *The Lark* (1922) . . . . E. NESBIT
FM21. *Smouldering Fire* (1935) . . . . D.E. STEVENSON
FM22. *Spring Magic* (1942) . . . . D.E. STEVENSON
FM23. *Mrs. Tim Carries On* (1941) . . . . D.E. STEVENSON
FM24. *Mrs. Tim Gets a Job* (1947) . . . . D.E. STEVENSON
FM25. *Mrs. Tim Flies Home* (1952) . . . . D.E. STEVENSON
FM26. *Alice* (1949) . . . . ELIZABETH ELIOT
FM27. *Henry* (1950) . . . . ELIZABETH ELIOT
FM28. *Mrs. Martell* (1953) . . . . ELIZABETH ELIOT
FM29. *Cecil* (1962) . . . . ELIZABETH ELIOT
FM30. *Nothing to Report* (1940) . . . . CAROLA OMAN
FM31. *Somewhere in England* (1943) . . . . CAROLA OMAN

FM32. *Spam Tomorrow* (1956) . . . . VERILY ANDERSON
FM33. *Peace, Perfect Peace* (1947) . . . . JOSEPHINE KAMM
FM34. *Beneath the Visiting Moon* (1940) . . . . ROMILLY CAVAN
FM35. *Table Two* (1942) . . . . MARJORIE WILENSKI
FM36. *The House Opposite* (1943) . . . . BARBARA NOBLE
FM37. *Miss Carter and the Ifrit* (1945) . . . . SUSAN ALICE KERBY
FM38. *Wine of Honour* (1945) . . . . BARBARA BEAUCHAMP
FM39. *A Game of Snakes and Ladders* (1938, 1955) . . . .
. . . . DORIS LANGLEY MOORE
FM40. *Not at Home* (1948) . . . . DORIS LANGLEY MOORE
FM41. *All Done by Kindness* (1951) . . . . DORIS LANGLEY MOORE
FM42. *My Caravaggio Style* (1959) . . . . DORIS LANGLEY MOORE
FM43. *Vittoria Cottage* (1949) . . . . D.E. STEVENSON
FM44. *Music in the Hills* (1950) . . . . D.E. STEVENSON
FM45. *Winter and Rough Weather* (1951) . . . . . . D.E. STEVENSON
FM46. *Fresh from the Country* (1960) . . . . MISS READ
FM47. *Miss Mole* (1930) . . . . E.H. YOUNG
FM48. *A House in the Country* (1957) . . . . RUTH ADAM
FM49. *Much Dithering* (1937) . . . . DOROTHY LAMBERT
FM50. *Miss Plum and Miss Penny* (1959) . DOROTHY EVELYN SMITH
FM51. *Village Story* (1951) . . . . CELIA BUCKMASTER
FM52. *Family Ties* (1952) . . . . CELIA BUCKMASTER
FM53. *Rhododendron Pie* (1930) . . . . MARGERY SHARP
FM54. *Fanfare for Tin Trumpets* (1932) . . . . MARGERY SHARP
FM55. *Four Gardens* (1935) . . . . MARGERY SHARP
FM56. *Harlequin House* (1939) . . . . MARGERY SHARP
FM57. *The Stone of Chastity* (1940) . . . . MARGERY SHARP
FM58. *The Foolish Gentlewoman* (1948) . . . . MARGERY SHARP
FM59. *The Swiss Summer* (1951) . . . . STELLA GIBBONS
FM60. *A Pink Front Door* (1959) . . . . STELLA GIBBONS
FM61. *The Weather at Tregulla* (1962) . . . . STELLA GIBBONS
FM62. *The Snow-Woman* (1969) . . . . STELLA GIBBONS
FM63. *The Woods in Winter* (1970) . . . . STELLA GIBBONS
FM64. *Apricot Sky* (1952) . . . . RUBY FERGUSON
FM65. *Susan Settles Down* (1936) . . . . MOLLY CLAVERING
FM66. *Yoked with a Lamb* (1938) . . . . MOLLY CLAVERING
FM67. *Loves Comes Home* (1938) . . . . MOLLY CLAVERING

FM68. *Touch not the Nettle* (1939) . . . . MOLLY CLAVERING
FM69. *Mrs. Lorimer's Quiet Summer* (1953) . . . MOLLY CLAVERING
FM70. *Because of Sam* (1953) . . . . MOLLY CLAVERING
FM71. *Dear Hugo* (1955) . . . . MOLLY CLAVERING
FM72. *Near Neighbours* (1956) . . . . MOLLY CLAVERING

Printed in Great Britain
by Amazon